5

'I have a quest
chief test pilot,

'I'm afraid w
tion on that mat
given out yesterday following the news of his tragic accident,' interrupted the girl.

The reporter seemed undeterred.

'My office has just telephoned me,' he said unnecessarily. 'The Federal Aviation Authority has just issued a statement following their initial enquiries into the crash. Major Westbrook's aircraft was sabotaged . . . has your company any statement to make on that?'

Also available in Star:

The Judas Battalion

AIRSHIP

Peter MacAlan

A STAR BOOK
published by
the Paperback Division of
W. H. ALLEN & Co. PLC

A Star Book
Published in 1985
by the Paperback Division of
W. H. Allen & Co. PLC
44 Hill Street, London W1X 8LB

First published in Great Britain
by W. H. Allen & Co. PLC 1984

Printed and bound in Great Britain by
Anchor Brendon Ltd, Tiptree, Essex

ISBN 0 352 31584 9

ACKNOWLEDGMENTS

Of the many people who supplied me with technical details as a background to this novel I would like to make a special acknowledgment to the following:

Denis Howe, Professor of Aircraft Design at Cranfield Institute of Technology; A.W.L. Nayler of the Royal Aeronautical Society and the Airship Association of London; Peter H. Molyneux B.Sc. (Eng.), C. Eng., M.I. Mech. E.F. Inst. Pet.; Eric Goodyer of the School of Mechanical Engineering, Cranfield; Miss L.M. Worley and K.G. Toal of the Civil Aviation Authority, London; Lauren D. Basham of the Federal Aviation Administration, Washington, DC; the Civil Aeronautics Board, Washington, DC; the Ministère des Transports (Direction Général de l'Aviation Civile) Paris; Anthony Roberts of *The Times*, London; John Carson of Cornwall, Ontario; Anne-Marie d'Ancona of La Chênerie, near Marigné, France; Donald M. Grant of Rhode Island and Judith A. Quinn of New York City.

Also, a special 'thank you' to Nick Austin who started the whole thing by suggesting I wrote a novel about the airship.

In thanking them for their essential information and invaluable suggestions, I assume full responsibility for all technical statements and would also like to stress that all characters, companies and corporations in this book are fictitious and any resemblance to actual persons, living or dead, companies or current airship projects, is purely coincidental.

Lastly, to Anne-Marie and Adrian d'Ancona this book is dedicated with affection and gratitude for allowing me the hospitality of La Chênerie so that I could finish it in the friendly peace of the Maine countryside.

Peter MacAlan

Lovers of air travel find it exhilarating to hang poised between the illusion of immortality and the fact of death.

Alexander Chase, *Perspectives*, 1966

PART ONE

Chapter One

The club steward hovered discreetly by the table.

Major Alec Westbrook looked up with a frown.

'A message from the airfield controller, Major Westbrook,' the steward said brightly. 'Your aircraft has been refuelled and your flight plan has been cleared for take-off at fifteen hundred hours.'

Westbrook thanked the man and smiled across the table at his wife, who was finishing her dessert.

'We should be back at the project site in time to join Garry and Helen for that game of squash.'

Jane Westbrook simulated a groan of anguish and pointed to the remains of her chocolate gâteau.

'Must we, Alec?'

'You're putting on too much weight,' admonished Westbrook, with a twinkle in his eyes. 'You need the exercise.'

Jane pulled a face across the table. She was an attractive, slim, thirty-year-old brunette. Her husband's comment about her weight was a ritual after almost every meal. She had an active metabolism and no matter how much food she consumed, she never seemed to put on any extra inches. The comment arose out of Westbrook's own enviousness because he had to be extremely careful of his food consumption and tendency to put on weight quite easily: a problem in his line of work. He was chief test pilot with a commercial aircraft development corporation.

He motioned to the steward for another coffee and sat back to survey the occupants of the restaurant of the Newport Aero Club with a quizzical eye. There were only a dozen other people there; no one he knew. A couple of pilot-tutors with their pupils and some others, probably businessmen who kept their private aircraft at the Newport State Airport. Strictly speaking, it was the Middletown Airport, on the island of Aquidneck, Rhode

Island—one of the three towns with Newport at the south and Portsmouth to the north, and Middletown situated where its name suggested. It was a small aerodrome, state-owned, although the state had hinted many times that it would like to wash its hands of it. Although it was two miles from the Newport City limits, the airfield serviced what was one of Rhode Island's popular resort centres whose suburbs contained many summer estates. As well as state airlines, private aircraft used the field regularly and, in a small section of it, the Newport Aero Club had their buildings: hangars for members' aircraft and a luxurious club-house with a fine restaurant.

Westbrook was not a member of the club but he was a regular casual caller at the airfield, usually when en route to somewhere else. The club officials knew him and always made him welcome. Right now he was on a practice flight in a brand new Mitsubishi Marquise which his company had purchased for executive use. The aircraft, a mixture of seventy per cent Texan and thirty per cent Japanese turboprop light aircraft, had been delivered to the company project site in Portland, Maine, the day before. Garry Carson, Westbrook's fellow test pilot, had flown it up from San Angelo, Texas, where the aircraft was assembled and completed from major airframe components made in Japan. Carson had been full of praise for the aircraft's capabilities and Westbrook had decided to take it for a spin, calling in at Newport for lunch en route. His wife Jane, always a flying enthusiast, had insisted on coming along for the ride. Garry Carson had been right. The twin-engine machine, capable of carrying ten people, flew like a dream. Westbrook found that the combination of smaller wing, big engines, and a lateral control system that used spoilers instead of ailerons, led to unusual handling qualities with a resultant high performance which he enjoyed.

'Thinking of me or your new toy?' Jane demanded, interrupting his thoughts.

Westbrook grimaced and then grinned. After five years of marriage he was still very much in love with his wife.

'I was just thinking. . . .'

'Alec!' cried a Boston voice, cutting into his sentence. 'Jane! Why, I didn't realise you were both here.'

A thickset man, topping six feet in height, seemed to push his way between the tables towards them like a battleship through a rough sea. He wore an untidy, crumpled suit. His fair hair was tousled and his craggy face and deep blue, almost violet eyes gave him the appearance of a mischievous schoolboy. He stopped and planted a smacking kiss on Jane's upturned cheek and aimed a friendly thump at Westbrook's shoulder.

'Hello, Al,' smiled Westbrook.

Al Volpe was the manager of the Newport Aero Club.

'I just came from the operations room and saw your flight plan,' said the big man, levering himself into a chair at their table, shaking his head as a steward came expectantly forward. 'Thought I'd say hello but didn't realise that you had Jane with you, or I would have had your take-off delayed and insisted you had a few drinks with me.'

Westbrook's friendship with Volpe dated from their service days in the Air Force when Westbrook was flying combat aircraft and Volpe was his base commander.

'No time, Al,' returned Westbrook. 'We have to get back to Portland for a squash match appointment.'

'Still with the airship project?' asked Volpe. 'Don't tell me that you are still expecting the thing to fly?'

Westbrook grinned.

'Damned right it will and before next year there'll be a whole fleet of them in operation.'

'Airships!' replied Volpe cynically. 'They went out with the *Hindenburg* in 1937. Jane, why don't you persuade this guy to get a real job?'

Jane smiled: she had known Volpe for five years and knew how to take his sense of humour.

'A real job? Such as, Al?' she countered.

'There's a job going at Fall River for a manager of the flying club . . . you'd be able to put your feet up, like me; able to relax and enjoy life instead of messing about with experimental machines. It's much too dangerous.'

'Retire, you mean?' Westbrook said. 'The day I retire from flying, Al, is when I qualify for a pinewood suit.'

Volpe nodded.

'Yeah, I guess you're a cussed sonofabitch at that! Is that your Mitsubishi that's just been refuelled?' he asked, abruptly switching the conversation.

'A beauty, isn't she?' Jane said.

Volpe stroked the side of his nose with a forefinger.

'I've heard a couple of pilots say they wouldn't bother with them.'

Westbrook shook his head.

'Aeroplanes are all the same—they ask to be understood and

flown properly. The Mitsubishi has its peculiarities but it's a damned good craft to fly.'

'Well, it's not what I've heard. I've been told that you have to spend too much time trimming . . . damn!' Volpe looked up belligerently as the steward came up and gave a polite cough. 'What is it?'

'Sorry, sir. I thought Major Westbrook would like to know that it's a quarter to three.'

Westbrook glanced at his watch.

'Damned right!' he said, ruefully. 'Sorry, Al. We have a scheduled take-off at fifteen hundred.' He stood up and held out his hand. 'Why don't you and Sally come down to Portland and join us for the weekend?'

'Yes,' Jane joined in, 'it's a long time since we've had a get-together.'

Volpe smiled.

'I'll get Sally to give you a call this evening. I don't think we have any plans for the weekend and it will be good to have a jaw. Maybe I can persuade you about taking on that Fall River job.'

'You can try,' chuckled Westbrook.

They went through the ritual farewells and walked across the tarmac apron to the aircraft. It was a warm, sunny July day. The barometer in the club-house registered 72.6 degrees, average summer temperature for the area. The Mitsubishi was cool and comfortable as they climbed in and seated themselves in the twin seat cockpit. Westbrook felt the strange sensation he had experienced earlier of climbing into a military rather than a civil aircraft, with its black instrument panel and array of functional switches, buttons, gauges, lights, levers and handles. After a quick word on the radio with airfield control he started the two AiResearch engines, hearing the angry growl of the straining 1,000 horse power in each engine, the equivalent of 157 pounds of jet thrust per side.

'Hello, Newport Control,' Westbrook flicked the r/t switch. 'This is Victor Papa Uncle Bravo requesting take-off clearance.'

'Newport Control,' came back a slightly bored voice, 'you are clear for take-off on runway two, west.'

Westbrook let the aircraft move forward slowly, taxi-ing on one engine to save fuel, making tight turns into the operating engine, and bringing the machine to the start of the runway. He turned to grin at Jane.

'All set?'

She smiled and nodded.

He began to accelerate rapidly down the runway. At 90 knots he gave a light additional increase in control back pressure to lift the nosewheel and the aircraft came unstuck at 100 knots. He raised his gear immediately and once the speed built a little he began to retract his flaps. They moved very slowly and in increments, so that there were no surprises and plenty of time for dealing with mild pitch changes and using trim. He preferred manual trim. The stall speed on the Mitsubishi decreased by 24 knots over the total 40 degree flap travel and so the gradual retraction was important.

Again he felt momentarily surprise as, in the first moments after take-off, differences between the Mitsubishi and other lateral control systems became apparent. It was almost like flying the aircraft by remote control. The feeling in the joystick or wheel that was associated with ailerons was missing and there was a new urgency to maintaining lateral and rudder trim. He knew enough about the aircraft to realise that if he failed to make the lateral trim in time, the tapping that followed could be Old Man Death knocking at the door. It took him a couple of minutes to get used to the controls again. He had to remember that when speed or power was changed, the aircraft needed to be trimmed, but this soon became second nature.

The aircraft climbed well, ascending at 2,000 feet per minute at 200 knots. The climb rate began tapering off at 13,000 feet, the engines reaching their maximum altitude, and in less than ten minutes Westbrook levelled off at 16,000 feet. He now turned into a gentle arc south to Rhode Island Sound with the grey, frothy Atlantic beyond.

'Beautiful,' cried Jane. 'Just like an elevator. Did anyone tell you that you should be a pilot?'

Westbrook stuck his tongue out at her.

It was as he was arcing back northwards over Sachuest Point, looking for the Sakonnet River to lead him northward towards the Massachusetts state line, that he felt a gentle thump. His eyes immediately sped along the rows of dials and gauges seeking an explanation. There was none. He waited tensely but the AiResearch engines continued to growl healthily. Below them were the rocky promontories and sandy lowlands of the smallest state in the union, with its U-shaped valleys, lakes, swamps and slow-flowing streams. Sunlight dappled the pleasant vista.

This time the thump was more pronounced, more violent. Jane gave an involuntary gasp and stared at him, her face white.

Frowning, he glanced over the controls again. The stick felt sloppy in his hands. Something was wrong. The aircraft was beginning to lose its forward momentum, the airspeed indicator moving backwards alarmingly.

Westbrook snapped on the r/t.

'Newport Control, Newport Control, this is Victor Papa Uncle Bravo.' His voice sounded calm, almost offhand, belying the tightness around his mouth. 'I have an emergency. Request landing clearance immediately.'

He was already beginning to turn the aircraft to the west.

'Newport Control to Victor Papa Uncle Bravo,' came a disinterested voice. 'What is the nature of your emergency? Say again, what is. . . .'

Something cracked with a force that sent the aircraft nose forward and rocketing downward. The control stick went completely slack in Westbrook's hand. The engines began to whine hysterically.

'May Day! May Day! May Day!' Westbrook found himself screaming into the microphone, but even as he did so he realised the hopelessness of it and the inevitability of death.

Al Volpe was in the Newport control tower when Westbrook's emergency request came through. He stood frowning as the controller replied requesting information on the emergency. Then came a garbled cry—it did not sound like his friend at all. Westbrook must have left his r/t switched on for suddenly his voice came over the speakers, strong and clear: 'Jane, oh God, Jane! I love you!' There was a woman's answering sob. A scream and then a roar of static before the radio went dead.

For several long seconds there was a stunned silence in the control tower before an Eastern Airways Merlin IVC pilot was heard requesting landing instructions. The controller turned, still pale, and automatically began to issue directions. Al Volpe was still standing in the same position, mouth slightly open, when a telephone shrilled. A second controller grabbed it, listened white-faced and scrawled something on a piece of paper. He turned to Volpe.

'A farmer from Tiverton . . . says an aircraft just went nose first into the marshy swamp area south of the town. It exploded on impact.'

Volpe stared at him, disbelieving. Then he started to swear in a harsh voice which he did not recognise as his own.

Chapter Two

Harry Maclaren halted his taxi at the corner of Madison and 28th Street, outside the huge black and silver edifice of the Pan Continental Airways Building. He paid off the driver with a sigh of relief. He hated New York and he hated travelling in New York. Since the Delta Airlines jet had touched down at Kennedy Airport, Maclaren had been loathing it all: the frenzied rush for the air terminal bus, the journey itself, wedged between sweating businessmen, frantic mothers, screaming children and garrulous old ladies. The arrival at the East Side Airlines Terminal on First Avenue and 37th Street was merely a repeat performance of the arrival at Kennedy. Then he had lost his place in the taxi queue because he had forgotten to get a 'queue ticket' from the machine which provided him with a number by which a burly attendant called him to the next available cab. Of course, Maclaren could have justified a taxi from Kennedy into New York, but being of a frugal disposition he had felt it a waste of money. Now he stood on the sidewalk outside the tall building and surveyed his destination with relief.

At 43 years of age, Maclaren looked nearer fifty. He was lean and wiry, with a shock of salt and pepper hair and grey eyes deepset in a weatherworn face. The face carried a semi-woebegone expression, an expression of permanent worry. He carried an overnight bag and an attaché case of tan pigskin which matched his light-coloured suit.

In the central foyer of the Pan Continental Airways Building he was greeted with an automatic smile from a small blonde receptionist.

'John G. Badrick's office, please,' he asked, adding hastily: 'He is expecting me.'

The girl did not bat an eyelid. Perhaps she was used to people wandering in off the street and demanding to see the executive president of the corporation.

'What name shall I give, sir?' she asked, reaching for an internal telephone.

'Maclaren. Harry Maclaren from Portland.'

It was a matter of a few moments before the receptionist established that he was expected. She waved to a uniformed porter.

'Take Mr. Maclaren to Mr. Badrick's penthouse.'

The uniformed man glanced at Maclaren with a certain amount of deference and offered to take his bags. Maclaren let him carry the overnight case and followed him to a special express elevator. It deposited him on the fifty-third floor with a speed which left him a little dizzy and breathless. Badrick's secretary, a grey-haired woman of about fifty, met them at the doors of the elevator.

'Hello, Mr. Maclaren.'

Maclaren's mind raced. What was her name? He struggled to drag it from his memory.

'Miss Shelley, isn't it?'

She smiled thinly.

'Mr. Badrick is waiting for you.' She turned to the porter. 'Just put Mr. Maclaren's bag down by my desk.'

She turned and preceded Maclaren across a plush-carpeted foyer through a large outer office and knocked softly on a door beyond. Without waiting for a reply she opened it and announced Maclaren.

Maclaren had the impression of walking into a carpeted cathedral. It was an enormous office, oak-panelled with purple drapes and full of antiques. He felt as if he were stumbling through a field of soft carpet pile towards a gigantic desk.

John G. Badrick, executive president of Pan Continental Airways, rose from a black leather swivel chair and came round his desk. He was in his early sixties, short, fat and balding, looking more like a stereotype business tycoon than the shrewd administrator that he was. He extended a hand to Maclaren. It was flaccid and held no warmth.

'Coffee, hot and black for two, Miss Shelley,' he growled over Maclaren's shoulder.

He motioned Maclaren across to a corner where there stood a couple of white fur-covered armchairs and flopped into one. He looked like someone with a problem.

'Well, Harry,' he began without preamble, 'let's have hard facts. How does it affect the project?'

Maclaren gave a long sigh.

'Pretty badly, I'm afraid,' he said, seating himself in the other armchair. 'Alec Westbrook was not only our chief test pilot but he had been with the project from its inception—he knew all there was to know about the ship.'

Badrick pursed his lips.

'But we must have a back-up team . . . ?'

Maclaren gave Badrick a hard look.

'It was decided by the board, in the interests of economy . . .' he paused to emphasise his words, 'that we should not commence the training of alternative crews for the airship until after the initial test flights. Colonel Garry Carson is now the sole qualified airship pilot on the project. He will, with his experience, naturally become chief test pilot, subject to your confirmation. But we will need a second qualified man as of right now . . . and I suggest we start recruiting and training our back-up crews immediately.'

Badrick passed a hand over his forehead and sighed.

'You know the board, Harry. Training pilots for the airship project before we know the results of the initial test flights is going to be a costly business.'

Maclaren snorted.

'The board doesn't seem to have much faith in the *Albatross*.'

'Harry, you know as much as I do about the costs of training pilots . . . what if we put these pilots on our payroll, begin expensive training programmes and then have to lay them off if the *Albatross* fails to come up to expectations?'

'The *Albatross* isn't going to fail. It's a wise investment to make. As project manager I have made my position clear all along: for the *Albatross* to do the Atlantic crossing, which will take about two and a half days, we need to carry two or three complete crews on board. That means two qualified pilots per crew. As it is, all we have at the moment is one solitary trained airship pilot, flight engineer and navigator. We should have been putting two more crews through simulator training while the initial testing on the airship was being carried out, then the problem due to Westbrook's death would not have arisen.'

Miss Shelley entered with a tray of coffee.

They waited in silence until she had left.

'As I see it, Harry,' said Badrick, lighting a Corona-Corona and exhaling deeply, 'we have one immediate problem. A replacement for Westbrook is needed to complete our test crew. I will certainly raise the matter of recruiting and training back-up crews at the next board meeting. In fact, we have some likely applicants who are already on our airline payroll but, frankly, the board is worried. We have spent a lot of money on this airship project. It's still an unknown quantity. The feasibility of large freight-carrying airships looks good on paper but it might prove otherwise in practice . . . you know what the public thinks of airships. They still haven't forgotten the *Hindenburg*, the R101 and all the other disasters of the 1920s and 1930s.'

Maclaren bridled.

'We both know that the early problems were mainly due to the fact that hydrogen-filled airships were prone to catastrophic fires. The public forgets that the *Graf Zeppelin I*, in spite of the hydrogen handicap, made one hundred and forty-seven safe crossings of the Atlantic during a period of eight years without any major incident. Inert helium gas was not available in sufficient quantities to. . . .'

Badrick held up a hand.

'You've no need to tell me, Harry. I know the history, but we mustn't blind ourselves to the problem. We have a tough job ahead of us. Even if the *Albatross* flies like a dream, we still have the investors and the public to consider. Anyway, let's get back to our main problem . . . we need a qualified airship pilot pretty quickly to fill Westbrook's place. Can he be found?'

Maclaren hunched his shoulders.

'I simply don't know at this stage. Goodyear operate three small airships—they might have some trained personnel who would be willing to cross to our company. Failing that, the only alternative is a head-hunt in Europe.'

'You're not suggesting that we try to poach from the French airship project?' Badrick frowned.

'Not necessarily. There are a few experimental companies in Britain. But it's not going to be easy. There would still be a lot of training involved—a dirigible pilot is about as rare as snow in Vegas.'

'How about people with balloonist qualifications?'

Maclaren shook his head.

'Not the same thing as flying a thousand-foot-long airship with a rigid hull.'

'Well, you know what you're looking for, Harry. I'll leave it to you to start head-hunting a suitable pilot to complete the test crew. In the meantime, I will do my best to get the board to approve the employment and training of your back-up crews. One point we've both got to remember . . . time is an essential on this project. We can't afford to let things get behind schedule. The French are well ahead with their project. I have reports that their prototype airship is nearing completion and may soon start its series of test flights. I want the *Albatross* first in the field . . . first to make the Transatlantic flight. John Public doesn't like people who come second.'

Maclaren nodded. Whoever made the first safe Transatlantic run would not only get public prestige, which would help certain commercial contracts, but would dominate airship freight transport during its new business awakening. That would more than compensate the capital investment on the project.

'Alright, Harry.' Badrick hauled himself to his feet. 'I agree with you that Garry Carson should be appointed your chief test pilot and I'll leave it to you to get cracking on the second pilot. I guess we are talking about days and not weeks?'

'Yes,' replied Maclaren, taking Badrick's proffered hand and letting the executive president guide him through the soft pile carpet jungle to the door.

'Leave the rest with me, Harry. Alright?'

'Fine,' muttered Maclaren with no conviction in his voice.

'Good. Well, my wife and I will expect you at eight o'clock tonight for dinner,' Badrick flashed an easy smile. 'Just a small affair—a few friends. Okay?'

Maclaren nodded. A few friends? With Badrick that usually meant about thirty or forty people, ranging from the mayor to local senators and anyone else who could be of use to Pan Continental's chief.

He went out feeling annoyed. The urgent call from Badrick for him to fly down to New York for discussions was nothing which a half-hour telephone conversation could not have resolved—apart from a half-hearted invitation to dinner. He felt he had wasted his time. Well, there was nothing for it. He couldn't fly back to Portland until early the next morning anyway. He scowled in annoyance.

'Oh, Mr. Maclaren.'

It was Miss Shelley.

'Don't forget your bag, Mr. Maclaren.'

He forced a grin as he turned to retrieve his overnight bag.

'I have booked a room for you at the Algonquin.'

Maclaren had to admire Miss Shelley's imperturbable efficiency.

'That's nice of you.'

'You're welcome,' she replied, turning with a smile of apology as a buzzer went on her desk.

Maclaren walked to the elevator and jabbed savagely at the call button.

Jesus! He suddenly realised the enormity of his task: find a qualified airship pilot within the next few days who could quickly become sufficiently skilled enough to take the *Albatross* through her initial testing.

Chapter Three

The group of reporters were seated in the board-room of Anglo-American Airships Inc., the subsidiary of Pan Continental Airways, at the company's project site. The site was really an extension of Portland's airport: a sizeable acreage of sheds and office buildings facing onto one of the larger inlets of the Fore River which cut through the city. Every month Samantha Hackerman, Anglo-American's press officer, made it a point to invite a dozen of the most influential aerospace correspondents to the project site. Here they were given an update on the corporation's progress in building their freight-carrying airship, the *Albatross*. The dozen correspondents had been wined and fed lavishly, and then led in a mellow, receptive mood into the board-room for the actual briefing.

Samantha, Sam to her friends, knew her job well; she was a professional to her marrow. At twenty-nine years of age, with a degree in science, she had worked on aviation magazines as a journalist before joining the press office of Pan Continental. She had only been a year in the job when she had been picked to head the press team on the airship project. She tucked a rebellious wisp of red hair behind her ear as she tried to marshal her experts to the top table.

There was Oscar Van Kleef, the chief designer of the *Albatross*, looking petulantly annoyed at being called away from his slide rules and computers. He was in his mid-fifties, a thin, worried-looking man with silver grey streaking his blue-black mane of hair. Van Kleef hated these monthly press conferences. Jack Lane, the assistant project manager, sat urbane and calm in the centre chair, filling in for Harry Maclaren, who had been called away on business to New York. Lane was a first-class administrator. Nothing ever seemed to worry or fluster him. He was one of the 'fixers' of the company, able to find solutions to the most difficult problems. Next to him was the chief electrical engineer of the project, Kurt Nieman, a man of medium height, stocky but not fat, with thinning fair hair. He had a fixed, pleasant smile but he always seemed absorbed in thought. He constantly drummed with his fingers on the table in front of him. On the far side of Nieman, sprawled in his chair, was Garry Carson. His face was grim. He had been a special friend of Alec Westbrook, whose death had stunned everyone who worked for Anglo-American. Thirty-nine years old, Carson was a tall, fair-haired Texan: a former colonel in the Air Force who had joined Pan Continental as a regular airline pilot before his knowledge of small dirigibles had caused his transfer to second pilot on the *Albatross* project.

Samantha frowned. She supposed Carson would become chief test pilot on the project now. Silently she prayed that the reporters would not dwell on the death of Alec Westbrook. She knew few details about the crash which had killed him and his attractive wife, Jane.

'Alright, ladies and gentlemen,' she called into the hubbub. Faces turned expectantly towards her. 'I am delighted to welcome you here to Anglo-American and hope you have enjoyed your lunch.'

There was an appreciative murmur.

'I would like to open this briefing with a short resumé of the project before handing you over to our experts, to whom you have already been introduced, for detailed questions.'

She paused, looked down at some papers and cleared her throat.

'Anglo-American Airships Incorporated was formed three years ago to develop a freight-carrying airship. Years of research by our parent company, Pan Continental Airways, revealed that it was feasible to design a large airship which had direct operating costs no greater than those of a subsonic jet aircraft. Research has shown that a large airship could transport immense payloads over useful distances with a minimum of handling: such an airship is particularly suited to the movement of containerised goods directly from departure to destination points without need for the intermediate handling stages inevitably associated with ground transport. As a result, Doctor Oscar Van Kleef,' she indicated the chief designer with a nod of her head, 'has designed our first ship which we call *Albatross*.'

Here she smiled broadly at the audience.

'I need hardly point out to the literary among you that we have named her after Jules Verne's famous airship creation in his books *The Clipper of the Clouds* and *Master of the World*.'

She paused to let the conscientious among the reporters make notes.

'Our *Albatross* is one thousand one hundred feet long and has an overall height and diameter of two hundred and twenty feet. She will be able to move a payload of five hundred tons and carry, at the same time, one hundred and fifty passengers and twenty-five crew. She will be capable of cruising between one hundred and one hundred and fifty miles per hour, and we estimate she will be able to cross the Atlantic in two to two and a half days. She is powered by eight Napier Nomad engines, a compound aero engine which was developed in Britain: a diesel pushing its exhaust through a gas turbine. It has a rating of thirty-one, thirty-five horse power maximum.'

One of the reporters frowned.

'What horse power rating?'

'Three thousand, one hundred and thirty-five,' repeated Samantha. 'You will find all these specifications in the publicity folders which have been distributed to you. Now I'll be quiet and let you ask the questions.'

A stocky man, she mentally identified him as the aerospace correspondent of *Time Magazine*, cleared his throat.

'Isn't history against a viable airship project?'

Samantha groaned inwardly. It was the inevitable question; always the first to be asked.

'I'll hand you over to Doctor Van Kleef to start the ball rolling on this one.'

Van Kleef shot her a disgruntled look.

'Would Mr. ah-er . . . be more specific?' His voice, slightly high-pitched and querulous, matched his sour expression.

'What I mean, doctor,' the man replied, 'is that while there has been sporadic interest in this class of aircraft over the years, and during the last ten years there have been any number of proposals for large cargo-carrying airships, not one has been successful. The history of airships prior to the 1940s was a story of one lamentable disaster after another.'

'It has perhaps been forgotten,' Van Kleef began, sounding like a teacher addressing a class of especially recalcitrant students, 'that during the 1930s the airship was the only type of aircraft which was capable of maintaining regular long-range commercial operations. Subsequent developments of the aeroplane have completely changed the situation . . . however, we believe that the new technology which brought about this change is also capable of profiting by the construction of modern airships, making them highly cost-effective against transportation by surface craft and aeroplanes, especially in light of current fuel and energy crises.'

'Yes, but what about all the disasters?' demanded a woman reporter who had identified her newspaper as the *Washington Times*. 'Surely airships have proved to be dangerous and that is why they have not been developed during the last forty years? They are archaic death traps.'

Samantha nervously saw Van Kleef's face whiten and stood ready to intervene, but it was Kurt Nieman who laid a hand on the chief designer's arm.

'Perhaps if I may . . . ?' he smiled slightly. 'Madam, it is true there were many disasters. Here, in the United States, the largest airships built—*Akron* and *Macron*—were wrecked in storms in 1933 and 1935 because of faulty structures. But let me point out that there was one company who successfully designed and built airships which were remarkably reliable in service: the German Zeppelin company. True, they had their share of accidents, but the problem was that the only lifting gas available to them was hydrogen, a highly inflammable gas. I would urge you to remember that the *Graf Zeppelin I* flew eight years, making one hundred and forty-seven crossings of the Atlantic, in complete safety. The *Hindenburg* had been flying safely for fourteen months before atmospheric electricity ignited a hydrogen leak . . . yet while the crash is depicted as a great horrific tragedy, let us consider the facts. Out of ninety-six people on board the *Hindenburg* at the time of the disaster only thirty-six actually died. How many survivors would there be from a comparable aeroplane crash?'

'Are you saying that the *Hindenburg* was a safer aircraft than an ordinary aeroplane?' demanded the *Time Magazine* man.

Nieman sighed.

'What I am saying is that it would have been a totally safe vessel had the inert gas helium been available instead of hydrogen. The Zeppelin company were the only organisation in the 1930s with sufficient experience to enable them to build economically viable airships, but they were denied the use of the safe gas helium because of restrictions imposed by the United States. The Zeppelin company were so sure of the viability of airships that even after the *Hindenburg* disaster they built the *Graf Zeppelin II*, designed for helium use, but were denied it.'

'There were political considerations at the time,' commented the *Washington Post* correspondent dryly.

Nieman looked puzzled.

'Hitler was then in power in Germany,' pointed out the correspondent.

Van Kleef interrupted.

'The point my colleague, Doctor Nieman, was making was that historically the airship was a highly successful passenger aircraft. Between 1910 and 1914, for example, the Duetsche Luftschiffahrts Aktion Gesellschaft flew 34,000 passengers a total distance of 108,000 miles in 1,600 flights in the company's seven airships within Germany. The main problem was, as Doctor Nieman stated, the lifting gases available. But no one in Anglo-American is suggesting that we return to the old methods of construction. The R100 contained more than fourteen miles of duralumin girders, the assembly of which is far too labour-intensive for today. Also, we have a ready supply of helium which was not available outside of the United States before 1940, and very sparingly used in the States at that time.'

There was a pause, during which Samantha pointed out:

'In a few moments you will be taken out to the construction area in order to see the *Albatross* and perhaps any technical questions on materials can be put then. Are there any more questions of a general nature?'

'How about noise levels?' asked a rather emaciated young man. 'My readers are especially conscious of the ecological considerations.'

Samantha looked towards Van Kleef but the designer seemed to have subsided into a brooding silence. Jack Lane, the assistant project manager, cleared his throat.

'The *Albatross*, like her predecessors, will be one of the most peaceful forms of travel ever devised. The old airships were never regarded as a noise nuisance. The maximum disturbance made by the *Hindenburg*, for example, was only sixty-one decibels. Modern airships, such as our *Albatross*, with modern silencing equipment and displacement of engines will be virtually silent. Likewise, unlike aeroplanes, pollution will be non-existent.'

One of Samantha's assistants, a dark-haired girl, entered the room, walked up to her and whispered in her ear. Samantha nodded.

'Is there a Mr. Ryan of the *Los Angeles Herald-Examiner* here?' she asked.

A man stood up, looking slightly uncomfortable.

'Your office is on the telephone, Mr. Ryan. They say it is urgent. Would you follow my assistant?'

The correspondent, with a mumbled apology, followed the dark-haired girl from the room.

'When will the *Albatross* take to the air?' the woman from the *Washington Times* was asking.

Jack Lane leaned forward and smiled.

'We hope to have our initial test flights shortly and a maiden Transatlantic run might be a feasibility within two months.'

'I was interested by the number you gave for crewmen,' said the *New York Times* reporter. 'The old airships had to carry large crews. What sort of crew will the *Albatross* be carrying?'

This time it was Garry Carson who answered. He had an easy, drawling way of speaking which left one in no doubt of his state origin.

'When the *Albatross* is operating normally it will carry three complete executive crews who will operate a six hours on and eighteen off watch period. They will consist of two pilots, a navigator and communications officer and the flight engineer. Four executive crewmen in all.'

'No more?'

'As it is planned to carry passengers there will be a further crew of ten stewards and stewardesses. They will operate under a chief purser and there will also be a cargo hold inspector who will be responsible for ensuring the cargo is stowed safely at all times.'

'Can I ask for some comparative dimensions between the *Albatross* and the *Hindenburg*?' It was the ecologically-minded correspondent.

Samantha looked at Van Kleef pointedly.

'The *Hindenburg* was 814 feet long with a volume of 7.1 million cubic feet. Our ship is therefore nearly three hundred feet longer and with a very much larger cubic capacity.'

The man was scribbling on a notepad.

'So what you are proposing is an aircraft that is larger than the *QE II*, five times the length of a Boeing 747?'

Van Kleef nodded.

'With so few crew to run it?' asked the woman correspondent. 'Only four executive crewmen, you said?'

'We have onboard computers,' replied Nieman. 'There are various control systems so that, even with four men, there is little which cannot be handled should an emergency arise.'

Van Kleef glanced impatiently at his watch. He had been through so many of these press briefings that he was bored and irritated and showed it. Samantha decided that it was time to conduct the correspondents to the airship construction site. Just as she was about to suggest it the *Los Angeles Herald-Examiner* reporter re-entered the room. He stood hesitantly.

'I have a . . . er . . . question.'

He paused.

'Go ahead, Mr. Ryan,' invited Samantha with an encouraging smile.

'It is about the death of your chief test pilot, Major Alec Westbrook.'

'I'm afraid we have no further information on that matter, other than the statement given out yesterday following the news of his tragic accident,' interrupted the girl.

The reporter seemed undeterred.

'My office has just telephoned me,' he said unnecessarily. 'The Federal Aviation Authority have just issued a statement following their initial enquiries into the crash. Major Westbrook's aircraft was sabotaged . . . has your company any statement to make on that?'

Chapter Four

Sir Ashley Ashton thrust aside his copy of *The Times* and gave an inward groan. He reached forward and pressed his intercom button.

'Alice, do you have any aspirin in your desk drawer?'

'Yes sir,' came his secretary's response. 'I'll bring some in.'

Ashton stood up and walked to his office window, looking down on the teeming crowds of people and slow-moving traffic which edged along London's Piccadilly. Thankfully, the roar they undoubtedly made was silenced by the double-glazing of his window. Ashton nervously rubbed the back of his neck. His head was splitting. First the domestic crisis last night and now . . . now this!

A soft knock at the door preceded the entrance of his secretary bearing a tray with a carafe of water, a glass and a packet of soluble aspirin. She set the tray down and expertly mixed two pills in a glass of water.

'Anything else, sir?'

Ashton shook his head.

The girl was halfway to the door when he changed his mind.

'Get my wife, will you?'

She nodded and closed the door behind her while he, gratefully, reached for the glass and drained it. A few moments later the telephone rang.

'Martha?'

'Yes, Ashley.' His wife's voice sounded cracked and strained.

'Has Claire rung you? Is there any news?'

There was a moment's hesitation.

'No, she hasn't. Did you expect her to after last night?'

'Not really,' sighed Ashton.

'You were a little heavy with her, Ashley.' There was a note of rebuke in Martha Ashton's voice.

'Damn it!' snorted Ashton. 'She's only twenty years old. How else do you expect a father to react when his daughter comes home and says she is going off to live with a man who is twice her age . . . and a man with the reputation that Allie Gray has? The Soho Porn King! That's what the gutter press call him.'

'You don't think that I am not concerned, do you, Ashley?' his wife's voice held a dangerously tremulous note. 'She is my daughter as well.'

'Yes, I know, dear. I know. It's just that I feel so damned impotent.'

'We'll just have to be patient,' returned his wife. 'If Claire doesn't contact us within the next day or two then I shall telephone Mr. Gray's place and see if she will speak to me.'

Ashton moodily replaced the receiver.

It had certainly been a bad scene last night. It had ended with his attractive blonde daughter, Claire, screaming obscenities at him because he had tried to forbid her to see Allie Gray again; she had finally announced that she was going to live with the man. Ashton had been beside himself with fury. He knew Gray from the newspapers as a Soho nightclub owner who ran a small empire of sex-shops, peddling pornography through the country, and who was also known for his underworld connections. Indeed, Gray had served time in borstal and prison as a young man. Ashton had found out about his daughter's affair with Gray just a few days before and his attempt to end it was met with hostility from Claire, whose temper was the equal of her father's. Late last evening Claire had flung some belongings into a bag and stormed out of the house.

Ashton wondered whether he should contact the police; but what could they do? Claire was twenty years old and her own boss. Should he confront Allie Gray in person? That would be rather Victorian and have a negative effect. Maybe Martha was right. Let Claire do her own thing for a while. She would eventually find out what sort of man Allie Gray was. But, by that time, she might be hurt . . . might be scarred by the experience. He sighed deeply, letting his eyes wander in distraction over his desk. They came back to the discarded copy of *The Times*.

The story he had been reading was about the sabotage of Major Westbrook's aircraft.

Ashton tried to dismiss Claire from his mind; picked it up and read it again, carefully. Then he pressed his intercom button again.

'Alice, get me a person-to-person call with John G. Badrick in New York.'

At fifty-six years of age Sir Ashley Ashton was the British vice-president of Anglo-American Airships, and was in charge of the company's London base. Ashton had spent most of his business life as an executive of British Aerospace Developments until his interest in the commercial use of airships had made him take up an offer from John G. Badrick to head the British end of his airship project. Ashton's interest in airships was passionate. In fact, the entire aviation business was a passion with him, so much so that his private and domestic life tended to suffer because of it. His telephone rang. It was Badrick.

'Good to hear from you, Ash. What's on your mind?'

Ashton always felt a surge of annoyance at Badrick's abbreviation of his name.

'Hello, John,' he replied coolly. 'Is it true about Westbrook?'

'The British newspapers are carrying the story about sabotage?' asked Badrick, after a slight pause.

'Yes.'

'H'mm. Well the FAA's initial findings show there was some tampering with Westbrook's machine. We don't know any more but I should imagine there'll be a federal investigation.'

'Does it affect the project at all?' pressed Ashton.

'Only in that it leaves us without a first-class test pilot for the *Albatross*. Maclaren is searching for a replacement right now . . . for a second pilot, that is. Garry Carson becomes our number one man. Do you have any ideas?'

Ashton snorted.

'For a qualified airship pilot? That's rather a tall order, old boy.'

'Well, if you can think of anything . . . even a long shot . . . get in touch with Maclaren.'

'You'll keep me posted about the sabotage?'

'Sure. See you, Ash.'

Claire Ashton let out a low shuddering moan as the man reached a frenzied climax. She clung, clung tightly to him, legs wrapped around his, fingers—like claws—biting deeply into his back. Her mind was swimming in an ecstasy of emotions—emotions she could only feel and not analyse. She had wanted the moment to last for ever, go on and on, but he had reached his climax all too soon and now lay inert and heavy upon her, heart thumping wildly against heart. Too soon, far too soon. Then he was rolling away from her—her hands reached out to detain him as he turned on his side. She lay spreadeagled, exposed and naked; she felt rejected and totally alone after the near-hysteria of her passion. She peered nervously into the darkness, at the dark mound of his shoulder, licked her lips and whispered: 'Wasn't it right? Wasn't I alright?'

The man made a noise, a quizzical sound deep within his throat like a stifled yawn.

'Wha . . . oh, sure. Yeah, you're okay, kid. Love you.'

One hand reached behind his recumbent form and patted the inside of her thigh, like a master petting his dog.

Then there was a silence.

Claire Ashton felt unhappy. It had not been like this the first time with Allie Gray. The first time? It seemed so long ago and yet it had only been three weeks, just after Claire had decided to drop out of university—bored with an attempt to gain a Bachelor of Arts degree in English Literature at Cambridge. She was a wilful girl, materially indulged by her parents but starved of love and understanding. Her father, Sir Ashley Ashton, had never had the time to be interested in what she thought and felt, nor even to be a companion to her, especially when she was growing up. Neither did her father believe in displaying emotion and her impression of him was a cold, austere figure who always held her at a distance and never really seemed interested in her. Her mother, Martha Ashton, was dominated by her husband. What he felt was right, was law to her. She was a timid woman who hardly ever went against Sir Ashley's wishes. The result was that while both parents provided anything Claire wanted within reason on a material level, they left her with a profound sense of dissatisfaction with her life and a strong streak of angry rebellion. Since adolescence she had tended towards outrageous behaviour in an attempt to attract her father's attention.

She had lost her virginity when she was only fifteen, more to spite her father than because she was attracted to the shy boy with the acne on his neck whom she had to coax into the act. She had enjoyed, far more, the beating that her father had inflicted when she confessed what she had done at breakfast the following morning. It was, as she recalled, the first time he had ever given her his undivided attention. She had been to bed with many men since then, experiences which left Claire usually cold and disinterested in them. There had been one man, a junior lecturer at college, who had made love to her coldly, mechanically, as if he were manipulating the buttons on a computer. True, he had pressed the right buttons; true, he had made her feel that sex was, for the first time, a pleasurable act in itself, not merely because it was forbidden. But Claire's demands for constant and undivided attention from the man made him quickly end the affair.

In her boredom and dissatisfaction she had decided to leave university without a degree and go to London with a friend to work as a model. At twenty years of age Claire had a slim, boyish body. Too slim to be attractive she had always felt, but her figure was well-proportioned. Her short cropped golden hair, wide blue eyes and permanently parted lips, giving her a surprised expression, added up to a 'little innocent' image. It was a deceptive appearance. Her friend, Rosabel, was older and had worked as a model before. Rosabel had assured Claire that her figure was what model agencies were looking for these days: voluptuous, heavy-breasted women were now unfashionable. So Claire had let herself be persuaded to accompany Rosabel to an agency in Soho. A bored-looking man, whose ability with make-up, especially in highlighting his eyes and cheekbones, made Claire a little envious, cast an appraising glance at her and suggested she try the Gray Shadow Club in Greek Street.

'Ask for Mr. Gray, love,' purred the man, stroking his blue-tinted curly hair. 'I'm sure that he'll be interested in you.'

Allie Gray was.

The interview took place in the penthouse apartment which he kept over the club. Gray was in his late forties, proud of his still athletic figure. During the day he always wore his shirt unbuttoned to the stomach, displaying a tangle of greying chest hair and proving his daily squash match and gym exercises stood his body in good stead. Claire didn't know anything about the lean, sun-lamp-bronzed Allie Gray at that time. When he appraised her, smiling in open admiration, she looked at his broad, handsome face and suddenly felt like a rabbit before a snake: helpless and afraid. There was a feeling, too, of excitement; an excitement that was also orgasmic as he reached forward to tilt her head this way and that.

'Yeah; yeah. I could really use you,' he muttered, and she was not even put off by his East End accent which her social background informed her was not 'nice' to be associated with.

'What,' she asked nervously, 'what sort of modelling job is it?'

Allie Gray's eyes widened.

'You've got to be kidding?' But he suddenly saw that she wasn't. 'How old are you?' he asked.

'Twenty,' declared Claire, tilting her head a little defiantly. 'I've just left university.'

'Not worked before?'

'No.'

Allie Gray smiled. 'I see.' He let his eyes run over her figure again.

'Well, I could really use you, love. But there's no rush . . . you see, I have interests in quite a few, er, enterprises. One of them, well, we are going to do some film work and I'm looking for someone . . . well, like you. But we can talk about that later. Let's talk about it over dinner.'

They had dinner that evening but they didn't talk about the job. Instead Allie Gray wined and dined her and then took her back to his apartment and made love to her with such a savage determination that Claire experienced her first mind-reeling orgasm. Allie Gray was an expert lover! he wanted the youthful body of Claire, wanted what it symbolised to his deprived boyhood, and he took her with the attitude of a Viking conqueror. The result was something which Claire had never experienced before, producing a mixture of physical pleasure and emotions which made her believe, in her immaturity, that she was experiencing that indefinable thing called 'love'.

For three weeks Allie Gray had sated himself with Claire, taking her to clubs, giving her meals, taking her gambling and allowing her to waste large bankrolls. By this time she had found out that her lover was rich and that the world he moved in was entirely alien to the staid and stable home-life she had experienced at her parent's house in Kent. Allie Gray's world made her feel nervous but also excited. It was like something from a storybook, romantic and intoxicating. She moved at his side through stripclubs, gambling casinos and sex-shops, protected by his far-reaching authority. Her excitement did not diminish even when she realised that he was party to many other vices and that the modelling job he was going to offer her had been a part in a blue movie. That didn't matter now. She was Allie Gray's woman.

Then she had gone to her parent's house in Kent to collect some things. Her father had been at home and had discovered that she had left university and was involved with Allie Gray. She didn't know how he had found out. The next thing was that he was ordering her, coldly and unemotionally, not to see Allie Gray again. She had shouted at him, defending herself and her lover. He had remained impassive—just gone on talking in that cold, sneering voice of his. She had started to scream obscenities, trying to stir up some emotion in him. He had turned, walked into his study and shut the door. In fury she had thrown some belongings into a bag and stormed out of the house.

When she returned to Allie Gray's apartment and told him, and talked about her love for him and about setting up home together, she had not understood the amused look in his eyes. He had not taken her out that night but made some excuse to spend the evening in his club without her. He had come in late. She was already in bed, drowsy and half-asleep. He threw off his clothes and climbed in beside her.

Now he lay on his side, snoring gently, leaving her strangely alone and dissatisfied. She felt used.

She must have dropped off to sleep for she started awake, conscious of a loud banging, of the lights flashing on and people milling into the room.

'Alright you two love-birds,' sneered a voice. 'Get out of that!'

She blinked and found herself focussing on uniformed policemen.

Beside her Allie Gray was swearing violently.

'That's enough, Allie,' admonished a voice. 'Plenty of time for that down at the station. And before you say it . . . yes, we do have a warrant.'

The speaker was a stocky man in civilian clothes, who was obviously in charge of the uniformed officers.

'Let me get my mouthpiece,' Gray was muttering.

'Later,' returned the detective. 'Get a move on, Allie.'

Confused, Claire was struggling to hold the sheet in front of her, hiding from the amused gaze of the policemen.

'I beg your pardon ma'am,' sneered the detective, affecting a slight Oxford accent. 'Had I known you would be embarrassed I would have rung the doorbell and waited outside.'

'Leave the kid alone,' Gray said. 'She don't know nothing.'

'Yeah, I believe you,' replied the man. 'Forbes!'

A policewoman came forward.

'Take charge of Allie's tart.'

Claire didn't have time to protest before the policewoman bustled over and gruffly ordered her to get her clothes on. Claire abruptly realised that Allie Gray was standing naked as the police milled through the room. She stared about in speechless confusion and, as the policewoman tried to get her out of the bed, she struggled to keep the sheet around herself.

'Don't try to kid me that you're bashful!' scowled the police officer. 'Get your clothes on!'

Claire found herself shivering with fear.

'What's . . . what's happening?' she whimpered.

'Got it, inspector!' cried a uniformed constable, entering the room. 'It was just where our snout said it would be. . . .'

The inspector turned with a triumphant smile to Allie Gray, now clad in a shirt and slacks.

'There now, Allie, and isn't that good news? A pound of heroin, all stashed neat and tidy in your private safe . . . a bit stupid, wasn't it? Especially when you know a number of your former comrades would like to see you doing a stretch somewhere safe like Parkhurst so that they can carve up your little vice kingdom between them.'

Allie Gray clenched his hands and swore.

'Tell me who the bastard was who grassed and. . . .'

The inspector laughed.

'And what? I'd calm down if I were you. You'll have plenty of time to meditate on the situation. You're on your way down, Allie. We are going to throw the book at you . . . drugs, porn and prostitution for beginners, and you haven't seen anything yet. Alright, constable, take him away.'

Uncomprehendingly, Claire watched as Allie Gray was led from the room. He did not look once in her direction. She was sobbing as she tried to struggle into her clothes before the amused gaze of the policewoman.

The inspector glanced round the room, then called to the policewoman.

'Get Allie's tart down to the car immediately, Forbes.'

The words stung Claire.

'How dare you!' she cried.

The inspector looked at her in amusement. There was also contempt on his face.

'A bit young to be on the game, ain't you?'

Claire flushed.

'I'm not!' she countered.

'Then what are you—Fairy Goody Two Shoes incognito? Come on, the sooner I get you to the station and charge you, the sooner I can get home to a meal and my beauty sleep.'

'Charge?' gasped Claire, going cold. 'Charge with what?'

'You're a bloody good actor, kid. I'll say that. What am I to be charged with?' he mimicked. 'Don't worry, we'll think of something. How about "accessory" for starters? I can promise you that you'll be in the slammer quite a while. Give you a holiday, won't it?'

Chapter Five

The two men were angry and Charles Renard took the opportunity of a lull in their highly technical argument to hold both hands upwards, like a priest bestowing a blessing, in an attempt to quell the tirade.

'M'sieurs,' he said, leaning forward over his large desk. 'If you will allow me? I am a businessman—chairman of this company—not a scientist nor a technician. I do not understand all your complicated technical jargon but, please . . . can we go through this more slowly?'

He paused and looked from one to the other of the two red-faced men who sat on the opposite side of his desk.

'Firstly, let Doctor Villemur explain his point,' Renard said quickly as it seemed, for a moment, as if they were both about to start a simultaneous monologue.

The elder man, with an untidy thatch of white hair, snorted and glanced in triumph at his colleague.

'It is simple, m'sieur,' he began slowly. 'You employed me two weeks ago as an acknowledged expert on aircraft metals and alloys. Is this not so? You told me your chief designer had resigned from your airship project and that you wanted to carry on with his design but needed someone of . . .' he paused, stuck out his chest and looked defiantly at the other man '. . . of authority to check over the project and point out any defective areas.'

Renard nodded wearily.

'You are entirely right, Doctor Villemur. But please come to the point.'

'It is simply this: you are using an unsafe alloy for the shell of the airship.'

'Rubbish!' snapped the second man, Doctor Le Braz, one of the designers working for Dirigeable-Commercial SA, the company of which Renard was chairman and executive director. 'The skin is perfectly safe . . . we have conducted countless tests on it.'

'One moment,' said Renard sharply. 'Let me get this clear. Doctor Villemur, you claim the skin is unsafe? You obviously have some reasons for this claim?'

The doctor jerked his head emphatically.

'Your design is of a honeycomb design skin made up of carbon-reinforced plastic.'

Renard acknowledged the fact.

'Carbon is a conductor of heat and electricity.'

'Elementary! Elementary!' muttered Le Braz.

'Should the airship be struck by lightning,' went on Villemur, ignoring him, 'there is no telling what the results would be. The charge of electricity or heat would be absorbed into the carbon of the alloy and that would generate heat. It is a dangerous structure. Most dangerous.'

Renard was right when he said he was not a scientist nor a technician. He was purely a businessman and, at thirty-four years of age, a young businessman at that. Born the younger son of a farm labourer in the Normandy village of Balleroy, Renard had been too poor to stay on at school to obtain his *baccalauréat*. He left without qualification and went to work at a local garage where he quickly learnt how to buy and sell cars at profit. Poverty had made him ruthless and ambitious: he owned his own garage by the age of nineteen. Soon he had two garages and then a concession on a nationwide string of gas stations. By the age of twenty-five he had invested in an engineering works, obtaining his first government defence contract for making fuel tanks for a series of fighter-aircraft.

By the time he was thirty Charles Renard's name was well-known in the aviation industry. His garages and filling stations had been sold off as his investment in aviation grew. His position had been enhanced by his marriage to the only daughter of Marshal Victor Dubray, one of the most wealthy and influential men in the Air Ministry. For Renard it had simply been a marriage of convenience; most people realised the fact except—at the time—Janine Dubray. People either liked or disliked Renard with a burning intensity. No one was indifferent to him. He was regarded as a 'whizz kid', a nine-day wonder. But whether people liked or disliked him, they all agreed that he managed to get things done. He was a hustler, unscrupulous and temperamental, who worked hard and played hard in alternative bursts of fierce energy.

The formation of Dirigeable-Commercial SA was his own pet project; he had used all his finances and those of many of his friends and business acquaintances to invest in the idea of building and launching a commercial freight-carrying airship. And now, with the prototype *Charles de Gaulle* almost ready, Renard faced near-bankruptcy unless the project could swiftly be proved successful. There had been many problems to overcome, the biggest of which had been Claude Lassay, his chief designer, quitting on him in protest against the safety margins being cut by financial necessity. Renard had hired Doctor Villemur, a leading authority on aviation metal stress factors, to get over the immediate testing problems, and now Villemur was telling him that the skin of the *Charles de Gaulle* was unsafe.

Renard turned to Le Braz and raised his eyebrows.

'You do not agree with Villemur?'

Le Braz cleared his throat. He was a fiery young Breton who had been with the project from the beginning and he disliked people who disagreed with his own pet theories.

'Theoretically, Villemur has a point. It is true that carbon-reinforced plastic is heat-absorbent because of its carbon content. However, he must realise that he is pointing out a very elementary factor and one which Professor Lassay and I considered months ago. The only danger is from a lightning strike and, naturally, our design therefore includes current-paths which would harmlessly discharge the lightning over the whole area of the ship instead of concentrating it at the point of impact. There is absolutely no danger of a lightning strike damaging the structure of the *Charles de Gaulle*.'

He sat back and glared at Villemur.

'I disagree! I disagree totally!' Villemur barked. 'We are working in the dark with carbon-reinforced plastic. I could not continue with this project unless sufficient safety precautions are taken. There are two alternatives—prolonged testing or reconstruction perhaps with a stainless steel skin, still based on the honeycomb sandwich method of construction. . . .'

Renard interrupted.

'Are you seriously suggesting that, because you are apprehensive about possible effects of structural damage caused by a lighting strike on the ship, you want to scrap eighteen months of construction work, not to mention research and design, and start rebuilding the *Charles de Gaulle?*'

Villemur shrugged.

'For the safety of the ship, it must be done.'

Renard bit his lip.

'Doctor Villemur, will you not accept that our design team has been through all these problems and that the ship is near completion, that any drastic alteration, such as you proposed, will cost about a third of our budget to date and put us another twelve months behind the Americans?'

Villemur grimaced.

'I speak as a scientist, not a businessman. Either you want me to take charge of the design with special responsibility for the safety factors of the hull and skin construction, or you do not.'

Renard's grey eyes met Villemur's excitable brown ones and remained locked for several long seconds.

'Le Braz, I will speak to you later,' he said slowly.

Le Braz nodded, picked up his papers, shoved them into his briefcase and left.

Renard continued to gaze thoughtfully at Villemur. Then he sighed.

'Doctor Villemur, are you suggesting that unless I let you do what you want on this project you will offer your resignation?' There was a coldness in the soft tones of his voice.

Villemur hesitated. He had not meant it to sound as drastic as that. After all, he had just resigned a lectureship in aircraft design at the Aerospatiale Centre Technique de Suresnes to join Dirigeable-Commercial. Positions were hard to come by and Villemur had too many pressing debts to make decisions lightly. Part of the reason, and a large part, as to why he joined Renard's company was the reimbursement.

'What I am saying is that I have studied outer shell designs on dirigibles and think I have sufficient knowledge to spot a weakness when I see one. Lack of knowledge of this form of construction has prevented the Americans from pursuing it —they are using fibre-reinforced plastic, entirely non-metallic and much safer, for the skin of their airship. A foam-backed light alloy skin has the advantage that all the shell material is in one surface but. . . .'

Renard stopped him.

'Doctor Villemur, I have told you that I am not a technician, only a businessman. It is as the chairman of this business enterprise that I must function. I have to make commercial decisions here and not scientific ones. So far as I can see, you are proposing the spending of millions of francs, the delay of the project for twelve months which would ensure that the Americans would be first in the field, and for what? Because you do not agree with the design and construction of the airship, a design which a lot of people have worked on, people at least as qualified in the field as you are.'

Villemur stirred uncomfortably.

'I don't argue with that. But we are dealing with theory, lack of knowledge and it is my belief that there is a danger. . . .'

'You have just put your finger on the problem, Villemur,' interrupted Renard, letting anger colour his voice. 'You *believe*. Your opinion is no better than anyone else's opinion in this field. I cannot make a commercial decision to do what you ask merely on speculation. Now, Doctor Villemur, I would hate to lose you from the project so soon after joining it, so I suggest you go away for a day and think this matter over quite seriously. Let me know your decision tomorrow.'

Villemur sat staring for a moment. The tone of dismissal in Renard's voice was final. Feeling like a naughty schoolboy who had been firmly ticked off by his headmaster, Villemur quietly picked up his papers and left the room. Outside he felt a surge of anger: anger that he had been so summarily dismissed by a man nearly twenty-five years younger than he; anger at being dismissed by someone who did not have the technical ability to appreciate what he was saying. He swore aloud and marched by Renard's astonished secretary.

Renard, too, was sitting at his desk seething with anger.

He did not need any more problems. His project had been beset with them from the start, mainly because of lack of finances. Almost everything he could scrape together had gone into the airship project, not mentioning his personal assurances to the friends he had persuaded to invest. He had to make it a success—he just had to! He certainly could not afford problems which cost time and money at this stage.

His secretary, Marie-France, entered.

'The doctor did not sound happy,' she observed with a smile, placing a tray on his desk with his morning coffee and a copy of *Le Monde*.

'He'll get over it,' muttered Renard.

'There was a telephone call while you were in conference,' went on the girl. 'The gentleman was insistent on speaking with you personally so I said that I would ask you to ring back when you were free.'

'Who was it?'

'A Monsieur Brisset. René Brisset.'

The name meant nothing.

'Never heard of him,' grunted Renard, sipping his coffee. 'What does he want?'

'He says he wants a private word with you. I suggest you ring him immediately.'

Renard stared at his secretary. There seemed to be some hidden meaning in her tone.

'Do you know something that I don't?'

'I know that René Brisset is an aide to the President.'

Renard's eyes widened.

'What would an aide of the President of France be doing ringing me?'

'Is that rhetorical,' asked the girl, 'or do you think I know?'

'No sarcasm, Marie-France. Get me Brisset on the telephone immediately.'

The girl pouted in mock anger and went back to her office. A moment later the telephone buzzed.

'M'sieur Brisset is on the line, sir,' came Marie-France's voice.

'M'sieur Brisset? You wished to speak with me?'

'Yes, M'sieur Renard,' came a rather high-pitched yet cultivated voice. 'It would be to our mutual advantage if we could meet somewhere soon for a discussion. Would this be agreeable to you?'

'Are you in Paris?' asked Renard.

'Naturally, but I am willing to come down to St. Lô, to your project site, if that is easier for you.'

Renard frowned.

'You say this matter is to our mutual advantage?'

'I can say no more at this stage, M'sieur Renard.'

'Well,' Renard flicked the pages of his desk diary, 'perhaps you could join me for luncheon tomorrow?'

'The rendezvous would be . . . discreet?' The voice was slightly anxious.

'Certainly. I know a little place called the Restaurant de Roches de Ham, it is in the countryside near Troisgots-la-Chapelle-sur-Vire, a few kilometres outside St. Lô. Would that be suitable?'

'Eminently suitable. At about one o'clock then?'

'Yes.'

'Until motorrow, M'sieur Renard.'

Renard replaced the receiver with a puzzled frown. What

would a presidential aide want with him that needed a discreet rendezvous and could work to their mutual advantage? It sounded very mysterious. Then he sighed deeply. It was no use wasting energy trying to work out what it was all about. He flicked on his intercom and asked Marie-France to book a table for him for the next day and then turned back to his coffee and newspaper.

It was a small news item on page three that caught his attention.

It brought a thin smile to his lips.

So Anglo-American's chief test pilot was dead?

Thoughtfully, he plucked at his lower lip and then whispered: 'That's going to put them behind a few months at least. We're in with a chance after all.'

Chapter Six

'Get up, *pigrone!*'

Maria Terrasino walked across the bedroom and chucked a handy cushion at the head of her gently snoring husband.

Terry Terrasino grunted and blinked.

'Wha . . . what'sa matter?'

'What's the matter, he asks?' jeered his wife in mock scorn. 'Breakfast is the matter. What d'you want me to do, let you sleep all day?'

Terrasino rubbed his eyes and grinned up at his wife.

He was four weeks married and still found it hard to believe. Maria and he had met while he was on holiday in Florence. She was an English-speaking tour guide: a twenty-three-year-old Milanese—red of hair, with a soft olive skin, blue eyes and a figure which, he believed, would have rivalled the young Sophia Loren. After the tour of the city was over, Terrasino had invited her to dinner. She had refused. He had invited her to breakfast. She had refused. He had invited her to lunch. To put an end to the flood of invitations, she had accepted. By four o'clock that afternoon, he had proposed marriage. By six o'clock he had met her family, who seemed to label all Italian-Americans as *mafiosi*. Yet a week later, with only five days of the holiday to go, Maria had accepted his offer of marriage. In spite of the protests of her family they had been married and, when Terrasino returned to his job at Portland, he had brought his bride with him. At thirty-three years of age, Terrasino, a former Air Force intelligence officer, was the chief of security for Anglo-American Airships.

Terrasino levered himself up in bed and held out a hand towards his wife. She took it and he drew her down to sit on the edge of the bed.

'What's the time, *mia tresora?*'

'Ten o'clock. Time you were at work, no?'

'No!'

He suddenly pulled her down and tried to kiss her.

She broke away, laughing.

'I do not think you are a . . . a serious man,' she said sadly, shaking her head. 'My family were right. I get up, I make your breakfast, which gets cold, and all you want to do is play games.'

Terrasino chuckled.

'Is there a better way to start the day?'

'Yes,' she pouted. 'With a cold shower. Now, I expect you in the kitchen in five minutes! Up! *Mettiamoci al lavoro!*'

She disengaged herself from his embrace and left the room, smiling at his assumed woe-begone expression.

She was pouring coffee when the back door buzzer whirred.

Frowning slightly, she opened the door and was faced by two sombre looking men in light-coloured lounge suits. They were both in their late thirties, with close-cut hair and clean-shaven faces. Maria thought they looked like the stereotype American —what was it Terry called the type? Ivy Leaguers?

'Mrs. Terrasino?' The taller of the two men smiled. 'Sorry to disturb you but is your husband at home?'

Terrasino entered the kitchen, straightening his tie.

'What can I do for you?' he asked, joining his wife at the door.

'Good morning, Mr. Terrasino. I'm Agent Hayes of the Portland office of the Federal Bureau of Investigation and this is Ken Vambrace of the Federal Aviation Authority, Investigations Department. Sorry to get you at home but we were told by your office that you were here and we wanted a word with you.'

Terrasino nodded, a little puzzled, turned and motioned them into his den. Maria followed with a tray of coffee and left them there.

'Now, what can I do for you gentlemen?' asked Terrasino as he helped them to coffee.

The FBI man glanced at his colleague.

'As Hayes here has told you, Mr. Terrasino, I'm with the FAA and you've probably guessed that we are investigating the crash which killed Major Westbrook.'

Terrasino made an affirmative gesture.

'Sure, the evening editions were screaming about sabotage.'

'What's your reaction to the news?' demanded Vambrace.

Terrasino sat back and looked thoughtfully at them.

'I gather you are confirming this? Westbrook's aircraft was sabotaged?'

'That's so,' Vambrace nodded.

'Do you have any details?' pressed Terrasino. 'The only official news that I've had is what I read in the *Evening Express*.'

'Your office will be getting a detailed report from our department but, briefly, our reconstruction showed that the controls of Westbrook's Mitsubishi had been tampered with . . . and tampered by an expert.'

Terrasino bit his lip.

'I see,' he said softly.

Hayes, the FBI man, leaned forward.

'Have you been experiencing sabotage connected with the project that Anglo-American are working on?'

'With the airship? No,' Terrasino shook his head. 'We've had one or two odd incidents during the period we have been constructing it—unresolved incidents, details of which I have on file at my office—but nothing which would make us unduly worried about the prospect of sabotage.'

He scratched his nose with a forefinger.

'What makes you think that the sabotage is directed against the project and not against Westbrook personally?'

'No reason at all,' returned Hayes, easily. 'At the moment we are pursuing all lines of enquiry. We thought we'd start with the easy options first. I would imagine that a lot of people would be against the airship project?'

'There are always a few nutcases about, those who are against things for the sake of being against them,' admitted Terrasino. 'Oh, we've had our share of threatening letters. Most of them are what you'd expect: a project of this sort attracts them.'

'Nevertheless,' interposed Vambrace, 'we would like to check them out.'

'Certainly. They've all been kept on file.'

'But, so far as you are aware, there has been no indication of sabotage connected with the project?' pressed Hayes.

'None,' affirmed Terrasino.

'And what about Westbrook himself?' asked Vambrace. 'Did he have any enemies that you know of? Any private threats, people he rubbed up the wrong way on the project . . . that sort of thing?'

Terrasino shook his head.

'Alec and Jane Westbrook were liked and admired by everyone on the project site. Westbrook was a nice, friendly guy, easy to get on with. Everyone was deeply shocked at the news.'

Hayes smiled abruptly and stood up.

'We'll drop by your office this afternoon to go through the files of threatening letters. Could we also look at Westbrook's personal file?'

'Yes; but I can tell you that there are no references to any personal enemies or anything like that. I was going through the file only yesterday to bring it up to date.'

Terrasino followed the investigators to the door.

'Will you keep me posted with developments?'

Vambrace nodded.

'We'll be co-operating very closely, Mr. Terrasino, and —naturally—will expect a similar co-operation from your office.'

'You've got it,' agreed Terrasino as he showed them out.

As the door closed, he turned to Maria and smiled apologetically.

'You were saying something about breakfast?'

He had to duck the wet kitchen cloth she hurled at his head.

'It's a helluva job, Harry,' observed Garry Carson, accepting the whisky which Maclaren had just poured for him and sprawling back in the leather chair opposite Maclaren's desk.

'The project must go on,' sighed Anglo-American's project manager. 'The French are too damned near completion and there is the old saying—first is best, second is nowhere. There's a lot of investment in the form of commercial contracts tied up with the first safe Transatlantic crossing, and I have pressure from above to ensure that the *Albatross* makes it.'

'That's all very well, Harry,' Carson said, sipping his drink, 'but airship pilots don't fall out of the sky.'

He paused in surprise, chuckling at his unconscious humour. 'Let's hope they don't, anyway.'

Maclaren's voice assumed a deep tone of woe.

'Your head isn't on the chopping-block, Garry. Pan Continental have put a lot of money in this development and I am the one left carrying the ashcan.'

Carson smiled pacifyingly.

'Understood, Harry. I'm sure there will be someone around somewhere with training enough to catch up with the *Albatross* development. You just need someone with some basic rigid hull dirigible experience and then put him through simulator training.'

'During the last twenty-four hours I have had our personnel team working round the clock. Everyone we have on file with airship experience is contracted to other development companies. I gather John G. has talked with Ashton in London and we are going to have to start checking out the European countries. It's going to create problems if we wind up with a non-English speaker for a second pilot. . . .'

Carson suddenly frowned.

'Are you trying outside of the States?'

Maclaren raised an eyebrow.

'Why? Have you got a touch of nationalism or something?'

'No, no. It just didn't occur to me. . . .'

'We *are* an international corporation,' went on Maclaren, a trifle sarcastically. '*Anglo*-American, remember?'

'I know, I know.' Carson drank some whisky. 'It's just that I wasn't thinking straight. If you are looking outside the States then I might be able to help you.'

Maclaren glanced at him with interest.

'Shoot,' he invited.

'About three years ago I was stationed in England when I was in the Air Force. I was commanding the Thirty-Third Pursuit Squadron which was based at Syderstone, an air-base in Norfolk. We were part of the NATO strike squadrons and we shared the base with an RAF squadron. The RAF liaison officer attached to our squadron was a guy called Saxon, Tom Saxon. We were pretty good buddies in those days. My wife, Helen, myself, Saxon and his wife . . . we would form a foursome every now and again.'

Maclaren made a gesture of impatience.

'Okay, okay. I'm coming to the point. Saxon had worked on British military "blimps"—non-rigid airships. . . .'

'We can get the services of any amount of non-rigid airship pilots or balloonists. What I want is a man with rigid frame airship experience,' interrupted Maclaren.

'Sure,' went on Carson, 'and this guy has. He was test pilot in a number of RAF experiments with small-scale dirigibles. I haven't seen him in three years. We never kept in touch after I was posted back Stateside but I did hear that his wife died and he left the RAF and went into civil aviation. A year ago there was an article in *Flying* about some experiments in producing small-type airships in Britain and it carried a photograph of Saxon. Said he was chief test pilot on the project.'

Maclaren was looking interested.

'It doesn't mean that we would be able to get him—he might be committed and he might not even want to join the project,' he said slowly.

'But it might be worth a try,' insisted Carson.

Maclaren buzzed for his secretary, Jean.

'Get a cable off to Ashton at our London office. Ask him to find out the availability of. . . .'

He looked a question at Carson.

'Wing Commander Tom Saxon, RAF retired,' supplied the pilot.

'Got that, Jean?' enquired Maclaren.

The girl repeated the name.

'Good, let me know the moment you get a reply.'

Maclaren turned back to Carson who was hauling himself to his feet.

'I'd better go and start minding the shop. Got a lot of work to do since. . . .'

He shrugged awkwardly.

'The FAA and FBI are working with our security on the sabotage aspect. Terrasino wants a head of department conference this afternoon to see if we can tighten up on security.'

Carson bit his lip.

'Let's hope they catch the swine,' he said softly. He had been a good friend of Alec and Jane Westbrook. He was almost through the door when Maclaren called him back.

'Just a thought, Garry. If this Saxon guy is available but needs some persuasion, are you prepared to act as head-hunter, go across to London or wherever and talk him into accepting the job?'

Carson hunched a shoulder indifferently.

'If it's necessary, Harry. But don't pin all your hopes on Saxon. It was just a thought. Maybe he won't want a job.'

Maclaren smiled absently.

'I'll let you know how it pans out but we've got to dig up a pilot from somewhere, and in a hurry.'

Chapter Seven

Sir Ashley Ashton turned his Daimler onto the Lewisham Way at the New Cross Old Town Hall, heading for the A21 and Kent. As he did so he glanced quickly at his daughter from the corner of his eye. She sat back in her seat, hands quietly folded in her lap, eyes staring forward and mouth set in a thin line. She had not spoken since Sir Ashley had picked her up from New Scotland Yard a short while ago. The woman police officer had been considerate and sympathetic. It had been three days since Claire had been arrested at Allie Gray's flat. The police had made their enquiries and had come to the decision that there was no case to be proceeded with against Claire. Nevertheless, the policewoman had delivered a stern lecture to the girl about the company she was keeping. Throughout it all Claire had remained impassive. She had hardly acknowledged her father and Ashton had left her alone for the first hour of their journey back to the Ashtons' home at Heaverham.

Now, as he drove into Lewisham, Ashton cleared his throat.

'I think we should talk, Claire.'

'Why?'

The girl's retort was like a pistol shot.

Ashton bit his lip.

'Something has to be done. . . .'

'All men are pigs!' the girl interrupted him.

Ashton frowned.

'Your behaviour is not exemplary, young lady,' he said. 'You have had everything you wanted. No other child has had the freedom . . . no, the *licence* . . . that your mother and I have given you. All I expected in return was respect and obedience.'

'Yes,' the girl's tone was a jeer, 'respect, obedience . . . never love! Who wants love and understanding?'

'Alright, Claire,' he said tightly, 'we won't talk about this unsavoury affair. However, the fact of the matter is that the story has appeared in several gutter newspapers. I don't suppose it even occurred to you that your actions would be seized upon by the press because of my position in society? It never crossed your mind how your actions would affect my standing?'

Claire said two words which she had never used to her father before.

Ashton whitened and gripped the wheel hard. He tried not to show how he felt. He hated showing emotion; he felt it was vulgar to display one's feelings in public.

'Listen, young lady,' he continued, trying to keep his voice even. 'You have brought enough disgrace on your family and made quite a spectacle of us. I have decided that the best course of action is for you to go abroad for a while. I have informed your mother.'

Claire remained silent, indifferent.

'I have had a word with Harry Maclaren, who is head of Anglo-American in Portland. As a very personal favour to me, he is going to fix you up with a job in the company's press office. Your ticket is already booked. You will fly to Portand via New York next week.'

Claire shrugged.

'I suppose it is as good a place as any other to go.'

The way she felt she did not care where she went. She just wanted to get away from the whole damned mess. She had never been so shocked and humiliated in her life as during the last three days. She did not blame Allie Gray so much as she blamed her father. Somehow, everything was his fault. She could not reason out why, it was simply an emotional judgment. She half-turned away from him and continued to stare out of the window, watching the built-up areas of the city lessen into the greener roads of suburbia until, once past Bromley, with a breathless abruptness, they were out in the country and into the Kent villages of her childhood—Pratt's Bottom, Badger's Mount, turning off the main A21 roadway to Otford and along the Pilgrim's Way to the hamlet of Heaverham. They drove up to the front of the old Restoration mansion and as the car halted Martha Ashton came out to greet them. But Claire was out of the car and brushing by her mother without a word. The girl ran straight up to her room and slammed the door.

Ashton looked at his wife and shrugged.

'She has turned into a selfish little devil.'

'She's upset,' countered his wife. 'She'll get over it, Ashley.'

Ashton turned and took the suitcases out of the boot of the Daimler.

'There's simply no communication with her.'

'Did you tell her . . . about America, I mean?' asked Martha Ashton.

He nodded.

'Yes. It's about time she stood on her own two feet, Martha. I've given her all I can. It's time she started to find out what life is really like. I can't keep helping her out of any mess she plunges into. I feel she does it to spite me. I've simply been too lenient with the girl.'

Martha Ashton frowned at her husband.

'I don't think that's the problem, Ashley,' she ventured.

'Of course it is,' replied Ashton. 'She has had everything she wanted in life and does she respect me for it?'

Martha Ashton sighed.

She vaguely felt that there was something wrong about her husband's attitude: his lofty coldness, his telling Claire what was best for her instead of asking her, dealing with her on the same level; that would not be her way of parenting. But her loyalty to her husband made her uneasy in questioning, even to herself, his attitude towards their daughter.

She nodded slowly.

'I expect you're right, dear,' she said, turning into the house.

Garry Carson came off the New Fore River Bridge and along St. John, past the Union Station. His vintage 1934 front wheel drive Cord automobile purred along the highway, causing people on the sidewalk to gaze enviously after him. The white and silver Cord was Carson's vice. He had spent a small fortune on its upkeep and drove it whenever he could. He loved the drive between the project site, by Portland's airport, to his home, a three-bedroom villa on Fernald Street, by Edward Payson Park, overlooking Back Cove. It was a nice area, away from the hustle and bustle of downtown Portland. A lot of the project site executives had houses in the district. Westbrook and his wife used to live four blocks away on Cummings and . . . Carson sighed and shook his head, trying to dismiss the subject of Westbrook from his mind. He still found it hard to believe that Alec and Jane Westbrook were dead, let alone that their deaths were caused by a deliberate act. Who could have done such a thing?

He turned from St. John into Devonshire, followed the road as it changed into Derring Avenue and then into Ocean Avenue before the railroad crossing. Ocean Avenue was usually a fast road and his speedometer edged dangerously over the speed limit as he coasted down towards Edward Payson Park.

His wife's automobile was not in the driveway and the garage door stood open, indicating that she was out. He wondered where Helen had gone to. He left his Cord in the driveway and entered the house. Helen had left a short note on the kitchen table. She was going out for the evening with Lesley Van Kleef, the wife of the project's chief designer, and Garry would find a TV dinner in the ice-box if he were hungry. Carson sighed. He wondered whether kids would help the situation. If Helen and he had . . . well, maybe it would stop her going out so much. She always seemed to be off somewhere these days—bridge clubs, women's golf tournaments, charity work and God knows what else. He went into the lounge, poured himself a bourbon and sank onto the couch. Hell! Helen was only twenty-nine years old, attractive, brunette and with a figure that produced wolf-whistles on the few occasions when she had visited him on the project site. What the hell was she doing living the sort of life that matrons of sixty-plus led?

He suddenly felt angry with her and with himself. Something had been going drastically wrong with their relationship in recent years and he could not understand what it was. They had not had sex together in six months and then once in the six months before that. Those odd occasions were half-hearted ones, when he was desperate and Helen was too tired to ward him off as she nearly always did. God, but she had grown expert at that. Attempts to discuss things always ended in bitter words. Helen never lost her temper but she had a ice-cold, biting tongue. Yet they could never get down to basics, never talk about why their relationship was floundering. They never seemed to be able to put their feelings into words—words were a language they did not understand or speak.

Carson set down his drink as the telephone buzzed.

It was Harry Maclaren.

'Garry, I've just heard from Ashton in London about your man, Tom Saxon. It looks as though we might have a chance. A slim one. It will need your help.'

'Oh?' Carson tried to bring his mind back to the problems of the project.

'You were right. Saxon left the RAF soon after his wife and kid were killed in an auto crash.' Carson frowned in surprise.

'I didn't realise both his wife and kid were killed.'

'No? Anyway, he had a good record with the RAF and, as you said, worked a lot with rigid hull airships. When he left he went to an airship company as test pilot. However, he's no longer there. In fact, he's had a few jobs since then. Maybe his wife's death unsettled him. Anyway, he is currently a flying instructor at a place which goes by the crazy name of Middle Wallop . . . it's near Andover in Hampshire.'

'A flying instructor?' Carson was surprised. 'I can't see Saxon settling into that sort of routine.'

'Apparently he has,' returned Maclaren. 'Ashton managed to ring him and put the proposition but he wasn't interested. Okay, so Saxon is playing hard to get. At the moment we need him. We need his experience with airships. So what I propose is this: you take a trip to England to look up your old Air Force buddy and do your damnedest to convince him to join us.'

Carson hesitated.

'It has been some years since we were last in touch, Harry. I told you. It may not be that easy. If he's not interested . . . well, what can I do?'

Maclaren ignored him.

'I'll get Jean to book you on a Delta flight for tomorrow. Why not persuade Helen to go with you and make a long weekend of it on company expenses?'

'She isn't here right now.'

'No problem. Ring Jean first thing in the morning if Helen wants to go along and she'll get the ticket. I'll also have Jean type up a copy of Ashton's comments, Saxon's address and resumé. Okay? See you before you go.'

For a moment Carson stared at the buzzing receiver before replacing it slowly on its hook.

He went into the kitchen and opened the ice-box, gazed in distaste at the TV dinner and suddenly slammed the door shut. He left the house and climbed into the Cord, starting it with an unnecessary roar of the engine, and raced down the road. He turned north onto Route 88 and put his foot down, feeling the vintage car's engine throb with power which fifty years had not diminished. Soon he turned off the highway before Yarmouth and raced along the road which led him to the Westcustogo, his favourite eating-place. But the steamed clams and seafood Newburg, which he threw down with a carafe of some unmemorable Californian white wine, did not alter his depressed mood.

When he returned Helen was watching television.

'Have a good day?' she greeted him, hardly glancing up from the quiz programme.

'Not very,' he said shortly, going straight to the drinks cabinet and pouring himself a bourbon. 'Drink?'

She shook her head and raised a still full martini glass.

'I'm going to England tomorrow on company business,' he said without preamble.

Helen raised her delicately arched eyebrows.

'What sort of business?'

'We need a new airship pilot on the project,' Carson said, swallowing a large part of his drink. 'I've got to interview a guy. Why don't you come with me, Helen . . . we could make a holiday of it? It would do us good . . . you know, maybe we could start getting things together and. . . .'

He hadn't meant to put the invitation that way. Helen was already shaking her head.

'I've already made plans, Garry. The day after tomorrow I have arranged to take Maria Terrasino to Niagara to see the Falls.'

'The Falls? Can't you put that off?' Carson's voice was almost a snarl.

'We've booked the hotel. I can't pull out now.'

'Hell!'

'Don't you think you're drinking too much, Garry?'

Carson had poured himself another drink.

'I don't see why the hell you can't alter your plans for me just once. What the hell is happening to us, Helen? We're growing further and further apart.'

'I don't know what you mean.'

Her voice was cold and brittle.

'Like hell you do!'

'Are you drunk, Garry?'

'Sure, oh sure. That's the easy answer, isn't it? Garry must be drunk. Hell, Helen, don't you realise that there's something wrong?'

'I'll get you some black coffee.'

Carson slumped into a chair and reached out for the automatic control to turn the television off.

'I thought you'd like a few days in London, Helen. We haven't been there since we were stationed. . . .'

'No one goes to England these days, Garry,' called Helen from the kitchen. 'It's too expensive and the service is awful.'

'The trip would be on company expenses,' returned Carson.

'So you said. Why did you say you are going?'

'Remember Tom Saxon?'

There was a clatter from the kitchen.

'What have you done, Helen?'

'I . . . I just dropped a saucer. What about Tom Saxon?'

'He's a qualified airship pilot. Harry Maclaren says we desperately need a qualified man as second pilot for the *Albatross*. We just haven't time to train our own personnel, even with the simulator.'

Helen had come to the door, looking at Carson with a slightly odd expression.

'You mean that you're being sent to ask Tom Saxon to come here and work on the project?'

Carson apparently did not hear the curious tone in her voice.

'Why not? We need him badly. It'll be nice to see that sonofabitch again. It's been a couple of years. We used to have great times in Norfolk—remember, honey?'

She nodded slowly.

Carson suddenly set down his drink, stood up and caught her by both hands.

'Look, honey, it would be really great if you could cancel this trip with Maria Terrasino. Come with me to London. We could do the town—do a little shopping—all on company expenses.'

He frowned as he noticed that Helen was trembling.

'I'm sorry, Garry. I can't. I simply can't.'

She broke away and turned into the kitchen.

'Damn it to hell!' he swore. Then he turned, picked up the bourbon bottle and stomped into his den, slamming the door behind him.

Ed Budmeyer unfolded his copy of the Portland *Press Herald* and settled down to read. Budmeyer was one of the two security guards whose job it was to patrol the structure which shielded the gigantic 1,100 feet long airship from public gaze. The structure consisted of a 350-feet high scaffolding, covered by tarpaulin, which formed four walls around the colossal aircraft. The structure acted not so much as a hangar—the top was open—but merely as a windbreak in which the men working on the shell of the airship could do their job with the minimum of hazard.

As security jobs went, Ed Budmeyer thought working for Anglo-American Airships was an easy one. He had usually been on payroll guard jobs for the Casco Bank and the Portland

Savings Bank. He hated payroll jobs—sooner or later some punk hoodlum was bound to try his hand at knocking off the shipment he was guarding. It was the law of averages. Budmeyer had seen a couple of his friends gunned down doing payroll guard over the years and he felt, fatalistically, that one day his turn would come. He had a wife and four kids to take care of and just paying insurance was not exactly a comfort. That was why he had jumped at the chance offered when Anglo-American Airships had started recruiting security guards for their project site. Hell! Who would want to knock over a goddam airship?

Budmeyer glanced at the clock on the desk in front of him. It was 1.30 a.m. He was in the guard hut at the north end of the giant construction. His routine was to patrol the area around the airship once every two hours, varying his routine as he thought fit. He swallowed the remains of a cup of coffee and decided he would do his patrol now. He stood up, stretched and yawned, putting on his hat, slightly askew over his grizzled curls. He hitched up his gunbelt and hooked on his nightstick, then flicked his hand radio.

'Silver Three to Control. Come in.'

There was a crackle of static.

'That you, Ed?'

It wasn't the official response that the chief night security guard should have made but Ed, usually a stickler for routine, let it ride.

'Yes, sir. Just about to start my walkabout.'

' 'Kay, Ed. Take it easy.'

'Silver Three to Control. Out,' retorted Budmeyer primly.

He left the hut and switched on his flashlight. He let it play for a moment over the enormous silver hull of the mammoth before him. He shuddered. The sight of the airship, resting like some great sleeping monster, always made him shudder. Scaffolding enclosed the long silver cigar-shaped creature which, for the most part, was shrouded in blackness. The airship, Budmeyer knew, was 220 feet in diameter and 1,100 feet in length. It dwarfed everything around it. He stood shaking his head slowly.

'Ain't gonna fly,' he muttered, as he had muttered every night for the last twelve months. It had become a ritual with him. 'Anyway, if it does fly they'll not catch me going up in it. Ain't natural.'

He turned and began to pace his beat in the blackness of the tarpaulin construction, the long slow beat to the far end of the ship where Pat Driscoll, his fellow guard, would probably be sitting in his hut, feet up with a good book. If Pat wasn't there, it meant he was patrolling the far side of the airship and Budmeyer would have to contact him by radio.

It was just a brief flash, a flicker behind the plastic of one of the portholes high up on the *Albatross*'s side. A small flicker of light.

Budmeyer halted and frowned.

Someone working late? Hell! They should have told him. Anyone working late in or on the airship, even the chief designer Van Kleef, had to sign a duty roster booking themselves in and out of the construction. So far as Budmeyer knew, no one had signed in to work that night. It meant that he would have to climb into that infernal thing to find out where the light had come from and who was not following security regulations. He flicked on his hand radio.

'Silver Three to Control. Come in.'

'What is it, Ed?'

'Going aboard the *Albatross*. Thought I saw a light. Anyone working tonight?'

'No one has let me know, Ed,' returned the imperturbable voice of the chief night security guard. 'Check it out and when you find out who it is give them a moan. They should let us know if they're working on the ship. Security regulations. Those damned scientists are all alike. Don't know the time of day.'

'Silver Three to Control. Out.'

Budmeyer walked to a gangway which led from the ground to the interior of the airship, whose belly nestled on ground zero. He walked up the slight incline into the ship. He presumed the area he was in was one of the cargo holds and peered round wonderingly. In spite of the darkness, he felt surrounded by a great spacious area. He stood and scratched his head. A few months ago, after the hull and the internal sections had been fitted, all the project site workers, including the security guards, had been given a tour of the ship, primarily in order to show them the extent of the creation. Now Budmeyer tried to visualise where he had seen the flicker of light. It had been the sort of flash one saw from a pocket torch momentarily reflecting against metal.

He made his way to a hatchway and opened it. There was a soft red glow from the ship's running lights. He climbed up a ladder to an upper deck and left the well by another hatchway. By the light of his flashlamp he made his way along the corridor and came upon a companionway ladder leading to another deck

—one of the spacious passenger lounges, he could tell by its rich furnishing. He paused and reflected before climbing upwards. The spot from which the light had come must be somewhere along the next corridor. He halted and switched off his torch. For a moment his world was plunged into blackness as he stood listening and straining his eyes for a tell-tale sign.

Yes, damn it! There it was! A faint flicker of light from the far end of the corridor, a flicker as if someone had swept a torch around a cabin and the ensuing light had shone momentarily out of a cabin door.

Budmeyer grunted.

He strode along the corridor, observing that he was in the electronics control section of the ship. Halting outside the cabin he found the door marked with the words 'Personnel Only: Back-Up Computers'. He pushed the door fully open and switched on his flashlight.

A man was crouched over a pile of wiring spewing from one of the computer control boards.

'What . . . ?' began Budmeyer.

He did not have the chance to finish the sentence.

As swiftly as a cat and with equal agility, the man wheeled round and threw, with all his might, the heavy torch in his hand. It struck Budmeyer straight and true between the eyes. The security guard's world exploded into a million coloured shooting stars before he slipped down a helter-skelter into a pool of velvet blackness.

Chapter Eight

Charles Renard swung his Mercedes off the main highway just past the village of Torigni-sur-Vire, dominated by the rebuilt Château Martignon, and headed down a narrow road towards the river. Before reaching the tiny hamlet of Troisgots-la-Chapelle-sur-Vire he turned along a rough trackway which wound through a forest of cedars before emerging, almost abruptly, onto a level stretch of ground on a small hillock. On this stood a large building whose façade resembled an enormous log cabin. The Restaurant de Roches de Ham was one of Renard's favourite eating-places, especially when he had to entertain. It was not overly expensive and, because of its setting, almost in the middle of nowhere, it was very discreet. The frontage of the restaurant, consisting of floor to ceiling windows, looked out across the Vire valley, across the thin strip of the river, towards the famous tourist attraction of the Ham Rocks, a magnificent escarpment of ancient shale rising to 150 metres.

Renard halted his car and then backed into a convenient parking place behind the restaurant building. He switched off and gazed about him. There were a dozen other cars parked and, apart from one Volkswagen, they were expensive vehicles among which his Mercedes was not out of place. Among them was a large shiny black Daimler bearing Parisian number plates in which a uniformed chauffeur sprawled, reading a magazine and munching a sandwich. Renard smiled and glanced at his watch. It was ten minutes after the appointed hour. His man was already inside. It was always good psychology to arrive a little late for a luncheon appointment. He climbed out of his car, stretched, locked the door and headed towards the restaurant foyer.

A girl in a black dress and white apron came forward as he entered and took his coat. She smiled as she recognised him as a regular. Then Gaspard, the *maître d'hôtel*, came bustling forward.

'*Bonjour*, M'sieur Renard. It is good to see you again. You are keeping well?'

It put Renard in a good humour to be recognised and made to feel as if his personal custom was all the restaurant cared about.

'I am well, Gaspard,' he replied.

Gaspard was holding open the door into the main dining-room.

'Your guest has already arrived, m'sieur. He is at the bar.'

'Excellent. We will have an aperitif.'

'*Bien*, m'sieur. Would you like to look at the menu while you are at the bar?'

Renard nodded absently.

Gaspard conducted him to the small cocktail bar, separated from the main restaurant by a decorative partition of pot plants. There was only one customer there, a tall man in his late forties. His raven-black hair was straight, with no hint of grey, and it made his pale features seem a trifle anaemic. He rose from his seat as Renard came up.

'Monsieur Brisset?' Renard held out his hand.

The man's grip was firm.

'I am delighted to make your acquaintance, M'sieur Renard.'

Gaspard motioned to the barman who left his post to hover by their table. Renard gestured to Brisset's nearly empty glass.

'Thank you,' replied the man to his unasked question. 'Another Byrrh Frappé.'

'And for you, m'sieur?' queried the barman.

'A Tom Collins for me, but with Bourbon not gin.'

'At once, m'sieur.'

Gaspard now moved forward and placed the menus on the table.

'The chef's speciality today, m'sieurs, is the *Noisettes des Tournelles* . . . fillets from the saddle of lamb, sautéed, covered with a little onion purée and then glazed under the grill and served with vermouth, sherry and butter.'

Renard nodded and Gaspard, with a hint of a bow, merged into the background as the barman brought their aperitifs.

'Did you have a good journey from Paris, M'sieur Brisset?'

The dark-haired man nodded. Renard knew Brisset was appraising him and he went on: 'Perhaps, if it is not rushing, we should get our orders out of the way first . . . ?'

'An excellent idea.' Brisset glanced at the menu. It did not take him long to decide. He announced that he would start with asparagus followed by *Truites Soufflées de Chez Garin*, a dish of trout stuffed with mousseline of pike flavoured with truffle. Renard, of course, knew the menu well and decided on a pâté of duck's liver flavored with armagnac, followed by the chef's speciality of lamb fillets. Gaspard appeared at his elbow a fraction of a second before Renard began to turn to indicate they had made up their minds. Renard gave the order, adding: 'And wine, would a bottle of Chablis Grand Crus suit you?'

Brisset smiled agreement.

'And now. . . .' Renard settled back in his chair and took a sip of his Tom Collins.

'Now, M'sieur Renard.' Brisset let a smile play around his thin, almost bloodless lips. 'You are doubtless wondering why I have requested this meeting and asked that we meet in a discreet rendezvous.'

'It has obviously crossed my mind,' agreed Renard solemnly.

'Monsieur le President is very interested in your airship project, m'sieur.'

Renard raised his eyebrows very slightly.

Brisset's eyes glanced around. It was the merest flicker but the action was not lost on Renard.

'Tell me, are you interested in politics, M'sieur Renard?' Brisset's voice dropped a tone.

Renard's mouth quirked cynically.

'I am interested in making money, M'sieur Brisset. In so far as a particular government or a particular party is able to help me in this matter, then I am interested in their politics.'

'You would tend to be conservative in your politics rather than a radical?'

'Radical?' Renard grinned, amused. 'I am a businessman.'

'There are many businessmen who claim to be radicals.'

'Then one should question who is paying their percentages. But, seriously, why does this question arise?'

Brisset leant forward a little.

'You will forgive me, m'sieur. I just wanted to hear your attitude from your own lips. We have, in fact, been a little deceptive in that we have made a careful scrutiny of you and your project.'

Renard stared at the man in surprise.

'You have investigated me?'

Brisset raised a pacifying hand.

'Just a precautionary measure, nothing more.'

'For what reason?' Renard began to feel indignant.

'Shall we say for a reason that could work to our mutual advantage?'

'Mutual advantage? To whom? For what?'

'To yourself, of course, and to Monsieur le President and his administration.'

Renard stared at Brisset and then finished his Tom Collins, regarding his empty glass thoughtfully for a few moments.

'I think you'd better explain yourself fully, M'sieur Brisset.'

Gaspard appeared and advised them their table was ready. The two men fell silent as they followed the *maître d'hôtel* into the main dining-room. Renard was thankful to see it was half-empty and that Gaspard had placed them at a corner table, near the window which gave them an uninterrupted view of the scenery of the Vire valley, away from the other guests.

The *hors d'oeuvres* were brought and the white wine served.

'Well?' prompted Renard.

'As you say, M'sieur Renard, you are a man of business and a political realist. Your rise to the chairmanship of the company you now run is proof of your capabilities. In three months Monsieur le President will have to go into an election to seek a further term of office. This time he will face some stiff opposition from ultra-left dissidents and far right extremists. It is the ultra-left that concerns us. They have formed a loose conglomerate of opposition groups to present a united front in an effort to oust him. They could create havoc in the primary elections. A dangerous situation could arise. Monsieur le President requires all the help he can get to win the election.'

Renard looked helpless.

'I don't understand what this is leading up to.'

'Monsieur le President requires your help.'

'I still do not understand. What help can I give?'

'By continuing exactly what you are doing at the moment,' Brisset smiled. 'I am, as you are probably aware, Monsieur le President's aide and adviser on matters pertaining to public relations. We must never underestimate the power of public manipulation. You will agree? Very well. If, just before the election, some historic event occurred to make France honoured in the world community, then that in itself would enhance the President's image not only in the eyes of France but in the international community. Such an event would be of tremendous help to the President when entering an election.'

'What historic occurrence?' asked Renard, still puzzled.

'Why, the successful Transatlantic flight of your airship the *Charles de Gaulle*,' smiled Brisset. 'If your airship could make that flight before the Americans—yes, we know all about the Anglo-American project—then it would be a tremendous propaganda boost for French technology and business achievement. Not only would your company's prestige be enhanced: France too would be honoured and Monsieur le President is the embodiment of France. What could be better for his image at a particularly vital time? Do you follow?'

Renard looked at Brisset's thin smile and found himself nodding.

'So that's it? The President wants to use my airship as an election gimmick?'

Brisset winced.

'Please, M'sieur Renard. That is a rather crude way of expressing it.'

Renard grinned cynically.

'That's the essence, isn't it? You have told me what I can do for Monsieur le President but you have yet to explain how this can work out to our mutual advantage.'

They were silent while their plates were cleared and the main course was served.

'Should this happen,' went on Brisset, after the waiters had left, 'should your airship achieve the first trans-Atlantic crossing and should Monsieur le President be equally successful in the election, then you could apply for government sponsorship for the expansion of your company with very favourable results.'

Renard smiled broadly.

'As simple as that?'

'Certainly. As simple as that.'

Renard signalled for a second bottle of Grand Crus to be brought.

'What guarantees would I have?' he asked after a short silence.

'Guarantees?'

'Yes. I could apply and be rejected and then what?'

'Such agreements can never be committed to paper,' replied Brisset. 'There would be nothing beyond my word here and now; a private, unwritten assurance.'

'I can appreciate that. But I would like something more tangible. Would, for example, the government help me out should problems arise before the *Charles de Gaulle* is ready to make the flight?'

'Within reason,' agreed Brisset.

'And afterwards, you say the government would help me expand my company to produce airships for them on a commercial basis?'

'Yes. The government have been following the British feasibility study for the military use of airships. The government would be interested in placing an order for an airship fleet with your company, the airships being suitably modified for military use. I understand airships seem to be suitable for roles requiring long endurance at low speeds and therefore have a potential for anti-submarine and counter-mine warfare, fishery protection, logistics support, and could even be used for missile launch and missile guidance systems.'

Renard nodded during the recital. He had spent long hours with his designers discussing the potentialities of his product.

'The government would guarantee a fairly big order?'

Brisset smiled.

'Unofficially, of course. The financial grants could be made to expand both military and civilian sides of the operation.'

'Government long-term loans at a moderate rate of interest?'

'Exactly.'

'And all I have to do . . . ?'

'. . . is ensure that Monsieur le President is able to bask in the publicity and prestige of an all-French achievement in opening the airways to airship traffic before the election.'

Renard grinned broadly.

'You may reassure the President on that.'

Brisset returned his smile thinly.

'He will be delighted to hear it. Do you have any immediate problems?'

'Everything is on schedule,' Renard assured him. 'We are awaiting a shipment of helium from America and as soon as we get it we can inflate the gas bags of our airship and begin our air tests.'

'Excellent. But what of the American project?'

Renard let his mouth droop.

'I am keeping a close eye on developments. Anglo-American Airships are too cautious. They are taking too long. I cannot see them completing their tests on their craft in time. Also, did you see the item in *Le Monde* yesterday?'

'What was that?'

'Anglo-American's chief test pilot was killed in an air crash.'

Brisset pursed his lips.

'Does that mean a substantial setback for them?'

'Trained airship pilots are at a premium,' observed Renard. 'I have made sure that I have three crews under training. The Americans, however, only had two such pilots. Westbrook, the pilot who was killed, was their chief test pilot and they won't be able to replace him in a hurry. It will take several months to train a pilot to Civil Aviation Authority regulations standard.'

'It is bad for them, eh?'

'But gives us an edge. We will be the first airship across the Atlantic. The President need have no doubts about that.'

Renard felt decidedly happy as he pushed away his empty plate.

His famous luck was holding. When he had gone into his office yesterday morning he had been in a black mood. The problems seemed insurmountable. Now Villemur had backed down over the safety regulations and Brisset had materialised with his offer of financial security once the *Charles de Gaulle* was launched. Renard would be able to pull through, he was certain of it.

Gaspard appeared.

'Have you enjoyed your lunch, m'sieurs? *Bien*. A sweet or coffee and liqueurs?'

Renard smiled.

'I think I will have a sweet today, Gaspard. How about you, M'sieur Brisset? Gaspard has a really special *Millefeuille Prince Albert*, it is. . . .'

He raised his fingers to his lips and kissed them with a resounding smack.

Brisset nodded.

'Good,' Renard said. 'And after the *Millefeuille*, coffee and brandy.'

Chapter Nine

Terrasino thrust the report away from him and sat back in his chair, gazing from Harry Maclaren to Hayes and Vambrace.

'I think the conclusion is fairly obvious,' he said after a pause.

Maclaren grimaced and turned to the FBI agent.

'Do you agree with Terrasino's conclusion?'

Hayes did not answer at once but lit up a Lucky Strike and frowned.

'I think it is too early to make a definite statement, but we cannot overlook the possibility.'

'Hell,' snorted the chief of security, 'Budmeyer is in hospital with the bridge of his nose smashed. He interrupted someone fiddling about with the back-up computer systems. The spaghetti that the guy was rummaging about in was all to do with the back-up controls. I had Kurt Nieman go over it this morning and he tells me that it will be at least five days' work to get it back in place. It's lucky there was nothing irreparable but I hate to think what would have happened if Budmeyer had not come along.'

'And Budmeyer didn't recognise the man?'

Terrasino shook his head.

'He says it all happened so fast and it was fairly dark. Not a chance.'

'Why are you reticent, Hayes?' asked Maclaren, turning back to the FBI agent.

Hayes exhaled smoke.

'It's an uncertain leap from the saboteur who beat up your security man, Budmeyer, to the saboteur who killed the Westbrooks.'

Terrasino frowned.

'Are you saying we have two saboteurs on our hands? That's a hell of a coincidence.'

'No; at the moment I'm not leaping to any conclusions. We've got to take this thing carefully. We are running through the computer all the various bits of information you have given us, such as the batch of oddball letters which have been sent to your company since the project was announced in the press. So we're checking on groups who have beefs about airships—the environmental nuts and so on. Frankly, it's a long shot. However, this business relies on checking and re-checking. We can't afford to leap to conclusions.'

'But,' sighed Maclaren, 'you do agree that someone tried to sabotage the *Albatross*?'

'Yes, of course. But I am not prepared, at this stage, to make the definite assumption that he and the killer of the Westbrooks are the same person.'

'I see.' Maclaren looked across to his security chief. 'How about the security angle, Terrasino?'

'I've tightened up procedures and doubled the security guards around the airship. My office is also fully co-operating with the FBI and FAA.'

Maclaren brushed his forehead with his palm.

'Any ideas of what else we can do?'

Terrasino glanced a little defiantly at Hayes.

'I think we have to start checking out our rivals.'

Maclaren stared at him for a moment.

'Are you talking about possible industrial espionage . . . sabotage?' he asked slowly.

'Let's put it this way,' Terrasino said. 'There are some powerful people in the aviation world who would like to see us take a bath over the *Albatross* project.'

Maclaren half-nodded in agreement.

'You may be right, but who the hell would go to the length of sabotage?'

'Desperate and ruthless men.'

Hayes and Vambrace were looking interested. Maclaren glanced apprehensively at them.

'Look,' said Vambrace, 'if you have any ideas, spill them.'

'Alright,' agreed Maclaren. 'Let's be open, Terrasino. Do you have a specific idea?'

Terrasino paused and then nodded.

'Charles Renard has a reputation for ruthlessness and it's common knowledge on La Bourse that he has sunk all his money into his airship project. He's bankrupt, penniless, unless he can get his airship flying before the *Albatross* takes to the skies.'

Hayes was looking puzzled.

'Common knowledge—where?'
'La Bourse, the Paris Stock Exchange,' explained Terrasino.
It was Maclaren who briefly filled in the FBI and FAA men about Renard's Dirigeable-Commercial and their attempt to build an airship called *Charles de Gaulle* which, in many ways, parallelled the *Albatross* in size and design purpose.
'You suspect this guy Renard might employ someone to delay your project?' Vambrace asked.
'From now on,' said Terrasino, 'I am suspecting everyone. You asked for a suggestion. You've got one. Right now we shouldn't overlook the fact that we have a security headache . . . and a bigger problem than finding out who might be behind the sabotage.'
'What do you mean?' demanded Maclaren.
'It's obvious from what happened last night with the back-up computer that the saboteur is right here on the project site. And although Hayes doesn't want to jump to conclusions, let's reflect on the ease with which poor Westbrook's machine was sabotaged. It was done by an expert and had to be done while it was parked on the project site airfield. We can conclude that the saboteur had easy access and a good technical knowledge.'
Anglo-American's security chief paused, over-dramatically.
'In a nutshell, gentlemen, the saboteur must be one of our top men.'

Oscar Van Kleef ran a worried hand through his mane of hair and frowned at the figures before him. In a sudden burst of energy he stabbed at the pocket calculator in his hand and eyed the resultant set of figures with evident annoyance.
'What do you make it, Jules?' he asked his assistant.
Jules Keller sighed. They had been over the figures seven times that morning and he didn't particularly care a damn for the result. At thirty-one years of age, Jules Keller, a French Canadian, was one of Pan Continental's regular aeronautical engineers who had been transferred to the Anglo-American Airship project without any intense feeling about the future of airships. He had been given a job to do and he did it to the best of his ability, but he could not bring himself to be enthusiastic about it. Aircraft were a different matter—aircraft, by which he meant aeroplanes, had a future—but airships! They were dinosaurs; they belonged to the past. He jabbed at his calculator and compared the results.
'The eight Nomad engines would have an empty weight of

377 tons; their fuel weight would be 158 tons. If we say our take-off weight for the *Albatross* is 1,020 tons and we want to get an average cruising height of 4,000 feet then we could maintain an average speed of 119 mph.'

Van Kleef sighed in annoyance.

'I was hoping we could push it up to 150 mph.'

Keller shook his head.

'Not with a full payload.'

'How about using cryogenic buoyancy control? That, of course, would increase the weight to another 150 tons.'

Keller made more calculations.

'Same result, Oscar. An average speed of 119 mph. There's no way you can push the figure up.'

The telephone buzzed and Keller answered it.

'Oh, hello, Mrs. Van Kleef. Yes, he is.'

Van Kleef's look of annoyance increased as he took the telephone from his assistant.

'Yes, Lesley?'

'Oscar,' Lesley Van Kleef's voice was a little shrill. It held a note of complaint. That was nothing unusual. 'Oscar, I couldn't remember whether I told you that Helen Carson and Maria Terrasino and I are heading to Niagara for a few days.'

Van Kleef exhaled deeply.

'Yes, you did.'

'We'll be away for three days. Maria hasn't seen Niagara and. . . .'

'You told me this morning,' Van Kleef interrupted.

'I wasn't sure whether you heard me or not,' replied his wife. 'You had your head buried in those ridiculous papers of yours. Anyway, you'll have to fend for yourself for the next three days. Sarah will be looking after the children, so you don't have to worry about them. Not that you would anyway. I'll be back on Monday morning.'

There was a click as Lesley Van Kleef hung up before her husband could make a suitable rejoinder.

Van Kleef stared at the telephone, seething with inward anger. Then he slammed it back on its cradle.

Why didn't Lesley understand? This last year had been an important one for him. The pressures had been great. It was probably the most important year of his life, with all the preliminary work which had gone into designing the *Albatross* suddenly bearing fruit. It was the pinnacle, the sum total, of his life's ambition—the design and successful launch of a commercial airship. Yet Lesley didn't really understand. Of course he had not been able to spend as much time with her and the twins as he should. It had been two years since they had gone on holiday together. But the work was all-important; the work had to come first.

'What did you say?'

He was suddenly aware of Keller speaking to him.

'I said, I think we must accept that all our calculations would have to be based on a speed varying between 95 mph and 120 mph, maximum cruising.'

Van Kleef ran his hand through his hair again and shook it, as if to get rid of the image of his wife and his domestic problems.

'I want to see if we can increase the capacity of our power plants, Jules. The size of the *Albatross* could warrant more powerful engines.'

'If we start to substitute the Nomads with bigger diesel units, it will be a lot of extra time and expense,' pointed out Keller.

'There is a good economic reason to increase cruise speed to the value which gives optimum work capacity,' muttered Van Kleef, gazing at his calculations once more. 'The extra fuel and power plant weight would be balanced against loss of payload, of course.'

Keller gave an inward groan and glanced at his watch.

'I'm going to grab some lunch,' he said in a tone of finality.

Van Kleef nodded absently.

'Yes . . . what? Oh. . . . You carry on without me. I'll just finish these calculations.'

Keller left the office, whistling softly.

In the corridor outside he bumped into Samantha Hackerman coming round a corner with her arms full of papers. They cascaded to the floor.

'Damn!' swore the company's press officer, gazing at the mess.

Keller grinned apologetically and bent to help scoop them up.

'My fault, Miss Hackerman. I'm sorry.'

Since joining the project Keller had seen Samantha Hackerman several times from a distance and met her only twice to talk to. He was attracted to her but was unsure of the best approach. She would make a damn good score. Keller always thought about women in terms of making a score; he had never matured in his attitude towards the opposite sex. In many respects he was still the carefree, insouciant student working his way through university on a football scholarship.

'That's alright,' replied the girl. 'They are only a load of old press releases. I was going to dump them.'

'Let me carry them to the garbage cans then,' smiled Keller smoothly.

'It's alright. Don't let me take you out of your way.'

'No trouble. I was just on my way to lunch. Oscar is minding the store.'

The girl fell in step with him.

'Doctor Van Kleef never seems to leave that office of his unless he's over at the construction site nursing his baby.'

It was a standard joke among the project site workers that Oscar Van Kleef regarded the monstrous construction like a proud parent with his firstborn.

'Yeah. I don't wonder at his wife getting upset,' mused Keller. 'He has a mistress, and one she can't compete with.'

Samantha shot Keller an amused look.

'I didn't know you were a philosopher, Mr. Keller.'

'Call me Jules, everyone does.' He pronounced it 'Jools' for her benefit.

'What makes you think Doctor Van Kleef and his wife are having problems?' pressed the girl.

'I work with the guy, don't I? She telephones when I'm there. It's pretty obvious Oscar's so wrapped up with his baby that he doesn't exist outside the project site. Can you imagine what that does for a woman?'

Samantha grinned broadly.

'You sound like an expert on the subject, Mr. Keller.'

'Jules,' he corrected. 'Why don't I stand you lunch over at the Greasy Spoon on Westcott and tell you my pet theories about the world and women?'

Samantha hesitated before smiling agreement. After all, why not? She was going out to lunch anyway and Keller seemed pleasant enough company.

Keller dumped the reject press releases into the garbage units and guided Samantha to his automobile. He turned out of the project site onto Western Avenue and joined the gentle flow of traffic southward.

'So you reckon that Oscar Van Kleef is too wrapped up in the *Albatross* to realise that his wife is getting fed up?' prompted Samantha after they had taken their seats in the Greasy Spoon diner and ordered lunch.

Keller shrugged.

'That's about the size of it.'

Samantha pursed her lips.

'And how do you cope, Mr. Keller?'

'Jules,' he corrected for the third time. 'Cope? Oh, you mean does my job cause friction with my wife?'

He laughed and shook his head.

'I guess not. I was divorced three years ago. I married her when I was working for Pan Continental down at San Antonio. Then the company decided they needed my talents up in Alaska. She wasn't keen to come. We drifted apart. That was it. No dramas, no great problems.'

Keller mentally glossed over the fact that the divorce had taken place because he had decided to go to Alaska with a pretty Pan Continental stewardess instead of his wife. Pan Continental had dismissed the girl and given Keller a warning; good aeronautical engineers were hard to find so the airline personnel officer merely lectured him on respecting the good name of the company. Stewardesses were easier to replace.

'And you?' asked Keller. 'Are you married?'

'At the moment,' she smiled, 'I'm married to my career.'

Keller chuckled.

'So it seems that neither of us have problems.'

Samantha thought his smile made him quite attractive. He was short, dark and wiry and, in a way, saturnine. Had she not known that he was a French Canadian, Samantha would have placed his ethnic origins as most decidedly south European. He had a charm that was very Latin. Her own origins were Nordic and she found herself wondering whether it was that fact that made her find swarthy Latin types attractive. Men of her own fair complexion repulsed her. She suddenly realised that Keller was returning her speculative gaze quite openly. She coloured slightly but did not lower her eyes. She realised, with a tinge of excitement quickening her pulse, that the speculation was mutual.

Chapter Ten

Tom Saxon's urge to have a drink was almost unbearable. His head felt as if it were splitting and he had difficulty concentrating on the instruments in front of him. He did not seem to be able to get them in focus for longer than a few moments. They kept blurring around the edges. He tried to focus on the altimeter. Eleven thousand feet.

'Watch your speed,' he grunted to his student pilot, seated alongside him in the Cessna Turbo Skylane.

'It's okay,' returned the slightly rotund sales executive whom he was instructing. 'True airspeed is 136 knots at 65 per cent power.'

Saxon grunted in annoyance.

'I'm the one who says if your speed is alright, mister,' he retorted.

The student pilot glanced at him and shrugged.

Sweet Jesus, how Saxon needed something for his head! He held his hands firmly in his lap to stop them from trembling. The hell with this job anyway! He wasn't cut out to be nursemaid to a lot of rich executives who thought flying was like taking a driving test. The four-seater aircraft suddenly hit some turbulence and started rocking, the student pilot over-reacted and, with a roar, the aircraft began to climb violently.

'Hold it steady, damn it!' snarled Saxon. 'Drop back, drop back to eleven thousand and hold her there.'

The student pilot scowled at Saxon. He had caught the smell of stale alcohol on his instructor's breath when they had met at the club-house. He knew that Tom Saxon already had a reputation among other students. The man was a boozer. Well, he was going to ask the club manager if he could change instructors just as soon as they were back on the carpet. It was either change instructors or change clubs.

Oblivious to the thoughts of his companion, Saxon peered wearily down onto the patchwork quilt of southern England. Ah, there was Andover below and to the starboard beam of the aircraft.

'Right, swing her to port and start your descent. We'll circle round Andover, down to Winchester and make our approach towards the north-east of the field.'

The student pilot signalled his agreement churlishly.

They circled, losing altitude.

Saxon glanced at his watch.

Thank Christ! The lesson was almost over and he would be able to have a few stiff belts before the next boy wonder showed up and demanded to be taught how to be another Billy Bishop or Eddie Rickenbacker. He watched the ground coming up to meet them with an anticipatory smile as the vision of a small amber-filled glass on the dark mahogany club-house bar swam into his mind.

'Damn it!' he suddenly snarled at his pupil. 'Neutral trim and apply moderate back pressure. I want that nosewheel just barely off the ground at touchdown. . . .'

He glanced anxiously over the instrument panels, wishing he could keep them all in focus at the same time.

'You bloody idiot,' he swore. 'Extend your approach flaps; you are well under 140 knots . . . are you trying to stall this kite? Prepare to retrim and then get your flaps down fully, we need to get down fast or you'll overshoot. Come on, you can get a steeper approach than this. Oh, sweet Jesus!'

The little Cessna wobbled onto the end of the runway, swinging this way and that, bumping down on the tarmac and then running towards the group of buildings which made up the Middle Wallop Flying Club.

The student pilot brought the aircraft to a halt and switched off. He gave Saxon a long look of pure hatred before he climbed out.

Saxon, oblivious to the man's anger, swung out after him.

'Are you trying to kill us both, you stupid bastard?' he demanded, as they reached the ground. 'Just how many hours have you had on this machine, you poor boob? You don't even know how to make a simple approach.'

The student pilot was red in the face with anger.

'Perhaps that's due to the way you instruct people, mister,' he said, his whole body shaking with an obvious attempt to contain his temper.

'What?' Saxon's jaw sagged as if he hadn't heard right.

'I have never been so insulted in my entire life!' snapped the pupil. 'I have never been subjected to the sort of language that you . . .' he fumbled for the right words. 'As for your capabilities, I've never flown with you without your being boozed to the eyeballs. . . .'

Saxon's fist shot out and sent the man flying backward across the tarmac.

The man's mouth became bloody with the impact of Saxon's fist.

'Saxon!'

Guy Lancaster came striding towards them. He was the manager of the flying club; a former Group Captain with iron-grey hair and steely eyes, set in a gaunt, angular face.

The student pilot was scrambling to his feet, incoherent with anger.

'Did you see what he did, did you see . . . ?'

Lancaster made a vain effort to pacify him.

'I'll sue. I'll sue this club, that man. . . .'

Lancaster tried to quieten him with a gentle hand.

'I really do apologise, Mr. Hamilton. I can only express the sincere regrets of the club that this has happened. Would you like to go across to the club-house? I'll join you there in a moment. . . .'

'I want that man sacked,' snarled the student pilot. 'I want that man dealt with!'

'Just so, Mr. Hamilton. If you will let me see to the matter and then we can talk about compensation for this unfortunate occurrence.'

The student pilot turned and stalked off, muttering, with little more than his dignity hurt.

Saxon, trying not to laugh, watched him go.

Lancaster swung round on him with a steely gleam in his eyes.

'Alright, Saxon,' he said coldly. 'You've had every chance that we could give you. It's just a bloody miracle that you haven't killed yourself or some poor luckless pupil during the last month or so. Don't think I haven't noticed the times you've come onto this field either as high as a kite or suffering from a colossal hangover. You've had more than enough chances to pull yourself together. You're fired! And I shall do my damnedest to see you never get another job in civil aviation in this country.'

Saxon shrugged indifferently.

'It was a bloody silly job anyway,' he gave a false chuckle.

Guy Lancaster watched him begin to walk away and stopped him after a few paces.

'For Christ's sake, Tom, can't you see a doctor or someone? You're cracking up, man!'

Saxon ignored him and walked to his MG sports car, parked behind the club-house. No use trying to get a drink there with everyone having seen what had happened. To hell with it! He didn't care. There was always something else to do; somewhere else to go. He started the car and roared away towards the village. He braked violently to a halt outside the pub and walked into the saloon bar. It was only eleven-thirty a.m. and the place was deserted.

'Hello, Gloria, my love,' he called to the slim, dark-haired barmaid, who glanced up from her copy of *Woman's Journal* with a look of irritation. When she saw Saxon her face broke into a smile.

'Good morning, Wing Commander. The usual?'

Saxon inclined his head as he slid onto a bar stool. He watched the girl place a glass of Jameson Irish Whiskey in front of him.

'You're in early this morning,' the girl said.

Saxon grinned.

'No hour is too early to partake of the nectar of the gods, Gloria,' he chided in a patronising tone.

The barmaid sniffed.

'Rotgut, more like,' she returned.

It was a pity, she thought, as she examined Saxon while he slowly sipped his drink. There was a look something akin to bliss on his broad, handsome face. Strange how one could tell alcoholics or near-alcoholics by the puffiness of their faces, the bulging eyes and flaccid mouths. It was a pity, because Tom Saxon was a handsome man. He was tall, with fair, almost corn-coloured hair, blue eyes and what had once been an athletic figure. It was slightly paunchy now. In other circumstances, Gloria felt she could have fancied Tom Saxon. Not that Tom Saxon would fancy her. She had heard village gossip. Something about his wife being killed a few years ago. That was the cause of his drinking, so they said.

'Fill her up again, Gloria,' commanded Saxon, pushing his empty glass somewhat distastefully across the bar.

'It is early, Wing Commander,' Gloria said with emphasis. She always called him Wing Commander, even though he was no longer in the Air Force. So did everyone in the village. Wing Commander Tom Saxon AFC. They said he had been quite a celebrity once—a hero. He had been awarded the Air Force Cross for, oh . . . something. She couldn't remember. He had been a hero. Such a pity.

'Another one,' grunted Saxon. 'I don't care what the bloody time is.'

The girl coloured.

'Sorry. I was only thinking. . . .'

'Well, bloody don't!' snapped the man.

'Now then, now then, Wing Commander!'

George, the landlord, emerged from a background.

'There's no call to use that sort of language to a young lady, is there, sir?'

Angered, Saxon hauled himself from the bar stool.

'Very well, if you don't want my custom. . . .' He turned and slammed out of the pub.

Behind him George gave a sneer.

'Damned souse! He's not to be served in here again.'

Charles Renard's house, in the hamlet of Balleroy, stood in the shadow of the old 17th-century château; a plain edifice whose long driveway majestically prolonged the village's single street. Renard's house was also of the 17th century, built by François Mansart, who had constructed the old château for the Marquises de Balleroy. Records showed that the house had been built for the mother of one of the Marquises as a dower-house. Renard, born of a small peasant farmer in the village, had made it his first ambition, when he acquired wealth, to buy the house. It satisfied some need within him. It was not enough for him to be successful but he felt the need to flaunt his triumph among the people who remembered him as a ragged-arsed little boy —especially the De Choisy family who were still regarded as the grand seigneurs of the village. If he had been able, Renard would have bought the old château itself with its extravagant library and its artifacts, but it had been turned into a museum. In fact, Renard was now fond of telling the story that as a poor peasant boy he had often gone to the château's museum to study its renowned collection of montgolfiers and gas balloons and made a vow that one day he, too, would build airships. There was absolutely no truth in the story: as a boy he had no interest in the old château nor in balloons, but the story looked good in the press interviews connected with the airship project.

Renard turned his Mercedes into the gravel drive which circled up to his house and felt a little proprietorial glow of pride as he surveyed it. He brought the car to a halt outside, climbed out with his attaché case and had not reached the door before Bernard Elbeuf, his manservant, opened the door and greeted him with a polite 'good evening'. Bernard helped him off with his coat but Renard stopped him taking his attaché case.

'There are some letters I must go through,' he explained. 'Is Madame Renard at home?'

Bernard bowed gravely.

'Madame is in the dining-room, sir.'

Renard went straight there.

Janine Renard was sitting before the fire sipping an aperitif.

'Hello, Charles.' She did not smile as her husband entered the room. Renard returned her greeting and, putting down his case, mixed himself a martini.

Janine Renard's age was difficult to place. In fact, she was only thirty but she disguised a good figure by wearing clothes that would have suited a far older woman. She gave the impression of being rather dowdy and nearer forty than her true age. Her tangle of mouse-coloured hair and lack of make-up heightened the effect. She had purposely stopped taking an interest in her appearance about six months after her marriage to Renard. She had become resigned to her marriage and resigned to her life. Resignation was the key to Janine Renard's character.

One evening, Renard had abruptly confessed that his marriage to her had simply been one of convenience—his own convenience. Her father, Marshal Dubray, was an influential man in aviation circles. Initially, Janine, who had always had a tendency to dowdiness, being bookish and introvert, had been swept off her feet by Renard's pursuit of her. She had generally been overlooked by men and, in fact, was still a virgin on her wedding night. Yet she was a girl with a great deal of emotional warmth and hidden sexuality. Her plainness as a child had produced in her an inferiority in that she had tried to suppress her natural feelings, would shun the company of men and had almost convinced herself that her role in life was to be a spinster.

Then Renard came along. It had begun when he had been invited to her father's house to a business dinner. Soon he was calling regularly not to see the Marshal but to see her. She could not believe it. Renard was quite an attractive man. There followed a whirlwind romance—a fiery courtship. What she had not known until after the marriage was that Renard had pursued and courted her because of her father's wealth and position. Renard was then a struggling aircraft industrialist and Dubray was the man who could influence the placing of air defence contracts. Renard's plan worked perfectly.

He did not become sexually bored with Janine until six months after the marriage. He had already become intellectually bored with her after a few meetings and had tried to keep up the pretence that he was interested in literature, films, ballooning (flying was only a means of transport to Renard) and other things which absorbed Janine. For Renard there was only one paramount interest—money and how to make it. Their worlds were poles apart and, finally, Renard, after a glass too much wine, confessed as much.

The confession did not make Janine angry. It merely reawoke in her all her feelings of inferiority. She turned in on herself, becoming a drudge, resigned to her role as Renard's housekeeper, being a wife in name only. Where other women would have sought a divorce or, at least, a lover, Janine retreated into her books, into her fantasies, away from the real world.

'Had a good day?'

It was an automatic question from Renard.

'Yes. I was reading *La Menace Invisible*. . . .' Janine loved fantasy tales, being so removed from her own drab existence. She was prevented from explaining further about the book by the bored expression on her husband's face. 'And your day? Was it good?'

'Could have been better,' Renard replied. 'What time is dinner?'

'In half an hour. My father is coming.'

Renard frowned.

'Your father? Why didn't you tell me? You should be dressed then. He likes things set out nicely. Have you warned Bernard and his wife?'

Janine nodded an affirmative.

'You'd better change then. Wear your blue dress and for goodness sake put on some make-up.'

Renard scowled as he went into his study.

Damn the woman! He wondered whether there was an ulterior motive to the Marshal paying them a visit. Could she have complained to her father about him? No. Janine didn't have the courage. Anyway, he didn't want the Marshal breathing down his neck over his domestic life at his stage. Perhaps the Marshal had heard about the unofficial agreement with Brisset? No, he would have to play that one close to the chest.

He sat down at his desk and began to go through the letters he had not found time to deal with that day. Ah, here was the letter of dismissal which he had already dictated and addressed to Villemur just in case the man stuck to his opinions about the safety of the construction of the *Charles de Gaulle*. Well, he didn't need it now. Thankfully, Villemur had stopped bellyaching about the design problems. Renard smiled. Money always talked. When he had threatened Villemur with accepting the design factors already agreed on the *Charles de Gaulle* or being thrown off the project, there was no question of the option Villemur would take. He screwed the letter into a ball and threw it into the fire.

There were a few letters from airship enthusiasts, one letter from a would-be investor—he would take advantage of that—and another from . . . he frowned. The postmark was Maine, America. It was a plain white envelope with neat, precise printing in black ink. He opened it. There was a single sheet of white typing paper on which was the same precise printing in English. Renard had managed to obtain a working knowledge of the language. It was essential in aviation circles.

'Airships are death machines: this was proved in the early years. God's will is paramount and these infernal and dastardly instruments of death will not be allowed to pollute the skies. Desist from your efforts to launch your airship. I have already shown my power once. Max Prüss.'

Renard chuckled, screwed the paper up and tossed it after Villemur's letter of dismissal.

There was a soft tap on his study door.

Janine entered. She had changed into her blue evening dress and had done something with rouge, powder and lipstick. The effect was not good, but better than before.

'Is it alright, Charles?' she asked anxiously. There was a plaintive note to her voice; a little girl seeking approval.

Renard uttered a sigh of exasperation.

'It's better, but why can't you . . . ?'

He was interrupted by the sound of a car drawing up outside, the slam of a car door and the peal of the doorbell.

'That will be your father,' he said. 'Now, for goodness sake, look a little happy.'

'Yes, Charles,' she said in a small voice.

Chapter Eleven

Tom Saxon struggled to open a bottle of Bell's whisky and pour himself a glass. For a moment he held up the tumbler to the light and studied the amber liquid reflectively. Then he intoned:

> Then trust me, there's nothing like drinking
> So pleasant on this side the grave;
> It keeps the unhappy from thinking
> And makes e'en the valiant more brave.

He laughed, perhaps a little too harshly, and tossed off his first drink of the day. One drink and that was all, that would steady him. He set down the glass and examined the kitchen of his cottage. Yes, today he would begin on the tidying-up. There was at least a week's dirty crockery lying about the place. He caught sight of a dozen empty bottles. Yes, time to pull himself together. Maybe he should ring up Lancaster at the club, see if he could get his job back. He bit his lip. No, that was no damned good. He wouldn't go bloody cap in hand to Guy Lancaster. There were plenty of other jobs about—plenty. Why, he strained to recall the incident, there was that fellow Ashton who rang up the other day—some job in America. He knew he had the telephone number somewhere. That was it. He would tidy up the cottage; spruce himself up and arrange to have a talk with Ashton. Why, with his experience . . . must be plenty of jobs.

The letter box vibrated.

He glanced at his wristwatch.

Ah, the morning post.

He hauled himself from the kitchen table and went through the lounge of the small Tudor cottage to the front door. There were two letters lying on the mat. One was an official brown envelope marked 'OHMS'. It was from the Inland Revenue. In disgust he tore open the envelope and glanced at its contents. A final demand for a tax bill. Well, they would have to go and whistle for their £2,000. Funds were getting pretty low. He glanced at the second letter. It was from Lancaster with the formal dismissal. He screwed it up and threw it towards an overflowing wastepaper basket. He suddenly became aware of the mess in the lounge. He would have to tidy up in here, too. Piles of bottles. Rubbish. Half-eaten scraps of food. That's right. Start tidying up.

He went back to the kitchen, his eyes coming to rest on the open bottle of whisky. That's right. A short nip to start the day. He must have had one already. No matter. He poured out another glass. . . .

There was a banging on the front door.

He set down the glass with a certain amount of hesitation and went back through the lounge.

Saxon blinked at the man who stood on the threshold.

'Garry Carson!'

'Hi, Tom!' Carson stood smiling. 'Jesus, you look a bit rough.'

Saxon gestured a little defiantly.

'A bit of a late night, old boy. What . . . what brings you here?'

'I've come a couple of thousand miles to see you, you sonofabitch. Aren't you going to invite me in?'

Saxon stood aside meekly.

The pungent reek of stale tobacco and alcohol hit Carson immediately he stepped over the threshold. He stared about him in surprised distaste.

'Had a party, Tom?'

Saxon seized upon the excuse.

'That's it, old boy. A party. Not had time to clean up. Sit down, if you can find somewhere.'

Carson removed a pile of dirty clothes and an empty glass from an armchair and sank gingerly into it.

'Well, well. How are you doing, Tom?'

'I survive.'

There was an uncomfortable pause.

'How are things with you?' Saxon asked.

'Just fine, Tom. I'm chief test pilot of a civil aviation company in Portland, Maine.'

'That's good. How's . . . Helen?'

'She's fine.'

'That's good.'

There was another pause.

'Drink?' Saxon asked.

Carson shook his head.

'Too early for me, Tom. Don't let me stop you.'

While Tom went to get the drink he had already poured, Carson peered round the interior of the tiny Tudor cottage.

'Nice place you have here. Have you had it long?'

'It's rented,' explained Saxon. 'I rented it when I moved down here and took a job with the local flying club. Pilot instructor and all that sort of thing.'

'Not your style, Tom,' observed Carson. 'That's why I came down to see you.'

Saxon frowned.

'What do you mean?'

'I told you I was chief test pilot for a civil aviation company in Portland, Maine,' replied Carson. 'It's a subsidiary of Pan Continental Airways—called Anglo-American Airships.'

'Oh?' Saxon's eyes narrowed. 'Anything to do with a character called Ashton?'

Carson smiled.

'That's why I'm here, Tom. I'm the head-hunter.'

Saxon pulled a face.

'I told Ashton that I wasn't interested.'

Inwardly, Saxon was cursing. What a damned golden opportunity. He was being offered a job on a platter just at a time he desperately needed one. He would never find anything worthwhile in England once Guy Lancaster started spreading the word. He had already been asked to resign from two previous jobs because of what they were pleased to call his drinking problem. Hell, he could go to the States and cock a snoot at them all. But he hadn't realised that Carson would be the fly in the ointment. Of all the people in the world—Carson!

'You're a qualified airship pilot, Tom. Anglo-American badly need your experience.'

Saxon gave Carson a penetrating glance.

'And what do you say?'

'I'm the guy who laid your name on the line when Anglo-American started pushing panic buttons. We badly need you, Tom.'

Could it be, wondered Saxon, that Carson didn't know? It seemed incredible. He had always assumed that Helen would tell him one day. Perhaps she hadn't. Maybe it was worth a chance.

As much as Anglo-American badly needed him, he needed them more, especially after yesterday's fiasco at the flying club. Of course, things might be awkward with Helen. He would have to try and live with it. He desperately needed the job. No rushing fences, though. He would have to play things in a low key.

'It's an exciting project, Tom,' Carson was saying eagerly. 'How about it?'

Saxon gazed at him for a while.

'It's ironic,' he said.

'How's that?' asked Carson, puzzled.

> 'What fate imposes, that men must needs abide;
> It boots not to resist both wind and tide.'

'Say again?' frowned Carson.

'Shakespeare, old boy. *Henry VI*.'

There was a brief silence and then Saxon exhaled deeply.

'Tell me about this airship project.'

Briefly, Garry Carson sketched in the basics, including the death of Westbrook. In spite of himself, in spite of his depressive thoughts that clamoured for his undivided attention, Saxon found himself excited by the idea. He started to throw some technical questions at Carson and soon they became embroiled in a discussion about the principles of airship economics. Eventually, Carson glanced at his watch.

'How about grabbing a bite to eat, Tom?'

Saxon looked up at the clock on the mantleshelf.

They had been talking for nearly four hours; four hours and he hadn't even touched a drop. Well, that proved it. He could lick this drink business any time he chose.

'Let me buy you a meal, Tom,' insisted Carson. 'On your new employers how about it?'

Low key, urged a voice in Saxon's mind.

'You can buy me a meal. But I haven't made up my mind yet. I want to hear more.'

'Okay, no sweat.' Carson stood up. 'Can you recommend a restaurant near here and we can go through the facts and figures?'

Saxon grinned. Not too near, just in case he bumped into anyone who might queer the pitch. He nodded and put on his coat.

'Okay, Garry, old boy. You fill me in and then I'll let you know my answer in twenty-four hours. How about that?'

'Fair enough, Tom,' agreed Carson as they passed out to Saxon's MG.

When the telephone rang on Terry Terrasino's desk it was Harry Maclaren. He sounded very tired and nervous.

'Terry,' he said, using Terrasino's first name, something he had never done before. 'Terry, can you get in here right away?'

Terrasino gave an affirmative and left his office, taking the elevator to the top floor of the administrative building. He smiled at Jean, Maclaren's secretary, who waved him through into the project manager's office. Maclaren was bent over his desk, head cradled in his hands. He started a little guiltily as Terrasino entered.

'Trouble?' Terrasino knew all the signs.

'Yeah, trouble,' returned Maclaren. He pointed to a sheet of paper and a envelope on the desk in front of him. 'Don't pick it up . . . it might be important to get fingerprints or something. I've just telephoned the FBI man, Hayes, to get over here.'

Terrasino walked around the desk and peered over Maclaren's shoulder.

The paper was an ordinary piece of white typing paper. On it were a few short sentences, neatly printed in black ink. Terrasino noticed how precise the printing was, each letter carefully formed, almost perfect.

'Anglo-American you have been warned. I am sorry about Westbrook and Budmeyer. I did not mean to kill Mr. and Mrs. Westbrook, only demonstrate my power. However, my previous warnings were ignored. I had to demonstrate my strength. Cease making this infernal machine or you will be punished. God's will is paramount. Max Prüss.'

Terrasino scratched his brow.

'A nutter?'

'A nutter with some knowledge, Terry,' replied Maclaren.

'What makes you say that?' asked the security chief, peering at the letter again.

'The news and speculation about Westbrook's death was common knowledge. But no one, apart from a few people on the project site, knew about the attack on Budmeyer.'

'Okay. I'll buy that. But it doesn't make it conclusive that the letter-writer and the saboteur are one and the same. It could be a weirdo who picked up some gossip. Or it could be someone trying to put us off the scent. It would take a lunatic to sign his name to the note. Max Prüss? Does the name mean anything to you?'

Maclaren shook his head, frowning.

'It seems familiar from somewhere but . . . no, I'm sure we don't have a Max Prüss working for us.'

The intercom buzzed on his desk.

'Mr. Hayes is here, sir,' came Jean's voice.

'Send him in.'

Agent Hayes came in looking a little excited.

He peered at the letter and then, producing a pair of tweezers from his pocket and a polythene envelope, he dropped the letter and its envelope in it and sealed it.

'I'll get our lab boys onto this right away.'

Maclaren pointed out the reference to Budmeyer.

'If this letter is genuine, it will help support Terrasino's theory that the saboteur is someone connected with the project site,' said Hayes.

'How's that?' demanded Maclaren.

'It was mailed in Scarboro . . . that's not far away and I guess a number of your men live there.'

Terrasino pursed his lips.

'If it is genuine, I can't see our saboteur being that dumb. He's not going to pull such a crude boner as to mail his letters from a mail-box near his home. Anyhow, how about the signature—Max Prüss?'

'I would imagine it is a false name,' replied the FBI man. 'I take it that you have started a check through your personnel files?'

Maclaren looked guilty.

'I'll get on to it right away but I certainly can't recall a Max Prüss on our payroll, and I've a good memory for names.'

'The writer also says that he has given previous warnings to Anglo-American.' Hayes turned to Terrasino. 'Is the letter, the paper, the printing and style, in any way familiar? Such letters would have come to you.'

Terrasino shook his head a little defensively.

'We had a whole batch of nutcases writing in over the last couple of years since the project has been developing. My office has passed over the file of letters to you for examination.'

Hayes smiled.

'In that case, we should be able to find Mr. Max Prüss's previous warnings. This might be the break-through we wanted. In the meantime, let my office have a list of the names and addresses of all employees who live in the Scarboro' area . . . just in case,' he added with a disarming smile at Terrasino.

Carson dialled Tom Saxon's number. Saxon answered almost immediately.

'Tom! Have you come to a decision about the job?'

Saxon's laugh rang a little hollowly on the line.

'As Seneca once said, old boy: Fate leads the willing and drags the reluctant. I shall be led.'

Carson frowned.

'Is that an affirmative or a negative?'

'Affirmative. I'll give it a try but with one condition.'

'What's that, Tom?'

'That your company advance me five thousand pounds to clear up some financial embarrassments here.'

Carson did a few mental calculations.

'That's about ten thousand bucks, eh? Well, I'm sure we can agree on that. When can you come to our London offices to sign the contracts?'

Saxon chuckled on the other end of the line.

'Any bloody time you like.'

Chapter Twelve

Terrasino drove his battered Ford convertible down Moulton Avenue and into the waterfront area across the Canadian National Railway Company's trackways. He found a parking space on Custom House Wharf. He wondered why Hayes had asked him to meet him at Boone's Restaurant on the waterfront. Why not? Maybe Hayes was a seafood addict. He grinned at the thought. He entered the restaurant and saw Hayes immediately. The FBI man was sitting deep in conversation with Vambrace. Hayes glanced up and spotted Terrasino before the waiter had time to go across to him, and he waved him over to the table.

'Glad you could join us, Terrasino.'

Terrasino exchanged greetings with both men.

'Want a drink?' asked Hayes.

A waiter materialised to take his order and he asked for a Cinzano, with ice and lemon. He looked at the two men curiously.

'You said it was important when you rang me,' he prompted.

The FBI agent inclined his head.

He reached down to a leather case by his chair and drew out a folder of stiff see-through plastic sheets. Inside were three letters. The last one Terrasino recognised immediately as the threatening letter which had arrived in Maclaren's office the previous day.

'The letter-writer, Max Prüss, was right,' Hayes began grimly. 'He *has* written two previous warnings.'

He handed the folder to Terrasino.

Like the other letter the first two were written on plain white typing paper and were neatly printed in the same careful, precise style. Terrasino read the first one.

'Anglo-American: desist from making these machines of death and destruction. Airships have been responsible for much unhappiness. They have taken happiness from me. Look to history and know that God Himself frowns on these machines and destroys them in fire. Make no more. You have been warned. Max Prüss.'

Luckily, when Terrasino's office had filed the hundreds of letters from various screwballs, the envelopes had also been filed. The datestamp bore a Scarboro' postmark some eighteen months previously. Terrasino could not recall the letter. He turned to the next one.

'You have ignored my warning. I shall now have to demonstrate my power and my serious intention. I shall act within seven days of you receiving this. If you are worried—I am sorry. But you have ignored my warning. Max Prüss.'

Terrasino put the folder down.

'Someone's got to be kidding. The quaint English! The phraseology! You can't take these seriously!'

Vambrace leant forward and jabbed at the second letter.

'Check the datestamp on that.'

Terrasino squinted at the envelope.

It was posted in Scarboro' again, exactly seven days before Alec and Jane Westbrook had been killed. Terrasino raised his eyebrows.

'Exactly,' said Hayes emphatically. 'That, coupled with the writer's knowledge about Budmeyer, makes me want to meet up with our Max Prüss.'

'So you believe they are genuine?'

'Yes. Vambrace and I are going to act on that assumption.'

'Did any prints show up?'

'A few,' Hayes said. 'But so few that they could only be those of whoever handled them after they were posted. We are onto a smart cookie, probably wrote them wearing rubber gloves or something. Anyway, we'll check those out—there's always the odd chance.'

'How about the name, Max Prüss?' asked Vambrace of Terrasino. 'I don't suppose it's on your personnel list?'

Terrasino shook his head.

'So the name is just a phoney,' sighed Hayes.

'Not necessarily,' Terrasino suddenly said, turning the letters over in his hands. 'The name Max Prüss must have some sort of significance for the writer. Look, if we are taking these letters as genuine then we'd do well to consider them carefully . . . the style, threats and so on. If the writer of these is our man then we are dealing with someone who has a grudge against airships. A paranoiac.'

Hayes and Vambrace exchanged glances.

'You mean we have a screwball on our hands who is doing this because he doesn't like airships?' Vambrace gave a wan smile.

'That's about the size of it,' admitted Terrasino, ignoring the levity of the question. 'Take those letters to a psychiatrist and get them analysed and I am sure he will diagnose a paranoid condition—a man who has a complex that airships have been responsible for hurting him or someone close to him.'

Hayes looked at the security chief in surprise.

'You seem to be pretty sure, Terrasino. How come you know about paranoiacs?'

'I did a degree in criminal psychology before I went into Air Force intelligence,' Terrasino admitted.

'You are pretty sure that it is a "him" rather than a "her"?' intervened Vambrace.

Terrasino shrugged.

'Okay, him or her. But the odds are that it's a male. Women don't usually develop this sort of psychosis.'

'So if Max Prüss is a paranoiac, how do you read them?' pressed Hayes. 'Who are we looking for?'

Terrasino sat back and sipped his drink thoughtfully.

'You want the textbook definition of a paranoiac? Paranoia is a chronic disorder of insidious development, characterised by persistent, unalterable, systematised, logically constructed delusions.'

Vambrace looked blank.

'Suppose you translate that into plain English for us?' he asked.

'Okay. Our saboteur's motivation is vengeance; he believes that he is on a crusade. Airships are, to quote his phrase, "machines of death and destruction". He must rid the world of them because God does not like them. Also, he believes he is seeking justice for a wrong done to him, allegedly caused by an airship. So the symptoms are almost classic. Also, it tells us a lot about him.'

'Such as?' demanded Hayes.

'Such as the fact that his problem was caused by some incident relating to an airship. There can't be many such incidents.'

'What time scale are you suggesting?' enquired Vambrace, making a note.

Terrasino shrugged.

'In paranoia the disorder develops slowly and steadily. The incident could have happened years ago. I'd say the man must be in his middle age at least.'

'How do you figure that?' Vambrace frowned.

'I've just said that the disorder develops slowly. Of course you *can* get young paranoids but it doesn't usually erupt in full force much before a person is in their mid-thirties. On the other hand, he may be considerably older. The disorder can last a long while—often a lifetime.'

Hayes drummed his fingers on the table-top.

'We'll have to get our own shrink to check out what you say. Even supposing you are right, you have nearly two thousand workers on the project site. From the list your personnel people supplied us with there are two hundred and thirteen of them living in the Scarboro' area. It will be like looking for a needle in a haystack.'

'Even if the saboteur lives in Scarboro', which I doubt,' replied Terrasino. 'My guess is that he mails the letters there because it is pretty safe for him to do so. Why, he might live anywhere . . . Cape Elizabeth, even Gorham.'

Hayes grimaced.

'We have to start somewhere. We have to work on the evidence that he has supplied us with.'

'And the important fact is that he's very knowledgeable about aeronautical engineering, especially electronics,' added Terrasino.

'So far as our investigation on Westbrook's Mitsubishi goes, you're dead right. Whoever messed with those control cables knew what they were doing,' agreed Vambrace.

'So we narrow our field to those people who have a knowledge of such things,' Hayes said. 'How many suspects would that leave us with?'

Terrasino made some mental calculations.

'About three hundred, at a rough guess.'

Hayes whistled.

'When does this airship of yours start its test flights?'

'The original schedule was for next week but with Westbrook's death. . . .' Terrasino shrugged. 'There's some scuttlebutt about an English pilot joining the team and Garry Carson, who's now our chief test pilot, is over in England at the moment.

If the man does join our project he would have to go through simulator training . . . I'd say the test flights are still a month off.'

'Well, we can do a lot in a month,' said Vambrace.

Hayes nodded agreement.

'We'll start on the spadework first. I'll get another couple of agents on the case and we can start checking through personnel files, trying to eliminate people.' He paused and frowned. 'Tell me, Terrasino . . . if this guy is a screwball, wouldn't it be noticeable? Wouldn't he be easy to spot?'

Terrasino grinned.

'You obviously haven't worked with scientists—most of them are screwballs anyway.' Then he looked serious. 'No, I wouldn't think so. The ordinary paranoiac doesn't get into trouble. His delusions of persecution and his search for revenge can often be expressed in a socially acceptable fashion. Contrary to popular belief, the typical paranoiac is not criminally inclined. It is only as a last resort that he turns to law-breaking, that is, only when other attempts to seek a redress of his imagined grievances have failed. Our Max Prüss is probably a very neat and proper man. It is a classical but often true picture. He would probably bend over backwards to avoid any appearance of flaw or fault. I expect he shows up for work each morning, neatly dressed, neatly shaven, lives a model life, never goes on a binge or gets involved with women and his professional life is probably exemplary.'

'Yeah, that's the thing which has been bothering me,' commented Vambrace. 'If the guy hates airships and wants to destroy the *Albatross*—then why is he working on the project and, from what you say, in a fairly senior position on it?'

Terrasino leant back.

'That's part of his problem. He has a schizoid personality. When working on the project, he gives his very best to it. One would assess him as a thoroughly reliable member of the *Albatross* team.'

'Surely the type of man you have described would stand out like a sore thumb anyway?' Vambrace smiled.

'Well, it certainly gives us something to work on,' agreed Hayes. He glanced at his wristwatch. 'Jesus! Let's order some food. . . .'

'One thing is sure,' Vambrace suddenly articulated Terrasino's thoughts, 'we'd better catch this screwball pretty soon. If he is someone in an executive position on the *Albatross* project, then he's going to infiltrate any security we can put up and when that big baby takes to the skies. . . .'

He pursed his lips and made a popping sound.

'You're looking tired, Charles,' observed Tanya Le Solliec as she brought a tray of crisp bread, paté, a bottle of wine and two glasses in from the kitchen and set them on the table.

Charles Renard sprawled back on the chaise-longue, loosening his tie and unbuttoning the collar of his shirt.

'Tired isn't the word for it,' he replied. 'It's been one hell of a week. Old man Dubray came to have dinner with us the other night. He kept looking at me very oddly. I have a suspicion that Janine has been complaining to him.'

Tanya poured the wine and handed him a glass, making a sympathetic clucking noise with her tongue.

'Poor *chéri*. The business does not go well either?'

Tanya had an unerring ability to go straight to those things that were truly important for Renard. His wife and domestic life could be an irritant but there was only one thing which really worried him.

'Things could be better. We are still awaiting the delivery of the helium gas to inflate the *Charles de Gaulle* for our test trials. I hear the Americans have another test pilot, some Englishman. That means they could be back on schedule again. They could be starting their tests before we do.'

Tanya pouted, perplexed.

'Why does it mean so much to you to be first across the Atlantic? Surely the days of Alcock and Brown and Lindberg are over? No one cares who crosses the Atlantic first.'

Renard regarded Tanya with a sense of pride and satisfaction, like a proud parent or owner. Tanya had been his mistress for eighteen months. A tall, willowy, red-haired girl from Rennes, she had been twenty-four when they first met. She had been entertaining as a folk-singer in a small Breton café near Montparnasse Station. It was strange how they had been drawn together. It seemed to have been a natural drift, two people oddly attracted by opposing characteristics. Renard, the hard, self-made opportunist, the hustler, the materialist, the man of little emotion. Tanya, full of the Celtic mysticism of her native Brittany, unmaterialistic, drifting through life like an untrammelled spirit; a butterfly, floating from one flower of experience to another. Calm, unflappable and highly intelligent. Had they ever bothered to analyse what had brought them together, and kept them together, they would have been unable to do so.

Renard felt completely at ease with Tanya; he could be himself without trying to observe social airs and graces which permeated his existence at Balleroy. At the same time he experienced an intrigue, a mystery, with Tanya; he strove hard to understand her views of life. He put more effort into his relationship with her than into that with his wife, Janine. Janine was of no importance to him; just a means to an end. He had no feeling for her. With Tanya it was different.

Soon after he and Tanya had embarked on their relationship, he had bought an apartment on the Rue Falguière, near the Gare Maine-Montparnasse. It was a simple one-bedroom apartment, not expensive, where he could stay on the occasional weekends or night when he could pretend he had to go to Paris on business. But it was regarded as strictly Tanya's apartment: he had allowed her to furnish it as she wanted and invite whomsoever she wanted there, provided it did not conflict with his arrangements. The situation would not have suited most women but it satisfied Tanya; it freed her from having to earn a living so that she could pursue her interests.

'Whoever makes the first airship crossing of the Atlantic will pick up a great deal of publicity,' explained Renard, pouring himself another glass of wine. 'And *chérie*, publicity ensures business.'

Tanya smiled.

'It is important to you that your *Charles de Gaulle* becomes the first airship to fly, isn't it?'

Renard looked serious.

'Very important. If it doesn't, then I shall be a pauper again. I will not have that.'

He patted the seat beside him and when she sat next to him he turned and took her face between his two large hands and kissed her softly.

'I promise you, *chérie*, that I shall succeed.'

He frowned suddenly.

'You did get your visa for tomorrow?'

'Yes. Don't worry, Charles. Everything is in order.'

His face relaxed. He knew how vague Tanya could be at times. He did not want the trip to Montreal to have any hitches. It was an important trip; a very important trip.

Chapter Thirteen

When the Boeing 747 landed at Kennedy Airport, New York, Tom Saxon was drunk. Not incapably drunk, but drunk enough for his slurred speech and slowness of response to be noticed by the stewardess. As she bade farewell to the passengers as they left the aircraft and walked down the covered gangway into the terminal building, she nudged the chief steward and nodded to Saxon's unsteady gait. The chief steward grimaced imperceptibly, and continued smiling and thanking the other passengers for flying with the company.

The immigration officer, seated in his cubicle, took the landing card and passport from Saxon and flicked it open. He looked up and saw Saxon leaning against the structure of the cubicle, swaying uncertainly. The immigration officer sniffed. There was usually at least one passenger, coming off the long haul of the Transatlantic flight, who had succeeded in drinking himself into a semi-coma. Not that the immigration officer was teetotal but, Jesus! you should learn how to handle your liquor when entering a foreign country. He sniffed again and the waft of stale alcohol confirmed his suspicions. He checked the visa stamp slowly. He hadn't really expected it to be out of order. He glanced at the landing card details and asked Saxon for his work permit.

Hell! The guy was an airline pilot, going to work for some company in Portland. He made a mental note not to fly with that company. Then he smiled charitably. Maybe the man had just been on a bender. Airline pilots worked hard and were known to go overboard once in a while.

'Will there be someone to meet you outside, sir?' he enquired politely as he stamped the passport.

Saxon frowned and tried to concentrate.

'What?'

'Are you being met, sir?'

'Oh, no.'

The immigration officer heaved a sigh and signalled to a porter.

'Tell Dave to process this guy as soon as possible, before he passes out. Get him to the lobby and into a cab, okay?'

The porter nodded. He knew the standard drill for anyone coming off a Transatlantic flight who had over-indulged themselves.

The immigration officer handed Saxon's passport across and smiled automatically.

'Hope you have a good stay, sir. Good luck.'

Saxon grabbed the passport and nodded.

The porter manoeuvred to his side.

'This way, mac. Which is your baggage?'

Saxon swayed after the man to the baggage claim area where what seemed a myriad suitcases were whirling around at alarming speeds on a circular conveyor belt. He pointed and the porter expertly grabbed two cases as they rushed by.

'This way, mac.'

He guided Saxon across to the customs tables. Dave, who usually dealt with 'floaters', the name given to inebriate passengers, was already processing a couple who seemed to resent his questions and his request to inspect their bags. The porter sighed. There was always someone who felt a customs office was an unwarranted intrusion into their private lives; they were usually people who had something to hide.

Across the concourse the immigration officer had processed two more people when he stared at the British passport he was proffered.

"Miss Ashton?'

He was looking up into the face of an attractive blonde.

'Yes.'

'It says on your documents that you are working for Anglo-American in Portland?'

'That is correct.'

The immigration officer glanced across to where the porter was steadying the swaying form of Tom Saxon as they waited to clear customs.

'Excuse me, miss,' he said, turning back to her, 'do you know a Wing Commander Saxon—he's a pilot with Anglo-American?'

Claire Ashton shook her head, frowning.

'I've only just arrived. I haven't started to work for them yet.'

The immigration officer shrugged.

'Sorry, it was just a thought, miss. That's Wing Commander Saxon over there. . . .' Claire Ashton looked in the direction he indicated. She saw a rather lean, handsome man, with an unruly mop of curly blond hair, standing supported by a porter. 'As you can see, miss,' grinned the immigration official, 'he is rather the worse for indulging too liberally in the inflight refreshments. I thought if you knew him you might be able to keep an eye on him until he gets to his hotel or makes his connection to Portland.'

Claire frowned.

'I'm afraid I don't know him. You say he's a pilot with Anglo-American?'

'That's it, miss.'

'Well, I'll see if I can help him.'

'Thanks, miss.'

The immigration officer stamped her passport, smiled and wished her good luck with her job.

Claire gathered up her suitcases, placed them in a trolley, and wheeled it across to where Saxon stood, trying desperately to focus in front of him. He looked rather like a little boy, lost and pathetic, thought Claire. He was also a very attractive man, lean and blond. A bit like her father when he was younger.

'Wing Commander Saxon?'

Saxon made the effort to turn, screwing his eyes up as he looked at her.

'Who are you?'

His speech was rather slurred.

'I am Claire Ashton. I work for Anglo-American. My father is Sir Ashley Ashton.'

Saxon tried to grin. The grin turned into a leer.

'Have you been sent to meet me?'

The girl shook her head.

'No; apparently we travelled over here on the same aeroplane without knowing it. I gather you are en route for Portland.'

The porter who was steadying Saxon grinned.

' 'Scuse me, miss, but this guy should be en route for a hotel and bed. He ain't in no fit state to make the connection to Portland in his condition.'

'What d'you mean?' demanded Saxon belligerently. 'Are you saying that I'm not sober?'

The porter gave a stage wink at Claire.

'Ain't implying anything, mac. But maybe this nice young lady would like to keep an eye on you until you get to a hotel, eh?'

Claire studied Saxon for a moment before nodding.

'I'm staying over in New York tonight and flying up to Portland tomorrow. It will help break up the jetlag.'

'Sounds reasonable,' conceded Saxon stiffly.

'Okay, mister,' the customs official called Dave was waving him through.

The porter whispered 'floater', laconically. Dave sighed, checked Saxon's passport and looked over his baggage. Then he glanced up at Claire.

'Are you with this guy, lady?'

'We've just met,' said Claire primly. 'But we are both employed by the same company so I'll make sure he gets to a hotel alright.'

'Okay, lady.'

Dave gave a cursory glance at her baggage and waved them through.

The porter escorted them outside the building and summoned a yellow cab. The large rusting vehicle lurched up and the porter dumped their bags inside. He grinned as Claire passed him a tip.

'Where to, lady?' demanded the driver.

'Can you take us to a moderately-priced hotel on Manhattan?' she asked.

The driver smiled broadly.

'English, ain't you? Want a cheap hotel? Okay.'

He threw the cab into gear and sent it speeding away from the terminal building like a frustrated racing-driver. He glanced into the mirror.

'Looks like the trip was too tiring for your husband, eh?'

Claire looked sideways at Tom Saxon. His head was bent forward on his chest and he was snoring gently.

She smiled.

'It seems to have been,' she replied.

It wasn't long before the driver deposited them on the sidewalk in front of the George Washington Hotel on Lexington and 23rd Street. He helped Claire in with the luggage and, having failed to fully rouse Saxon, half-walked, half-dragged him into the lobby.

Claire never reasoned out why she decided to book one room under the name of Mr. and Mrs. Saxon. She was impulsive and hardly ever questioned the reasons why she did anything. The man at the reception desk handed her a key.

'Fifth floor, ring down if you don't like the room,' he said disinterestedly.

A porter helped her with both the luggage and Saxon.

They deposited him on the bed and he lay sleeping while Claire showered and changed her clothes. Then she went downstairs and found a small fast-food restaurant next door to the hotel and ate a meal. When she returned to the room, Tom Saxon was still deep in an alcoholic sleep.

She stood examining his face for a while. So he was a pilot with Anglo-American? She didn't even know whether he was married. Was he a permanent drunk or was he just recovering from a once-off bender?

Well, she did not want to be alone; not alone in a strange country. She had no qualms about taking a room with this strange man if it meant she didn't have to be on her own. She wished he would wake up, talk with her, but it was enough that he was there.

She began to haul off his jacket and trousers. She took off his tie and loosened his shirt, removing his shoes and socks. Then she struggled to get him between the sheets. He did not wake once.

Claire looked at her watch. It was only seven o'clock in the evening, New York time. That was midnight English time. It had been a tiring day. She locked the door, slipped out of her dress and slid between the sheets by Saxon's side. There was something comforting about being in bed with a warm body next to you. She lay looking at him for a moment before turning off the bedside lamp and cuddling up to his recumbent body.

It was still dark when she was awoken by his movements. She was not alarmed, only excited as she felt his hands moving over her breasts and across the flatness of her stomach. She began to respond. They made love anonymously, in the dark, with only their physical selves as a connection. Then it was over. She smiled sleepily and whispered something but he seemed to have fallen asleep again.

When she woke in the morning, she found that Saxon was in the shower. She lay in bed until he came out, a towel around his waist.

'Hello,' she smiled.

He looked down at her quizzically.

'Hello, er . . . ?'

'Claire Ashton, remember?'

He bit his lip and looked abashed.

'My memory isn't all that good, I'm afraid. Oh. . . .' he struggled hard to recall. 'Sir Ashley Ashton's daughter. Er, look, Miss Ashton. . . .'

'Claire,' the girl grinned at his obvious confusion and embarrassment.

'Look, er, Claire . . . did I . . . did I . . . ?'

She gave a peal of merry laughter.

'You were the perfect gentleman, Tom Saxon, apart from a tendency to fall asleep due to an excess of alcohol. No, it was I who brought you here and put you to bed and. . . .' she grimaced in amusement.

He looked more bewildered now.

'*You* did? Why?'

'Because I thought you would make a damned good screw,' returned the girl primly.

Saxon's mouth tightened.

He was still quite inhibited about some things. Anyway, the blonde was young enough to be his daughter.

'And did I?' he asked sarcastically.

The girl sighed.

'Not bad, I suppose. But I would need to conduct a few more tests before I could make an informed judgment.'

She chuckled as Saxon coloured.

'You're a bit of a prude, aren't you?'

Saxon sat on the edge of the bed.

'No. I'm just rather old-fashioned.'

'Old-fashioned?' A hard look came into her eyes. 'My father is old-fashioned. It's just another way of saying that you want to dictate and can't bear it when others make the running.'

Saxon raised his eyebrows.

'It means that I prefer to do my screwing sober and I prefer to choose my own screws too.'

Claire lay back, hands behind her head, the action causing the sheet to slip so that her small breasts lay naked to his gaze.

'Well, you're sober now. . . .'

The invitation in her voice was unmistakable.

He couldn't make her out. She was young and very attractive. There was no denying that. And she was Sir Ashley Ashton's daughter! He didn't want to blot his copybook with the company right away but. . . . Well, it hadn't been his fault. The girl was making all the running. She must be some type of nymphomaniac and. . . .

He suddenly leant forward and threw back the sheet from her body.

She did not move; just lay watching him with a half-triumphant smile on her lips.

He bent his mouth to hers.

'Yes, damn it!' he whispered. 'I'm sober now.'

Chapter Fourteen

Samantha Hackerman pressed the doorbell with a decisive gesture. The buzzer sounded faintly and she heard footsteps. Jules Keller, clad in jeans and a check sportshirt, opened the door and smiled warmly at her.

'Right on time,' he greeted her. 'Come in.'

She stepped into the apartment and looked round curiously. Her first impression was of neatness to the extent that it did not resemble a normal bachelor apartment—at least not the ones she had experienced. The place appeared newly swept, polished and tidied. Books on the shelves were ranged in orderly rows, no book stood out from the others and each was placed in sequence of size. All the cushions were placed at appropriate angles on the chairs and couch. Nothing seemed to have been left casually lying around: the room had an unnatural, unlived-in feeling.

Keller shut the door and followed her in.

'Let me take your coat,' he said. 'Would you like a drink? I've a wide selection.'

He motioned to a neatly-positioned cocktail cabinet.

She asked him for a Campari and soda. He took her coat, placed it carefully on a hanger and hung it with equal care in a cupboard. Then he proceeded to mix the drinks.

She felt a little guilty as she dropped onto the couch.

'Did you tidy up especially for me?' she asked, peering round.

Keller laughed disarmingly.

'No. Most of my friends reckon I have a phobia about untidiness. I just like to keep the place neat and smart, that's all.'

Samantha took her drink from him with a grin.

'Well, I've known very few bachelors who keep their apartments this tidy,' she said. 'In fact, I haven't known any.'

'Yeah? Well I did say that I was married once, so I guess that excludes me from the usual run of bachelors, eh?'

He poured himself a whisky and tipped some ice cubes into the glass.

'Here's to us, Sam,' he said, raising it.

'Us,' she replied, returning the gesture. After sipping the drink she asked: 'Where are we going for our meal tonight?'

Keller smiled mysteriously.

'To a place that is the very mecca of gourmet delights. A place where you can get the best French cooking in America. Chez Jules.'

She frowned.

'Chez Jules? I don't . . .' her eyes suddenly widened. 'Oh, you mean . . . ?'

He walked across the lounge and opened a swing door which obviously led into a kitchen. A scent of aromatic cooking pervaded the air.

'Tonight I have decided to put my culinary reputation on the line and cook you a meal.'

Samantha answered his grin.

'I didn't realise you added cooking to your other talents.'

Keller assumed a pose.

'Ma'am, I am so talented that I bore myself. Electronics wizard, aeronautical genius, superb cook, expert tennis-player and lover and a wonderful all-round warm human being.'

Samantha chuckled deeply.

'I'll let you know my opinion of your talents later,' she quipped, colouring as she suddenly realised the double meaning to her words. She had meant, after she had tasted his food, but. . . . He saw her embarrassment and, smiling, sought to cover it up by excusing himself to go into the kitchen.

She stood up and started to examine the books in his bookcase. There were quite a few on aeronautical engineering, electronics and other related subjects. There was a whole section on airships. Many of them were historical outlines and accounts of airship disasters, but there were also new studies such as Hartcup's *The Achievement of the Airship* and Kirschner's *The Zeppelin in the Atomic Age*. She was turning away from the bookshelf when she suddenly noticed a half-dozen books on psychiatry: titles by Freud, Reich, Laing, Rollo May and Jung. She stared at them in surprise. She wouldn't have thought Keller would have been interested in that sort of subject.

'The food will be ready in a moment,' announced Keller, re-entering the lounge.

Samantha pointed to the books.

'I'd never have guessed you were into psychiatry.'

For a moment Keller looked uncomfortable.

'Yeah. I had a passing interest.'

'A bit odd for an electronics man.'

Keller shrugged.

'I guess we all should know a bit about what motivates us, don't you?'

'I hadn't really thought about it before,' admitted Samantha.

Keller suddenly sniffed and hurried back into the kitchen.

The telephone buzzed.

'Shall I get it for you?' Samantha called.

She heard Keller say something within the kitchen and took it for an affirmative.

'Hello?'

'Is that Mister Keller's residence?'

The female voice was friendly and bright.

'Yes. He's busy right now. Can I take a message?'

'Yes please. This is Air New England calling. Would you tell Mister Keller that we rang to confirm his booking on the noonday flight to Montreal tomorrow?'

'Oh yes. Thank you.'

'You're welcome.'

Samantha replaced the receiver as Keller came back into the room.

'That was Air New England confirming your flight to Montreal tomorrow at noon.'

Keller frowned.

'Oh . . . thanks.'

Samantha went back to her drink.

'I didn't know you were off to Montreal tomorrow.'

'Just a two-day trip,' Keller grimaced. 'Back home to see the folks.'

'Oh. I keep forgetting you are French-Canadian.'

'*Je suis Québecois*,' intoned Keller. '*Ma père est canadien mais ma mère est française*.'

Samantha smiled apologetically.

'French is not one of my languages. Now had you spoken Spanish—been a Mexican or from somewhere down that end of the continent. . . .'

'I was just saying that I was born in Quebec. My father was from there but my mother was a Frenchwoman. They still live near Montreal. I'm just going up there to perform my filial duty.'

He pronounced Montreal as a French-Canadian would.

'But now,' he changed the subject abruptly, 'dinner is served.'

He led her into the kitchen which doubled as a dining-room.

There was no sign that Keller had been cooking, only the simmering pots and pans on the hob. Everything had been cleared away. The table was neatly laid and a bottle of white wine was standing in an ice-bucket.

Samantha sniffed appreciatively.

'Smells great.'

Keller motioned her to sit, helping her with her chair, before serving her with a mushroom starter.

He poured the wine and took his seat.

'You seem to live in comfort, Jules,' Samantha commented, encompassing the apartment in a motion of her hand.

Keller's face grew serious.

'Yeah. I was born in Joliette, that's halfway between Montreal and Quebec City. We lived in a poor part of town. My dad was a farm labourer but he had a bad accident when I was young and couldn't work. There wasn't much money about. I had to get through school and college as best I could. That meant working every goddam hour there was in a day. I was determined that when I was able to earn my own living I would adopt a lifestyle that . . . well, I would luxuriate in the things that I never had as a kid.'

He laughed, a little too harshly.

'Anyway, you don't want to hear my problems. Eat up.'

Afterwards, she had to admit the meal was exceptional. Jules Keller was a good cook and excellent company. She had never giggled so much in her life. He was full of witticisms, of quick retorts and amusing anecdotes. She could not remember when she had had a more enjoyable evening. When Keller brought the coffee she found his face had become serious again. He was staring at her with that same speculative gaze she had noticed when he had taken her to lunch a few days ago. She returned the gaze steadily.

'Will you stay the night, Sam?' he suddenly asked.

To her surprise, she found that she was not shocked. It was inappropriate to feign any false modesty or pretend that she did not want to stay.

'Alright . . . yes,' she found herself answering in a small voice.

Garry Carson looked at his wife across the breakfast table.

'Tom Saxon flew into Portland last night,' he said.

Helen did not glance up from the morning newspaper.

'Maria Terrasino told me.'

'He's staying at the Sheraton in South Portland until he finds a suitable apartment.'

'Oh?'

Her voice was polite and disinterested.

'I thought we could organise a barbecue this evening to welcome him. I could invite the Terrasinos, and some others from the project—Harry Maclaren, Danny Macmillan, Billy Heath, the guys he will be working with.'

Helen raised her eyes from the newspaper and stared at her husband. Her face looked a little strained.

'Tonight, Garry? That's rather short notice.'

'I wanted to tell you last night,' there was a touch of bitterness in his voice. 'But I understood you were at a movie with Lesley Van Kleef.'

Helen nodded absently.

'She's having trouble with Oscar. I think she might be leaving him.'

Carson was not interested in the domestic problems of Oscar and Lesley Van Kleef.

'Anyway, I've already mentioned tonight to a few people. It would be nice for Tom to meet a few friendly faces.'

He couldn't understand Helen's lack of enthusiasm. Tom and Jan Saxon, Helen and himself, used to be such good friends in the old days. Knowing Tom, and about the tragic death of Jan and Tom's kid, Tom Junior, he would have thought that Helen might have gone out of her way to make him feel at home.

'There's also the English girl,' went on Carson, 'Claire Ashton. She's the daughter of our British vice-president. I've invited her across as well. She arrived on the same flight as Tom.'

Helen Carson drew a deep sigh. It seemed there was no getting out of the party. It had to happen, she supposed, sooner or later she would have to meet Tom Saxon. She wished it had been later, though.

'Well, I suppose I better see what I can dig out of the freezer.'

Carson smiled, partly with relief.

'We'll just rustle up some barbecue chicken, corn on the cob, a few snacks. Nothing grand.'

'I'll ask Maria to come over and help me prepare.'

She began to tidy away the breakfast things.

'What's this Claire Ashton doing on the project?' she asked, trying to make conversation.

Carson finished his coffee with a gulp.

'She's a secretary or something. Going to help out Samantha Hackerman in the press office, so far as I can gather.'

He stood up.

'Gotta go. We're showing Tom round the *Albatross* today.'

Helen watched the kitchen door slam shut. Carson hurried out of the house and climbed into his Cord automobile.

Damn it! It was so unfair, she thought. Just when she had dismissed Tom Saxon from her mind, he had to reappear. And the irony was that it had been due to Garry that Saxon had been offered a job on the project.

Charles Renard turned his black Thunderbird hire-car off the main highway and along the road to Pointe-aux-Trembles, the northern suburb of the city of Montreal. Beside him, Tanya was peering at the city guide on her knees and glancing, now and again, at the street signs.

'Ah, *voilà*!' she cried and pointed to an old colonial French-style building which they were approaching. A large, peeling notice hung outside. *La Ratière*. Renard grinned as he swung the Thunderbird into the parking lot alongside the building.

'The rat-trap, eh? An appropriate name for our rendezvous.'

Tanya put the street-map back into the glove compartment and stretched.

'How long will you be, Charles?'

'Not long. A few moments if the man I am to meet is not late. Will you be alright waiting in the car?'

'Certainly.'

Renard left her and walked into the bar. It was fairly dark and smoky inside. He stood on the threshold, allowing his eyes to grow accustomed to the gloom. He spied his man sitting near the door. There was a bottle of wine on the table before him and two glasses, one of which was nearly full and which he was sipping.

'Hello, Keller,' Renard greeted him, slipping into the seat opposite.

'Welcome to Montreal, M'sieur Renard,' replied Jules Keller. 'A glass of wine?'

Without waiting for an answer, Keller filled the empty glass and pushed it across.

'What is the news?' asked Renard.

'Saxon, the English pilot, arrived the other day. He will go through a familiarisation programme, a course of the simulator and then the *Albatross* will start her flight tests for her airworthiness certificate.'

'How soon?'

'Probably by the end of the month.'

Renard swore.

'We are still held up on our shipment of helium for the *Charles de Gaulle*,' he explained. 'The gas hasn't even left the suppliers yet.'

Jules Keller pulled a face.

'Well, the parent board at Pan Continental have also approved the training of two aircrews for the *Albatross*. I understand that the crews have already been chosen and should start their training schedule in about a week's time. For the Transatlantic flight the *Albatross* will need at least one complete back-up crew.'

'Do you know the schedule for the flight tests, Keller?'

'Sure. The first test will be along the coastline from Portland north to Grand Manan Island, turning before they cross into Canadian airspace. Depending on the problems they encounter on that flight, they will carry out a training flight down to Washington, D.C. That flight will be the big prestige, publicity flight for the *Albatross*, with the presentation of an airworthiness certificate and the President going aboard to inspect the airship and so on. After that, a few more tests, and then the big one —the Atlantic flight.'

'Do you think they will keep to their schedule?'

Keller was non-committal.

'There's a lot of talk about sabotage.'

'They don't suspect you of playing a double game?'

Keller grinned.

'I'm keeping a low profile, as they say. Anglo-American already have their hands full. Westbrook's death didn't delay them, however. I initially thought it would put them way behind schedule but they managed to get hold of this English guy pretty quickly. He's a qualified airship pilot and knows his stuff.'

'I know about him,' nodded Renard. 'Did you bring me the specifications on the engines?'

Keller gave a quick glance round before reaching into his inside pocket and bringing forth an envelope.

'These are the modifications on the Nomad engines but there might be other alterations before the final test flights.'

'Modifications?' frowned Renard. 'What do you mean?'

He took the envelope and thrust it into his pocket.

'Van Kleef wants to try to boost the speed factor to 150 mph.'

Renard looked apprehensive.

'Does he have a chance of succeeding?'

'That's my field, remember?' Keller's assurance was bland. 'Have some faith in me, Renard.'

Renard drummed his fingers on the table.

'You know that the *Charles de Gaulle* is equipped with only six commercial high-speed diesel engines which would give the ship a maximum speed of 118 mph. We would have no way of competing if Van Kleef found a way to can more power out of those compound aero engines of his.'

Keller was reassuring.

'Don't worry, Renard. I won't let you down. . . .'

He shot a meaningful glance at the chairman of Dirigeable-Commercial and raised his left hand, slowly rubbing his fingers together. Renard gave a gesture of disdain and took a small package out of his inner pocket. It looked like a fairly thick book wrapped up in brown paper.

'Ten thousand American dollars in small denominations,' he said. 'That's your second payment.'

'It's a pleasure doing business with you, M'sieur Renard. I sincerely hope we can do some more in the future.'

'You may count on it,' grunted Renard.

'I hope you have a good trip,' smiled Keller, as Renard stood up. 'Are you over here for long?'

'Just ten days. We will be going to see the helium people at Lake Charles. The delayed shipment is holding us up.'

'The *Albatross* has already had her tanks filled,' mused Keller. 'She's only waiting on getting a trained crew.'

Renard suddenly sat down again and stared at Keller.

'You're pretty unscrupulous as they go, aren't you, Keller?' he asked softly.

The French Canadian chuckled.

'You have exactly the same traits. I know your history. Poor background, like me. I was not meant to be poor, either, Renard. To make money you cannot afford to be a moralist. Money and morals don't go together.'

Renard lowered his voice but he spoke intently.

'If the *Albatross* can be delayed from making her test flights on schedule and, above all, from making the Translantic crossing before the *Charles de Gaulle*, there will be a fifty-thousand-dollar bonus credited to whatever bank you like.'

Keller stared thoughtfully at Renard and then grinned.

'Don't worry, M'sieur Renard. The *Albatross* will not beat your ship . . . you can leave it safely in my hands.'

Chapter Fifteen

Harry Maclaren's first reaction as he stood up to shake hands with Tom Saxon was a favourable one. Saxon seemed to be the stereotype airline pilot: tall, well-built, tousled blond hair and an air of boyish handsomeness. Yet Maclaren also noted the dark skin under the eyes, the drooping of the lids and the slackness of the mouth as if the man had made a night of it. He motioned Saxon to be seated.

'Coffee?'

Saxon smiled. It was an easy smile, thought Maclaren.

'Anything stronger, old boy?'

Maclaren drew his brows together. He didn't approve of early-morning drinking. However, he went to the drinks cabinet without commenting.

'What'll it be?'

'Whisky, if you have it.'

'How about a shot of Old Grand-dad Bonded?'

'Suits me. That'll do the trick.'

'Heavy night?' enquired the project manager.

'You could say that. Jetlag and all that.'

Maclaren handed him the drink and poured a coffee for himself.

'Well, er, Tom . . . let's get right down to business. Garry Carson is delighted to have you as his second pilot. I've seen your dossier and it's very impressive.'

Saxon's mouth quirked. It was apparent that Anglo-American's dossier on him was a little outdated, or maybe Guy Lancaster hadn't shot his mouth off after all.

'It's very impressive,' Maclaren was saying. 'I'm glad you decided to join us. Your work with dirigibles is invaluable to us. I presume you have read through all the project reports which Garry gave you?'

Saxon placed his attaché case on Maclaren's desk and drew out a number of folders.

'Yes; you better have them back as they're all marked "secret".'

Maclaren grimaced as he took the files.

'We are more security-conscious here than in military aviation, Tom. Don't let it worry you. Anyway, how do you feel about the project?'

'It's a development in aviation that was bound to come,' Saxon replied with consideration. 'Had there been a few far-sighted people about, we would have seen commercial airships flying in the late 1960s. Heaven knows, there were certainly enough designs and proposals going about at the time. I gather you have some pretty strong competition from France?'

'Yeah,' admitted Maclaren wearily. 'There's a guy called Renard who has built a similar ship in design, size and payload capacity, called the *Charles de Gaulle*, which is getting near completion.'

'How near?'

'Last time I heard they were arguing structures again. Their chief designer, a man named Lassay, resigned a few weeks ago but has shut up like a clam. Rumour has it that he was not enamoured with Renard's safety requirements. He was replaced by a man called Villemur.'

'I know of both Lassay and Villemur. They are top men. Villemur is an expert on metal and alloy stress.'

'We understand that he's not all that happy with Renard's whizz-kid techniques,' observed Maclaren.

'Well, I'd say you have certainly got some strong competition to face. Forget the hustler. If Lassay and Villemur built the *Charles de Gaulle* then it's going to be competition.'

Maclaren looked slightly irritated and then relaxed.

'Yeah, I suppose you're right, Tom. You know a lot about the European experiments?'

'As much as most people who have been in the field. When do I get to see the *Albatross*, though?'

'Right now,' replied Maclaren. 'We're joining Garry Carson and the rest of the test crew over at the construction site in a moment. But let me get you prepared. The *Albatross* is not like any airship that's flown before. It is the last word in improved fabrics, metals, plastics and other structural materials. It has better engines and more streamlined ground-handling techniques than any other dirigible.

'Remember the *Hindenburg* which crashed at Lakehurst back in 1937? That carried a crew of sixty-one, most of them riggers who had to crawl and scramble around inside the great airbag at distances as far as 400 feet from the main control room, having to take orders over intercoms. The *Albatross* will carry a flight-deck crew of four—the normal flight-deck crew of any modern long-distance aircraft. We have a pilot-captain; a co-pilot; a navigator and communications officer and an engineering officer. The whole ship can be controlled from the flight deck simply with advanced computer back-up. Even the slightest gas leak will register on the flight-deck control system.'

Saxon sat back, relaxed. He had read the specifications.

'What about ground-handling crews?' he asked. 'That has always been a problem. In the old days it needed up to four hundred men and sometimes hours to secure an airship at her moorings.'

Maclaren grinned.

'That's the beauty of the *Albatross*. We envisage a ground crew of a couple of men because our vectoring propeller system will bring the ship down to ground zero and anchor it there. It does away with mooring masts and the like.'

'What about ancillary crew?'

'The *Albatross* is primarily designed as a freight-carrying ship. She will have to carry three complete flight-deck crews, twelve people, on the Transatlantic run for safety. However, it is also designed to carry 150 passengers. To cater for those we have the equivalent of a cabin staff of ten under a chief purser. As well as passenger cabins or staterooms—we are going back to the old nautical phraseology, I'm afraid—the ship contains recreation rooms to make the two-and-a-half-day trip pleasurable. There's a small cinema, a promenade and observation deck, two lounges and a restaurant and a special "sky room" at the top of the ship which our designer reckons will become the hub of social activity on board.'

'And you reckon all this can be run by a cabin crew of ten?'

Maclaren nodded emphatically.

'Sure; most things, as you will see, are heavily computerised. It will be like staying in a small, discreet hotel. The passengers, don't forget, are just ancillary to the ship's main operation—freight-carrying. Now,' he stood up, 'let's go across and meet the *Albatross*.'

Figures can be deceptive. Tom Saxon knew very well the height and diameter of the *Albatross*; he knew the figures by heart from the specifications. He knew theoretically one could lose a dozen Boeing 747 Jumbo Jets inside its giant interior; knew that the ship dwarfed the biggest ocean-going liner. But it was hard to translate figures into reality, theory into tangibility. Tom Saxon experienced a feeling of awe as he stood under the belly of the monster and peered up at the outsize silver cigar.

Harry Maclaren stood regarding his expression with a smile. He had seen the same expression on the faces of countless people—the sceptics who had come to sneer and the believers who had come to worship. The feeling of utter awe silenced them all.

'Oscar! Just the man,' called Maclaren as the harassed-looking designer came by. He halted and shot a look of annoyance at the project manager.

'What is it, Harry?' he said irritably. 'I'm rather busy at the moment.'

Maclaren gave him a pacifying pat on the arm.

'You are always busy, Oscar. I know. But I want you to meet our new test pilot. This is Tom Saxon who arrived from England yesterday. He is going to be Garry Carson's second pilot when we lift your baby into the air. Tom, this is our chief designer, Oscar Van Kleef.'

The two men shook hands, each warily weighing the other up. Van Kleef's eyes narrowed as he inspected Saxon.

'I am told that you have had experience in piloting airships before—that you are highly regarded.'

'I've had experience piloting airships,' replied Saxon.

'Well, forget that,' Van Kleef made a gesture of dismissal. 'You will have to learn all over again with the *Albatross*. She is a very special baby.'

He turned abruptly and stalked off.

Saxon turned to Maclaren with a puzzled expression.

'Is it something I've done or is he like that with everyone?'

Maclaren smiled and took him by the arm, leading him along to the main gangway into the airship.

'Oscar Van Kleef is like that with everyone. If he had his way he would not only design, but build and fly this bird if he could. He is like a jealous husband, protective of his wife's honour . . . except the *Albatross* is a little outsized for a wife. Come aboard.'

At the gangway into the ship's interior they were halted by two security men who checked their passes and made them sign a book logging them into the ship. Maclaren explained that since security had been tightened, everyone had to sign on and off the ship.

'Garry Carson must have told you we were having some trouble,' said the project manager.

'He did say that the cause of your chief test pilot's crash was sabotage,' admitted Saxon, 'and that there was an attempt to cripple the back-up computers the other night. I understand that there's talk of some screwball trying to gum up the whole works.'

'I'm afraid so. We have a good security man named Terrasino on the job and the federal investigators are looking into the matter.'

They passed into the ship and for a moment Saxon felt as if he had boarded an ocean-going vessel; it was like stepping onto the main deck of the *QEII*.

'Plenty of time to take a trip through the staterooms and lounges later,' Maclaren told him as he made his way to a small elevator. 'We'll go straight up to the flight deck.'

He pressed a button. Saxon noticed that it said deck level ten and he counted twenty-one deck levels marked. He tried to make some mental calculations but before he could work out an answer, the elevator deposited them in a corridor. The sign said: 'Restricted Area: Flight Deck Crew Only'.

'The flight deck is placed at the nose of the ship, on a central level,' explained Maclaren, as he led him down the corridor. 'On this level you have the crew's cabin and recreational quarters so that the personnel are never too far from the flight deck.'

'It seems very spacious,' observed Saxon, noting that a series of cabin doors carried such legends as 'central communications cabin'; 'emergency engineering cabin'; 'computer back-up systems'; 'chart room'; 'captain's cabin' and so on. They approached a central door which simply said: 'No Admittance'. A red light shone above it. Maclaren pushed a button at the side. After a moment the red light changed to green and Maclaren opened the door and ushered Tom Saxon inside.

The interior, apart from large tinted windows giving an extensive forward vision, reminded Tom of a larger version of a flight deck on a modern jetliner. The atmosphere was very familiar. Garry Carson rose from the chief pilot's chair. There were two other men in the cabin.

'Hello, Tom,' smiled Carson. 'I understand you've settled in your hotel, okay?'

'Yes, thanks. It's very comfortable.'

'Good. Let me introduce you to the rest of the crew. This is Billy Heath, our navigator and communications officer. Billy, this is Tom Saxon.'

Billy Heath was a small, wiry negro. He greeted Tom in a soft southern accent.

'And this is Danny Macmillan, our flight engineer.'

Macmillan was about twenty-seven, lean, angular and dark-haired. Although his eyes twinkled with bubbling humour, he was hollow-cheeked which gave him a superficial appearance of mournfulness. He had a firm handshake which made Saxon wince slightly.

Maclaren waited until the introductions were complete before speaking.

'As you see, Tom, this is the main flight deck. We can control the entire ship from this point, provided the computer works alright. But as every computer system has five back-ups, going through five support computers, and every computer must be in synchronisation before we lift off, what can go wrong?'

'Like the computer systems on those space-shot rockets,' grinned Billy Heath.

'Pre-lift-off checks must be carried out thoroughly,' agreed Carson. 'So there is no way that any mistakes occur with malfunctioning hardware.'

'When the *Albatross* is in service she will carry three flight-deck crews with her,' went on Maclaren. 'We would try to maintain a six hours on-watch and a twelve hours off-watch duty roster.'

'Do you have that number of trained flight-deck crews?' asked Saxon with interest.

Maclaren shook his head.

'Until you are trained, we don't even have one fully trained crew,' he admitted. 'However, our parent company have just approved crew training and next week the back-up crews will start their training in the simulator.'

'Simulator?'

'An interesting piece of hardware, Tom. Just like an ordinary aircraft simulator flight deck but built to the *Albatross* specifications. We have worked out that a minimum sixty hours simulator experience is preferable before you are let loose on the real thing.'

'How long will that take?'

'Oh, about a couple of weeks,' smiled Maclaren. 'It will be

just like flying the real thing anyway. You'll be presented with the same problems that you will encounter in actual flight. You'll go through with Carson, Heath and Macmillan here so that you can get adjusted to each other before you start making the flight tests in earnest.'

'Feel confident about it, Tom?' asked Carson.

'Certainly,' returned Saxon evenly. 'That's what I came for.'

'Good,' Maclaren clapped him on the back. 'I'll let you know the training schedules first thing tomorrow. Now let's show you around the rest of Oscar Van Kleef's baby.'

Bernard entered the lounge after softly tapping on the door.

'Excuse me, madame,' he said softly. 'There is a Captain Barjonet from M'sieur Renard's er, factory.'

Bernard never knew what to call the Dirigeable-Commercial's project site.

'Will you see him, madame?'

Janine Renard looked up in puzzlement.

'He wishes to see me?'

Bernard coughed.

'Not exactly, madame. He came to see M'sieur Renard but when I told him that monsieur was in Canada for a few days he said he would like a word with you.'

Frowning, Janine set her book down and stood up.

'Very well, Bernard.'

The man whom Bernard ushered in was tall, broad-shouldered but with a slight stoop. He was muscularly built with merry, light blue eyes, a rather heavy jowl, which suited his raven-black hair, and a tanned complexion. His smile was warm and pleasant and Janine found it was natural to return it. His handclasp was powerful—She could feel the strength of his character in that grip.

'Captain Barjonet?'

'Jacques Barjonet, Madame Renard. I am most sorry to disturb you but I understand that your husband is away?'

'That is so, captain.'

She motioned him to sit down.

Barjonet did so, looking slightly contrite.

'It is my fault, madame. I should have enquired of his secretary but I was passing by and. . . .'

He shrugged.

'Would you like a drink?'

Barjonet smiled.

'A Pernod, thank you.'

Janine went to the cocktail cabinet and poured it for him.

Barjonet raised his glass slightly in salute before taking a sip. Janine acknowledged the salute with a bob of her head. She waited politely and then asked: 'What can I do for you, captain?'

Barjonet started.

'Forgive me, madame,' he apologised, setting down his drink and raising his attaché case of his knees. 'As I say, it is my fault. I should have realised that your husband was away. I should have enquired at the project site. I had these papers, you see. Papers that have to be returned to Monsieur Renard. I was motoring by, suddenly realised I was near his home and thought . . . well. . . .' He shrugged and smiled.

'It is no trouble,' smiled Janine. 'I can ensure that my husband gets the papers when he returns.'

'Wonderful. But you will forgive me for trespassing on your privacy, madame?'

'Of course,' returned Janine. 'You say you work with my husband?'

Barjonet chuckled. It was an infectious chuckle.

'I work for him, madame. I am the chief test pilot of the *Charles de Gaulle*.'

'Oh?' Janine felt a little lost. Charles never spoke about the personnel on his airship project. 'You are the pilot?'

'Indeed, madame. I am the captain of the airship.'

He turned to his attaché case and drew out the papers.

'We have been carrying out some tests and I have all the reports here.'

Janine took the buff-coloured file from the man, acutely aware that he was appraising her.

He was thinking: what a pity! Janine Renard could be a very attractive woman if only she took more care with her make-up and clothes. At the moment she was giving an impression of a drab housewife with a tangle of mouse-coloured hair and an appalling lack of clothes sense. He would like to take her out and tell her how to dress and. . . .

He became aware that she was saying something.

'Pardon?'

'I said, if you give me the papers, I'll place them in my husband's safe.'

In startled embarrassment he realised that they were both holding onto the buff envelope.

He let go of it hastily and followed her with his eyes as she went across to a portrait which hung on the far side of the room. It came away from the wall on hinges. Barjonet grinned.

'Why is it, madame, that people hide safes in such predictable places?'

Janine frowned. It was her turn to ask: 'Pardon?'

'In all the best mystery movies,' explained Barjonet, 'the safe with the jewels or important papers is hidden behind a portrait, usually a very hideous portrait.'

The portrait that hid Charles Renard's safe was of Charles Renard.

Janine suddenly found herself giggling with amusement.

'You are quite right, Captain Barjonet,' she smiled as she manipulated the combination.

'Will Monsieur Renard be away long?' asked the pilot, as he watched her deposit the papers in the safe and push the picture back in place.

'Probably until the end of next week,' replied Janine. Seeing that Captain Barjonet made no movement to go she offered him another Pernod, which he promptly accepted. Barjonet was wondering whether the rumours that he had heard about Renard and his Parisian mistress were true. If they were, it was rather unfair. Janine Renard only needed a little attention to be quite attractive—very attractive, he corrected himself. If only. . . .

His eyes fell on the book she had discarded when he had entered. It was a horror tale. *Les mains d'Orlac* by Maurice Renard.

'Any relation?' he asked, picking up the book.

Janine looked uncomfortable.

'Oh no . . . not that I am aware of. Maurice Renard came of a prosperous family with roots deep in the French legal hierarchy, whereas Charles's family were. . . .'

She hesitated, realising that she was sounding patronising.

Barjonet pretended not to notice.

'You like such tales, Madame Renard?' he enquired politely.

Janine felt embarrassed. It was perhaps childish to admit to her fondness for fantasy tales.

'I enjoy such things—it sounds ridiculous, I know. . . .'

'Not at all,' Barjonet assured her. He had read the classic horror tale some years ago. It was a *grand guignol*, a terrifying and ingenious story centred around a world-famous concert pianist named Orlac whose hands are horribly mutilated in a train accident. An eminent surgeon grafts on a new pair of hands with ghastly results, for Orlac finds himself possessed by strange and terrible impulses. The hands he has been given are those of a man guillotined for murder, and his spirit survives in his hands to live again in the unfortunate pianist.

'I, too, like fantasy literature and films, madame,' admitted Barjonet. 'I find them a superb way of relaxing.'

At that moment Bernard knocked on the door.

'Excuse me, madame, your father is on the telephone from Paris.'

Janine rose to her feet and Barjonet followed her example rather reluctantly.

'Many thanks for bringing the papers round, captain.'

She extended her hand.

Barjonet took it, bowed low, brushing it with his lips.

'The pleasure has been mine, Madame Renard. I shall look forward to meeting you again.'

Tom Saxon sprawled in an armchair in his suite at the Sheraton Inn and sipped a whisky. He had to admit that he was excited by the prospect of flying in the *Albatross*; excited enough to have completely forgotten, for a brief space of time, his anxieties about meeting Helen Carson at the party that evening. He still wondered whether he should try to invent some excuse and not go. But the barbecue was in his honour and it would be pretty churlish, suspicious even, to cancel and say he didn't feel well or something equally ridiculous. Now he had started to think about it, now he had turned his mind away from the *Albatross*, which had filled his thoughts for most of the day, he acknowledged a sinking feeling of depression. It was going to be some ordeal meeting with Helen and Garry Carson . . . meeting Helen with the ghosts of Jan and Tom Junior hovering like accusing wraiths forever haunting him. He reached for the bottle with an angry grimace and poured himself another drink. He would have to try to stop thinking about it.

There was a knock on his door. With a sigh he hauled himself up and went to open it.

Claire Ashton stood there, pert and attractive in a summer frock. She grinned at Saxon and pushed past him into the room. They had not seen each other since they had travelled down to Portland together on the Delta Airways flight out of Kennedy. So far as Tom Saxon was concerned, the night spent in New York was a brief interlude—not that he could remember much about it. He was vaguely grateful to Claire for probably saving him from being rolled into some New York gutter and robbed.

Whatever else followed left him with no other feelings. It was freely offered and accepted in the spirit of the time and place. That was all.

'Hello,' he said, as he shut the door behind her.

'You don't look ecstatically happy to see me,' she replied with a cynical smile.

'I'm not ecstatically happy to see anyone right now,' he admitted. 'Want a drink?'

Shaking her head, she dropped onto the couch and examined him carefully.

'You look as though you have a large head start.'

'What can I do for you?' he demanded harshly.

'Oh, touchy about it?'

There was an irony in her voice which made Saxon feel a sudden and intense dislike for the girl.

'None of your damned business,' he replied. 'What do you want?'

'I've been invited to Colonel Carson's party. I understand that you are supposed to be the honoured guest. I thought I'd call by and we could go together.'

He made no movement.

'Well?' pressed the girl. 'Are you ready?'

Claire Ashton, gazing into his eyes, suddenly realised that she had made a mistake; damn it, she was always making mistakes. The other day, in New York, she had acted on impulse, out of an immediate physical attraction to Saxon. She had also fantasised a little, perhaps. Now she saw that Saxon wasn't in the least bit interested in her. She had simply provided him with a good lay in New York—if he had been sober enough to remember—but he was more interested in the booze bottle and whatever it was that had driven him to it.

'I need a shower first,' replied Saxon slowly when she repeated her question.

Claire Ashton stood up and assumed a look of indifference.

'Fair enough,' she said.

Saxon watched her slam out of the room and bit his lip. Maybe he should have handled things more gently. He was not too impervious to the situation to realise that Claire Ashton was a rather unstable young woman. In fact, when Carson had picked him up from Portland Airport the previous day and been introduced to Claire, he had shot a strange kind of look at Saxon. Later, after they had dropped Claire, and Carson had driven him down Maine Mall Road to the Sheraton, he had asked Saxon pointedly:

'How well do you know Claire Ashton?'

'Not very,' he had answered. 'We just met in New York and discovered that we were heading for the same destination.'

Carson had pulled a face.

'You know that she is the daughter of our British vice-president Sir Ashley Ashton? Scuttlebutt says he has sent her over here because of some trouble back in England.'

'Some grapevine you have, Garry,' Saxon had laughed.

Now, as Saxon threw off his clothes and went into the shower, he realised that the last thing he wanted was to get embroiled in some affair with someone like Claire Ashton. And he certainly didn't want trouble in the guise of an irate father who just happened to be one of the executives of the company he was working for. Not with all the other crises in his life. Damn! Should he go to Carson's barbecue or not?

Chapter Sixteen

The 'Town Taxi' cab deposited Tom Saxon outside the low bungalow whose address Carson had given him. He paid off the driver and tried to saunter nonchalantly up the short driveway to the door. He could hear the sounds of music and noisy laughter from somewhere at the back of the house. He pressed the doorbell and waited, trying to steady his racing pulse. How would Helen react to him? What would he say to her? The door opened.

Smiling at him was a very attractive negro woman.

'Hi,' she said.

'Is this, er, Garry Carson's house?'

The woman's smile broadened.

'Guess you must be Tom Saxon,' she replied. 'Come on in, I'm Lisbet Heath, Billy's wife.'

Saxon awkwardly held out his hand.

'How d'you do?'

Lisbet Heath chuckled.

'Couldn't mistake you for anything but English,' she commented. 'Come on through. The folks are expecting you.'

She guided him through the lounge and kitchen where food and drink was spread on tables. A few people he didn't know, but who nodded to him as he passed, were hovering around. In the yard beyond the French windows about twenty people or so were gathered—talking, laughing, seemingly enjoying themselves. Saxon gave a panic-stricken look around but did not see Helen. Lisbet Heath was propelling him to where Garry Carson, in a loose shirt, slacks and baseball cap, was turning over pieces of chicken on a smoking barbecue fire.

'Hi, Tom. Glad you could make it.'

'What'll I get you to drink, Tom?' asked Billy Heath's wife.

He asked for whisky.

'The barbecue sauce is my own recipe, remember?' grinned Carson. 'Mind you, I've improved on it a bit since the old days.'

Saxon took his whisky and looked round the garden again. He still couldn't see Carson's wife. Harry Maclaren was there and introduced him to his wife, a small homely and pleasant woman named Anne. Just the sort of wife a man like Maclaren would have, mused Tom. Stable. Secure. No problems. Jack Lane, the assistant project manager, a staid north country Englishman who had worked for ten years in America, was also there. Saxon had met him earlier in the day. He also caught sight of Oscar Van Kleef in a corner, looking very unhappy. He was staring moodily at a vivacious red-haired woman who was dancing very closely with a rather suave-looking man. Billy Heath was standing by the food table, tackling the snacks as if he hadn't eaten for weeks, and Danny Macmillan, the *Albatross* flight engineer, was engaged in conversation with Claire Ashton. The English girl seemed to be making a point of ignoring Saxon—not that he cared. Carson was introducing him to other people—names and faces no longer meant anything to him. He smiled automatically, shook hands or said 'hello' and passed on. Carson was called back to his chicken and Tom Saxon found himself manoeuvred into a corner of the yard.

'Hello, Tom.'

He turned with an uneasy lurch of his stomach.

She had not changed at all during the intervening years. She was still as slim, dark and attractive as ever. She stood regarding him with those big, ice-grey eyes; a faint smile on her lips.

'Hello, Helen.'

'Have you been keeping well, Tom?'

He gestured defensively.

'I made out, Helen. And you?'

'I've made out, too.'

She did not ask whether he was happy. She could read the answer in the lines around his mouth and eyes; they had not been there two years ago.

'I was surprised when I heard that you had accepted Garry's offer.'

He shrugged off her question with its hidden meaning.

'I needed the job. It was a great opportunity for me.'

'Helen!'

Garry Carson was waving to her across the yard.

She smiled apologetically.

'I'll see you later, Tom.'

He raised his glass in acknowledgment.

It had been restrained, so much left unsaid. Well, at least he was sure that Carson did not know. Perhaps things might turn out alright; perhaps his feelings of unease were unjustified.

'Well, Saxon, what do you think of her?'

Saxon turned to meet the dour face of Van Kleef. It took him several seconds before he realised that the designer was talking about the *Albatross* and not Helen Carson.

Saxon smiled winningly.

'She's a beauty, doc. Really impressive.'

Van Kleef accepted the compliment as his natural due.

'Aeronautical engineers have been talking about such a ship for years but I have made the concept into a reality.'

Saxon accepted that most designers were egocentric.

'What made you go for a ship as big as the *Albatross*, doc?' he asked.

'Back in the 1960s it was agreed that while aeroplanes had proved to be extremely efficient for carrying large numbers of people at high speeds, airships were the only craft able to carry large quantities of cargo quickly and efficiently to any point you cared to name. Aeroplanes were more or less obsolete when it came to carrying cargo. Aeroplanes carry only 0.04 per cent of the world's total cargo tonnage. Just think of that! They invariably suffer from the mathematics of the square cube law. That's why a big airship was the answer.'

Saxon looked at him blankly.

'The square cube law,' explained Van Kleef, like a teacher instructing a particularly backward pupil, 'is that lift or carrying capacity rises as the square of their linear size but the structure weight increases as the cube.'

'Oh,' commented Saxon, trying to work out the equation.

'On the other hand,' went on Van Kleef, 'an airship becomes more efficient as it gets bigger. That's why the *Albatross* will be one of the most efficient cargo transports the world has seen.'

They were joined by Jack Lane.

'Talking about the efficiency of airships as freight carriers,' he interposed, 'airship cargo would travel faster than seaborne cargo but, of course, slower than aeroplane freight. Now where the *Albatross* can become really cost-effective is by carrying medium bulk and weight goods . . . all manner of manufactured products, mainly in containers. You know the sort of thing: smaller consignments will probably always go by aeroplane while primary products will always go by sea. But airships can take over the middle and biggest chunk of freight-carrying work.'

''Scuse me,' Lisbet Heath caught Tom Saxon's arm and guided him away, smiling an apology at Lane and Van Kleef. 'There's someone I want Tom to meet.'

Once in the lounge of the house she grinned.

'I thought you might like to get away from those two. They can become absolute bores when they get going about the *Albatross*. You'll have plenty of time for talking shop but this is supposed to be a get-to-know-you party.'

Saxon answered her grin.

'I'm grateful.'

'Well, you can show your gratitude by dancing with me. Everyone here seems to just want to talk, including that everloving husband of mine over there. Will you look at him! You'd think I starve him all week the way he's wolfing down that food.'

Saxon indicated the vivacious redhead who was still dancing with the suave young man.

'Not everyone seems to want to talk,' he observed.

Lisbet Heath sighed.

'That's a fact.'

'Tell me, why does Van Kleef keep looking at that redhead like a fox who hasn't had a square meal for some time?'

'The redhead is Lesley Van Kleef, Oscar's wife,' explained Lisbet Heath. 'Now, are we going to dance or not?'

'I . . . I'm not very good,' protested Saxon. It was years since he had danced. Not since. . . . Lisbet Heath was taking charge again, propelling him into the middle of the floor.

Across the room, Helen Carson was talking to Harry Maclaren and his wife but watching Tom Saxon out of the corner of her eye.

She was thinking that he had not changed a great deal in general appearance. Superficially, he was still the same athletic, tousle-headed Englishman she had welcomed to her home when she and Garry were based at the USAF airbase at Syderstone in Norfolk. Garry had been commanding the 33rd Pursuit Squadron and Tom Saxon had been the squadron's RAF liaison officer. For a few months Garry and Helen, Tom and his wife, Jan, had enjoyed a friendly foursome—parties, dinners, explorations into the countryside. Then Garry had been away on a squadron-training flight to West Germany. Tom had called by to organise a golfing weekend. After a few drinks—it seemed quite natural at the time—they had gone to bed together. It was then that Helen had realised that her marriage to Garry Carson was a sham.

She had married Carson soon after she had left high school, having dated the young Air Force officer since she was sixteen. The Carsons had been neighbours and friends of her family since she was born. Everyone assumed that she and Garry would eventually get together. She had grown up with that assumption; Garry, too, had grown up with it and neither of them had ever questioned it. Not that Helen had been unattracted to Garry. They had been friends, very good friends, but, being young, did not realise that simple friendship was not in itself an adequate basis for marriage. They had drifted into an engagement because it was expected of them.

After they had been married for a year, Helen began to feel dissatisfied and bored with her relationship. She had no yardstick to judge by, no other experiences she could compare. She suffered her feelings without articulating them. One thing she did make clear—she wanted no children and now, six years later, she still refused to contemplate the idea in spite of a natural pressure from Garry, the sly remarks of Garry's mother and the more pointed questioning of her own mother.

When Garry had introduced her to Tom Saxon, Helen had felt an immediate physical attraction, a fluttering in her stomach. That first night, when Tom and his wife, Jan, had come round for a meal, she had gone to bed and made passionate love to Garry who, unused to such fervour, had been surprised and delighted, thinking that he had finally managed to stir the dormant passions of his bride. Helen, however, was fantasising that she was making love to the English Wing Commander.

When Saxon and Helen did go to bed together, the experience had been shattering for both of them. The affair grew in intensity; they shared not only physical passions but intellectual ones as well. Tom was everything Helen had ever wanted in a relationship with a man.

At the time Tom Saxon had been married four years and had a four-year-old son, Tom Junior. He told Helen, somewhat guiltily—he was always guilty when he talked about Jan and Tom Junior—that Jan was a nice enough person but was too involved with domesticity, too involved with her child. Jan never referred to Tom Junior as 'their child' it was always 'hers'. Nor did she ever make any attempt to share Tom's flying interests or hobbies. On the other hand, she demanded that Tom's interest in herself and her home should be total. At one stage Tom had admitted that he should have had an affair with Jan and ended it while they were still ahead and happy. But when Jan had become pregnant they had both allowed themselves to use it as an excuse to marry and, instead of finding that the child, marriage and a home was a bond to cement their relationship, they discovered it was divisive, a means of levering everything apart. They presented a superficial front to the world while their marriage inwardly rotted.

The affair between Tom and Helen continued for several months until Garry Carson announced that he was being posted back to the States for demobilisation. He was planning to join Pan Continental Airways as a pilot. Tom and Helen discussed the situation. Both talked of divorce. A day or so later, Tom Saxon had gone home and discovered that Jan had found out about the affair; how, he didn't know. She had left a curt note and gone, taking Tom Junior with her. She was going to stay with her parents in Perth until things were sorted out. Hardly had Tom Saxon recovered from the surprise when the police were on his doorstep. Jan's car was a mangled twist of wreckage on the M1 motorway. She had driven into the back of a lorry. Both she and Tom Junior had been killed outright.

Helen had seen Tom Saxon just once after that: a pitiable figure of guilt and remorse, already trying to dull his senses with whisky. There was no talk about divorce between them then; no talk of making a new life for themselves. Tom simply wanted to drown his guilt. Frustrated at his attitude, Helen had gone back to the States with Garry, secretly hoping that Tom Saxon would pull himself together and come after her. He had not. She then tried to forget him. At first it had been a hopeless task. Tom Saxon became a vague shadow, a dark symbol of her frustrations, and her relationship with Garry had gone from bad to worse.

Now, almost out of the blue, Tom Saxon had reappeared. It was ironic to think that it had been Garry who had brought this about. Garry, still innocent about her affair with Tom; still ignorant of the events which had led to Jan Saxon's tragic death. The situation had the quality of a Greek tragedy.

She looked across the room and studied Saxon once more. No, he had not changed much. Not physically, that was. But he brought with him an aura of tragedy. His eyes held a deepset self-accusation which two years of boozing had not eradicated. The ghosts of Jan and Tom Junior still sat firmly on his slightly stooped shoulders.

It was at that moment that she realised that for her the intervening two years had been mysteriously wiped away as if they had never passed; with a sense of astonishment and perhaps excitement, Helen realised that she was still in love with Tom Saxon—if love was the correct word. As much in love with him as she had been during the days of their tempestuous affair in England.

'Hey, *pigrone!*' yelled Maria Terrasino. 'We're going to be late for Helen and Garry's party. Is that nice?'

Terrasino came out of the shower, wiping soap from his eyes with a towel, and grimaced in amusement at his wife.

'Okay, okay. What do you want me to do . . . go to the party smelling like a *paesano* straight from the farm, huh?'

Maria Terrasino grinned.

'Why not?' she countered mischievously. 'You look like one.'

She dodged behind the door laughing as he threw his towel at her. Then she poked her head round the door and rolled her eyes theatrically at his nakedness.

'*Rapidamenti!* Hurry now, eh?' she urged.

'Not before you come here and give me a kiss,' insisted Terrasino.

Maria put her hand over her heart and assumed a virgin-like expression.

'What? Enter the bedroom of a naked man to kiss him? Oh, signore, you cannot be serious. I have my honour to protect!'

Laughing, Terrasino made a run at her, but she dodged behind the door and slammed it shut.

'*Buffuno!*' she yelled. 'Get ready!'

The telephone rang.

'That will probably be Helen and Garry to find out where we are,' she called in dismay and went to answer it.

'*Pronto?*' she said, then, correcting herself, 'yes, hello?'

She frowned, trying to understand the voice on the other end of the line.

'A minute, please.'

She turned to where Terrasino stood uncertainly in the doorway, a towel wrapped round him now.

'Someone from the project site,' she said, holding the receiver towards him.

Terrasino pulled an apologetic face at her and reached for the phone.

'Yeah?'

'Terrasino?'

'Yeah. Who's this?'

'It's Kurt Nieman. Can you get over to the project site immediately?'

Terrasino glanced at the clock on the mantleshelf.

'It's late, Kurt. We were just off to Garry Carson's party. Is it important?'

There was a pause at the other end of the line. The project's chief electrical engineer seemed to have trouble finding the right words.

'I think so . . . I think I've discovered a bomb on the *Albatross*. Can you get here soon?'

Terrasino swallowed hard.

'I'm on my way.'

PART TWO

Chapter One

Kurt Nieman met Terrasino by the guard's hut at the end of the gigantic canvas construction which shielded the *Albatross*. The project's chief electrical engineer looked nervous.

'I haven't told anyone else,' he said, 'but I'm pretty sure it's a bomb.'

'Where is it?'

'It's on deck level six in a recess by the junction of the fuel leads and gas valves.'

Terrasino frowned.

'How much damage would that do if it explodes?'

Nieman looked puzzled.

'I wouldn't know. It depends on how much explosive the device contains.'

'Sorry, I meant is the device placed in a vital position?'

'It will blow the valves off the major gas cell controls but with the ship not being fully gassed up as yet that would not create an insurmountable problem. The most important area is that of the fuel leads. If there is enough explosive then the fuel reserve tanks could be ignited.'

Terrasino bit his lip and sighed.

'Okay, let's go and see this device.'

Nieman led Terrasino into the darkness of the ship's hull. It took them ten minutes to make their way to deck level six where the chief electrical engineer took Terrasino along the corridors to a section which housed the complicated control systems for every gas cell in the ship. He halted before a particular series of panels and pointed at a recess.

Terrasino bent forward.

Lying in the recess was what, at first, he thought was a piece of metal pipe. It was about six inches long and an inch in diameter and there were plugs screwed into the ends. Terrasino's brow puckered as he knelt down to examine it carefully with his flashlight.

'Is it a bomb?' Nieman asked.

Terrasino pursed his lips and nodded slowly. In the Air Force he had been on a course in bomb and incendiary devices and his trained eye picked out the wire soldered to the metal casing and clipped to the terminal of a flashlight battery which lay alongside the casing. Another piece of wire ran from the second terminal into the pipe through a spark gap, and out to an insulated mounting on a cheap watch which, so far as he could see, had its minute hand removed. When the hour hand reached this mounting and touched the wire it did not take an expert to see that the circuit would be completed and the spark would detonate the bomb.

Terrasino broke out into a cold sweat and was about to back off when he suddenly realised something.

The watch was not ticking.

He licked his lips which were incredibly dry.

'I . . . I think this is a dud,' he said slowly. 'The watch is not working.'

'Are you sure?' Nieman demanded apprehensively, peering over his shoulder.

Terrasino set down his flashlight and, carefully and with deliberation, yanked the wires from the torch battery. Nothing happened for a few long seconds. Then he gave a deep sigh.

'Our saboteur goofed on this one,' he said finally, looking at the construction. It registered with him that it was a beautifully wrought piece of work. The saboteur, whoever he was, was certainly no mere oddball amateur.

'Hey, there's a piece of paper under the device,' he said reaching forward and gingerly taking a corner of the paper between thumb and forefinger to draw it out. It was plain white typing paper and the message on it was printed in black ink. It was small, neat and very precise printing. It said:

'Anglo-American, this is for you. Stop making these murder machines. You have been warned. Max Prüss.'

Terrasino shook his head slowly.

He examined the device and then the cryptic message. There was something curious about the note. If the device had exploded the message would have been destroyed. Why write it?

The telephone gave several long peals before Janine Renard remembered that she had given Bernard and his wife the evening off. She laid her book aside with a frown of annoyance and picked up the receiver.

'Hello?'

'Madame Renard?'

'Yes.' She thought she ought to know the voice on the line.

'This is Jacques Barjonet.'

'Oh?'

She wondered what the Dirigeable-Commercial's chief test pilot wanted. He knew that Charles was still in Canada until the end of the week.

'Madame Renard, this may seem rather forward of me . . . in fact, very forward. I would like to invite you to come to the cinema with me.'

There was a pause before Barjonet plunged on.

'You see, I have just noticed that there is a cinema in Caen which is showing a programme of two versions of *The Hands of Orlac*: the 1924 silent version by Robert Weine and the 1935 version with Peter Lorre. Tomorrow night is the last showing. Will you come?'

Janine Renard's reaction was confusion. She had not been asked out by a man since Charles had courted her.

'I . . . I couldn't possibly . . .' she said but there was no conviction in her voice. She just didn't know what to say to such an invitation. She was surprised to realise that her refusal was not out of loyalty to Charles but simply because she did not want the routine of her life to be altered.

'Oh come,' Barjonet's voice was enthusiastic. 'You would love these films. You know you would. I'm going anyway, so why not come?'

He made it sound ungracious to refuse; made it sound so . . . was 'innocent' the word she wanted? Well, why not? She was abruptly defiant. She hadn't been to the cinema in years. Not since she married Charles. He never took her any more. On the other end of the line, Barjonet could almost sense her mind coming to its conclusion.

'I'll pick you up at six-thirty,' he prompted.

'Very well,' Janine reached her decision. 'I'll be ready.'

When she replaced the receiver she realised that she was tingling with excitement. She felt mischievous and improper, as if she were about to do a forbidden thing.

Tom Saxon entered the lobby of the Sheraton Hotel, where he had his suite, and was crossing to the elevator when a voice called softly.

'Tom!'

He swung round.

Helen Carson had been sitting on one of the couches in the lounge foyer. She rose and came across to him.

'Hello, Tom. I've been waiting nearly an hour for you to come in.'

Saxon frowned slightly and then shrugged.

'I was eating out.'

'Can we go somewhere to talk, Tom?'

He took her by the arm and guided her across to Dunfey's Lounge, the saloon bar which was part of the hotel complex. He found a secluded corner table and ordered some drinks.

'I just had to come to see you, Tom.'

Saxon made no reply. He fixed his gaze on the table top.

'It isn't easy for me,' Helen went on, a slight tone of desperation in her voice, but he made no attempt to help her.

'I . . . I just wanted to know how things were with you; *really* were.'

He raised his eyes to hers and let his lips droop in a grimace.

'I survive, Helen.'

'Haven't you been able to come to terms with things?'

Saxon's brow puckered.

'Terms?' There was an abrupt harshness in his voice. 'How am I supposed to feel? Jan and Tom Junior are dead because of me. If she had not run away, if she had not found out. . . .'

Helen's face hardened.

'If, if, if . . .' she said bitterly. 'How long are you going to play that record, Tom? The whole world revolves on "ifs".'

Saxon gave a harsh bark of laughter.

'What was it that Shakespeare wrote? "Your If is the only peacemaker; much virtue in If." Much virtue!'

He sighed deeply.

'I'm sorry, Helen. Sorry about everything.'

For a moment Helen recognised a genuine note of regret in his voice.

'That's what I'm saying, Tom. There's no need to be sorry . . . just accept things and learn to live with them.'

'Easier said than done, Helen.'

'Tom, I came here to tell you that . . . oh damn!'

She stood up, almost knocking the drinks over, and turned abruptly, leaving Saxon gazing after her with an astonished expression on his face.

Chapter Two

'Hi, Tom.'

Garry Carson grinned at Saxon as he entered the simulator. Saxon stared around him in amazement and let loose a low whistle of appreciation. The simulator was an exact replica of the *Albatross* flight deck.

'It even works like the real thing,' Oscar Van Kleef informed him with a ghost of a smile on his thin features. 'Computer tapes respond to controls and navigational information and you will feel exactly as if you were really flying the *Albatross*.'

'We have to log a minimum of forty-five hours on the simulator,' explained Carson. 'Maclaren is cautious, of course, and wants sixty hours.'

'Have you been familiarising yourself with the flight theory?' Van Kleef asked.

'Yes but there are a few questions I'd like to ask. I noticed that while you have a manual back-up system, practically everything is computerised.'

'That's right,' agreed Van Kleef. 'The *Albatross* is controlled in very simplistic terms compared with the cumbersome airships of fifty years ago. As you see, this is like the flight deck of any Transatlantic aircraft—like a 747, for example. Everything is compact and workable by a small crew.'

Saxon nodded. 'It does come as a bit of a surprise that a ship of this size can be controlled by a normal aircraft flight deck crew.'

'The controls of the *Albatross* are the result of nearly a decade of testing in wind tunnels and operational conditions with small models,' there was pride in Van Kleef's voice. 'Before the operation of a large airship could become an economic possibility, the production of a structure of sufficiently low weight with acceptable airworthiness qualities had to be achieved. It is essential for structure weight to be minimised, representing as it does by far the largest item of total empty weight. With the *Albatross* we set ourselves a design target of no more than 30 per cent of the gross lift.'

'What exactly is the *Albatross* made of?' Saxon asked.

Van Kleef smiled proudly.

'All earlier craft used a fabric outer covering which was supported by a complex skeleton of frames, longitudinals and bracing wires. The gas bags were separate and mounted internally and so difficulties with these and the coverings were not uncommon. We have solved those problems by using a fibre-reinforced glass and foam-supported single face panels. The *Albatross*, therefore, is of a reinforced plastic construction.'

'Doesn't that imply a prohibitively high constructional cost?' Saxon asked.

Van Kleef laid a finger against the side of his nose.

'That's an Anglo-American secret I can't reveal.'

'I also expected there to be a terrific amount of framework inside the ship.'

Again Van Kleef allowed himself a thin smile.

'I decided to base my design concept on the old ZMC2 airship.'

Saxon looked puzzled.

'It first flew in 1929 and was scrapped in 1942, having flown thirteen years without any mishap,' explained Van Kleef. 'The basis of the design was what we call monocque, a streamlined fuselage shaped like an elongated egg with the structure forming a continuous shell or envelope. It cuts out all the braced framework such as was used in the Zeppelin designs or, for example, the British R101. You know the sort of complicated structure of polygonal cross-sections with a longeron at each vertex to provide bending strength and stiffness? Well, while that type of structure was easy to maintain, I found it was severely limited by the need to provide separately for the transverse shear and. . . .'

He broke off as he caught sight of Saxon's blank face and tried to simplify the explanation.

'Well, this girder structure added immensely to the airship's weight and it complicated the interior of the structure of the ship. The structural basis in the *Albatross* lies in the outer covering, the fibre-reinforced glass panelling.'

'How about gas capacity?'

'The *Albatross* encloses a volume of 39,300,000 cubic feet

or, if you like, 1,110,000 cubic metres, which gives it a total available lift at sea level using helium of 970 tonnes.'

Van Kleef paused and then went on: 'You will see that instead of using the old gas bag idea, we use gas cells. The gas is the source of the relatively cheap static lift which is the main benefit of the airship against any other aircraft. The advantage has been that the gas cells can be any shape within reason which is not dependent on internal pressure. They become structurally more efficient with increasing size and can tolerate minor gas leaks. So our lifting gas cells are like a series of large rooms filled with helium. Each room is specially lined and so we have another improvement over the old airships by avoiding chafing between actual gas bags and rigid structure. According to our information, the French airship, the *Charles de Gaulle*, has opted for the old gas bag idea—a series of ballonets within the airship structure. It's my belief that they'll run into trouble with that design.'

Danny Macmillan and Billy Heath joined them. After a brief exchange of greetings, Saxon pressed on with his questioning.

'As I see it,' he said, glancing over the control panels, 'the problem is low-speed handling.'

Carson grinned.

'Dead right, Tom. In fact, many designers working in this field have tried to avoid the subject. One of the modern pioneers in the field, Morse, designed a passenger-carrying airship which had to work in conjunction with a small ferry aircraft.'

'Which,' interposed Van Kleef, 'is going to introduce more problems than it resolves.'

'So what happens with the *Albatross*?' demanded Saxon.

'Simple,' replied the chief designer. 'We have a vectoring propeller system and the airship itself will work like a gigantic helicopter. The pilot positions the craft over the mooring area and the ship then sinks to ground zero where it is secured in much the same way as helicopters are held to the decks of ships. The ground facilities are not too complex either.'

Carson nodded and added: 'All payload handling is done from ground zero . . . a drive on and off situation via ramps.'

'All that can be done with a vectoring propeller system?' Saxon was surprised.

'The right control forces can be obtained by varying the magnitude and direction of the propeller thrust,' explained Van Kleef, 'especially if—as we have on the *Albatross*—propellers are located at the extremities of the craft to give the maximum effect. You see, Saxon, vectoring the propeller thrust is no different from the technique employed for large hovercraft, and it does not give rise to any new mechanical problem. With the *Albatross*, the propellers are shaft-driven with the powerplants remotely located, and fail-safe requirements are used with a minimum number of thrust units dependent upon the layout adopted.'

'It sounds simple.'

'The best ideas are simple.' Oscar Van Kleef allowed himself a self-satisfied smile.

Saxon examined the flight-control system and glanced at Carson.

'What about control ability at cruising speed and height?'

Carson grinned.

'The *Albatross* suffers from a relative reduction of control power as size is increased, just like an aeroplane. The overall aerodynamic lift at a given speed is approximately proportional to the surface area and it decreases relative to volume. So the effect on control power is even more pronounced since moments of inertia are a function of length to the power of five, whilst the control moments vary as length to the power of three. Increases of speed can be used to compensate for these effects. The ratio of velocities required to maintain the same aerodynamic lift to displacement ratio is the displacement ratio to the power of one-sixth, whilst maintaining control moment ratio requires the square of that figure. But hell, don't worry, everything is worked out by computer. In other words, you press the button and the computer flies the airship.'

Saxon nodded slowly.

'I suppose the effect of low-speed control is somewhat similar?'

'Sure,' agreed Carson. 'Speed cannot be used to compensate for size increase, so relatively greater power must be installed. For the same time response characteristics, the thrust of the control rotors is required to increase in proportion to length to the power of four, that is the installed power-weight ratio has to increase in proportion to the cube root of the relative displacement.'

'Now,' interrupted Van Kleef, 'I think we ought to go over to the ship so that I can explain about the electronics. Have you met Kurt Nieman, our chief electrical engineer?'

Saxon shook his head.

'Well, he will be able to brief you how the computer systems work as well as the electronics side of things. We have, in fact, several power systems, including solar panelling on the topside of the ship which can supply emergency running power during any nine-hour period in twenty-four. We are hoping we can gradually improve that performance.'

With Van Kleef leading the way, Saxon accompanied Carson, Macmillan and Billy Heath across to the *Albatross*, which lay dark and inert like some sleeping monster, and inside to the electronics centre of the ship. Kurt Nieman was introduced and carefully described all the circuits and controls so far as they concerned him as a pilot. Nieman, Saxon found, was a very precise man who explained things slowly and carefully, pausing to ensure that he was being understood before going on to the next step. Saxon was silently amused by the man's pride in the electronics section, but then Nieman had every right to glory in the incredible systems which helped run the colossal vessel. Saxon himself was astonished at its size, its complexity and its awesomeness. In fact, Saxon realised with some amazement that he had been thinking of nothing during the last two hours but the *Albatross*. For him, that was a truly disconcerting discovery.

'We'll make the first simulator run this afternoon at fifteen hundred hours,' Carson told Saxon, as they prepared to leave the airship. 'Have you seen everything you want to see at this stage?'

'I think so,' Saxon replied.

As they reached the main ramp they met Maclaren ushering four wide-eyed men into the *Albatross*. They all wore Pan Continental flight crew uniforms.

'Ah, Garry,' Maclaren smiled, 'I want you to meet the first back-up crew . . . they'll be starting on the simulator training programme next week.'

Carson was already smiling at a lean, dark-haired man who wore the four stripes of a Pan Continental captain.

'Hello, Art. I knew it wouldn't be long before you joined this outfit.'

The man took Carson's outstretched hand and grinned.

'Good to see you, Garry.'

Art Stein had begun his career as a pilot with Northwest Airlines, much to the indignation of his parents. Loeb and Jessica Stein had set their hearts on their only son going into the family law business. 'Arthur, my boy, you want that you should cause your mother grief?' his father had asked him on the day he left university and announced his intention. 'What career is this flying? Just a bus driver in the sky. Is that a career?'

'I aim to be an airline pilot, pa,' Art had said.

'And don't call me that. Have you no respect?' snorted Loeb Stein.

'I am going to be an airline pilot,' repeated Art doggedly.

'It's a crazy thing you do, boy,' his father had assured him. His mother had gone so far as to demand that her rabbi say Kaddish for him. It took her five years to forgive him. Now, fifteen years later, Art Stein was a four-striper Pan Continental airline captain who had volunteered to join the company's subsidiary to train as an airship pilot. Art Stein loved adventure, especially adventure in flying, and the idea of piloting a giant dirigible appealed to him enormously.

The *Albatross*'s new back-up crew were introduced all round. For Saxon the names did not register, just a surprising feeling of excitement which he had not experienced in years; a feeling of coming together for a purpose, of joining an enthralling and important project.

Chapter Three

'I don't like it,' Terrasino said, glancing at Hayes, the FBI agent. 'Something doesn't quite fit.'

They were seated in Hayes's office, with Vambrace an interested spectator.

'I'm not sure what you mean,' Hayes said, as he turned the pipe-like explosive device over in his hands.

'I think that the saboteur wanted us to find that bomb.'

'What makes you say that?'

'I believe that this device was just a warning. When he does strike in earnest, he is not the sort to forget a simple thing like winding up his trigger mechanism.'

Vambrace moved his head in agreement.

'I can see Terrasino's point, especially about the note.'

'There's another explanation,' pointed out Hayes. 'Working on the assumption that we are dealing with a psychopath, the man might be so far out of touch with reality, so far along his paranoic path, that the fact that no one would read his note after the explosion never occurred to him. Maybe he simply wrote it to satisfy some compulsion within himself.'

'No; you could be right but I don't think so,' Terrasino replied. 'I say he planned this bomb to fail because he only intended to make a point.'

'The point being that Anglo-American are totally vulnerable to his attacks?' asked Vambrace.

Terrasino nodded.

Hayes sighed.

'Is this guy Nieman outside?'

'Yeah. I brought him down with me just in case you wanted to question him,' said Terrasino. In fact, Nieman was rather upset at being asked to accompany the chief of security to the FBI office. He confessed to Terrasino that he tried to avoid any dealings with the police or related agencies, but the security chief had convinced him that his help might lead to them tracing whoever had planted the explosive device. Nieman entered Hayes's office looking nervous.

Hayes rose, introduced himself and tried to put the man at his ease.

'We just want to ask some questions about how you found this mechanism,' he gestured to his desk on which the device lay. 'We've heard the story from Mr. Terrasino but you might be able to fill us in a little more.'

'What can I tell you?' Nieman asked. 'I found it merely by accident and telephoned Mr. Terrasino immediately.'

'How did you find it?' prompted Vambrace.

'Well, I had been working on the section in the afternoon with Keller. . . .'

'That's Jules Keller, Doctor Van Kleef's assistant,' interposed Terrasino.

'. . . yes, Jules Keller.' Nieman frowned at the interruption. 'We packed up early. I was going to Garry Carson's party. Well, as I was getting ready I suddenly remembered something which had been worrying me—some circuits that didn't seem to be connected correctly. On my way to Carson's place I thought I would look in and check, see whether my memory was playing up. I went to my office, took out the plans and examined the circuits. I was sure that something was wrong and decided to make a thorough comparative check while the problem was in my mind. I took the plans with me to the section. I checked them out. As I thought . . . there were a few minor mis-connections. Nothing serious. The valve system would not have functioned correctly on gas cells seventeen and eighteen, that's all. It was while I was making these checks that I found the device and then rang Terrasino.'

'Is that a section of the airship which is in constant use?' asked Hayes.

Nieman shook his head.

'There is no reason for anyone to go there apart from the electrical engineering personnel.'

'You and this Jules Keller were working there during the day?' Vambrace asked.

'No, Keller didn't start work until late. He had only just returned from a trip to Montreal about midday.'

'No one else?'

'No. Mind you, Keller continued working after I left, so I

wouldn't know who else was there between the time I left and the time I went back.'

'Can you be specific about the times?' Terrasino queried.

'Certainly. I packed up a little after five o'clock and returned there just about eight o'clock.'

'I see,' smiled Hayes. 'Well, I guess that's all, Mr. Nieman.'

Kurt Nieman nodded, stood up and went to the door. Then he hesitated and half-turned.

'Of course, when I left Doctor Van Kleef had just arrived to inspect the section.'

Terrasino glanced up.

'Van Kleef?'

'Yes, that's right. He wanted to check the amount of leakage in the fuel valves. I can't think why. The checks had been thoroughly carried out the day before.'

'So Doctor Van Kleef was there when you left?'

'With Keller,' returned Nieman and then smiled softly. 'You don't suspect either Keller or Van Kleef, do you?'

It was nearly three o'clock in the morning when Jacques Barjonet halted his Mercedes sports car before the Renards' house in Balleroy. Janine sat back feeling blissfully happy. She had, in spite of her initial feelings, enjoyed the trip to Caen with Barjonet; had enjoyed the movies and only made a minor protest when he suggested they move on to a restaurant afterwards. The meal had been marvellous, helped with two bottles of a dry light white wine. Barjonet was excellent company, keeping up a flow of jokes, light banter and anecdotes, gently pushing her into the conversation until she suddenly realised that she was doing most of the talking. She had never talked as much in her life as she had done during the evening.

In the car, on the way back home, she began talking about Charles. She did not know exactly how it had happened. She found herself confessing to Jacques Barjonet her frustrations and annoyance at the lack of compatibility between Charles and herself. Barjonet was sympathetic and Janine, for the first time for a year or more, didn't feel lonely.

When Barjonet drew up outside her house, he climbed out and, to her surprise, politely bade her 'Goodnight'.

It had crossed her mind a few times during that evening that Barjonet was making a play for her. She resolved that when he did so she would act the enraged faithful wife. Now, strangely, she discovered that she was disappointed as she watched him climb back into his car. She stood hesitantly.

'I enjoyed this evening very much,' she said.

Jacques Barjonet smiled up at her.

'So did I. Perhaps we can do it again soon?'

She found herself eager, excited.

'I'd like that,' she said, trying to sound noncommittal and failing.

'Fine,' he put the car into gear. 'I'll give you a ring soon . . . goodnight.'

She stood watching the red tail lights disappearing down the drive and turned for the house with an odd feeling of anti-climax, of dissatisfaction.

Jules Keller and Samantha Hackerman came out of DiMillos on Commercial Street and walked to Keller's white convertible.

'It's been a great evening, Jules,' smiled Samantha happily, as she slid into the passenger seat.

Keller grinned.

'Why end it now?'

Samantha glanced towards the early dawn sky. Catching her gaze, Keller laughed.

'See what I mean? Why end things just as the most interesting part of the day is beginning?'

'What do your have in mind?' she demanded warily.

'Oh, a drive down to Cape Elizabeth to pay our respects to the Portland Head Light and watch the dawn come up properly and in style. Then we can breakfast in an all-night diner I know on the shore road. Neither of us has to be at work tomorrow . . . rather, today.'

'Okay,' Samantha sighed as she relaxed against the car upholstery.

They soon left downtown Portland and drove south over the bridge and into the still sleeping streets of South Portland, then out into the country along the coast road.

'Sam,' Keller said after being silent for a while as he negotiated his way out of the city, 'how about us—the two of us—packing up here after the *Albatross* does its thing and going to Europe for a year or two?'

Samantha stared at him in surprise.

'What do you mean, Jules?'

'How about a tour of Europe—one end to the other?'

'I couldn't afford to do that.'

'Who's asking *you* to afford it, Sam? I'll do all the affording.'

The girl was startled.

'It would cost a fortune,' she whispered.

'So?' grinned Keller.

'You can't afford it. You've alimony payments among other things.'

'I said I can afford it.'

Samantha laughed.

'On what Anglo-American pays? Come off it, Jules.'

Keller looked hurt.

'The hell with Anglo-American. I have a little going on the side. Enough for us to spend a year lazing in the Mediterranean sunshine.'

The girl frowned at him.

'We can't afford to be away from our jobs for a year. It's a nice idea. I'd love it. But you have to be practical.'

'I'm being realistic, Sam,' he said soberly. 'I tell you, I'm doing a little job for which I am being paid well. When it's over I also have a job offered me in France.'

'France?'

'Well, it's not the end of the world,' he protested at her surprise. 'I'm French Canadian, you know.'

Samantha shook her head.

'What is this job on the side, Jules? You know that if you're under contract to Anglo-American you're not supposed to be working for anyone else.'

Keller laughed.

'So who's going to tell Maclaren? You? Come on, Sam. Relax. Let's start living instead of being hung up on this damned work ethic bit. Why should everyone else have the fun while we poor suckers do all the work, eh?'

Samantha gave Keller a worried glance. She wondered what job he was doing which would enable him to take her on a twelve-month vacation to Europe and not feel concern for the future.

'You've got to be kidding,' Hayes said, looking at Terrasino in amazement. 'You really want us to check out Oscar Van Kleef?'

Terrasino had presented himself in Hayes's office first thing that morning with the proposition. The FBI man was still trying to wake himself up with a pot of hot coffee.

'I'm not saying that he's our man,' Terrasino insisted, 'but of all the names we've come up with, he is a strong possibility. He has the opportunity and the knowledge.'

'What about motivation?' demanded Hayes sourly. 'Jesus, why the hell would the man who designed the *Albatross* want to destroy his own creation?'

Terrasino grimaced.

'You have just asked a question to which hundreds of people have tried to supply answers. There've been countless books on that particular subject.'

'So enlighten me,' suggested Hayes, sprawling in his chair.

'Okay,' replied Terrasino, sitting down. 'The guy we are after is, I believe, a schizophrenic paranoiac. Trying to destroy the thing he created would be a fairly logical response in certain cases of this type. No one on the project is ruled out as a suspect . . . certainly not Oscar Van Kleef. We must start somewhere and I say let's start with him.'

Hayes bit his lip thoughtfully.

'Okay, Terrasino. We'll check out Van Kleef. Then Keller. They seem to be the two possibilities at this stage.'

'If it was a choice between Van Kleef and Keller,' mused the security chief, 'I'd come down on Van Kleef. He is more the type which fits in with my image of our man. And he's got domestic problems, too. I understand that his wife has finally left him. It's been on the cards for some time. Ran off with an air steward who works for one of the local lines.'

'That hardly puts the finger on him,' Hayes pointed out.

'No, but it's another piece in the jigsaw. Domestic pressure could be one of the triggering factors in our friend Max Prüss's condition. Incidentally, have you been able to get a trace on the name at all?'

Hayes shook his head and poured himself another cup of black coffee.

'What about this guy Nieman? How about a check on him?'

Terrasino laughed.

'Now it's you who has to be kidding.'

'And why should the proposition that Nieman is the saboteur be so ridiculous?' asked Hayes. 'Surely he is just as good a suspect as Van Kleef?'

'Yeah, excepting Kurt Nieman drew our attention to the bomb—our psycho would not be that crazy.'

Hayes suddenly exhaled deeply and put down his coffee.

'I'm wondering just how crazy our bomber is.'

'What do you mean?'

'Our psychiatrist agrees with your diagnosis,' admitted the FBI man, 'but only on the evidence presented, and maybe we are being too selective in that evidence. What if the situation is more complicated?'

'I'm not sure that I follow,' frowned Terrasino.

'What if the bomber merely wants us to believe he is a psycho when all the time he is a cold, calculating saboteur acting for someone or some faction who would like to see the *Albatross* project fail?'

Terrasino shrugged but took the suggestion seriously.

'Could be . . . you're talking about a financial or political motivation? Sure, but would such a person go to the lengths that this man is going to? He is, he must be, very well placed among the technicians working on the project. That fact alone could cause tremendous difficulties in tracing him without his resorting to any other subterfuge and the laying of false trails. That's why I wonder about Van Kleef. He has been around airships a lot of his life and could very easily have suffered some accident which now produces paranoia. . . .'

Hayes was still sceptical.

'I don't think the evidence we have is enough to take action over Van Kleef.'

Terrasino looked at the FBI man pointedly.

'Van Kleef, Keller and Nieman, if it makes you happy,' he said. 'Check them all out. What can it do except eliminate three suspects?'

Chapter Four

Charles Renard and Tanya Le Solliec took a taxi from Orly airport and sat silently as it sped through the southern suburbs of Paris to Tanya's apartment on the Rue Falguière. Renard paid off the driver as Tanya went to open the door. After ten days, the apartment was a little stuffy and Tanya went through it opening all the windows.

'Let's go out for a meal,' Renard said, dumping the suitcases in the hallway.

'Aren't you tired, *ma mie*?' Tanya asked. 'You didn't sleep on the aeroplane.'

'Food first,' shrugged Renard, 'then we'll come back and sleep.'

Tanya glanced worriedly at Renard. He had become morose and almost monosyllabic during the last few days. She knew that something was worrying him. She decided to make a frontal attack.

'What's wrong, Charles? You can tell me.'

Renard looked momentarily annoyed.

'Business, just business,' he grunted.

'The airship? The *Charles de Gaulle*?'

'What else?' he laughed bitterly. 'Now come on, let's go out and eat.'

She did not bring the subject up again until they were in bed a few hours later.

'Why are you worried about the airship, *ma mie*?'

Renard was lying on his back, hands cupped behind his head, staring at the ceiling. Tanya turned on her side to look at him.

'No need for you to worry.'

'If you are worried,' declared the girl, 'then so am I.'

Renard grimaced with brusque affection.

'I am worried that the Americans are going to beat me to it.'

'Is that such a catastrophe?'

'I've done a lot of things in my life, Tanya; I've hustled here and there, done a little of this and that. I've made money, that's true, but I have never really made it big. This is my chance, a real chancc to pull it off, become really secure. That's what the *Charles de Gaulle* means to me.'

Tanya grinned cynically.

'Secure, *ma mie*? You have more money than anyone I know.'

Renard shook his head.

'Tanya, my finances are like a card house . . . one breath of wind, one puff . . . and. . . .'

He snapped his fingers.

'Everything depends on the success of launching the *Charles de Gaulle* before the Americans. It's no use coming a poor second.'

'Why do you think the Americans will beat you?'

'Because I'm being faced with union problems, design problems and supply problems. Anglo-American are more advanced than we are. They'll soon be starting their tests.'

There was a silence.

Tanya felt a little helpless. Such things did not mean anything to her. She was not even interested in the project except in so far as it affected Charles. She tried to say the right things, make the right sympathetic noises but, underneath, she wished Charles did not have this hang-up about materialism. She could rationalise and understand it well enough. He had come from a very poor background and it was probably the memories of poverty that gave him the urge to strive and measure his progress by material landmarks. Yet she hoped that one day he would come to the realisation that there were other things in life; other measurements of progress.

'How long will you stay in Paris, *ma mie*?' she asked.

'Until the day after tomorrow. Time enough to recover from jet-lag and go to see one or two people at the Ministry of Transport.'

'Then you will go to St. Lô?'

'Yes; I must bring our flight tests forward ahead of the Americans.'

Tanya sighed.

'You'll succeed, Charles. I know you will.'

He nodded absently.

'Perhaps, but. . . .'

Tanya silenced him by bending over and kissing him.

'No buts, *ma mie*. Not now.'

Danny Macmillan had just taken his seat at his favourite Italian restaurant on Congress Street—the Roma. Terrasino and his wife, Maria, had taken him there one evening and Macmillan had fallen in love with Italian food. The head waiter, Bruno, had greeted him in friendly fashion, given him a menu and taken his order for a Cinzano aperitif. When Macmillan had first gone to the restaurant, Bruno had mistaken him for an Italian. At twenty-seven, Macmillan was dark-haired, lean and angular, with hollow cheeks which gave him a superficial impression of mournfulness until one glanced into his twinkling dark eyes. Macmillan turned to contemplate the main task of the evening, examining each dish on the menu.

'Hello.'

Macmillan glanced up. It was a willowy blonde, the English girl who was working with Samantha Hackerman. What was her name? Ashton. She stood by his table smiling down at him. Confused, Macmillan rose to his feet.

'Hi. It's Miss Ashton, isn't it?'

'Claire Ashton. We met at the Carsons' party. You're Danny . . . ?'

'Danny Macmillan,' supplied Macmillan.

Claire gestured towards the empty chair at his table.

'Are you expecting anyone? Can I join you? I came in for a meal on my own but it's much more fun to eat with someone.'

Macmillan hesitated a moment and then moved round the table to pull out the chair for her.

'I haven't been in America long and it still gets lonely at mealtimes,' she told him.

Macmillan gave a half-smile. Not if the rumours he had heard about Claire Ashton were correct, he thought. Apparently the English girl had already propositioned some of the men on the project site. Rumour had it that she liked older men. Well, at his age he probably didn't qualify. Looking at her attractive face he wondered whether the rumours were true or just scurrilous gossip. The girl didn't have the hard expression of a whore. He suddenly felt guilty. Why should a whore look any different from anyone else? He was abruptly aware that she was asking him a question.

'Sorry?'

'You were miles away,' she said. 'I was asking you what you recommended.'

He reddened and glanced at the menu, then realised that Claire had not got a drink. He waved to the waiter, asking her what she wanted. She chose a Campari and soda.

'How about a prime sirloin *alla Pizzaiola*?' he suggested. 'It's a steak sautéed with fresh green peppers and tomatoes.'

'Sounds good.'

Macmillan ordered for both of them.

'How do you like working for Anglo-American now?' he prompted, after a short silence.

Claire Ashton shrugged expressively.

'It's alright. I've never been a press officer before. What do *you* do? I think you told me at the party but I've forgotten.'

'I'm a flight engineer. When the *Albatross* takes off, I'm her chief engineer.'

'Oh.'

She did not sound especially interested or impressed. However, Macmillan turned the conversation to her impressions of America and Portland in particular. Whatever else he had heard about her, Macmillan decided that Claire Ashton was a very intelligent and attractive girl. He wondered again whether the rumours he had heard could be wrong. No; he knew one of the men whom Claire Ashton had apparently propositioned. He was a forty-year-old, happily married man whose strict Methodist upbringing had made him indignant about her behaviour. He wouldn't have made up the story.

Macmillan suddenly realised that he was gazing speculatively at the girl. He became aware of some indefinable expression in her eyes . . . a sort of hurt, a grief. He felt sorry for her, but whatever kind of problem she had was not his concern. She was good company for the evening, that was all. He insisted on paying for the meal and she did not really object. As they left the restaurant Macmillan motioned towards his car.

'Can I give you a lift?' he offered.

'I've just moved into an apartment on Bay View Drive,' Claire smiled.

'Good. That's on my way,' replied Macmillan. 'I live further round in Back Cove.'

They drove to Bay View Drive mostly in silence. Macmillan felt it strange that the girl suddenly withdrew in on herself and only answered his questions in monosyllables.

As Macmillan slid into a parking space before her apartment block, Claire asked abruptly: 'Like to come up for a coffee?'

Macmillan's eyes flickered to the dashboard clock. It was still early and he had no plans beyond watching the ball game on television.

'That'd be nice,' he agreed.

Claire Ashton betrayed no reaction as she climbed out of the car, led the way into the building and took the elevator to her floor. She had a small two-room apartment on the fourth floor. There was a small kitchenette off the main living-room and a bathroom. She started the coffee machine without a word and went into the bedroom.

Macmillan lowered himself into a chair and picked up a magazine, assuming that the girl had gone to freshen up. His mind was not on the pages before him. He was still wondering about Claire Ashton. He had to admit that he was attracted and impressed by her intelligence and reserved warmth. But he kept remembering the strange, haunted look on her face—a hurt animal look. He shook his head and sighed.

'Well?'

The sharpness in her voice made him glance up, startled.

She stood in the bedroom door with just a loose silk dressing-gown on. It hung open, and Macmillan could see that she was not wearing anything underneath.

His mouth dropped open as he stared in astonishment.

'Well, do you want to screw me or not?'

Macmillan slowly rose to his feet. There was a cynical, almost sneering expression on the girl's face as she watched his reactions. He felt a tremendous anger surge through him. The girl misinterpreted the look and gave a hard laugh.

'Shocked?'

Macmillan shook his head slowly.

'Why?' he demanded.

'Why? Should there be a reason or do you want a lesson in biology?'

'You're attractive and intelligent. . . .' Macmillan fought for the right words. 'Why go round acting like a goddam whore?'

'Do men expect women to act like anything else?'

'What happened to you to twist you up like this?' Macmillan asked quietly.

She detected the sympathetic note in his voice and bridled defensively.

'Finish the small-talk. What are you waiting for?'

Macmillan stood staring at her for a moment and then shrugged. He turned and walked out of the apartment, slamming the door behind him. He could hear Claire Ashton's voice raised: 'What are you, a queer or something?'

His face burning, he went down to his automobile and sat for a few minutes trying to gather his scattered thoughts. It was not that he didn't feel like taking up Claire Ashton's offer. What man wouldn't? But he discovered, to his surprise, that he felt a compassion, a sympathy towards the girl. It was that fleeting look of a hurt animal in her eyes—so fleeting—that made him realise that she was a prisoner of her own emotions. Damn it! He should have stayed and tried to talk with her, tried to. . . . Who was he kidding? It would take more than an amateur psychologist to get under Claire Ashton's skin.

Almost savagely, he set his car in gear and, with a scream of tyres, sent it into the night streets.

Charles Renard sat behind his desk gazing moodily in front of him. He had just spent two hours with the representatives of the Syndicat National des Pilotes de Ligne discussing the training of pilots for his prospective airship line, and was unhappy with the results. The SNPL people were demanding more simulator training and a higher degree of practical experience before allowing their members to take responsibility for flying the type of aircraft which the *Charles de Gaulle* represented. Renard could do no more than promise to consider their proposals at the end of two hours' fruitless discussion. With the costs of extra training too prohibitive, he was going to have to find a way round the union objections.

Earlier that morning his plant manager had informed him of another union problem. Dirigeable-Commercial SA employed its own small transport fleet of trucks. Two of his drivers, both members of the Confédération Française des Travailleurs, had been discovered breaking transport laws by working over the maximum daily times and falsifying documents. They had done this by taking out the EEC running disc which allowed the authorities to check times of loading and unloading, starting times, period of driving, rest periods and speeds. The transport manager had discovered that the two drivers had been using the same disc for a period longer than the prescribed twenty-four hours, which was illegal. He had sacked the men on the spot.

Within the hour representatives of the CFDT had been howling victimisation and demanding reinstatement immediately.

The transport manager had referred the matter to the plant manager and now both managers and union officials were demanding to see Renard. Renard's immediate reaction was to back his managers, but he was in a vulnerable position. He just couldn't afford a strike: even a day would put his schedule so far behind that he wouldn't have any hope of catching up with Anglo-American. He bit his tongue, simmering in rage as the flushed-faced Breton union official made his demands.

'Very well, Kerouac,' he sighed at length. 'Your men will be reinstated. In return I shall want full union co-operation and support about the application of rules and regulations. The CFDT supports EEC regulations on long-distance hauls and I would have thought that any contravention of the rules would be condemned and our company's stance supported.'

Kerouac shrugged.

'It is not a clear-cut case in this instance, M'sieur Renard.'

'And what would be a clear-cut case, if this was not?' grunted Renard.

The union man smiled disarmingly.

'I trust you are asking a hypothetical question, m'sieur?'

'Alright, Kerouac,' Renard said, ringing for his secretary to show the union officials from the room, 'but remember, the next time there is a breach of regulations, I shall not be in a compromising mood.'

Marie-France hesitated on the threshold after the delegation had left.

'Doctor Villemur wishes to see you, sir.'

Renard, with great effort, controlled himself.

'Send him in.'

Villemur entered looking nervous and worried.

'More problems?' demanded Renard, glancing at his face.

'I'm afraid so,' the designer said, 'a big problem this time.'

'Well?' prompted Renard when the man paused.

'The helium consignment which you cleared when you were in America . . . there are more delays in delivery. We will not be able to inflate the *Charles de Gaulle* in time for the scheduled tests.'

Renard's face went white.

'But the tests are already behind the Americans' schedule!' His voice was dangerously high-pitched.

'I know it,' replied Villemur nervously. 'The supplying

company in America have a new union dispute on their hands. They don't know how long it will be before they can supply us.'

'What about alternative sources?' demanded Renard.

'We have started to make the necessary checks but . . . well, you know how difficult helium is to get, especially the amount we require for our purpose.'

'So what do you suggest, doctor? Do we all sit round and give up?'

'We are doing what we can.'

Renard swore, startling Villemur to red-faced silence.

'Marie-France,' he said, pressing his intercom, 'get me M'sieur Brisset on the telephone.'

He glanced back to Villemur.

'I'll send for you when I have worked something out.'

Renard's talk with Brisset was short and unfruitful. There was no way even the French government could use their influence to obtain a large consignment of helium for commercial use. Renard put down the telephone and added colourfully to his vocabulary of invective. The Americans were going to beat him after all. Then he paused and frowned. Maybe not. Maybe there was a way. . . .

Chapter Five

Tom Saxon was drunk when he left Justin's Lounge in the Executive Inn on Congress Street. What's more, he was belligerently drunk. He paused outside the hotel to take his bearings. Congress Street was a long main thoroughfare stretching nearly the entire length of downtown Portland. He looked around for a cab but could not see one. He had difficulty seeing anything amidst the enraged onslaught of bright neon which attacked his aching eyes. He blinked and swore aloud. How the hell was he to get back to—where was it?—South Portland? He stood swaying uncertainly. Several people passed him by, carefully avoiding him. The hell with them!

He began to walk along; at least he thought he was walking. Onlookers saw him swaying and staggering. One woman passing by with her timid spouse in tow loudly declaimed about 'drunken bums' spoiling the city centre. Saxon turned with a leer and told her to perform several gymnastic gyrations which made her go bright red and hurry on, dragging her pale-faced husband with her.

'If I had not been warned about my heart, Claudine. . . .' Saxon heard him wailing as they disappeared.

Suddenly, a man was at his side, a hand firmly holding onto his arm.

'Want some help, mac?'

Saxon tried to bring the man into focus and failed.

'Wanna cab,' he muttered.

'Sure, mac, sure. Got some money for it?'

'Course!'

'You're drunk, mac. Helpless as a baby. Sure you got some money?'

Saxon was vaguely aware that the man was laughing at him; vaguely aware that the man's hand was inside his coat, feeling for his wallet. It suddenly dawned on his alcoholic befuddled mind that he was being 'rolled'. He struck out at the man, who yelped but succeeded in dragging Saxon's wallet from his pocket.

'You bastard!' cried Saxon, and tried to grab at the thief, but the shadowy figure ran off.

'Bastard!' screamed Saxon.

'Now then, mister,' another hand caught his arm.

Saxon swung round to meet the new attack, and lashed out wildly. Two dark shapes grabbed him. One of them twisted his arm behind his back with a painful jerk. He bent double against a car. He dimly saw a flashing red light, felt something metal being put on his wrists.

'Okay, mister, get in the car,' a heavy voice was saying. Then, in an aside: 'Jesus, this guy smells like a distillery.'

Carson answered the telephone.

'Colonel Carson?'

'Who's this?'

'My name is Sergeant Twoomy of the Portland Police Department, sir. We are holding a man who says his name is Saxon. Sounds English. Says you know him.'

Carson's jaw dropped.

'You are holding him? For what?'

'Do you know him, sir?'

'Yeah, I know him. Wing Commander Saxon is a fellow test pilot with Anglo-American Airships here in Portland.'

'Wing Commander? What's that?' The policeman sounded puzzled.

'A British Air Force rank, sergeant. A colonel.'

'Jesus!' came the voice on the other end of the line. 'Don't that beat all? Well, sir, this Colonel Saxon is soused—but really soused. We picked him up in Congress Street and he tried to assault the arresting officers.'

'Oh Christ!' moaned Carson.

The sergeant was obviously pleased with the response.

'When we searched him this guy, er, Colonel Saxon, had no ID on him, no billfold or anything. Says he was robbed . . . at least that's as far as I can understand. Can't tell too much on account of him being soused and his limey accent. The lieutenant here says if he is who he says he is, then maybe you'll come down and go bail for him . . . if not, we'll keep him in the caboose until we can get some real sense out of him.'

Carson groaned.

'It's okay, sergeant. I'll be down there in half an hour. Tell me, does this have to get into the local papers? Colonel Saxon holds a prominent position with Anglo-American and . . . well. . . .'

The sergeant was understanding.

'The guy from the *Press-Herald* usually checks with us in, say, about another two hours. If you can get this limey, er, Colonel Saxon, out of here by then we could neglect to mention his arrest. But there'll be charges before the judge in the morning, I'm afraid.'

'I'd be grateful for the extra time, sergeant.'

'Okay, colonel. Do you know where the PPD is? Congress Street, southside, just past the Eastern Cemetery.'

'I'll be down there in half an hour.'

Saxon faced an angry Garry Carson in his hotel room. Carson had gone bail for him and driven him back to the Sheraton, pumped coffee into him and finally drawn out his side of the story.

'Alright,' Saxon grunted belligerently. 'So I got smashed, was rolled and had a brush with the law, so what?'

'Dammit!' swore Carson. 'You're in a sensitive area, Tom. If the papers get hold of the story . . . *when* they do, how long do you think you will be employed by Anglo-American? How will Anglo-American's image appear?'

'Oh . . . *their* image is what you're worried about,' Saxon smiled cynically.

'I sure as hell ain't worried about yours, brother,' snapped Carson. 'A drunken test pilot, assault on the cops . . . that really is going to give the public confidence in the *Albatross* project.'

'Go lecture elsewhere, Garry,' replied Saxon, yawning deliberately. 'I'm going to bed.'

Carson bit his lip. He could see that Saxon had not entirely sobered up.

'Alright, Tom. I'll be by here about ten o'clock tomorrow. You're due to appear in court at midday on the drunken assault charge. I'll ring Samantha Hackerman first thing . . . maybe she'll know a way to keep this out of the papers.'

'And the best of British,' sneered Saxon, as he slammed the bedroom door shut.

Maria Terrasino woke up to find her husband getting dressed. It was still dark outside.

'What's up, *caro*?' she asked, sitting up in bed and turning on the side lamp.

Terrasino looked apologetic.

'Sorry to disturb you, love. Something has just occurred to me. I have to go down to the project site.'

Maria Terrasino looked at his worried face.

'It is about . . . how do you call him . . . the psycho, the mad bomber?'

Terrasino nodded.

'There's something that doesn't make sense. I feel that there is some clue which is just staring me in the face and I can't see it.'

Maria Terrasino sighed.

'You be careful, no?'

Terrasino leant over the bed and kissed her on the forehead.

'I'll be careful, yes,' he said lightly.

Parish was on duty as chief night security guard. He greeted Terrasino respectfully as the security chief entered his hut by the great canvas shroud which cloaked the *Albatross* from public gaze.

'I'm just going to have a look round,' Terrasino explained, as he signed his name in the security book. He had tightened up security so that each time a person went on board the *Albatross* they had to sign in and out, giving times.

He made his way straight to the area on deck level six where the explosive device had been discovered by Kurt Nieman. It was as good a place to start as any. He went to switch on the cabin lights. Nothing. That was funny. He flicked the switch up and down several times and then felt his way to the emergency cupboard. In each section were similar cupboards containing tools, flashlights and other useful equipment.

There was a sudden footfall behind him.

Terrasino went to turn and his world went black: utterly black. His last conscious sensation was that of something striking the back of his head.

When he came round, which seemed like a second or two later, the thin and concerned face of Oscar Van Kleef was peering down at him.

Terrasino felt a blinding pain in his head and he groaned.

'What happened?' demanded Van Kleef. 'Did you trip and fall?'

Terrasino screwed up his face and shook his head.

'When did you get here?' he demanded, ignoring the other's question.

'A second or so ago. You were lying flat out. What happened?'

'Someone hit me from behind, dammit!'

Van Kleef looked shocked.

'You mean the saboteur . . . ?'

It was then that Terrasino noticed that the cabin lights were on.

'Were the lights working when you came here?'

'Yes. Why?'

'No matter.'

He groaned again. His head was painful and there was a sticky trickle down the side of his face. He put his hand up. It was blood.

'I don't suppose you saw anyone else about?'

Van Kleef made a negative gesture.

'Alright,' Terrasino gave him a suspicious glance. 'Let's have a look round.'

They spent half an hour examining the adjoining cabins.

'It looks like you disturbed whoever it was,' ventured Van Kleef. 'I'll have the engineers make a thorough check first thing in the morning.'

'You do that,' replied Terrasino, feeling angry with himself. 'Whoever it was is long gone.'

'Think so?' replied the security chief laconically. 'We'll see.'

He left Van Kleef staring strangely after him. Jesus! Maria was not going to like this. He'd better not say anything to her. He signed out without saying anything to Parish and went across to the administrative buildings and up to his office. First he went to the washroom and began to clean himself up. He hoped that Maria would not notice the bloodstain on his jacket. He'd better take it to the local laundry before she saw it. He was going to leave without going into his office but he heard his telephone start to ring. Maria, he thought. He entered his office and lifted the receiver.

'Yeah? Terrasino here.'

'It's Hayes,' replied the FBI agent's voice. 'Your wife said you'd be at the project site.'

'What's up?'

'I thought I'd let you know that we've got a trace on the mysterious Max Prüss.'

'Yeah?' Terrasino's voice rose a fraction in excitement.

'I guess you were right when you said our saboteur was a psycho.'

'What makes you say that, Hayes?'

'The real Max Prüss has been dead fifty years.'

'And you know who he was?'

'Max Prüss was the captain of the airship *Hindenburg*.'

Tom Saxon was dreaming; no, not dreaming—remembering. Remembering in a sweat-soaked, alcoholic-induced sleep; recalling with vivid nightmare clarity. He twisted and turned in helpless unease.

The Wessex Mark IV helicopter was spinning to the ground. It seemed to be spinning slowly as if all time and motion had slowed, slowed to a near standstill. Saxon watched impotently, unable to co-ordinate his muscles, unable to react quickly. The terrorist rocket had struck the helicopter just below the rotor, snapping one of the blades and twisting the entire section at an awkward angle; the controls were slack and useless. Saxon experienced a feeling of detached fatalism. Yet the soldiers in the machine—six of them—were screaming, unwilling to face death even in the face of its inevitability.

Saxon was a young flight lieutenant, only a week out from England on his first posting to Northern Ireland. He was flying a squad of soldiers into Cullyhanna in the 'bandit country' of South Armagh, in which the Irish Republican Army operated almost with impunity. Crossmaglen, the little village which republican resistance to British rule had made world-famous, was the next village to Cullyhanna. British troops could only move along the hedge-bordered lanes of South Armagh in strength and in armoured personnel carriers, and even then not be entirely assured of their safety. Too many mines and booby traps had exacted a heavy toll of British lives. Army and RAF helicopters were now used to ferry the men to strongly fortified military posts within the area.

The rocket attack had been totally unexpected. Tom Saxon's orders had been not to fly too close to the ground in case of such an attack, but he had only been a half-mile from the Cullyhanna military post and preparing to land when it had happened. The Wessex had bucked under the impact and slewed slowly groundwards.

The impact snapped Saxon's safety belt and threw him from the cockpit into a thick thorn hedge, thereby saving his life, though he felt a searing pain in his left leg and back. His face was cut and sticky and when he put his hand up to clear his eyes he realised, with a detached curiosity, that the stickiness was blood.

The Wessex had buried itself in the ground and there was an odour of petrol, the hiss of fuel dripping onto a scalding hot pipe. Someone, far away, was screaming with high-pitched monotony.

In spite of his pain, Saxon heaved himself upward and crawled the ten yards towards the jumbled mass of wreckage. The mangled piece of machinery bore absolutely no resemblance at all to the flying machine it had been a few moments before.

In the remains of the cockpit, a glance told Saxon that his co-pilot was dead. Crawling round to the main cabin, he felt momentarily nauseated at the sight which met his eyes. It was the squad's lance-corporal, who was screaming horribly. In his right shoulder a jagged piece of metal stuck like a grotesque spear. The man was pawing at it feebly and screaming in that awful monotone. The RAF sergeant lay a few yards away. He was still and his neck was twisted at an awkward angle. Saxon surmised he was dead, although he couldn't really be sure. Another soldier lay on his side moaning softly. The others sprawled in various prone positions like a collection of rag dolls.

Saxon caught the strong smell of escaping petrol once again.

He grabbed the lance-corporal first, trying to ignore the throbbing pain in his own leg and back, and crawled, pulling the man until he was some twenty yards from the wreck. Then he repeated the same painful journey with the moaning soldier. Finally, he managed to drag the other bodies some way from the remains of the helicopter before unconsciousness overtook him.

When he came to, someone was bending over him. He realised he could have only been unconscious a moment.

The figure above him was that of a bearded young man; fresh-faced, freckled and red-haired. He was looking down with a compassionate gaze in his grey eyes. Saxon was aware that the young man carried a rifle slung in the crook of his arm and wore a camouflage jacket. For a moment Saxon thought he was a soldier—a British soldier.

Then he realised that he was the enemy.

Saxon blinked and gazed up curiously.

'Are you going to kill me?' he asked.

The young man stared for a moment and then shook his head.

There came a muffled explosion nearby and a flame abruptly

twisted out of the wreckage of the helicopter and started to devour it.

'You got your friends out just in time,' observed the Irishman softly. 'Are you alright?'

Saxon stared at him angrily.

'What the hell do you care, you bloody murderer!' he snapped.

The young man ignored him and pursed his lips as he looked him over with those oddly compassionate grey eyes.

'You'll be alright,' he said. 'A couple of armoured cars are coming down the road from Cullyhanna. There'll be here in a minute.'

A violent pain shot along Saxon's back and leg and he groaned.

'You'll be alright,' muttered the Irishman again.

'Murderer!' replied Saxon through gritted teeth. '*They* won't be alright!'

He flung out a hand to the bodies of his dead companions.

'It's war and the moral right is on our side,' replied the young man imperturbably. 'But I'm not going to argue politics.'

He jerked his head to the road. Saxon could hear the noise of engines.

'Maybe one of these days we can sit down and discuss it over a beer, but not before you Brits get out of my country and start running your own affairs and stop poking your noses into other people's countries. The sooner you do that the sooner we can all go home in peace.'

He vanished.

Soon after that they gave Saxon his medal; for bravery, they said, bravery beyond the call of duty in that he had returned to a highly dangerous wreck, in spite of a broken leg and rib, and saved the lives of two of his comrades and the bodies of his other men, all of whom would have been incinerated when the machine erupted into flame.

Now the remembrance changed in Saxon's uneasy sleep.

He was crawling painfully to the wreck, fighting against delaying obstacles, fighting to get in. The bodies lay like abandoned rag dolls splashed with red paint and there, among them, were the bodies of Jan, his wife, and his young son, Tom Junior. He gave a cry and reached out, trying to drag them away from the wreckage. But he could not. No matter how hard he tried, no matter how much effort he used, he could not pull them from the wreck.

He cursed and cried and pleaded with them as he pulled but the obstacles were insuperable.

He woke up in his hotel room whimpering like a baby.

Saxon was still in bed when Garry Carson came to the Sheraton the next morning.

'You look lousy,' smiled Carson vindictively.

'I suppose I must feel it, too,' replied Saxon. 'Not that I can feel much at the moment, old boy. What's the time?'

'A quarter after ten.'

Carson reached for the phone and asked room service to bring up a pot of black coffee and ham and eggs for two.

Saxon winced.

'First the good news.' Anglo-American's chief test pilot sprawled in a chair, as Saxon walked unsteadily to the bathroom. 'You're off the hook so far as a court appearance is concerned.'

'What did you do, bribe the judge?' called Saxon cynically.

Carson raised his voice above the sound of running water.

'No; your thief was picked up by the cops last night as he was about to dispose of your billfold.'

'My what?' Saxon frowned.

Carson delved into his memory for the English equivalent.

'Your wallet. There wasn't much money left but all your ID and credit cards were intact. With a little help from the local patrolman, the guy admitted to rolling you just outside the Executive Inn. The lieutenant decided, in view of all the circumstances, not to press charges . . . so long as I smack you on the knuckles and give you a sermon on drinking and throwing punches at cops.'

Carson dropped Saxon's wallet on to the table.

Saxon, having splashed his face, came out of the washroom and sank into a chair opposite Carson.

'Well, I'll just have to thank our friendly neighbourhood cops.'

He paused.

'You said, "first the good news". What's the bad?'

'A warning, from me,' replied Carson curtly. 'I'm going to keep this incident from Maclaren and Anglo-American. In return, you lay off the booze. I don't want to see the *Albatross* project fouled up. If I even think you're taking a swig then I'll boot your arse back to England so quickly that you won't even need an airplane to get you there! And when that happens, Tom, you won't have a future in aviation. No way!'

Chapter Six

As Janine Renard picked up the telephone she knew who it was going to be.

'Janine, this is Jacques Barjonet.'

She felt extraordinarily pleased.

'Hello,' she replied warmly.

Charles had just left for a weekend in Paris—some business conference, he had said—and Janine had wondered, with a growing excitement, whether Jacques would take the opportunity to telephone her.

'It's such a beautiful day today. I was thinking of driving over to the coast for a picnic; to St. Pair-sur-Mer, there's a lovely beach there.'

Janine smiled as he paused.

'Would you like to come? It's a perfect day for swimming.'

'I'd love to, Jacques,' she replied immediately and a little breathlessly.

'I'll pick you up in half an hour.'

As she put down the telephone Janine experienced a tremendous sense of happiness. The feeling of doing something naughty, something forbidden, had vanished now. Instead she was genuinely pleased at the prospect of being in Jacques Barjonet's company. She had not reasoned it out entirely as yet, but she could not deny the feeling. She admitted to herself that she was attracted to Barjonet—firstly, so she told herself, it was an intellectual attraction; then she had tried to reason that it was merely his friendship that she delighted in; finally she found herself wanting Barjonet to take her in his arms. So far Barjonet's behaviour was impeccable. But it was surely just a matter of time. Janine Renard hummed gaily to herself as she went to fetch her swimming suit.

Saxon still felt rough as he slid into the co-pilot's chair on the simulator flight deck. He should have had a drink before coming to the project site. Damn it! Of all the mornings to have a simulator test. Garry Carson looked across at him with a sympathetic expression.

'You look tired, Tom. Do you feel okay?'

Saxon shrugged.

'I'll be alright.'

'You knew this test was scheduled this morning. There was nothing I could do about it.' There was a querulous note in Carson's voice.

'Yes; sorry.'

Carson sighed and turned back to the flight controls and his check board.

'Right,' he turned to encompass Danny Macmillan and Billy Heath as well as Saxon. 'This is going to be a three-hour simulator flight and hopefully our last simulator experience before we take out the *Albatross* for real. Billy, our course will be a take-off from Portland heading for Toronto via Montreal. I want an exact course, speed and height.'

'What about weather conditions, skipper?' demanded the navigator.

'The information is in the flight instructions in the sealed brown envelope in front of you.'

Carson turned back to Saxon.

'Right, let's run through the pre-flight checks, Tom.'

Saxon sighed and reached for his check board.

They lay on the golden sands of St. Pair-sur-Mer. It was, as Jacques had said, a perfect place for swimming. The long strip of golden sand bordered by a breakwater promenade with its small yet impressive church, said to have its origins in a monastery founded by St. Pair and St. Scubilion, made a picturesque setting. Janine Renard and Jacques Barjonet lay on their towels, the sun bathing their bodies in a golden glow. There was no one else on the beach.

'Any more wine left, Jacques?' inquired Janine, turning on her side.

Barjonet had been admiring Janine's beautifully proportioned figure, her light golden skin offset by her dark blue bikini. He kept having to quell uncomfortable but pleasant sensations as he devoured her body with his eyes. He had been right. When

Janine Renard discarded her dowdy clothes, which she wore in her role as Charles Renard's wife, she was quite a beauty.

He forced himself to sit up, reach across to the picnic-box, which was a special thermostatic container to keep food cold, and draw out a bottle of Muscadet. He poured the soft yellow liquid into two glasses.

'It's a perfect day,' smiled Janine, taking one of the glasses.

Barjonet nodded thoughtfully.

'Doesn't Charles ever take you on picnics?'

Janine pouted.

'No,' she replied shortly.

Barjonet realised that he had made a mistake in mentioning her husband.

'Look,' he said, distracting her attention, 'look out to sea, over there! See that tiny white sailing ship; my God, I wish I was as free as that.'

Her eyes followed his extended hand.

'So you will be once your airship flies,' she smiled. 'I think flying in an airship is *really* flying.'

He grinned at her in slight bewilderment.

'How do you make that out?'

'Well, I should imagine that it would be a similar sensation to gliding or ballooning . . . flying like a bird with a sense of freedom and relaxation as opposed to that awful sensation of being hurtled through the air in a machine.'

Barjonet gazed at her in astonishment.

'Have you been gliding?'

She nodded.

'Don't forget my father is an air force general. I used to go with him before . . . before I married.'

'Would you like to go again—tomorrow?'

She laughed loudly at the eagerness in Barjonet's voice.

'I'd love to go tomorrow.'

He raised his glass.

'To tomorrow . . . and tomorrow and tomorrow,' he said softly.

She lowered her gaze but continued to smile and pretended to adjust her bikini top.

'Right, Tom,' said Garry Carson, sitting back at ease in his command chair. 'We're locked in now to the automatic pilot. That should do most of the work but sing out when we come to the course changes.'

'Right, skipper.'

Saxon confirmed his switches were locked on and gazed at the cumulus that was 'floating by' the cabin windows. The simulator was video-fixed so that processed sky and cloud wafted in front of the window spaces to give the sensation that the simulator was really flying. The simulator was a very costly piece of equipment. No expense had been spared by Anglo-American to present an approximation of an authentic flight deck for the training of its crews. Saxon gazed moodily out at the sky. He found himself thinking that it was more turquoise than blue. Jan had a dress of that colour. She had been wearing it on the day she had left with Tom Junior. . . .

A vision of a young police constable swam before his gaze. The constable was very young and looked embarrassed.

'Are you Thomas Saxon?'

There was a falter in his voice.

Saxon admitted he was, wondering what the policeman was doing at his door at that time of night. He had wanted to be left alone, to plan what he was going to do now that Jan had left him. It was probably better this way—Jan going instead of making that final terrible scene, with him moving out to join Helen.

'Is your wife's name Janice Joy Saxon?' the young policeman was saying, staring with a strange intensity at a grease stain on Saxon's shirt collar.

Oh Christ! Saxon had thought. Surely Jan had not involved the police in a domestic quarrel?

'I . . . I'm sorry, sir. I have some bad news for you.'

The policeman's voice wavered.

'I regret to inform you that your wife, Mrs. Janice Joy Saxon, and your son, Thomas Saxon, were killed in an incident on the northbound carriageway of the M1 motorway earlier this evening.'

The young constable's gaze momentarily flickered from the grease stain on Saxon's shirt collar to meet his gaze, wavered with a look of frightened compassion and fell away.

Saxon had simply stared. The words had not meant anything at the time.

The policeman's compassionate stare dissolved to the compassionate gaze of the IRA man.

'You'll be alright,' the man said. 'You'll be alright.'

Then Saxon was clawing his way into the mangled wreckage. They lay there—the crumpled bodies—like blood-splattered rag dolls. Little Tom Junior lay as if he had fallen asleep in his cot except he was covered with a red sticky substance, one hand flung out in a pleading gesture. Then Jan. Jan lying face turned towards him, eyes staring, eyes wide in accusation.

Saxon found himself staring at the blue sky and sweating.

Garry Carson was saying something. Asking Billy Heath something.

'Our position is forty-five north, eighty west, skipper. Georgian Bay should be to our starboard.'

'Damn!' swore Carson. 'We should have already started our turn. We'll come over Owen Sound and down to Toronto.'

Saxon looked at the instruments before him and bit his lip. He should have been checking the course readings and have given Carson the changes five minutes ago. Damn it! He wanted a couple of aspirins. His head was pounding. Maybe he should have had a drink before. . . .

'Saxon!'

Carson spoke sharply.

'Sorry,' he mumbled.

'Where's that goddam course change?'

'I've got it, skipper,' sang out Billy Heath.

'No, dammit! It's Saxon's job.' Carson's voice was savage.

Saxon reached forward and pushed the console buttons. Hell, had Billy Heath said eighty north and forty-five west or. . . . He banged the buttons again.

'Sonofabitch!'

The vehemence in Carson's voice made him pause.

'You've just made a course change north-west for Manitlouin Island instead of south-east for Toronto. That's a bloody expensive mistake.'

Carson swivelled round and called the flight controller on the intercom.

'We're aborting this simulator flight test,' he growled.

Macmillan and Billy Heath looked uneasy. Carson's face was a mask of anger.

'You two go off and be ready for another test at the same time tomorrow.'

Carson waited silently until the navigator and flight engineer had left the simulator flight deck and then he turned to Saxon. Saxon sat quietly, staring at the instrument panel in front of him.

'You screwed up, Tom.'

Saxon didn't say anything.

'You screwed up.'

Carson's voice was more insistent.

'I heard you. So I screwed up. It's only a bloody simulator flight,' Saxon replied defensively.

'Only a. . . .' Carson was angry; more angry than he'd been in a long time. Suddenly he slumped forward.

'Okay, Tom. We're all keyed up—all a little tense. It's important the *Albatross* lifts off on schedule. After last night I can appreciate how you feel today. But hell, I want a first-class crew with me and that means everyone on the team has to pull their weight. There's no room for passengers. Now I told you earlier that last night will not get back to Maclaren, not from me anyway. But don't goof up on me, Tom.'

He paused and looked hard at Saxon.

'You've changed from the old days. Why the drinking?'

'Hell!' snapped Saxon. 'I went on a bender last night and had a few drinks too many; a few drinks and everyone is labelling me a bloody drunk!'

'So long as it *is* a few drinks,' replied Carson. 'If there's some problem, why not talk to me about it? Come out with it before someone else does and you get hauled up before a disciplinary board of the APA. You can't afford to lose your pilot's ticket, Tom.'

Saxon climbed stiffly out of his co-pilot's seat.

'I'm sorry I screwed up the test flight. Is that all, skipper?'

Carson looked at him for several seconds and then shrugged in resignation.

'Yeah; yeah, that's all.'

As Tom Saxon left the simulator an explosion shattered the administration offices on the project site.

The blast blew in the windows of Terrasino's office and sent him flying to the floor where he bumped his head on the corner of his desk and lay for a moment stunned.

He became aware of voices shouting, of a woman's thin scream, then the whining sound of a fire-tender rushing across the Anglo-American site towards the administration block. He smelt the acrid tang of smoke and heard the crackle of fire. Groaning, he raised himself to his hands and knees. There was smoke all over the place.

The door suddenly burst open.

It was Harry Maclaren.

'Terrasino! Christ! Are you okay?'

The project site manager hauled the security chief to his feet and stared at him anxiously.

'Yeah,' grunted Terrasino, his mouth dry. 'What the hell was it? Not the *Albatross* . . . ?'

Maclaren shook his head violently.

'No. . . .'

Parish, one of the security guards, burst in. His gun was out and he looked white-faced.

'Cool it!' snapped Terrasino. 'What's the score, Parish?'

Parish looked bewildered for a moment and then his face cleared.

'Explosion. Part of this office building has been demolished. Looks like a bomb hit it.'

'A bomb?'

Terrasino gave a sudden groan and held his head. It throbbed as if it was on fire.

'Has our mad bomber struck again?'

No one answered him. He turned and made for the door, finding himself limping. Parish was right. Outside it looked as if the three-storey administration building had been partially demolished, as if it had received a direct hit from a bomb. One end of the building had vanished, the floors and walls dropping away within yards of Terrasino's own office. Flames were flickering up part of the building.

'We'd better get the hell out of here,' muttered Terrasino as a nearby wall crumbled into the inferno below. He led the way along the corridor towards the safer end of the building. Already some of the project site firemen were coming up the stairwell.

'Are you folks okay?' demanded their leader as they met him at the head of the stairway.

'Yeah,' grunted Maclaren.

Down on the ground firemen with hoses were training jets of water on the smoking building.

Someone thrust a brandy flask at Terrasino but he waved it away.

'Tiny' Small, the project's chief fire officer, was directing operations as Terrasino limped up.

'Casualties?' he snapped.

Small gestured helplessly.

'We've taken out six people—they're on their way to the Mercy Hospital on State Street.'

'How bad are they hurt?'

'A couple with broken legs, I figure.'

'No dead?'

'None so far but we're still digging in the rubble.'

'Do you know what happened?'

Small shook his head and backed away.

'You'll have to ask someone else, Terrasino. I've got a job to get on with.'

He turned, shouting orders to his men.

Terrasino gazed round. There were a couple of girls sitting on the grass nearby. One of them was a receptionist in the building. She was sobbing. Terrasino went across. Samantha Hackerman was trying to comfort her.

'Hey, Mandy,' he tried to speak kindly but the urgency in his voice made him seem gruff. 'Did you see anything?'

The girl did not reply; her body was straining under her choking sobs. Samantha Hackerman, face begrimed with smoke, looked up at Terrasino.

'There wasn't much to see, Terry,' she said. 'Just a big flash and a bang and then. . . .'

She lifted a shoulder and let it fall, eloquently.

'Thanks, Sam.' Terrasino turned away to where Maclaren was standing, gazing stunned at the burning debris.

'Sounds like a bomb, Harry,' said Terrasino.

Maclaren swore colourfully.

'We've got to get the murderous bastard.'

'Sure we will. I will.'

There was shouting from a group of firemen who had been digging among the rubble. They were bringing something out of the wreckage.

'Tiny' Small, his face white, came across to them.

'The first body,' he said without preamble.

Maclaren bit his lip.

'Who is it?'

'Mr. Lane.'

'Jack Lane? The assistant project site manager?'

The fire chief nodded dumbly.

'Don't worry,' Terrasino said quietly. 'I'm going to nail the bastard who did this.'

Chapter Seven

Tom Saxon had just emerged from the shower and finished towelling himself when his doorbell rang. He glanced at his travelling clock and frowned. It was only eight-thirty. He threw on a robe and went to the door, wondering who could be calling this early on a Sunday morning.

Helen Carson was standing there.

He gaped in surprise.

'Hello, Tom,' she said, awkwardly. Then, with a defensive gesture, added: 'I couldn't keep away.'

Silently, he stood aside and allowed her to enter. As he shut the door he said: 'You shouldn't have come here, Helen.'

'Don't worry,' she replied, 'Garry is working at the project site today. He won't know.'

Automatically, Saxon turned to the drinks cabinet.

'Want a belt? 'Fraid I've only got whisky.'

Helen shook her head.

'It's eight-thirty in the morning, Tom,' she rebuked.

'Yes it is,' he agreed, as he poured himself a shot and then added a liberal splash of water. 'Don't worry, it's just to brush my teeth in.'

Helen watched with sad eyes as he went into the bathroom.

'Look, Tom,' she said, raising her voice slightly so that he could hear, 'we didn't part on good terms the other day. I just wanted to say how sorry I was. . . . Can't we sort this thing out together?'

She heard Saxon gargle and then he came out of the bathroom rubbing his face on a towel.

'Sort it out? What's there to sort out? We are prisoners of fate, you and I, Helen.'

He struck a bad dramatic pose and intoned:

'These struggling tides of life that seem
In wayward, aimless course to tend,
Are eddies of the mighty stream
That rolls to its appointed end.'

Helen just shook her head.

'Fate, kismet, providence, destiny,' Saxon gave a bitter laugh.

'Fate is just an excuse, Tom. Whenever we feel limited or do not wish to act, we shrug and call it fate. It's an excuse for us not facing up to things.'

Saxon smiled wryly.

'Helen, I do believe you are being profound. You're too intelligent to argue with.'

'Tom,' there was a slight note of desperation in her voice, 'I've tried to forget you during these past couple of years. It has not been easy. In fact, it's been impossible. I still love you.'

He stirred uneasily.

'That's ridiculous.'

'Ridiculous? Why?'

'Garry. . . .'

'Don't use Garry as an excuse. He wasn't an excuse two years ago.'

'A lot has happened since then.'

Helen decided to be brutal.

'A lot? Your wife and son died and you've become a near-alcoholic. Has anything else happened?'

He winced but did not reply.

'You have to face it sooner or later,' she went on remorselessly. 'Jan and Tom Junior are dead. You can't go on living with the dead. You have to exorcise them.'

At her words, agony came into his eyes.

'It's all very well telling me to exorcise them, Helen. Tell me how . . . . just tell me how!'

He looked so helpless and pathetic that she instinctively moved towards him and raised a hand to touch his face.

'Oh Tom, I want to help you. I do so want to help you. . . .'

He closed his eyes for a moment, feeling the soft cool caress of her hand on his cheek. Then he drew himself back.

'It's no good, Helen. It won't work out.'

She felt hurt, rejected. Then she realised that Tom Saxon was still too weak to be able to help himself. She had to be strong enough for both of them. She abruptly tried to summon up a false enthusiasm.

'Come on, Tom. This is Sunday—a day off. I'm going to take you on a tour of Portland. We'll start with a boat trip to Fort Gorges.'

She gave him a gentle shove.

'Now get dressed.'

He looked dubious.

'What about Garry . . . ?' he began.

'Look, Tom,' she faced him squarely, her jaw stuck out aggressively. 'My marriage with Garry has been on the rocks for a long time. I should have done something about it years ago. Alright, we are all moral cowards. After you and I split up . . . well, I should have left him then. I was frightened, I suppose. Afraid of being alone. Maybe I'm using you as an excuse now but I'm sorting out my problems, the problems of my own marriage. I am going to leave Garry and get a divorce.'

Saxon looked worried.

'Don't do anything because of me, Helen.'

'Damn you, Tom Saxon! I'm doing it because of me.'

There was a break in her voice as she turned and slammed into the bathroom. Saxon hesitated, wondering whether to go after her. Instead, he decided to get dressed. By the time she came out of the bathroom, she had remade her face and was wearing a smile—a smile that was perhaps a little too fixed.

'Ready? Or do you want breakfast first?' she asked.

'I hardly ever eat breakfast.'

'Let's go then.'

It came as a surprise to Saxon how quickly and pleasantly the day went. They hired a small dinghy with an outboard motor from a boat-hire place on Long Wharf. Helen acted as navigator. There were many imposing forts and old gun emplacements round the entrances to Portland harbour which had been built to protect it from raids by the British. Once, in 1775, a British naval squadron under Captain Henry Mowatt had levelled the town during a twelve-hour bombardment and during the subsequent War of Independence and the War of 1812 the people of Portland resolved to protect themselves against further incursions by a string of fortifications. Fort Gorges was the largest and most imposing of these, situated in the centre of the harbour. Although the fort was never attacked, its solid granite construction and intricate stonework made it a place of tourist pilgrimage.

After the visit to the fort, they lunched at a café which specialised in oyster dishes on Portland Pier and then Helen took Tom to Longfellow's house in Congress Street, the boyhood home of the famous poet. After a tour of the house, inspecting its artifacts and furniture, Helen drove him through southern Portland out towards Cape Elizabeth.

She drove down through the tall pines of Crescent Beach State Park and halted the car on the lip of the long sandy beach looking out to the broad sweep of the grey Atlantic. Yet here the ocean swell was strangely tame, whispering its way up the sloping beach with a gentle insistence.

'How about a swim?' Helen asked.

Saxon paused.

'No costume.'

Helen gestured to the empty expanse of beach and smiled mischievously.

'So what? I've a towel in the back of the car anyway.'

Saxon answered her smile.

'Alright,' he said.

He took off his shoes, socks and jacket, leaving them in the car, and followed her across the broad strip of sand which was broken by a rocky section complete with tide pools. Helen halted and pointed.

'Along there, beyond that freshwater marsh, is where most of the tourists go. There are picnic tables, parking spaces, restrooms and a regular bus service. Everyone goes there and no one comes here. I always swim here. Here you can smell the spruce and oak . . . you can pretend that civilisation is a million miles away.'

In spite of it being late afternoon, the sun still shone down fiercely. The sea hardly stirred and the gentle breeze kept the air a moderate temperature. It was a perfect sea for swimming. Saxon was suddenly glad that Helen had made the suggestion.

Without any self-consciousness, they both stripped and walked down the beach, plunging into the foamy waves. It was slightly cold, making then gasp momentarily. Then Saxon was swimming for a short distance with powerful strokes before turning on his back and floating. Helen came up and playfully splashed him. He grinned and made a half-hearted attempt to duck her. For a while they splashed happily before reluctantly leaving the water and making their way back to the spot where they had left their clothes.

Saxon flung himself down on his back.

Helen flopped down beside him, turning on her side to gaze at him. She noticed that his body was pale. It had obviously been a long time since he had lain in the sun. She remembered his deeply tanned, muscular body without an inch of surplus fat. Now there were strong indications of a paunch; she could tell that his body was soft, a little fatty and out of condition. He was breathing heavily from the exertion, a sure indication that he was no longer used to such physical exercise.

'I haven't been swimming in years,' he said suddenly, as if reading her thoughts. 'I suppose I'm out of condition.'

She smiled.

'We'll soon have you in condition here. There are some really great beaches.'

Saxon glanced at her and let his gaze wander over her body. It was as perfect as he remembered it. It was something of a shock to realise that he did remember it, in spite of his attempt to obliterate it from his mind. She lay there, allowing his eyes to wander over her body, happy and content at just being with him. He was thinking, a little surprised, how easily and pleasantly the day had passed; an entire day with Helen and not once had he thought of Jan or Tom Junior. The guilt feelings came back with a rush. Helen saw a cloud pass over his features.

'What's up, Tom?'

He shook his head and closed his eyes.

With a savage abruptness he realised that he still desired Helen, physically and mentally. He sat up suddenly.

'It's time we were getting back,' he muttered, as he started to towel himself vigorously, trying to ignore the startled hurt in her eyes.

Harry Maclaren waited until his secretary, Jean, had left his office before giving Carson a quizzical glance.

'One goddam problem after another, eh Garry? It isn't enough to be sweating out my guts trying to get the *Albatross* off the ground but I have to contend with a bloody maniac who's running round planting bombs in an effort to destroy the project. That's two colossal problems. But d'you know what? Now I'm landed with the job of being a goddam schoolmaster!'

Carson reached for the coffee Jean had just brought in.

'Okay, Harry, what's the new problem and how does it concern me?'

'Two problems!' snapped Maclaren. 'First, there's Claire

Ashton. Hell, Garry, if she weren't Ashton's daughter I'd have given her the bum's rush out of here some time ago.'

Carson frowned.

'Why? And why does it concern me?'

'Why? I can't have a woman going round offering herself as an easy screw to every goddam male over thirty—what's more, she usually has a public screaming match with the guy after a couple of days.'

'Is that a fact, or just local gossip?' queried Carson. Anglo-American was such a tight-knit concern that he was well aware of the gossip about Claire Ashton.

Maclaren looked uncomfortable.

'Well, I haven't proof, if that's what you mean. But there's too many stories flying about for there not to be some basis.'

'So why don't you send her home?'

Maclaren raised his hands hopelessly.

'Sir Ashley Ashton's daughter? What do I tell her father who just happens to be our vice-president? What do I tell Badrick?'

'How about the truth?'

'Oh yeah; 'scuse me, Sir Ashley, I'm getting rid of your daughter on account she set herself up as the project's number one unpaid whore and it's upsetting some of the younger guys because she won't screw with them, only men over thirty and preferably married.'

Carson clicked his tongue sympathetically.

'It's interesting what you said. From the stories I've heard I gather Claire Ashton doesn't go in for younger men.'

Maclaren's brows met.

'So what's interesting? She just likes older men. Hell, I've got enough psychiatric mumbo-jumbo on my plate with Terrasino and his pet theories about our mad bomber.'

'Anyway, what's Claire Ashton to do with me?' demanded Carson.

'I was wondering whether you could ask Helen to have a word with the girl?'

'Helen's not a particular friend of hers,' replied Carson. 'She's only spoken to her a couple of times.'

Maclaren sighed.

'Well, who is friendly with the girl?'

'She works with Samantha Hackerman.'

'I've already spoken to Sam. She says that they are not that close.'

'Well, I'll have a word with Helen if you want me to.'

'I'd be grateful, Garry,' Maclaren paused. 'That brings me to the second problem.'

'What's that?'

'Tom Saxon.'

Carson looked uncomfortable. There was a pregnant pause before Maclaren spoke again.

'How serious is his drinking, Garry?'

'Serious?'

Maclaren waved an expressive hand.

'I know Saxon is a damned fine pilot and his record and knowledge of dirigibles puts him into the Number Two spot, after you, on this project. But if he's a lush then he's about as much use to us as a looking-glass to a blind man. Come on, Garry, I pick up the local gossip as well as the next guy. I hear he's always carrying a bottle. Is it true?'

Carson's face was serious.

'Harry,' he said, considering his words, 'the moment I think Tom Saxon is a liability to this project, I'll boot his arse out of here myself.'

'So you don't think his drinking is serious?'

'He's a bloody good dirigible pilot.'

'That's not what I asked. I heard he fouled up on one of the simulator tests because of misjudgment. Was that due to booze?'

Carson gave a sharp look.

'Where did you hear that?'

Maclaren grimaced.

'I wasn't born yesterday, Garry. There's also rumours going round about a drunk he went on in town. I gather you had to bail him out of jail and hush things from the press.'

'He was rolled and robbed. Not his fault. Anyway, he's not the first guy to be picked up from the gutter after a skinful.'

'Not on my project, Garry; not among my pilots.'

'I've had a word with him. He's been having trouble adjusting since his wife and kid were killed. He tends to knock the booze back a bit. But I've warned him, Harry, and he knows that I'm watching him. As chief test pilot he's my responsibility.'

'A crew doesn't like to fly with a lush.'

'My crew is okay,' Carson returned defensively. 'Look, I'm not likely to put my neck on the line for a lush. But Saxon's my pigeon and when I feel that he's a danger to the project, then I'll put the skids under him so fast that he won't know what's happening to him.'

Harry Maclaren sat back and toyed with his pen for several long seconds. Then he gave a deep sigh.

'Okay, Garry. I have the utmost faith in you. He's your pigeon. But for God's sake try to kill those rumours.'

Agent Hayes threw a buff-coloured folder on the desk in front of Terrasino and dropped into the wicker chair by the security chief's desk. The office had been hastily prepared for Terrasino in another block of the project site. It was littered with haphazardly placed cabinets and files. Terrasino made no attempt to pick up the folder.

'The cause of the explosion which demolished the administration block was a carefully placed device,' said Hayes.

Terrasino smiled cynically.

'Brilliant! I could have told you that without an investigation.'

Hayes was unperturbed.

'Could you have told us that the explosive device was packed with home-made dynamite?' he asked. 'Or that it was placed in the men's room on the second floor? The second floor happens to be where Oscar Van Kleef had his office. Coincidence?'

Terrasino pursed his lips and gave a soundless whistle.

'Home-made explosive, you say?'

'Yeah,' Hayes confirmed, 'that's why the explosion was stronger than a normal charge. Its basis was nitroglycerine.'

'How could anyone have manufactured that?'

'I'm told it would be fairly simple for someone who knew about explosives. You need nitric acid, sulphuric acid and glycerine.'

'But then what?'

'Get a bath-tub, fill it full of ice, then pour a beakerful of nitric into it. Add the sulphuric and then add more ice. You get the temperature down to about ten degrees centigrade. The nitroglycerine will start forming on the top but you have to beware of the temperature rising above fifteen degrees. And if your hands tremble while you are taking off the nitro—pow! Instant detonation!'

Hayes paused.

'The explosives seem to indicate that our mad bomber is a pro when it comes to knowledge about explosives.'

'Yeah? Well, we can forget Van Kleef for a start,' Terrasino's voice was almost regretful.

'Why? You were the one who was routing for him as Suspect Number One.'

‘I’ve discovered that he was attending an aeronautical engineering seminar in Ottawa when the Westbrooks were killed. That rules him out.’

Hayes tugged at his lower lip and exhaled deeply.

‘Well, we have a mad bomber who’s a top technician. First the Westbrooks and then Lane are killed and seven others injured. We’ve got to stop this madman before he goes for broke.’

Chapter Eight

The telephone woke Danny Macmillan from a deep sleep. He lay for fully half a minute listening to its buzz, lying in a semi-stupor and wondering first where he was and then what the time was. He groaned and finally reached out for the offending instrument, glancing at the luminous dial of the bedside clock. It was twenty minutes after two o'clock in the morning.

'Danny? Danny Macmillan? This is Mike, Mike Pullen.'

The voice sounded worried.

Mike Pullen was the flight engineer in Art Stein's back-up crew. Macmillan did not know him that well. They had shared a few drinks over the last week or so and talked about their common professional interest. Nothing else.

'It's late, Mike. What is it?'

'I know, I know. But I just didn't know who else to ring. I'm speaking from Claire's apartment . . . Claire Ashton.'

Macmillan blinked in surprise.

'What is it?' he repeated.

'Danny . . . she locked herself in the bathroom and threw back a bottle of pills on me! Jeeze! I got her out but she's so goddam sleepy. I don't know what to do.'

Macmillan was wide awake now.

'Have you rung the hospital?'

'Christ, Danny, I can't do that. You know I'm married . . . I can't let Diane know. What about my kids?'

'You should have thought of that before,' sneered Macmillan.

'Aw come on, you know the score, Danny.'

Macmillan bit his lip. It was no time for a moral lecture.

'Okay,' he said. 'Keep her walking up and down, try to keep her awake. I'll be round there in five minutes.'

He was already throwing on his clothes as he slammed down the telephone. It did not take him long to make the five blocks from his apartment to Bay View where Claire Ashton lived. Mike Pullen, a florid-faced man, met him at the apartment door looking anxious.

'Christ, Danny, nothing like this has ever happened to me before. How did I know that the stupid bitch was leading up to an overdose?'

Macmillan brushed him aside and looked round the apartment. Claire was lying on the couch in her silk robe. The way she was sprawled over the couch allowed the robe to fall so that she looked indecent.

'Did you try to keep her awake?'

'Yeah; but she keeps falling asleep.'

'Where's the bottle she took the pills from?'

Pullen gestured towards the bathroom.

Macmillan swept past the girl's sprawled form. In the sink was a small empty bottle. He picked it up and glanced at the table. Scorbital. The name meant nothing to him but the instructions seemed to imply they were sleeping pills. He carried the bottle outside and showed it to Pullen.

'Is this it?'

Pullen nodded.

'Look, Danny, what the hell am I going to do?'

'You can tell me what happened.'

'We . . . Claire and I . . . we've been screwing a couple of days. You know what an easy lay she was. Christ! She almost raped one guy. We all knew the score. Well, tonight we had a meal, bought a couple of bottles of bourbon and came back to her apartment. Apparently it was her birthday 'cos there was this card from her parents lying in the box. The next thing I know is that she starts getting upset. I reckon the girl is loco, has gone round the bend. Suddenly she locks herself in the john. When she doesn't open up after a while I push in the door. She's on the floor and the empty bottle is in the sink.'

'So you wouldn't know how many tablets she's taken?'

'Christ, no!'

Pullen looked helpless.

'What am I to do, Danny?' he repeated.

Macmillan looked at him bitterly.

'I'd face up to paying for my fun and get myself a clean pair of pants.'

Pullen's face almost puckered.

'Christ, Danny, why take it out on me? I didn't cause her to go round the bend, did I? I didn't do anything. We all knew the score with her.'

'You just took advantage of the poor bitch,' Macmillan said sharply, then he glanced at his watch. 'Get your things and get the hell out of here. I'm telephoning the hospital right away.'

Pullen shot Macmillan a look that was half hate and half gratitude and seemed to scuttle out of the apartment. Macmillan was already onto the Maine Medical Centre.

A cold impersonal voice informed him that a Paramedical Unit would be with him within ten minutes and that he should try to keep the OD moving.

'OD?' Macmillan was puzzled.

'Overdosed person,' came the laconic reply before the phone went dead.

Macmillan tried to haul Claire's body into an upright position. She was a dead weight and looked deathly pale.

'Poor bitch,' he muttered compassionately. Then loudly: 'Okay, Claire . . . okay . . . we are going for a little walk. Come on, move . . . move. . . .'

For ten minutes he walked up and down the room, cajoling, threatening, trying to keep her from slipping into a complete coma.

There was a bang on the door and suddenly two men in white coats, carrying some equipment, hurried into the room. They were followed by a policeman. The paramedics grabbed the girl and made a quick examination.

'What did she take?' demanded the elder of the two, a grizzle-headed man with a deeply lined face.

Macmillan held out the bottle.

'Scorbital,' said the paramedic. 'Was it full?'

'I don't know,' replied Macmillan. 'I wasn't here when she took it.'

'Shit!' swore the younger man, who had a mop of fair hair. 'A pump job?'

'Yeah,' replied the other. 'Let's get her into the bedroom. You,' with a glance at Macmillan, 'stay here.'

The two medics took the girl and their equipment into the bedroom and shut the door.

The policeman, a heavy-jowled sergeant, had dropped into a chair and was shoving a piece of gum into his mouth while contemplating his notebook moodily.

'Okay, mister,' he said. 'Let's have it. Your name first.'

Macmillan told him.

'Who is the OD?'
Macmillan gave details.
'What's your relationship to the OD?'
Macmillan hesitated.
'A friend.'
'Okay. How did it happen?'
Macmillan chewed his lip a moment as he tried to think the story out.
'I wasn't here. It was an . . . an accident. She rang me half an hour ago saying that she had been having trouble sleeping and was taking some pills which hadn't worked. She told me that she had taken some more and that she wasn't feeling too good. She realised that she must have taken an overdose. That's why she rang me. I got over here as fast as I could and then rang the Medical Centre.'
The policeman looked at him suspiciously.
'An accident, you say?'
He made some more notes.
The bedroom door opened and a medic came out. It was the fair one.
'How is she?' demanded Macmillan.
The medic sighed and pulled out a packet of Lucky Strike, lighting one up and inhaling deeply.
'Cigarettes can ruin your health,' he said conversationally. 'I must give them up sometime but not on this job. How is she? She'll survive. She'll wake up with one hell of a stomach-ache tomorrow but she'll survive.'
Macmillan gave a sigh of relief.
'You got the details, sarge?'
The policeman handed his notebook to the paramedic who read it through and nodded. He pulled out his own notebook and made some notes, then he handed the policeman's notebook back.
'Seems straightforward this time,' said the man. 'You'd be surprised how some of these OD cases turn out—real complications.'
He glanced at the bedroom.
'You through in there, Charlie?'
The elderly man came out with the equipment.
'Yeah; all through.'
Macmillan looked at them in surprise.
'Is that it?' he asked.
The elderly man chuckled.

'What else is there? We've cleaned her out. She'll sleep, maybe twelve hours if she's lucky. When she wakes up she'll feel lousy. Just give her liquids for the next twenty-four hours and then she'll be as right as anyone else on this goddam lousy planet.'

Macmillan nodded dumbly.

'Oh, and mister, I presume you will be staying with her for the next twenty-four hours? Yeah? Well she should see her own doctor or go to a clinic as soon as she feels up to it.'

They all trooped out, slamming the door and leaving Macmillan with a tremendous sense of unreality.

He went across to the bedroom and peered in. The girl was lying hunched up in the blankets on the bed. She looked pale and pathetic. Macmillan suddenly remembered her frightened, hurt animal look and shook his head. What was Claire Ashton's problem; what was twisting her up? He switched off the bedroom light and went to the kitchenette to make himself some coffee.

'You are behaving very strange of late,' remarked Samantha Hackerman as she placed a plate of pasta in front of Jules Keller. They had just returned to Keller's apartment after seeing a late-night movie show and Samantha had produced a spaghetti supper. Keller glanced at her almost furtively, Samantha thought.

'What do you mean, Sam?' he countered defensively.

'I don't know what I mean,' she admitted. 'Ever since you came back from Montreal . . . well, you seem so preoccupied.'

Keller forced a grin.

'I'm sorry, love. It's just that Van Kleef has been on my back a bit lately. You know, a few design problems to be sorted out before the *Albatross* makes its first test flight next week.'

He picked up his fork and began to tuck into the plate of spaghetti as though the subject were closed. Samantha sighed. The last really serious conversation she and Jules had had was when he had mentioned his idea of going to Europe on an extended holiday. Since she had pointed out the practical difficulties, Jules had not discussed the plan again. Recently he appeared almost totally absorbed in his work—which seemed a little out of character with his usual easy-going manner. Well, she supposed he was getting uptight along with everyone else. The entire project staff were feeling apprehensive as the day approached when the *Albatross* was due to make her first flight.

'You seem far away.'

She glanced up from her food and found Jules gazing at her thoughtfully.

'Yes,' she smiled. 'I was just thinking—only a few days before the *Albatross* lifts off for the first time. That's going to be a lot of extra work for me in dealing with the press and public.'

'Have you thought any more about my suggestion—about coming with me to Europe?'

The question startled her by its unexpectedness.

'Not really,' she admitted. 'I just don't see how we can afford it.'

A ripple of anger crossed Jules Keller's face.

'I told you to leave that part of it to me. All you have to do is make the decision. You can't imagine that I'm sticking with this project much longer. I want my freedom. I don't want to spend my days as a minor anonymous cog in a big wheel. I want to be able to breathe.'

She gazed at him in surprise for a moment.

'Isn't that what everyone is working for—freedom in some form or another?'

'Yeah? Well, with most people it's just an illusion, a dream. With me . . . well, you'll see what I mean.'

He fell silent and returned to his food. For some time Samantha, puzzled, continued to study him from the corner of her eye.

A groan from the bedroom caused Danny Macmillan to set down his coffee cup and stride across to the door. Claire Ashton lay on her back, one hand across her eyes, shielding them from the sunlight which now streamed into her uncurtained bedroom window. The paramedics had been right. She had slept almost twelve hours. She groaned again.

'Hi,' said Macmillan. 'Do you want a glass of water?'

'I feel awful,' moaned the girl. She removed her hand and tried to focus on his face.

He moved to the bedside, poured a glass of water from a jug and handed it to her. She took a gulp and heaved.

'Oh God! My stomach!'

Macmillan looked sympathetic.

'It's going to hurt for the next twenty-four hours,' he said. 'Take it easy, huh?'

Her face was a blotchy yellow colour, drawn and haggard; the eyes red-rimmed.

She frowned as she tried to focus on him again.

'You're not . . . you're not . . . whatsisname.'
Macmillan smiled.
'I'm Danny Macmillan. Remember me?'
She sank back against her pillows with a groan and closed her eyes.
'I still have some of my faculties left. What happened to whatsisname?'
'Mike Pullen?'
Macmillan gestured.
'He took off like a bat out of hell when you overdosed yourself.'
Her eyes flickered open and for a moment her face blazed with anger.
'Who says I overdosed myself?' she demanded harshly.
'I do, for one,' replied Macmillan calmly. 'Pullen for another and the two paramedics who had to pump the muck out of your stomach.'
Her head jerked round. She stared at him with wide eyes and open mouth.
'I can't remember . . . I had my stomach . . . ?'
Macmillan nodded.
'What happened?'
'Pullen rang me last night. Said you had gone to the bathroom and thrown back a bottle of tablets. Scorbital, they were called. Mike was scared shitless because of his wife. I came over. He left. Then I called the Medical Centre and two paramedics and a policeman arrived. The medics pumped you clean while I told the policeman that it was all an accident.'
'So your friend whatsisname was protected?' she sneered.
It was the sort of attitude Macmillan expected.
'No. So that you were protected until you have time to sort out your problem. Trying to make away with yourself is not looked kindly upon by the police in this country. And Pullen isn't a friend of mine.'
'So what?' returned the girl. 'What's it to do with you or the police for that matter? I can do what I like. Leave me alone.'
Macmillan shrugged.
'You're right. If you want to kill yourself that's your business.'
The telephone rang.
Macmillan went into the living-room and answered it. It was Mike Pullen.

'Diane's just gone out into the garden,' he said breathlessly. 'What's happened?'

'Nothing for you to worry about,' the contempt in Macmillan's voice was obvious. 'She's okay—just.'

There was relief in Pullen's voice as he said: 'That's dandy. But Christ, Danny, we all knew the score about that dame. Anyway, you can tell that screwball to stay away from me in the future.'

'You can count on it,' replied Macmillan, putting down the receiver.

'Who was it?'

Macmillan turned to see Clare framed in the doorway of the bedroom, holding unsteadily to one side of the door.

'Pullen,' he said.

She looked blank.

'Whatsisname.'

'Oh . . . good old whatsisname. Get me a drink.'

Macmillan shook his head.

'Against medical advice.'

'Damn medical advice!' She lurched to the kitchen and poured herself a straight bourbon. Macmillan made no attempt to stop her as she swigged the neat alcohol.

'I think you will be sorry in a minute,' he said softly.

It was slightly less than a minute when she bent double and threw up.

Somehow Macmillan got her to the bathroom and, with a sigh of resignation, began to clean up the place. After a while he went into the bathroom. She was huddled over the sink sobbing with deep, retching sobs. The sound was so like an animal in pain that it made Macmillan shudder. He took her gently by the shoulders, then stooped and picked her up and carried her into the bedroom. It was like putting a child to bed. He tucked the clothes around her and sat silently in a chair by her, just holding her hand. It was some while before the sobbing died away and was replaced by stertorous breathing. She had cried herself to sleep.

Macmillan was making himself a sandwich in the kitchenette when she woke two hours later and moaned for some water. He cradled her head and held the glass to her lips, letting her have no more than a few sips. She gazed up at him with a troubled expression.

'Why?'

He looked puzzled.

'Why are you doing this?'

The question threw him. He had no answer. He had not even reasoned out his actions and concern to himself as yet.

'Someone's got to.'

'That's no answer,' she replied. 'Why you . . . after, well, after what happened between us?'

He grinned.

'Nothing happened between us. Anyway, let's say that I hate to see an attractive and intelligent woman flush herself down the tubes for no reason.'

She lay back on the pillows.

'No reason?' She smiled bitterly. 'Ah well, to hell with reasons. To hell with everything. Nothing really matters. The whole damned world doesn't matter.'

Instinctively, Macmillan reached forward and found her hand.

'Listen to me, Claire. I want to help. Can't you tell me what's bugging you?'

She gazed at him, perplexed.

'That brings me back to my first question. Why the hell would you want to help me?'

Macmillan reflected for a moment.

'Because, Claire, you are a young, attractive and obviously intelligent woman and you have a problem which you don't appear to be able to deal with. Whatever the problem is, you can't resolve it by asking every goddam male in Portland to screw you and you can't resolve it by opting out, by flushing yourself down the tubes with a bottle of whatever happens to be handy. I think I might be able to help you sort yourself out . . . if you let me be your friend.'

'Friend?' she looked at him suspiciously. 'Is that a long-winded way of saying that you want to get into bed with me?'

'Dammit! No!'

'You want to help me and yet you don't want payment in kind?'

There was an incredulous note in her voice.

'Your experience with men must be very limited, Claire,' he said sadly. 'But everyone who does something for you does not necessarily have to do it because they want to lay you.'

She sneered.

'That's been my experience. People use people. What's your angle?'

'As soon as I figure one out I'll let you know.'

Claire stared at him for a moment and then smiled slightly.

'Alright, *friend*,' she said. 'Will you do me a favour?'
'Sure—what?'
'Can you make me a cup of tea—English tea?'
Macmillan grinned.
'I can try but I won't guarantee the result.'
Claire Ashton's mouth drooped wistfully.
'No one can guarantee anything in this damned awful life, Mr. Danny Macmillan,' she said softly.

Chapter Nine

It seemed that the entire world was there to watch the first flight of the *Albatross*. By six o'clock in the morning the streets around the Anglo-American project site were crowded with spectators, many from out of state, all eager to catch a glimpse of the gigantic airship. Police were already trying to cope with numerous traffic jams as enthusiastic people tried to park their cars as near to the site as possible. Television cameras were everywhere: NBC, ABC, PBS and CBS crews dominated the television platforms while foreign camera crews struggled for the remaining good angles of view. There were also special facilities for the fourteen local radio station commentators, many of whom found themselves being broadcast nation-wide, and crowds of other press representatives were vying for places. Samantha Hackerman and her press team had been working overtime to provide the special facilities and information. It had been decided that no press men would be allowed on the airship during its first flight. Only essential personnel and FAA and CAA officials were to be on board.

The first flight was to be a fairly short one. The airship would take off over Fore River and then turn northward up the coast to Newfoundland, leaving American airspace at Moncton, New Brunswick, one of the Canadians' main air-traffic controller centres. Moncton would pass the airship on to Gander in Newfoundland and then the *Albatross* would turn back to Portland. If this short haul was successful after a few days the airship would make a second trip, this time to Washington carrying a full load of press, aviation officials and businessmen. The plan was to set her down at Andrews Air Force Base where the President would come on board and officially name the ship.

The weather experts had chosen the day of the first flight well. By nine o'clock there was not a cloud to be seen against the azure sky. The sun was quite hot. At a few minutes past nine, the great canvas shelter and network of construction girders were moved away from the airship by tractors to provide more space for the lift-off. So far no one who stood outside the canvas shelter could see the colossus. Inside three specially constructed portable gangways were being towed away from the airship's main entry ports, and the doors were closed as the last of the personnel went aboard. Then, at a given signal, the engines of the ship started to whine and the vectoring propellers lifted the massive aircraft, slowly, inch by inch, until it began to appear over the three-hundred-feet high canvas shelter.

There were screams and gasps and applause from the spectators as the sun glinted wickedly on the mammoth's silver hide.

'Imagine, imagine,' a radio commentator was trying to capture the scene in words, 'a giant beast, a monster, a dinotherian creature floating in the air which could swallow the *QEII* in its mighty maws . . . the world has seen nothing like this. Nothing. An immense, herculean, titanic. . . .'

He groped for endless synonyms.

Slowly upwards, almost blackening out the blue sky, the *Albatross* rose.

Charles Renard, sitting in Tanya Le Solliec's apartment in Paris, watched the take-off on the television, a live broadcast over the satellite. He was far from happy as he saw the airship rise into the air over Portland.

'Damn bastards!' he muttered. 'I thought Keller was supposed to be doing something about it. They've beaten us to the first test flight.'

Tanya glanced at him with a frown.

'Who's Keller, *ma mie*?'

'It's not important,' Renard replied, concentrating his gaze on the television. He studied the vectoring propeller system as it allowed the ship to rise into the sky, accompanied by an enthusiastic commentary from a French reporter. There was excitement in his voice as he described the main features of the aircraft and its commercial potential. Renard bit his lips in annoyance as the man made no mention of the *Charles de Gaulle* or the French developments in the field.

On the television screen the airship rose spectacularly to a height of a thousand feet and then its propellers ceased abruptly. It stopped, floating motionless, hanging in the sky like some strange vessel from another planet. Then slowly, majestically, the mammoth silver cigar-shape began to move away.

On the screen there flashed an assortment of publicity stills, of the interior of the ship, its freight holds, private staterooms, lounges and restaurants. Renard swore with a violence that startled Tanya and reached forward to snap the set off.

The first flight of the *Albatross* had been an unqualified success. No problems or hitches had arisen. Even John G. Badrick had moved around the project site congratulating everyone with his face wreathed in smiles. Garry Carson carried a echo of a smile as he debriefed his crew in the administration building, and before he had time to finish Oscar Van Kleef hurried in to pump them by the hand. 'Terrific!' he kept saying over and over again. 'Terrific!'

The slightly pompous Federal Aviation Administration official who was checking their individual reports allowed himself to smile thinly.

'Well, Colonel Carson, if your second flight goes as well, I can see no reason why we won't be granting a certificate of airworthiness.'

'It certainly went smoothly,' observed Tom Saxon, handing the man his report.

'Airships,' the FAA man said in a dry monotone, looking at Saxon, who, as an Englishman, he probably considered was not acquainted with FAA regulations, 'being aircraft are subject to Federal Aviation Regulations Part 91, General Operating and Flight Rules, when operating within the United States. This rule prescribes the conditions and limitations for the operation of aircraft within the national airspace system.'

'Oh really?' Saxon smiled broadly.

'Oh surely,' continued the man, who apparently lacked a sense of humour. 'In order to conduct a freight and passenger airship operation for compensation or hire, any company, either private or one backed by public funding, would be required to comply with Federal Aviation Regulations Part 121, Certification and Operations. Er, that is where I come in. Airworthiness standards for construction and manufacturing of large airships do not exist and the certification of such a ship as the *Albatross* is being handled on a case basis utilising the experience of similar projects that have been started over the past.'

Danny Macmillan was doubled up in laughter.

Even Van Kleef was trying to suppress a grin as he drew the FAA official out of the debriefing room.

Carson slapped Macmillan on the back.

'Jesus! And it depends on that guy whether the *Albatross* gets an airworthiness certificate!'

'Just so long as it's allowed to fly, skipper,' grinned Billy Heath. 'Well, I'm going up to the celebration party that Badrick's throwing. Anyone coming?'

'Yeah,' said Macmillan. 'Count me in.'

Carson nodded.

'I'll be along later.'

Macmillan and Billy Heath exchanged glances and left. Carson waited until they had gone before he looked at Saxon.

'Thanks, Tom.'

Saxon was puzzled and said so.

'Thanks for pulling yourself together for this trip. I hope it keeps up. You've been worrying me, and Maclaren, about your fitness to fly.'

Saxon's features suddenly became moulded in anger.

'How did Maclaren hear?'

'I didn't tell him, Tom. But Harry is pretty attuned to project site gossip. Anyway, you did fine. I'm glad you're laying off the booze. See you up at the party.'

He turned and left before Saxon could reply.

'The hell with them!' he muttered as he grabbed his kitbag. Bloody pious bastards. Well, he wouldn't go to their pain-in-the arse party. He'd have his own.

'Sorry to drag you away from the celebration,' Hayes apologised as they entered Terrasino's office. The security chief grunted as he switched the light on. He was still carrying a glass half-filled with bourbon. He sprawled in his chair and motioned Hayes to take a seat.

'Well,' said the FBI man, 'that's one headache less.'

Terrasino looked annoyed.

'Not for me, it's not. Because our mad bomber didn't strike on this occasion does not mean to say that he's given up. I wouldn't want to go through the last twenty-four hours again. The tension nearly killed me.'

Hayes lit up a Lucky Strike.

'You don't think the fact that the mad bomber didn't strike is at all significant?'

'I'd have thought that he would have made his move on our first flight. But maybe that's what he figured as well.'

'How's that?'

'Maybe the guy is a little too clever. He knew that we were

waiting for him to strike and that we had a security blanket on this first flight. Maybe he thought—hell! Let 'em stew a while. Spend all their time and energy sweating it out for me to drop the big one while I simply put my feet up and smile. Then, when they have grown tired of waiting, when they least suspect it . . . zowie!'

Hayes looked at him hard and then slowly nodded.

'It makes sense, I guess,' he said.

'Sure it does,' replied Terrasino. 'Our mad bomber is highly intelligent. We know that. He'll wait until the time is right for him, not for us. In the meantime, the boys on the project have been getting a little jumpy since poor Jack Lane was killed. Badrick and Maclaren keep pestering me for results.'

'My chiefs too,' rejoined Hayes moodily.

'No luck in tracing a connection between Max Prüss and any of our men?'

'Not so far,' admitted the FBI agent. 'But our computer is only as good as the information we feed into it.'

'It's an angle that doesn't seem to make sense,' replied Terrasino.

'We haven't got much else to go on. Since you discovered Van Kleef was in Ottawa when the Westbrooks were killed that seems to rule him out. Though one thought . . . it depends when the electronic scrambling device was planted in Westbrook's aeroplane. Van Kleef took the flight to Ottawa on the morning that Westbrook was killed. Still, Van Kleef is so tied up with the *Albatross* project that the whole thing would be unlikely. He doesn't even have time for his wife.'

'Is that why she left him?'

'Seems so.' The FBI agent shrugged. 'Let's face it, our checks show that Van Kleef leads a comparatively blameless life. The same with Nieman and with Keller—except that Keller is young, woman-crazy—but they all three seem nice guys.'

Terrasino did not look convinced.

'Our mad bomber is going to be precisely that sort of person, Hayes. He will have led a blameless life. He will look pretty ineffectual and the very opposite of what most people think is the type who goes round planting bombs and killing people.'

Helen Carson was just about to have a shower prior to going to bed when the telephone rang.

'Is Colonel Carson there?' asked a male voice. She didn't recognise it.

'No, he's still at the project site. They're holding a celebration party there.'

'Oh,' the voice sounded blank. Then: 'Is that Mrs. Carson?'

'Yes.'

The voice became apologetic.

'You don't know me, Mrs. Carson. My name's Ed. I'm the barman at the Black Eagle Bar on the corner of Congress and Locust.'

He paused to let the information sink in and then hurried on: 'We have an English guy down here . . . his ID says his name is Saxon, Tom Saxon. He's had a mite too much to drink. If I let him out of the bar he's either going to get rolled, arrested or killed trying to drive home. I went through his billfold and the only local telephone number I came up with was Colonel Carson's. Do you know the guy?'

Helen felt an odd sense of resignation.

'Yes: yes, I know him.'

'Well,' said the barman called Ed, 'I don't like bothering a lady but is it possible you could pick him up before the cops do?'

Helen hesitated only a fraction.

'Yes; yes, I'll be down there in ten minutes.'

'Thanks a million, lady. The poor bastard seems to have a problem. He's been sat alone at the same bar stool for the past three hours tossing back bourbon like the world was ending.'

'I'll be down there.'

Helen went to the mirror to patch her make-up. She wouldn't bother to leave a note for Garry. After all, he didn't like driving when he had been drinking and knowing how late the project site party would doubtless finish, Garry would probably spend the night there. It occurred to her in passing to wonder why Tom Saxon was not at the project site party and instead drinking alone in a bar on Congress and Locust. Puzzled, she took her car keys and went out to her Chevrolet.

The Black Eagle Bar was nearly empty when she went in. Tom Saxon was perched at the end of the bar, head slumped forward in his arms.

A pudgy, dark-haired man was wiping glasses behind the bar.

'Mrs. Carson?' he asked as she entered.

She nodded and went across to Saxon. The barman reached over the bar and shook him by the arm.

'Wakey-wakey, mac. Your chauffeur is here.'

Saxon groaned and half-raised his head.

'I didn't order a bloody chauffeur!'

The barman, Ed, grinned apologetically at Helen.

'He's a bit cantankerous, Mrs. Carson.'

She smiled thinly and laid a hand on Saxon's arm.

'Come on, Tom. I'll take you home.'

Saxon raised his head and blinked blearily at her.

'Home? What home . . . oh, why it's *Mrs*. Carson.' He laid an emphasis on the prefix. 'Hello to you, *Mrs*. Carson . . . have a drink . . . let's all have a drink. Come, landlord, what kind of hostelry are you running?'

He suddenly slumped forward, laughing stupidly.

Helen glanced at the barman.

'Can you help me get him out to my car?'

'Sure,' returned the barman. 'Will you be able to manage him at the other end?'

'I'll manage him,' she replied.

They heaved Saxon, protesting but too helpless to do anything, onto his feet and out of the bar, across the sidewalk, and pushed him into the back seat of her car. Helen thanked the barman and climbed behind the wheel.

Saxon was trying to sing.

> 'Drink today and drown all sorrow;
> You shall perhaps not do it tomorrow!'

Helen sighed as she drove through downtown Portland and out on the South Portland road towards the Sheraton. Looking in her driving mirror she saw that Saxon had levered himself into a sitting position and was trying to focus on her.

'Why . . . dear old Helen . . . love of my life! What are you doing here?'

'I'm driving you back to your hotel, Tom,' she replied evenly.

'Saving my life again, eh? Everyone wants to save me . . . poor Helen. You know I love you Helen? That's the saddest thing of all. I love you and yet I can't love you. Got to consider Jan. Got to consider Tom Junior. Jan . . . but she's dead. Dead! It's her damned ghost that I'm afraid of. Accusing me. Can't get rid of it. Helen. Love you. But Jan's always there . . . always. . . .'

Helen glanced into her mirror.

Saxon had slumped down in the back seat. His eyes were closed and he was breathing deeply in an alcoholic sleep.

Helen reached up to wipe away the tears which were stinging her eyes.

She drove swiftly through the city and across Portland Bridge into South Portland. At the Sheraton she enlisted the aid of a grinning porter to take Saxon up to his suite. The porter had to get help to carry the inert body. She tipped them both and ordered a pot of hot coffee to be sent up. The porter looked at Saxon and shook his head.

'Coffee won't bring him out of that, lady. The only thing that will bring that guy round is a twelve-hour sleep.'

An hour later Helen was forced to agree with him.

She left Saxon sleeping soundly on his bed and let herself out of his suite.

Driving home through the deserted night streets she realised that there were odd similarities between Tom Saxon and herself. Saxon would not face up to the realities of his life, would not lay the ghost of his dead wife and son, while she had not made any attempt to sort out her own problems. Oh, she had talked and thought about it for a long time. Yet, somehow, seeing Saxon's helplessness, she suddenly found how amazingly simple it was to make the most important decision of her life. She had decided what she had to do long before she reached home.

Chapter Ten

'I don't believe it!' gasped Charles Renard.

The voice on the other end of the telephone line was apologetic.

'It's true nevertheless. The consignment of helium for your airship was cleared by the suppliers three days ago, sent to the Yarmouth Docks for shipment and is now held up by a longshoreman strike which is effectively blocking the eastern seaboard ports.'

'But this is incredible!' shouted Renard. 'Is there no way you can get that gas offloaded and put onto another form of transport?'

'No way this side of hell. The gas is safely stored in the docks until the dispute is over.'

'Alright,' Renard was breathing heavily. 'See what you can do.'

He slammed the telephone receiver back on its rest and gazed moodily across the desk to where his secretary, Marie-France, was sitting nervously, halfway through a dictated letter.

Abruptly, Renard banged the table.

'I want Villemur, Le Braz and Barjonet in my office immediately.'

Renard realised that there was only one thing to do now if the *Charles de Gaulle* was going to be in with a chance against the Anglo-American airship. The *Albatross* had already caught world attention by making its first successful test flight. At the moment the *Charles de Gaulle* lay with only ten per cent of her gas capacity filled with helium. Now it seemed impossible that the rest of the helium supply would arrive at St. Lô in time to lift her off before the *Albatross* announced its first Transatlantic run. Unless. . . . Even with a supply of gas it would still take seven days to ready the *Charles de Gaulle* for her first test flight, but

Renard determined to ensure that the flight would be a spectacular one.

Tom Saxon moaned aloud in his dream-infested sleep.

Norfolk. A lonely whitewashed cottage with a yellowing thatched roof and small windows which let in hardly any light. A scene like an animated picture postcard. A structure like an Irish croft rather than an East Anglian cottage. So long ago. In another life.

Tom Saxon and Helen Carson lay curled up on the big couch before a roaring log fire which scattered now and again in a shower of sparks as the cold winds whistled across the chimney top. Outside the rain whispered against the dry thatch and tapped persistently on the window panes.

'What should we do, Tom?' Helen was asking.

'Decision time,' Saxon said solemnly. 'Yes, we must make a decision.'

They both stared awhile into the crackling yellow glare of the fire. Then Saxon asked:

'If I were free and you were free, would you marry me?'

Helen laughed.

'That's hypothetical.'

'Seriously, though.'

'Perhaps,' she said tantalisingly. 'But we have to deal with the realities of the situation, Tom, and not talk about our dreams.'

'Perhaps we should put our dreams into reality.'

Helen gave him a serious glance.

'Can we?'

'Why not? It is simply a question of practicalities. Once the heart has decided, then the rest is easy.'

She was a little nervous now.

'Are you sure, Tom? Is it what you want?'

'It's very much what I want.'

She leant forward and kissed him.

'It's going to be difficult. Garry won't be home until the end of the week. I'll tell him then.'

'I'll start the ball rolling by telling Jan tonight. Let's not pretend that it's not going to be difficult, or that Jan and Garry are not going to feel hurt.'

'What shall we do then . . . afterwards?'

'I'm still a serving RAF officer,' Saxon mused. 'I'll have to move out of my house but maybe we could hire a cottage or a flat near the airbase—just to start with. Then I'd like to get out of the service and get into civil aviation.'

'Like Garry plans to do?' Helen broke off and looked uncomfortable for a moment.

'Yes, like Garry,' Saxon smiled softly.

'I wish we didn't have to hurt people,' Helen said.

'It would probably hurt them more, and us as well, if we were not honest about our emotions, about what we feel for each other.'

'I hope your wife will understand. No one meant this to happen.'

Saxon glanced at his watch.

'I'd better be going back now. I'll ring you in the morning.'

Then a kaleidoscope of images.

The deserted house. The note of accusation from Jan. She knew about his affair with Helen. She had taken Tom Junior and gone to her parents in Perth to think things over.

Then the nervous compassionate policeman.

The compassionate terrorist.

The mangled corpses in the wreckage of the helicopter. No, the wreckage of a car. The bloodied, distorted remains of Jan and Tom Junior. Everything merging into a misshapen whirlpool in which red was the predominant colour.

Tom Saxon moaned aloud in his sleep.

Helen Carson arrived at the Sheraton early the next morning and went unannounced to Saxon's suite. She let herself in with his key, which she had retained from the previous night, and found him still asleep. She rang room service and ordered a light breakfast for two and plenty of coffee. Then she set about waking Saxon. He came unwillingly from his sleep and lay blinking in bewilderment at her.

'Helen . . . what time is it?'

She told him as she sat on the edge of the bed.

'Oh hell,' he groaned. 'I promised Maclaren I would be in early today to go over some specifications.'

'After what I heard about last night's celebration party at the project site, I would not imagine that anyone will be in early this morning. Anyway, you'd better ring up and say you overslept or something.'

Saxon stared at her for a minute and then groaned.

'Christ, my throat is like sandpaper.'

'Coffee is on its way up.'

Saxon rubbed his forehead as if trying to get his bearings.

'Did you . . . you came to the bar last night? What happened?'

'Nothing much,' she replied. 'The barman rang me. I went, collected you and brought you back here.'

'You stayed all night?'

'No; I went home. You were dead to the entire world.'

There was a knock on the door and the room service boy wheeled in a trolley. Helen signed the check. While she was doing so, Saxon climbed out of bed and went into the bathroom. In a few moments he was out, having had a cold shower and wrapped a towel around himself. He lowered himself onto the couch and grabbed for a cup of black coffee.

'How long can this last, Tom?' she said directly.

He winced.

'No lectures, Helen. Not until I'm repaired a bit.'

'No lectures. No recriminations. But what of the future? You won't last long like this. If Garry or Harry Maclaren found out that you are just a lush. . . .'

'I'm not!' Saxon snapped, stung by the realisation that she spoke the truth.

'You're doing a pretty good imitation, Tom,' Helen smiled. 'I know and understand some of the reasons but you have to let the dead bury the dead eventually. You can't live in the past.'

There was an awkward silence before she went on.

'Anyway, speaking for myself, I'm beginning to see things more clearly and I reached a decision last night.'

He glanced up curiously at her.

'Oh, it's absolutely nothing to do with us. It's something I should have done a long, long time ago. I am going to leave Garry. I'm moving out in a day or two after I've talked to him.'

'Oh.'

Saxon didn't know what else to say.

'It was all over with Garry and me a long time ago—in fact, I don't think we ever got started but we never admitted it. So don't think that it has anything to do with us, Tom. It hasn't.'

'No; I see.'

He hesitated, as if trying to make up his mind to say something, then:

'I'd better call the project site to say I'll be in late.'

She bit her lip. She had been expecting a little more reaction to her news. She watched him dialling then, as he was put through to Maclaren, she stood up and left. Why should she expect anything from Tom Saxon?

'Hydrogen?'

Villemur stared aghast at Charles Renard.

'Why not?'

It was Le Braz, doodling on a jotting pad, who spoke.

As Villemur, Renard and Barjonet turned to look at him, Le Braz shrugged.

'We must accept that even if we were able to get our immediate supply of helium, we would face a long-term problem. It must be acknowledged that the natural supply in North America is limited and that helium released into the atmosphere escapes into outer space and is lost. Eventually, the United States Government will reimpose an export embargo on it as they did during the 1920s and 1930s. Whereas hydrogen is easily obtainable and, at the moment, stands at one-tenth the cost of helium.'

Villemur looked angry.

'I know about costs . . . but helium as the necessary lifting gas for the *Charles de Gaulle* is essential. Surely you must have ensured the availability of an adequate quantity before you undertook the construction of the airship?'

He turned and stared accusingly at Renard. The head of Dirigeable-Commercial sat back and spread his hands.

'Even I cannot foresee union problems in the United States, Villemur.'

'There is only one thing for it, the tests must be delayed until we can obtain an adequate supply of helium. Hydrogen is out of the question.'

'Sooner or later,' interposed Le Braz, 'we will be forced to use hydrogen as an alternative gas.'

'Nonsense!' returned Villemur. 'The public won't stand for it. It is going to be difficult enough to sell them the idea of safe airships in view of their history. But even the smallest child knows just how dangerous hydrogen can be. Why, every major incident connected with airships can be attributable to hydrogen gas.'

'The use of hydrogen in a passenger-carrying airship might well be ruled out by public opinion,' replied Le Braz excitedly. 'But there is no reason why it should not be made as safe as any other commonly accepted fuel, and successful experience with a freight-carrying airship would dispel such fears.'

Renard held up his hands like a priest bestowing a blessing.

'There seems a division of opinion among you men of science,' he said paternally. 'The problem is simple. At the moment we can inflate twenty per cent, one-fifth, of the gas cells with helium from the supply we already have. Now, as you know, and I am not an expert in such matters, the *Charles de Gaulle* was designed on the same lines as the *Hindenburg* and *Graf Zeppelin II*. That is, they were initially designed to carry hydrogen as well as helium for buoyancy. If I recall correctly, the hydrogen was contained in separate gas cells located entirely within the helium cells. So we could carry out this form of inflation with the *Charles de Gaulle*.'

Le Braz nodded eagerly.

'The perfect answer! Use the helium we have to encompass the hydrogen-filled cells. And we would still be in with a chance of competing with the *Albatross*!'

Renard suddenly stared hard at Villemur.

'Well, Villemur? Yours is the final decision as our chief designer. The entire project, and the economic solvency of this company, stands or falls by your decision.'

Villemur shuffled uncomfortably.

'I . . .' he coughed nervously. 'I have already said that I have my reservations. However, if we can ensure that all the hydrogen gas cells are surrounded by helium gas cells . . . well, I suppose. . . .'

'Excellent!' declared Renard. 'That is excellent. You agree, of course, Le Braz? Yes. And you, Barjonet? What do you say?'

Jacques Barjonet shrugged.

'I am not a scientist, m'sieur. I'm merely a glorified bus-driver. Give me the ship and I'll fly it.'

'Good. Very well, gentlemen, we shall start the inflation process the day after tomorrow.'

'We shall still be a long way behind the Americans,' Villemur complained.

Renard smiled.

'No; I have a plan that will put us in advance of them.'

'How?' demanded Le Braz.

'As soon as we have completed our inflation process, when the *Charles de Gaulle* lifts off on . . .' Renard glanced at his calendar, 'on next Monday, she will start her maiden voyage to New York. No preliminary testing. It will be done en route.'

There was complete silence. Villemur looked astounded while

Le Braz and Barjonet exchanged glances. Barjonet cleared his throat. Renard looked up.

'You have a problem?' he said softly.

'Not exactly,' he replied, 'but surely we will not be able to make that flight without more extensive tests of the ship under actual flight conditions and before we get a certificate of airworthiness?'

'That's right,' Villemur chimed in. 'It would not be legally possible.'

Renard smiled smugly.

'Gentlemen, you build the ship and fly it. Leave the legalities to me. That's my function. Of course we must get a certificate of airworthiness. Of course testing has to be done. But do not think I put forward ideas without background knowledge. There are no rules or regulations applicable to an airship which specify exactly where a test flight can take place, or the duration of that flight. It can be done on a trip across the Atlantic just as well as a trip up and down the Seine. Is that not so?'

He waited for a contradiction. When there was none, he continued.

'The maiden voyage of the *Charles de Gaulle* will start next Monday. We will not carry any fare-paying passengers or cargo. We will simply carry personnel, aviation officials and members of the press, at their own risk, for a test flight. I have already spoken with officials at the Ministry of Transport and they will be on board to chart the flight and results, and grant an airworthiness certificate to be effective on our entry into American airspace to comply with international law.'

'In that case,' Barjonet observed slowly, 'we will have to avoid flying over any part of the British Isles or any foreign airspace before reaching American airspace.'

'Captain Barjonet is quite correct,' Villemur supported him. 'No civil aircraft is allowed to fly over the United Kingdom unless it holds a certificate of airworthiness from its country of origin. It is part of the British Air Navigation Order of 1974.'

'Then we will do precisely what Captain Barjonet suggests,' smiled Renard. 'We will merely avoid British airspace.'

'It would be a safer route to fly across southern Britain and Ireland and then up to Greenland and Newfoundland. A straight trip avoiding those countries presents more hazards.'

'Are you saying that it is more dangerous?' demanded Renard.

'Not exactly,' admitted Barjonet. 'But making a sea crossing out of sight of land always has an element of risk.'

'If it is not dangerous then we have no problem,' Renard said with an air of finality.

Villemur did not look happy.

'But will our government allow the *Charles de Gaulle* to take off on such a flight without a certificate of airworthiness? France is a member state of the International Civil Aviation Organisation and has agreed to the international code. . . .'

'Crap!' Renard answered him crudely. 'I've already told you that I am handling that side of things.'

In fact, Renard had just spent an hour on the telephone with Brisset, the presidential aide, who was even now pulling every string in the government bureaucracy to ensure that the *Charles de Gaulle* could undertake its flight and beat the Americans. It was vital to enhance the prestige of France and its President, now facing a difficult election.

Chapter Eleven

The small band had just finished playing 'Hail to the Chief' when the tall, thickset figure of the President of the United States strode into the lounge of the *Albatross*. He had to squeeze through a huge crowd of reporters, television crew and selected Anglo-American officials and guests as he made his way towards the podium which had been placed at one end of the great cabin. There was a small burst of applause, respectful and deferential. When it had died down, the President coughed. He always coughed before beginning a speech. It was a gesture as widely known to the American television audiences as his nervous habit of brushing some imaginary loose hair away from his forehead.

The President made no preamble.

'I am deeply honoured to come here to Andrews Air Force Base today to witness with my own eyes a great achievement of American . . .' he paused and turned to smile winningly at the British ambassador who was standing next to John G. Badrick, 'and British technology; honoured to be able to glimpse a new and exciting future in the history of aviation, a future made possible by our two great countries. I am also proudly aware of the distinction I have in being allowed to officially name this great ship *Albatross*, a ship—so I am informed—that will be the first of many, the first of a grand fleet. And in so naming this ship, I am delighted to present to Mr. John G. Badrick, chairman of Pan Continental Airways and chief executive of Anglo-American Airships, a certificate of airworthiness for this most remarkable vessel.'

He turned, amidst renewed applause, towards an aide. A scroll was handed to him as Badrick moved forward to the podium. There were smiles. Handshakes. Loud congratulations. The band then struck up 'The Star-Spangled Banner' and followed it with 'Rule Britannia'. A few people mistakenly thought this was the British national anthem and tried to stand respectfully among the milling press men. Then the President took a step backwards to allow Badrick to address the gathering.

Badrick began with effusive thanks. The *Albatross* had completed the strict FAA and CAA testing requirements and had flown from Portland to Washington. Now the gigantic airship was ready to make her first Transatlantic flight and mark a new step forward in the history of aviation. The *Albatross* was, at this moment, about to take off for a short circular tour of Washington, and before he left to accompany the President on a tour of the airship, Badrick told the reporters that he wanted to say a few words about the ship.

Samantha Hackerman glanced at Harry Maclaren and raised her eyebrows. Badrick was deviating from the itinerary. The chairman of Pan Continental had agreed simply to thank the President and start the tour. She knew that Badrick liked to hear the sound of his own voice and was inclined to long boring speeches. Maclaren gave her a sympathetic look.

Badrick was smiling expansively at the reporters.

'We, in Anglo-American, are determined to develop a fleet of freight-carrying airships on the same design pattern as the *Albatross*. Our company believe that the *Albatross* has a promising role as a general cargo carrier in competition with conventional transport. As you gentlemen, beg pardon, ladies and gentlemen, know, most time-sensitive shipments are transported by aircraft for long distances and by truck for shorter distances. Let's examine costs. Current costs may run as high as twenty-five cents per ton mile and trucking costs at nine cents per ton mile. For slow bulk traffic we have railroads making a cost of two to three cents per ton mile and barge traffic at about one-point-five cents.'

The President's smile was still fixed but Samantha Hackerman saw him glance anxiously at his wristwatch.

'In terms of speed the *Albatross* is superior to surface modes of transport but inferior to aircraft. In terms of capacity, the *Albatross* is superior to trucks and aircraft but inferior to large trains, barge tows or ocean transport . . . at the moment, that is. I hope you will take note of that. Costs of transportation by airship will be less than aeroplanes but greater than trucking. Under current costs I'd say costs would be twelve cents per ton mile. At that price, with our speed factor, I would say that we will capture that portion of the current air freight market that is semi time-sensitive—traffic that must move faster than truck but does not have to travel at jet speeds; traffic that currently moves by aeroplane because there is no alternative.'

'That's all very well, Mr. Badrick,' a *Washington Post* reporter standing near the podium took Badrick's pause as an opportunity to interrupt. 'But don't you have to face the fact that the word "airship" has become a synonym with air disasters? Mention "airship" and everyone starts thinking of the blazing infernos of the R101 and the *Hindenburg* and all the other airship disasters.'

Samantha Hackerman inwardly groaned. The Presidential ceremony was going to get out of hand because Badrick had wanted to sound off; he was opening it up into a press conference. She glanced in desperation at Maclaren.

Badrick was floundering.

'Ah, a'hmm . . . well, it can't be denied that the *Hindenburg* disaster was an accident of major proportions for its time and for the state of the air industry of that time. I . . . er . . . I. . . .'

Badrick desperately caught Maclaren's eye.

Harry Maclaren sighed and moved forward.

'What Mr. Badrick is trying to say,' he gave a scornful glance at the Pan Continental chairman, 'is that it's our job to get you gentlemen of the press . . . ladies and gentlemen of the press . . . to put the matter in perspective for the public. What we have to impress on people are the facts. Nothing else. Between 1900 and 1937 the total casualties due to airship accidents were only 349—and that's about the same number that can die in one major airline accident today.'

Badrick wiped his brow and looked a little relieved.

'And now,' he forced his smile, 'I understand we are due for take-off so. . . .'

'What about the mad bomber tales that are going about?' It was an anonymous reporter from the back of the crowd. 'Is it true that someone has it in for Anglo-American? Are you expecting an attempt to destroy the *Albatross* on its Transatlantic flight?'

Before Badrick could answer, Harry Maclaren swung round angrily.

'Like many major companies we receive our share of threatening letters. It is also true that our company has sufferened a couple of tragic accidents resulting in the deaths of two of our key personnel. The matter is under police investigation. We can say no more at this stage.'

'Yeah, but you can say . . .' began another reporter.

'I'm sorry,' Maclaren snapped. 'That's as far as we can go at this stage. Now we are due to take off for the trip around Washington. Why don't you all relax now and enjoy the view from the observation windows?'

He turned and began to hustle Badrick, the British ambassador and the President out of the lounge, leaving Samantha Hackerman to deal with the questions now being shouted. Outside the lounge Badrick heaved a sigh of relief.

'We certainly don't want any scare-mongering publicity.'

'It shouldn't have developed into a press conference,' Maclaren said. There was a strong tone of rebuke in his voice which was not lost on Badrick.

'Don't you think you should have issued a denial instead of saying the matter was under police investigation?' he countered.

'No.' Maclaren was emphatic. 'Once a reporter has an idea for a story, unless you can positively contradict him, it's best to let sleeping dogs lie by not antagonising him.'

The President interrupted with his bad joke about the press which had now become a White House cliché.

'Not better to let lying dogs sleep, eh?'

Maclaren smiled politely.

'If you'll come this way, sir, we can start our tour of the ship.'

Garry Carson could scarcely restrain his enthusiasm.

'She is the sweetest thing I ever saw,' he exclaimed, as they manoeuvred five hundred feet above Andrews Air Force Base. 'This is exactly like flying the simulator. No problems.'

Tom Saxon glanced at him from the co-pilot's seat.

'You didn't expect her to handle in any other way, did you, skipper?' he said as he punched the computer controls for a course change to head them towards Suitland Heights. Saxon was feeling a little testy. He was confused and vaguely unhappy. He had not seen Helen Carson for several days; not since she had visited the morning after his last drunk. He had an overpowering urge to see her again but he lacked the courage to call her. He glanced at Carson out of the corner of his eye. The man never talked about his private life these days. He wondered whether Helen had moved out yet. Wondered whether Carson suspected that Helen and he had once had an affair. Wondered whether Carson realised that Helen had been in touch with him and still loved him. Saxon suddenly started. Yes, that was true. Helen had said it. She still loved him and he had only just realised what that meant. Damn it! He must speak with her.

'Tom!'

He looked up and saw that Carson was apparently waiting for an answer to a question.

'Sorry, skipper.'

'Didn't you notice the delay on the computer reaction?'

Saxon shook his head.

'I did,' interposed Danny Macmillan. 'I thought I was dreaming but I thought there was a sluggish response with our last course change.'

'We'd better try a sample course change and watch the readings,' suggested Carson.

They were at a thousand feet moving parallel to the Capital Beltway, the ring road which encircled Washington. Saxon fed a course change to the west, towards Capitol Heights, and switched on the timing response device.

'I make it a full second out, skipper,' he said, checking the figure.

Carson bit his lip.

'Once more,' he said. 'Try switching back to the original course.'

Saxon did so.

'Yes; a full second out.'

'Okay, okay,' muttered Carson. 'Try the course change on the second computer channel.'

Again Saxon punched the figures in. This time the response was immediate.

'Secondary channel working fine, skipper.'

'Right,' there was relief in Carson's voice. 'Switch to secondary channels. Danny, will you go and find Van Kleef and, if he is with anyone, diplomatically tell him we have a problem and its nature.'

'Sure, skipper.'

Badrick was sitting with a worried expression in Maclaren's stateroom. Both men had taken the opportunity for a private conference while the President and British ambassador were being conducted to the upper observation lounge by Samantha Hackerman. The worried expression sat on Badrick's face like a wreath at a funeral.

'So what's the score, Harry?' he grunted moodily. 'How is Terrasino making out on this sabotage business?'

'The last forty-eight hours the *Albatross* has been wrapped up tighter than a drum. Christ, what with Terrasino's men, the FBI and the President's secret service men, there is absolutely no way anything can happen to the *Albatross*. You can't go to the john without a couple of security men sharing the can with you.'

'But we still haven't caught this maniac?'

'Terrasino is giving us as good a security coverage as he can manage,' replied Maclaren.

Badrick pulled out a Corona-Corona and lit up.

'Sure, I know that Terrasino is a sound man. Incidentally, how's Art Stein and the back-up crew shaping?'

'They'll be ready for the Transatlantic flight.'

'Excellent. I am going to authorise the commencement of training for three more crews on the strength of the initial reports. And, just between ourselves, once the Transatlantic trip is out of the way the board is going to authorise the building of two more freight airships.'

Maclaren smiled broadly.

'That's good news. But it's early days. We must walk before we can run.'

Badrick waved his cigar.

'Yeah, I know. I'd be a damned sight more happier if we could nail this mad bomber.'

Maclaren shot Badrick a vindictive glance.

'Well, so far the press haven't latched onto the entire story. But the reports which have managed to leak out have been harmful enough.'

'Well, let's hope Terrasino can nail this creep soon.'

Oscar Van Kleef looked up from his instruments and gazed at Danny Macmillan with a thoughtful expression.

'There is a slight power surge on the primary computer circuit, nothing positive but enough to throw out the timing by . . .' he glanced at his gauge '. . . point eight nine of a second. My guess is there's an exposed wire touching somewhere.'

He turned and began stripping off the casing of the primary computer circuits. Macmillan helped him.

'You reckon the electricians haven't wired up properly?' he asked.

'Could be, but the delay would have showed up before now,' mused Van Kleef.

It was Macmillan who saw it first. A tool-precisioned piece of piping which was almost an exact replica of the one Kurt Nieman had discovered. It was six inches long and an inch in diameter with a timing device, circuits and battery. A wire from the battery was attached to the power supply for the primary computer terminal. Van Kleef stared at it with disbelief on his face.

Macmillan reached for the inter-ship telephone and told Carson.

'Don't touch anything, Danny,' snapped Carson. 'I'm on my way down and I'll get hold of Terrasino and that FBI man —Hayes.'

Macmillan and Van Kleef didn't have long to wait before Carson came in and took a brief look at the device.

'How is it wired to ignite?' he demanded.

Van Kleef shrugged.

'I don't know. So far as I can see, it isn't.'

'What do you mean?' Carson snapped. 'I can see one wire from the battery twisted onto the computer terminal.'

'Right, and the juice from the battery is what is creating the slight power surge to the computer and throwing it out of timing,' replied Van Kleef. 'But I can't see how any juice is getting to the timing mechanism to ignite the bomb.'

Carson was considering the problem when Terrasino and Hayes joined them. Both men looked pale and worried.

It was Terrasino who confirmed Van Kleef's theory that the bomb was not armed. He untwisted the wire connected to the computer terminal and withdrew the device. Underneath was a note. It was written on plain white typing paper with the characters printed in black ink, neat and very precise.

'Understand,' it read, 'that I can destroy the *Albatross* at a time of my own choosing. Only my intense patriotism forbids me to destroy it while the President is on board. I could do so. I will not. You have already forced me to destroy human life. I did not want to do so but you have ignored my previous warnings. Ignore this, my final warning, at your peril. The *Albatross* will be destroyed unless you give up this blasphemous project. Max Prüss.'

Terrasino whistled slowly.

'I'd better see what we can do about prints. Not that I expect he's left any,' Hayes said morosely, taking out a plastic bag to deposit both device and note in.

Van Kleef was staring accusingly at Terrasino.

'How can this happen? You are supposed to be chief of

security, yet this mad bomber is running rings round you? How can he plant a device like this when you are supposed to be saturating this ship with security?'

Terrasino gazed evenly at the outraged chief designer.

'Because the mad bomber is not only very clever but he is highly placed in Anglo-American . . . he is one of us.'

Van Kleef's jaw dropped as he stared at Terrasino in astonishment.

Carson was also staring at Terrasino in surprise.

'Doesn't that make it easier to nail him?' he said after a pause.

'Don't worry,' replied the security chief slowly, still gazing at Van Kleef. 'We'll nail him soon.'

The inter-ship telephone buzzed and Carson picked it up.

It was Tom Saxon.

'We are turning south over Silver Spring, skipper. I thought you'd want to know.'

'Okay, Tom. Will you carry out a check on the primary circuit now? It should be clear.'

'Roger, skipper.'

Carson replaced the telephone and looked thoughtfully at Terrasino.

'If this madman had triggered that bomb . . .' he said slowly.

'Thank God he only meant it as a warning,' interposed Macmillan.

Terrasino nodded and plucked at his lip.

'Yeah; but as he says, it is the final warning. We've got to find the bastard quickly . . . and we will.'

Chapter Twelve

Janine Renard turned over in bed to face Jacques Barjonet.

'Why do you work for my husband?' she asked.

Barjonet blinked his eyes, yawned and smiled sleepily.

'Why do you live with him?' he countered.

He grunted as she gave him a light punch on the shoulder.

'Don't answer a question with a question,' she admonished.

Barjonet reached towards the bedside table for a cigarette and lit up. He and Janine had been spending the night in his cottage just outside Carentan on the flat Cotentin Peninsula. The cottage had belonged to his parents, a refuge during the holidays for the family had lived in Paris. Now his parents were both dead and Barjonet had made the cottage his home, travelling down to St. Lô each day by car. He propped himself up against the pillows and exhaled.

'Why do I work for Renard?' he mused aloud. 'Because, at the moment, he is the only person who can offer me what I want.'

'What do you mean, Jacques?' frowned Janine, nestling into the crook of his arm.

'I've dreamt of piloting an airship ever since I was a kid,' Barjonet replied. 'Flying machines is alright but flying an airship . . . that's something different. That's why I go hot air ballooning most weekends, *ma biche*. It gives me a tremendous sense of freedom, that freedom of floating free in the air, not having to rely on speed and machinery to keep you airborne.'

She smiled at his enthusiasm.

'I know exactly what you mean, darling. Last weekend, when we went gliding, it was fantastic. I haven't enjoyed myself so much in years.'

Barjonet turned an abruptly serious face to her.

'But once this Transatlantic flight is over, I shall be resigning from the project, *ma biche*.'

'Why?' she asked in astonishment.

'Because I have found something I want even more than being captain of an airship.'

She could not pretend to misunderstand.

'Sooner or later your husband will find out about us,' went on Barjonet. 'I will save him the trouble of getting rid of me.'

'What makes you so sure that he will find out about us?' demanded Janine.

'Because, *ma biche*, I am in love with you. I do not want you to be simply my mistress. I want you to be my wife.'

Janine stared hard at him.

'You are not joking, Jacques? You mean it?'

'I am very serious.'

She gave a half-sob, half-laugh and reached up to hug him.

'You will leave Renard?' He spoke quietly. 'You will ask for a divorce?'

She nodded eagerly.

'When?' he demanded.

She pursed her lips in thought.

'I shall not tell him face to face,' she said, after consideration. 'You don't know what he's like, Jacques . . . how ill-tempered and nasty he can become.'

Barjonet smiled.

'I work for him, Janine. I know.'

'Well, I shall wait until he is away and then I shall simply pack my bags and leave. I'll get my father to tell him. He won't dare try to intimidate my father. I shall go down to my villa at Fréjus and when you come back from America you can join me there until we decide what to do. I think we need to be away from Normandy and Charles until things are sorted out.'

'Won't Charles follow you to Fréjus?'

'The villa there is mine. My father gave it to me. It is nothing to do with Charles. I shall make sure my father warns him not to come near me.'

Barjonet nodded.

'You think he will be unpleasant?'

'Perhaps; he can be very nasty at times, especially when his plans are thwarted. But if I tell my father everything he will make sure Charles does not trouble us. Charles is scared of my father.'

'Renard is a snob. He has dropped several hints about the high position your father has in the government and how well-connected he is.'

'Charles is certainly a social climber,' agreed Janine. It was the first time she had ever voiced her real opinions about her husband. 'I didn't realise how much he was using me until after our marriage.'

'Why did you marry him?'

She frowned.

'I suppose because he was attractive, because he was so different from everyone I knew, because he was full of ambition and promised an exciting life.'

A silence suddenly fell between them.

'What will you do when you leave the airship project? Aviation is your whole life.'

Barjonet lit another cigarette.

'It will be enough that I have captained the *Charles de Gaulle* on its first major flight. After that . . . well, there will be other airship companies. Once people recognise that airships are the transport of the future, there will be others who will start developing and building dirigibles. They will need experienced pilots.'

'You say that the first flight of the *Charles de Gaulle* will be next Monday?'

Barjonet nodded.

'Renard has let it be known to a few of us that when the airship takes off, he plans to make the Transatlantic run. He hopes to steal a march on the Americans.'

Janine was surprised.

'You mean Charles plans to fly straight to New York without any preliminary test flights?'

'So Renard has not spoken to you about this?' asked Barjonet. Janine shook her head, and he sighed. 'Renard is a little crazy, a little ruthless, but he might succeed in giving the *Charles de Gaulle* a place in history.'

'Won't it be dangerous?' she asked.

'Dangerous?' he smiled broadly. 'No more dangerous than doing a series of short-distance test flights.'

Janine sighed.

'I suppose Renard has a flair for these things. It will be an important achievement for him to beat the Americans.'

'And for me to be captain of the airship that does so.'

Janine suddenly sat upright.

'The flight of the *Charles de Gaulle* will be the beginning,' she said solemnly.

'Eh?' frowned Barjonet.

'When Charles sets off on the flight then that will be the time I shall choose to leave him. So, my darling, when you return from America you will find me in Fréjus . . . and we can start our new life together.'

Barjonet chuckled.

'What is it?' demanded Janine.

'I should be grateful to Renard. He has provided me with the two things I wanted most in my life . . . the captaincy of an airship and the woman I love.'

Janine reached across and kissed him.

'Let's make the most of our time, darling. Charles will be in Paris until this evening. He's at some aviation conference there.'

Garry Carson was whistling a tune as he turned his Cord along by Edward Paysons Park and braked before his house. He was feeling particularly pleased with the performance of the *Albatross*. He let himself into the house and stopped short. There were half a dozen suitcases in the hallway. He was looking at them when Helen came to the door of the lounge. She had her coat on.

'Hello, Garry.'

Her voice was quiet. Only her hands twisting over her bag betrayed the tenseness in her body.

Carson said nothing. He sensed what was coming.

'I was waiting until you came back before I left . . .' she began. 'I . . . I am leaving you, Garry.' Her words suddenly erupted in a torrent. 'I have to leave you. The marriage hasn't worked out. It never worked out. We tried for too long, ignoring the problems. Now we both have to make fresh starts. I . . . well, I'm going to stay with some friends. After a while, when things are more settled, when we can see things in perspective, we can meet . . . talk about a divorce. . . .'

Carson said nothing. He just stood staring at her.

Strangely enough, he realised, he was not surprised. He had been half-expecting Helen to make some move like this for at least a couple of months. The tension had been growing almost unbearable.

'Well, say something,' Helen said nervously. His face was an expressionless mask.

'What do you want me to say?' he finally replied. 'What is there to say?'

'Garry, we've known each other a long time; too long not to feel emotional now it's over. We were good friends once. Our mistake was getting married. It *was* a mistake, a bad mistake. But can't we remain friends still?'

There was a pleading note in her voice.

Carson saw it as a sign of weakness. He felt a cold, bitter anger surge through him.

'No, Helen. You want me to make things easy for you. That's not my style. I loved you. We had good times together. I'm not just going to say "goodbye and good luck" and leave it like that.'

'Garry, there's nothing you can do. It's foolish to think there is.'

'Maybe so. Maybe not. I guess you've been playing around with someone behind my back. Well, you'd better pray that I don't find out who the bastard is.'

He turned abruptly and went out, slamming the door.

Helen stared after him for a while, her lips trembling. She did not really want it to end this way, with bitterness and hostility. Yet, perhaps, it was inevitable. She had her own survival, her own happiness, to consider. Slowly, she began to carry her cases out to her car.

The reception for those attending the International Aeronautical Association's Technical Symposium on Airship Travel was in full swing in the Hôtel Central des Écoles. To call it a reception, however, was rather ridiculous, thought Sir Ashley Ashton as he peered around the crowded room. The Symposium was over and this was really the final party for those who had survived the four days of boringly predictable papers on various aspects of airships, from the economic problems of running freight airships to their technical construction. Now the grey-bearded professors, earnest would-be designers, aviation company directors and aviation enthusiasts were gathering to swap gossip and get drunk. It was always the way, year after year. Ashton wondered why he bothered to attend—he always did. It was a tax write-off and a good excuse to spend a weekend in Paris visiting his favourite restaurants and picking up the latest aviation gossip. It was an important way of finding out what was going on in the world of aeronautical design.

This time he had not picked up much. He had seen Doctor Villemur briefly and Charles Renard had attended one session, but there had not been any way of pumping them about the progress of Dirigeable-Commercial. Still, judging from what the aerospace correspondents were saying, the *Albatross* was far in advance of the *Charles de Gaulle*, which had not even made its first test flight yet.

By coincidence Charles Renard entered the room at that moment and weaved his way unsteadily to a waiter, lifting a glass of champagne off his tray. It was obvious that he had been drinking already and the young girl with him was tugging at his sleeve and seemed to be trying to persuade him to leave, gesturing towards the door. Ashton frowned. Rumour had it that she was Renard's mistress. Renard shook off her hand angrily. As he did so he caught Ashton's eye. The Englishman was about to turn away when Renard hailed him.

'Hello, Ashton! And how is my rival, eh?'

Ashton assumed a mask of tolerant diffidence.

'Good evening, Renard . . . Ma'mselle.' Ashton bowed slightly to the embarrassed-looking girl.

Renard reached forward and patted his arm.

'So when is the *Albatross* going to make its maiden flight across the Atlantic?'

Ashton arched an eyebrow.

'It was announced in the newspapers yesterday, Renard. Next Thursday.'

Renard gave a little giggle.

'Well, I'll make a bet with you, eh? I'll bet you that my *Charles de Gaulle* will make the Atlantic run before the *Albatross*, eh?'

Ashton showed no expression.

'Really, Renard?'

'Really, Ashton,' smiled Renard. He turned and reached for another drink, ignoring Tanya's protest.

'If you will excuse me, Renard . . .' Ashton was backing away.

'No,' Renard snapped. 'You at Anglo-American think that you are in advance of me. Well, I'd like to let you into my little secret. . . .' He giggled again. Tanya looked at Ashton and made an apologetic grimace. Renard ignored her.

'How would you like a little trip to New York at the expense of Dirigeable-Commercial, Ashton? How would you like to fly on the maiden flight of the *Charles de Gaulle*?'

Ashton suddenly realised that Renard was deadly serious.

He smiled, coldly polite.

'That's very kind of you, Renard. It would be a most interesting trip. But I understand you have not yet started on your test flights. Perhaps you will let me know when. . . .'

Renard jabbed him in the chest with a finger.

'When? I'll tell you when. The *Charles de Gaulle* will take off at seven o'clock on Monday, that's when. Be at St. Lô at three o'clock.'

Ashton looked at Renard curiously.

'You are seriously telling me that the *Charles de Gaulle* is ready to make a Transatlantic flight?'

Renard nodded with a smug smile.

'You are going on Monday?' Ashton asked.

Renard poked Ashton in the ribs.

'You thought we were held up with our supplies of helium gas, eh? Oh, I know you have your informers. Well, you're wrong. We are going to beat your *Albatross* across the Atlantic. Monday. Be at St. Lô at three o'clock and I'll reserve you a stateroom on the *Charles de Gaulle*.'

Ashton made a lightning decision.

'Very well, Renard. I'll be there.'

Renard grinned and then allowed Tanya to guide him unsteadily away. For a few moments Ashton did not move from the spot. Then he shook himself and, with a muttered apology to one of the reception's organisers, he went out into the hotel lobby and found a phone booth.

'Get me a person-to-person call—John G. Badrick, chairman of Pan Continental Airways in New York City.'

Helen Carson and Maria Terrasino were sitting in Maria's kitchen having coffee. Maria was studying Helen with some surprise.

'It's strange,' she was saying, 'but Terry and I always thought you and Garry had a good marriage.'

Helen shrugged ruefully.

'Well, that's the situation, Maria. I'm sorry to inflict it on you. I know I have a nerve but I couldn't really think of the next step.'

'Well of course you can stay with us for a few weeks, Helen,' she replied warmly. 'Stay as long as you like while you sort things out.'

'Thanks a million, Maria. I guess my first job will be to start searching for an apartment and then a job.'

Maria was pouring more coffee.

'Do you want me to keep things from Terry?'

Terrasino was out at the project site.

'That's hardly possible,' smiled Helen.

'I don't mean about your leaving Garry. I meant what you said about Tom Saxon.'

'Oh,' Helen hesitated. Then: 'Well, it might be best that he doesn't know. You see, my leaving Garry has absolutely nothing to do with my feelings for Tom. Perhaps Tom and I will never ever get it together. That's a million years in the future. Tom has to sort his own life out first.'

Maria nodded.

'I know that Terry doesn't really like your Tom Saxon,' she said.

'Oh?' Helen was suddenly defensive.

'He calls him a *beone*.'

'A what?'

'A drunk, how you say in America, a lush?'

'Tom has a problem,' admitted Helen, 'but I hope he will be able to overcome it.'

'Sure,' agreed Maria. 'It's understandable, how you told me. I feel sympathy, eh?'

Helen was still defensive.

'Tom doesn't need sympathy—he basically needs to be shocked out of his guilt and self-pity, that's all.'

'Sure he does. Tell me, Helen, do you really love him? Is he worth what you are doing for him?'

Helen shook her head.

'What I am doing, Maria, is firstly for myself. I'm not leaving Garry for Tom. I'm leaving Garry because it is wrong that I should be with Garry. But as to your first question—yes, I love Tom. Very, very much. But things can't happen between us until he has worked out his own problems. I'm a little older and maturer than I used to be, Maria. I'm not going to run from one goddam mess into another.'

Maria smiled sympathetically and reached forward to press Helen's arm.

'I pray you do the right thing, Helen.'

Chapter Thirteen

When the call came from John G. Badrick, Harry Maclaren was still in his office on the project site, trying to catch up on the paperwork before the weekend. He listened in astonishment as the chairman of Pan Continental outlined his telephone conversation with Sir Ashley Ashton.

'So Ashton is accepting Renard's offer?'

'Yes,' replied Badrick. 'In one way it will be the perfect opportunity for one of our men to study the *Charles de Gaulle* and its potential at first hand.'

The project manager whistled soundlessly.

'Well, this certainly puts the French in advance of us by four days.'

There was a pause.

'Not necessarily. Harry . . . I want the *Albatross* ready to take off a day in advance of the *Charles de Gaulle*. I don't want Renard using his cowboy tactics to beat us.'

Maclaren exploded in protest.

'Take off for the Transatlantic run on Sunday? There is absolutely no way that we can do that. Fuelling, maintenance checks, victualling . . . even rushing it we will need at least forty-eight hours. No, the way our schedule is arranged, Thursday is the day.'

'To hell with the schedule!' Badrick retorted angrily. 'This isn't a request, this is an order. I can make it a board decision within the hour.' His voice became calmer. 'Look, Harry, I appreciate your problems. Okay. You say you need a minimum forty-eight hours? Right. You have it. The *Albatross* must be scheduled to take off at one o'clock Monday afternoon. That will make us level pegging with the *Charles de Gaulle*. If Renard wants to play race games, we will damn well give him a race to remember.'

'Why one o'clock?'

'Because the *Charles de Gaulle* will take off at seven o'clock French time . . . that's one o'clock our time.'

'What about the state of readiness of our people in England? Can their airfield be prepared for the arrival of the *Albatross* in time? And what about Air Traffic Control clearance?'

'You concentrate on getting the *Albatross* ready and I'll concentrate on those details,' Badrick assured him.

'Well, frankly, I don't like the idea of getting involved in some goddam publicity race.' There was still annoyance in Maclaren's voice.

'Nor more do I, Harry,' Badrick's voice oozed charm. 'But Renard has thrown down the gauntlet. We'd cut our own commercial throat if we let him get away with it. Don't forget what is involved with making that first Transatlantic crossing.'

'I know. I am also thinking of our mad bomber.'

'Terrasino and his men will have to make sure maximum security is given to the preparations.'

It was obvious that Badrick had made up his mind and had the backing of the board. Maclaren sighed deeply.

'You're the boss.'

'Right,' acknowledged Badrick. 'Now let's get the show on the road, Harry. We go with just a selected group of press and VIPs on board. No cargo.'

'The press we can arrange,' muttered Maclaren. 'Samantha Hackerman will have to start work briefing them on the new date, but you can't start mucking about with VIPs' schedules.'

'Leave that to me. There's some British government official over here visiting our Secretary for Air. I know the Secretary very well. I might be able to persuade them to take a little trip. Leave it to me.'

Maclaren hung up and sat gazing down at the telephone for a while.

'Sonofabitch!' he breathed at last. 'Forty-eight hours!'

FBI agent Hayes, accompanied by the FAA investigator Vambrace, entered Terrasino's office and exchanged greetings with the harassed-looking security chief.

'What brings you by so late in the evening?' demanded Terrasino, glancing at his wall clock.

Vambrace eased himself into the only spare chair while Hayes perched on the deck and lit up a Lucky Strike. Terrasino sat back and watched him quizzically.

'Just to report a big fat zero,' sat Hayes, exhaling smoke.

'How's that?'

'The device we took off the *Albatross* at Washington. No prints. No traceable components.'

'And,' added Vambrace, 'we've come to the end of the computer checks with the name Max Prüss. No connections with any members of the project staff. We tried to trace all known descendants and relatives of Prüss. Negative. We might know who Max Prüss was but that does not solve our problem in connecting him with the mad bomber.'

Terrasino sighed and reached for the coffee percolator.

'I didn't really think our man would give himself away quite so easily,' he said. 'An immediate connection with Max Prüss would be too much of a miracle. Your forensic guys have been able to come to no conclusion on the explosive devices?'

Hayes shook his head.

'I reckon our Max Prüss is playing with us,' said Vambrace.

'Well, playing or not . . . I've just had Maclaren, my boss, on the phone. The *Albatross* is scheduled to make its first Transatlantic flight in forty-eight hours. I reckon that if Max Prüss hasn't been caught by then, he is really going to pull the plug on the *Albatross* and perhaps a hundred lives along with it.'

Hayes let out a low whistle while Vambrace's eyebrows shot up.

'Can't the flight be delayed?' he asked.

Terrasino shook his head.

Hayes drew deeply on his cigarette.

'Well, I have a whole section working round the clock. We've interviewed the members of the project site twice on average and each time . . . zero!'

Terrasino swore abruptly.

'I bet our mad bomber is laughing up his sleeve at us . . . wherever he is.'

Jules Keller had difficulty being put through. Finally Renard's voice answered. Keller thought his speech sounded slurred, and wondered whether it was some distortion of the Transatlantic telephone cable. Keller did not identify himself.

'Anglo-American know about the flight of your ship,' he said tersely. 'They have scheduled their own ship to take off within forty-eight hours. They plan to give you a race.'

There was a long pause. Then:

'Listen carefully, my friend,' said Renard. 'I want Anglo-

American delayed by at least twenty-four hours. Do you understand?'

Keller was silent.

'Are you there?' asked Renard.

'Yeah,' Keller acknowledged. 'It will cost you.'

'I had no doubt it would. How much?'

'One hundred thousand dollars.'

'That's very high.'

'So are the risks. It's very dangerous now. Police and security activity on the project is pretty frenzied after the killing of Jack Lane.'

'Very well. It will be paid into the account in Geneva.'

'I want a cable of confirmation from the bank before I act.'

'You will have it.'

Keller replaced the telephone receiver and went to the window of his apartment to stare thoughtfully out on the city. Delay the *Albatross* twenty-four hours. That was going to be a tall order. He took out a wooden toothpick and absently began to pick his teeth. Twenty-four hours delay. It was risky. But he needed that money badly.

Danny Macmillan had enjoyed the last two weeks in the company of Claire Ashton, enjoyed them as he had never enjoyed a relationship with a woman before. Who was it who had said that friendship was a contract in which people rendered small services in expectation of big ones? That was nonsense. His friendship with Claire had developed without any end or obligation in sight and without the slightest inclination for a physical consummation of that friendship. He had nursed her over the first twenty-four-hour period after her overdose and, being young and physically healthy, she had recovered quickly. Even Anglo-American did not know the cause of her two days away from the office. Just a flu bug, Claire had explained to Samantha Hackerman.

When Claire felt up to it, Danny embarked on a series of trips to the beaches and picnics to Bradbury Mountain, Wolf Neck State Park, Scarborough Marsh Nature Centre and Crescent Beach. Evenings were fully booked too, spent in the Lyric Theatre, the Portland Stage, or the City Hall Auditorium to listen to the Portland Symphony Orchestra. Claire was not given a chance to be alone and dwell on her problem.

Danny had come to know a great deal about Claire and to suspect a great deal more. There were certain areas of her past, experiences that were pertinent to her behaviour, that she would never dwell on. He knew that she disliked her father, Sir Ashley, that he was a remote, cold man and that Claire was a very emotional and warm girl who was starved of a father's natural love. In her search for the affection of older men, father figures, she had had bad experiences and had grown cynical about all men and their motivations.

Macmillan realised at the end of the second week that he was falling in love with Claire; it was a slow realisation. He tried to suppress it, but he had to admit it eventually. Even so, he knew that he must hide it from Claire. Claire needed more than anything a simple and ordinary friendship. She had had lovers before but never friends. She needed someone who was concerned for her but wanted nothing in exchange, someone who made no demands on her. Macmillan's amateur pyschology was right. All the support and concern that Claire had never received from her father when she was a child, or from the men who had used her for their own ends, came as a surprise to her when supplied by Danny. She had never experienced the pleasure of being taken out for her own sake. Gradually she became used to unwinding and not waiting for her companion to make the inevitable suggestion or merely to grab her at the earliest opportunity. For the first time she found herself feeling loose and relaxed, enjoying life.

Late that Friday evening they returned to Claire's apartment after a concert of the Portland String Orchestra at the Phyllis Thaxter Theatre in South Portland. Claire offered him a coffee.

'Yeah,' smiled Macmillan, 'but I can't be late. I have some flying training schedules to go over with Carson tomorrow.'

As Claire went into the kitchenette the telephone rang.

'See who it is, Danny,' the girl called.

It was Maclaren. He was surprised at finding Macmillan at Claire Ashton's apartment. He didn't think that Macmillan was the type to . . . well, from what he had heard Claire Ashton had been behaving herself during the last two weeks. That had been one worry less.

'I did want Claire,' he explained, 'but I'm glad I caught you, Danny. Has Carson been in touch with you during the last hour or so?'

'No,' Macmillan was puzzled. 'We've only just come back from a concert. What's up?'

Maclaren told him. Macmillan was unable to suppress his astonishment.

'We've all got to hustle this weekend, Danny, so I'll see you at the project site early. Can you tell Claire what's in the wind? Samantha Hackerman is going to go mad tomorrow with the extra work reorganising press schedules and so forth. Claire will be needed in the office all weekend, I'm afraid. Also, she will have to accompany Samantha on the trip to wipe the noses of the press people and generally look after them. Okay?'

Macmillan put the telephone down in a daze.

'What was that all about, Danny?' demanded Claire, bringing in the coffee.

He told her.

'Oh Lord!' she groaned. 'I don't know how I'll cope.'

'You'll cope fine,' grinned Macmillan. 'Sam's a real pro, she'll not put too much on you.'

'Yes, but I mean, flying on the *Albatross* across the Atlantic. . . .'

Macmillan laughed.

'Jesus, don't make it sound like a death sentence, Claire. Remember, I'm the chief engineer on the trip.'

The girl grinned.

'I suppose it is rather exciting, isn't it?'

'Yeah; it was exciting enough as it was, but trust Badrick to throw in a little extra drama. One would think we were back in the 1920s and 1930s racing against rival companies.'

'Well, I can see how important it is to be the first to make the crossing and prove airships are safe and economically viable.'

Macmillan sipped his coffee.

'I guess you've been reading Samantha's press handouts.'

She pouted.

'I've been writing them,' she replied. Then: 'It will be nice to see England again. How long do you think the *Albatross* will be there? I mean, we won't just fly there and then fly back like an aeroplane, will we?'

'No,' Macmillan shook his head. 'According to the schedules we drew up originally, we should be there seven days because there'll be a lot of checking out to be made after the flight.'

'Seven days,' breathed Claire. 'Where will we be—Heathrow? London Airport?'

'No, some place called Cranfield, a little aerodrome just north of London.'

'Will you and I be able to have a few days off?'

Macmillan smiled.

'I suppose so, why do you ask?'

'I'd like to show you some of England, Danny—especially Kent where I grew up.'

'I'd like that a lot, Claire.'

The girl suddenly reached forward impulsively and caught one of his hands in hers.

'Danny, did you ever read Nietzsche?'

He looked at her in surprise.

'Nietzsche? No, I can't say I have.'

'He once wrote that women can form a friendship with a man very well; but to preserve it a slight physical antipathy would help.'

She paused and gazed directly into his eyes.

'Well, Danny, I want you to know that I don't feel any physical antipathy towards you.'

Macmillan stirred uncomfortably.

'Claire, I value our friendship very much. I don't want to destroy it.'

'If our friendship ends, it can never have started.'

'Claire. . . .'

She moved forward towards him.

'Kiss me, Danny . . . please.'

Conflicting emotions racing through his mind, Macmillan reached forward. The girl's mouth was soft and warm and opened hungrily under his.

For the second time in an hour Samantha Hackerman woke up wondering what had disturbed her. The first time it had been the telephone and Jules Keller had answered it. His conversation had been short and monosyllabic. Now the bed beside her was empty. She squinted into the darkness and then reached out for the bedside lamp and switched it on.

Jules Keller was dressing in the darkness.

'Where are you going?' she demanded in a grumpy voice, still sleepy and annoyed at being disturbed. 'Don't you realize I have to be in the office at eight o'clock? Hell!' She peered at the bedside clock. 'It's two-thirty in the morning!'

Keller grinned apologetically.

'I was hoping I would get back before you woke. I didn't mean to disturb you.'

'Where in hell are you going?'

'I have some work to do down at the project site.'

She frowned.

'At this hour?'

'Yeah; it's important. I had these series of equations to work out for Van Kleef and it went clear out of my head until. . . .'

'Was that Van Kleef on the telephone earlier?'

Keller hesitated. It had been the Transatlantic Cable Service with an important cable from Geneva.

'That's right, Sam,' he smiled.

'Damn!'

Samantha Hackerman turned over and snapped off the light.

Chapter Fourteen

Tom Saxon came out of the shower, grabbed a bathrobe and sauntered to the television. He pressed the channel finder until he came up with an all-night programme of old movies. Tense and irritable, he did not feel at all like sleep. The shower had not relaxed him. He needed a drink. He was about to telephone room service when he changed his mind. Maybe not. He had not exactly reached the stage when he was consciously a *kamikaze*. Still, one drink wouldn't notice, would it? Then one drink would lead to another and another and. . . . Oh hell! What did it matter, anyway? Again he hesitated as he reached towards the telephone. He knew Carson was watching him and that Maclaren was suspicious. Not that he cared about them but he'd better not foul up at this time. If he was booted out of Anglo-American that would put an end to his flying career . . . career such as it was. It had to come sooner or later. He couldn't stand the strain. Better to hang on as long as he could, though. This time he picked up the telephone and when room service answered he ordered a pot of black coffee and some alka-seltzer.

As he put the telephone receiver down, he was startled by its immediate ring. With a frown he picked it up. To his astonishment Helen greeted him.

'I'm glad you're not asleep, Tom,' she said. 'I'm down in the lobby. I was, er, passing by. I want to see you before you go.'

He hesitated.

'Do you want to come up?'

'Yes. If that's alright with you.'

'See you in a minute.'

A moment later the door buzzer whined. Helen stood there, her face a little tense, but she forced a quick, nervous smile.

'Hi, Tom.'

He swung the door open.

'Are you coming in?' he asked as she made no movement.

'For a moment,' she said hesitantly. She brushed by him and he caught the fragrance of her perfume—a musky smell. 'Opium' by Yves St. Laurent. Strange how he could remember. He closed the door and motioned her to take a seat.

'I've left Garry and moved in with the Terrasinos for the time being,' she said.

'I heard.'

The doorbell buzzed again. It was room service with the coffee and seltzer. Saxon mixed the concoction and threw it back, feeling sick. He reached for the coffee pot.

'May I have a cup?'

He poured it for her while she loosened her outdoor coat but did not remove it. When he placed the cup before her she made no move to touch it.

'Tom,' she said, after what seemed a long, uncomfortable pause, 'what I've come to tell you is that I've started to make a few decisions.'

'Oh?' He felt a little helpless, as if he had to flow with a situation over which he had no control.

She nodded.

'The first decision was leaving Garry. I told you before that it had absolutely nothing to do with us. What has happened between us merely threw my problem into a sharper relief.'

He made no comment.

'Garry and I were good friends once,' she went on, 'and we had some fun together. But there was nothing more in our relationship than friendship. For many people it would have been the basis for a good marriage. For me, it was not enough. I didn't really understand that until I met you in England. Then came all the drama. . . .'

Saxon stirred uncomfortably, waiting for her to refer to Jan and Tom Junior. She didn't.

'Even though we split up, even though we didn't make it together . . . well, I should have left Garry then, a couple of years ago. But I was a coward. It takes a lot of nerve to alter your lifestyle suddenly and drastically. I was emotionally exhausted when our relationship came to an end. So I decided on an easy option. I stayed with Garry. I tried to pretend that everything was alright with us. I tried to bury my head in the sand. But you can't go on living a lie all your life. Something had to give. Our relationship was almost split up when you arrived, only I still had not built up enough courage to make the important step.'

Saxon raised his eyes to hers.

'Now you have? For good?'

'Yes. Your coming put a lot of things into a clearer perspective for me.'

'Does Garry know about us?'

She shook her head.

'What do you want from me, Helen?' Saxon asked quietly. 'I'm pretty loused up, you know.'

'I know.' There was sympathy in her voice.

'Well?' he prompted, after waiting for a reply.

'I said that your coming had put things in a clearer perspective for me. By that I don't mean that I see you as an avenue of escape. No, it's the reverse.'

'What do you mean by that?' He was puzzled.

'I mean that I am not leaving Garry simply because I think I have a better deal going with you. To leave Garry for you would be no solution. But what I am saying is that I love you, Tom. I would like to make a life with you. However . . . I can't.'

He stirred uncomfortably.

'You have problems and I have problems,' she continued. 'We need time to sort them out. I'm going to work on mine. At the same time, though, I want you to know that I love you and that I think that we could possibly have a future together. . . .'

'If?' It was Saxon who conjured the word.

'If you can lay the ghosts which are haunting you, Tom. It can only be when you've stepped off the elevator that's carrying you down into the pits. You don't really want to spend the rest of your days as a lush . . . but that's where you're headed.'

He could summon no reaction to her words. He felt mentally drained. Deep inside him, Tom Saxon—the old Tom Saxon—agreed with her, agreed with her every word. Yet he found himself wondering whether he really cared.

'What I am saying, Tom, is that if and when you've laid the spectres of your past, when you've stepped off the liquor merrygoround, I'll be there. Then, perhaps, we can make it together. Who knows? But it can't be under the present conditions.'

Abruptly, she stood up.

'Well, I just thought I'd tell you.'

Buttoning her coat, she walked purposefully towards the door.

Saxon, sitting in the chair, did not move. He sat, gazing into space.

Helen paused at the doorway.

'And Tom,' there was suppressed emotion in her voice, 'for all I've said, I hope to God that you can get things together soon, really soon.'

When he glanced up the door was banging shut.

Terrasino was still working late in his office. Maclaren had presented him with one hell of a problem: to finalise security plans in time for the *Albatross*'s take-off. It was an almost impossible task to provide one hundred per cent security cover. Terrasino could not even guarantee a fifty per cent cover until the mad bomber was found. Badrick must be mad himself to let commercial decisions overrule the safety of the airship, its crew and passengers. The only method of frustrating the designs of the psycho would be frequent searches—body searches and searches of the airship. That, in itself, was a near impossibility, for the *Albatross* was like a gigantic floating city . . . and it was obviously the saboteur's home territory. In his anonymity and with his technical knowledge, the mad bomber could roam at will. If he wanted to hide explosives on board he had a million and one places to choose from. The bomber was dictating the ball game. Terrasino turned a baleful eye on the plans of the airship. He cursed Badrick for putting too much responsibility on him.

There was a tap on his door and Parish, one of his security guards, entered. He carried a clip-board.

'What is it?' demanded Terrasino irritably.

'I thought you might like to see the list of people who have checked on board the *Albatross* for maintenance duty tonight.'

Terrasino frowned.

'Why should I see that, tonight especially?'

Parish stood hesitantly.

'Well. . . .'

'You have something on your mind, Parish?' Terrasino encouraged.

'Usually the duty roster for night work on the ship is listed during the morning, right? And any changes on that list are confirmed by department heads to the security duty officer.'

'What are you getting at, Parish?'

'Maybe it doesn't mean anything in particular, these scientists are a bunch of weirdos anyway, but one of the engineers showed up tonight whose name was not on the duty roster. He said he had forgotten some work which had to be done before Doctor Van Kleef arrived in the morning.'

'So?' sighed Terrasino, 'aside from the bureaucracy of his name not being on the list, what is so goddam suspicious about that?'

Parish bit his lip.

'It was just the way the guy acted. I was a cop for twenty-five years before I came into security, Mr. Terrasino. You develop an instinct for things which aren't right.'

Terrasino looked at the man and stroked the side of his nose. He had been in security long enough to respect 'instincts', especially from old pros like Parish.

'Okay, who is the engineer?'

'Keller, Van Kleef's assistant.'

'Keller?'

Keller, with Van Kleef and Nieman, had been one of the first to be checked out by the FBI.

'What section has he signed in to work on?'

'Section 5CB.'

Terrasino checked his plan of the airship and identified the area.

'Okay, I'll go and have a word with him just to ease your mind, Parish.' The security chief smiled. 'I can't see our mad bomber giving us cause for suspicion like this. The man is too clever.'

'I just got this feeling,' replied Parish in an aggrieved voice.

As Terrasino went aboard the airship, through the main companionway entrance, he checked with the security guard there that Keller had not left. Then he made his way up to Deck Level 5. Section CB was towards the rear of the ship, one of the stabiliser units. Most of this level was deserted and only the red running lights lit the now gloomy corridors. Terrasino reached section CB and peered around. No one was in sight. He unclipped his transistor two-way radio.

'Evans?'

The main companionway guard answered immediately.

'Are you sure Jules Keller has not left the ship?'

'No way, sir,' was the response. 'This is the only exit open now.'

Terrasino flicked off the radio and frowned. Keller was breaking security rules by signing in to work on one section and then leaving it. He walked along the corridor to the nearest toilet facilities but Keller was not there. He stood for a moment, mystified.

It was the slight noise that caused him to glance up. It had been a shuffling step on the deck immediately above. The corridor in which he stood ended in a spiral staircase leading to Deck Level 6, which contained areas for the fuel systems for the ship's heating and lighting. It was a restricted area. He heard the sound again. This time he moved forward and cautiously began to climb the stairway.

As his head came level with the deck above, he halted and peered round before climbing on. The corridor was deserted. Something made him reach to his Berns-Martin belt holster and pull out his Walther PPK 7.65 mm automatic. He began to inch his way along the corridor, peering into the side cabins.

Jules Keller was bent over something by one of the control boards in the fuel induction unit control.

Terrasino glanced at what was in Keller's hand, recognised it and felt a fierce elation.

'Freeze, Keller!' he hissed.

Keller's body tensed.

'Put down the explosive, gently, then stand up slowly with your hands on your head.'

Keller did as he was told.

Still holding his automatic on Keller's back, Terrasino unclipped his radio and called Evans.

'Get a security detail here fast, Deck Level 6CB,' he snapped.

Then he glanced down at the two sticks of dynamite which Keller had laid on the ground. By them was a timer and battery.

'Two steps backward, Keller. Then turn around slowly. After the Westbrooks and Jack Lane my finger is very itchy, so just give me an opportunity to blast you. . . .'

Slowly, very slowly, Keller stepped backwards and turned around as instructed. His face was white, eyes staring.

'Terrasino . . .' his voice was dry and harsh. 'I didn't kill the Westbrooks or Lane. I wasn't responsible for the previous bombs. Honest to God, Terrasino!'

'Yeah?' sneered the security chief. Again he spoke into his radio. 'Evans, get Agent Hayes, FBI headquarters. Tell him we've caught our bomber.'

'No!' protested Keller. He looked desperate. 'I'm not the bomber. You can't pin that on me!'

Terrasino gestured to the dynamite.

'What's that, Keller? Your usual tool kit?'

'No, no. I can explain.'
Keller moved a hand in emphasis.
Terrasino swung up the muzzle of his gun.
'Hold still, dammit!'
Keller snapped his hands back on his head.
Parish and two other guards came hurrying along the corridor. Acting on Terrasino's orders they seized Keller and handcuffed him. The engineer was silent.
'Take him down to my office and stay with him,' Terrasino ordered, as he holstered his gun.
Parish motioned the two guards away and turned, grinning, to the security chief.
'I just knew the guy wasn't acting right,' he said.
Terrasino had dropped beside the explosives and was examining them without picking them up.
'He hadn't time to wire them up,' he murmured. 'Strange though, this seems a crude construction compared with the previous devices. This was going to be a pretty sloppy job.'
'Effective enough,' commented Parish, peering over his shoulder.
'Get a plastic bag and bring those things down to my office,' replied Terrasino as his radio buzzed.
'Evans here. Agent Hayes and Mr. Vambrace are on their way. They'll meet you in your office in five minutes.'
'Right.'
Terrasino turned and walked through the silent corridors of the airship. Something was nagging at him. Like most pieces of detective work the tracking down of Jules Keller had been a fluke, a piece of absolute luck, an ex-cop's reliance on an indefinable instinct rather than a brilliant piece of detection. Well, that was the way it usually happened. Yet, at the same time, Terrasino felt uneasy. Why? Something was wrong. He couldn't figure out what it was. But something was wrong.

Chapter Fifteen

Samantha Hackerman was still asleep in Jules Keller's bed when the FBI and local police broke into the apartment. She started screaming until Terrasino came forward to identify them and calm her down. The project's security chief pushed the officers out of the bedroom and told her to get dressed immediately.

'What's with the kid glove idea, Terrasino?' grunted Hayes as they waited outside the bedroom for Samantha to put on her clothes. 'She's probably in this with Keller.'

'No way,' Terrasino disagreed. 'Study the whole M.O., Hayes. Max Prüss alias Keller is a psycho. That's been agreed. They work alone. The girl wouldn't know a thing.'

Hayes looked dubious but held his tongue until Samantha, looking shocked and bewildered, came out of the bedroom and stared around at the police now going carefully through Keller's files.

'What's wrong?' she demanded of Terrasino. 'What's going on? Has anything happened to Jules?'

Terrasino poured the girl a brandy and told her to sip it.

'What's happened to Jules?' she repeated.

It was Hayes who answered.

'Keller has been arrested. He is the saboteur.'

The girl stared at him in disbelief.

'It's true, Sam,' Terrasino told her gently. 'I caught him in the act of setting up a bomb in the *Albatross* tonight.'

'I don't believe it,' she said slowly.

'It's a fact,' replied Hayes.

Samantha stared with a white, shocked face at him.

'You . . . you are not saying that Jules is the mad bomber?'

'I'm afraid that's exactly what we are saying, Sam.' Terrasino sighed.

'But Jules couldn't kill anyone . . . he wouldn't. . . .'

Her voice ended in a gulping sob.

'He's apparently deceived a lot of people, Sam,' Terrasino replied. 'How long have you been going with him?'

The girl sank abruptly into a chair.

'Three, maybe four weeks.'

'Do you know much about him?'

'Sure. . . .' She suddenly realised that she didn't know all that much about Keller's past.

Hayes caught the hesitation in her voice.

'Nothing he's done or said during the weeks that you've known him has made you suspect him . . . made you suspicious about him?'

'Suspect him in what way?' demanded the girl.

'Well, suspect that he, maybe, was not all there. That he was off his head.'

'Jules is as sane as. . . .'

She caught herself.

'Jules can't be the bomber. I won't believe it.'

'He's made no reference to anything which you thought was out of the ordinary?' insisted Hayes.

'No . . .' she suddenly remembered about Europe. Once again the hesitation was not lost on Hayes.

'But you do remember something?'

'Only that Jules said he was expecting to leave the project soon, that he was going to have enough money to spend a year in Europe and wanted me to go with him.'

Hayes exchanged a glance with Terrasino.

The FBI agent smiled apologetically at the girl and motioned to a policewoman who had entered the apartment.

'Miss Hackerman, I'm afraid that I'm going to have to ask you to go with this officer here. I'll have to take you into custody for a while for questioning. This officer will read you your rights but you are not really under arrest. If you want to help Keller I would advise you to co-operate all you can.'

The girl nodded dumbly and raised a worried, tear-stained face to look from Hayes to Terrasino. The security chief smiled and patted her shoulder.

'Don't worry, Sam. I know you haven't done anything wrong. We'll get things sorted out as soon as we can. Okay?'

Samantha sniffed and nodded.

As she was escorted out of the apartment by the policewoman, Hayes looked thoughtfully after her.

'Yeah, I guess you are right, Terrasino,' he said at last. 'I don't think the girl knew what Keller was up to. She wouldn't have made a damaging admission that Keller was preparing to leave the project if she was covering up.'

'Yet,' mused Terrasino, 'Keller sleeping with Samantha Hackerman doesn't fit in with the traditional pattern of a psychotic; not the type of character who would write those notes, a man with a deep-felt grudge and paranoia.'

'Maybe you've misjudged his character.'

'Maybe. . . .'

The police psychiatrist entered Hayes's office, nodded in acknowledgment at Terrasino and Vambrace, and dropped into a chair. He took the cigarette that Hayes offered and lit up. He was a worried-looking man in his mid-thirties, short and muscular with a square face and jutting jaw. He looked as though he would be more at home on a football field than in a psychiatric hospital.

'Well?' It was Hayes who gave the prompt.

'If that guy is suffering from schizophrenia or paranoia then I am Napoleon Bonaparte,' was the emphatic response.

Hayes gave an amused glance at Terrasino.

'He's legally sane?'

The psychiatrist smiled.

'He's as sane as anyone is in this goddam mad world we live in.'

Terrasino scowled in disbelief.

'You don't believe he's a paranoid schizophrenic?'

'Nope. You can get any other opinion you want but I guess we'll all agree on this one.'

'He's not deluding you?' pressed the security chief.

The psychiatrist shrugged.

'There's always the possibility . . . but I would say that the odds are ninety-nine per cent against it. We can all make mistakes. He might actually be a psychopath who has cleverly play-acted for two hours, but it isn't easy for a man to fool someone trained to spot these things.'

'Can I question him again?' asked Terrasino, speaking to Hayes this time.

'If you want,' Hayes agreed. 'But I guess this puts the lid on your psycho theory.' Terrasino didn't answer.

Keller was still sitting in the interrogation room, head cradled in his hands, leaning forward on the table.

He started up as Terrasino entered.

The security chief drew out a packet of cigarettes and offered it to him. Silently, Keller lit one up and exhaled deeply.

'Well?' he forced a smile. 'Am I mad or what?'

'No, you're not mad, Keller,' Terrasino said softly. 'At least, that's what the shrink says.'

'But you still reckon that I'm the bomber, eh?'

Terrasino gazed at him thoughtfully before replying.

'If the shrink had diagnosed schizophrenia, I would have had no hesitation.'

Keller glanced up. There was a sudden gleam of hope in his eye.

'But now?'

'Now I say that you are either a very clever actor, in which case we'll find out soon enough because there'll be shrinks in to see you like the proverbial locust swarm. . . .'

'Or?'

'Or you are telling the truth.'

Keller bit his lip.

'It is the truth, I swear it! I was a fool, sure enough. I was prepared to damage the *Albatross*, to prevent her taking off on schedule. What I did was simply for money, no other reason. But I never planted an explosive before. I did not kill the Westbrooks or Jack Lane.'

The earnestness in his voice made Terrasino even more uneasy.

If Keller was merely mad, trying to get out of things, he would not be admitting enough to send him to prison for a long time. It was going to be a ten to fifteen year stretch anyway.

'How's Sam?' Keller asked abruptly.

'She was released a few hours ago. She's been cleared of complicity. Maclaren has ordered her to take a long holiday with her parents down in Florida. She took some persuading. I will say this, she is loyal to you, Keller.'

Keller sighed.

'What's going to happen to me?'

The security chief shrugged.

'You are in the number one hot spot. If we can prove you are not the mad bomber then things will be easier. If not. . . .' He made a dismissive gesture. 'Whatever happens, the least you'll get is a ten to fifteen year stretch and no prospect of a career when they let you out. Was it worth it?'

Keller looked at him for a moment, remembering the Geneva bank account, and slowly smiled.

'Perhaps,' he said. 'Perhaps.'

Terrasino bumped into Harry Maclaren as Maclaren was leaving his office after lunch on Sunday.

'Hi, Terry. Were you looking for me?'

Terrasino grunted.

'What's up?' Maclaren frowned as he turned to lock his office door.

'It's about Keller.'

Maclaren straightened up and grinned.

'A damned good job, Terry. At least we'll all be able to sleep nights now.'

'I don't believe he is the mad bomber.'

Maclaren started and gazed in astonishment at the security chief. Terrasino's face was set in sombre lines.

'You've got to be kidding,' the project site manager said at last. 'You actually caught him planting a bomb.'

'Yeah,' admitted Terrasino. 'But nothing else ties up. The man who has been planting bombs and leaving notes is a psycho . . . I'll bet my bottom dollar on it. Keller is not off his head. He's cold, ruthless, cunning but a psycho he ain't.'

'Well, perhaps you're wrong about that.'

Terrasino kicked at the floor.

'Sure, sure. That's exactly what Hayes keeps trying to tell me. He's so cock-a-hoop that he has someone in the can he's closed his mind to any other possibility.'

'I can't see there is another possibility if you caught Keller in the act.'

'Keller admits trying to delay the *Albatross*. He admits that he has been working for someone else, supplying them with information about our project. A purely financial transaction.'

'Someone else?'

'Yeah. We don't need to look far. My guess is that Renard was meeting the payroll. Keller is small fry. A little man indulging in industrial espionage. He's not the mad bomber.'

Maclaren was frowning.

'It's a pretty big coincidence to have two saboteurs on the same project.'

'Maybe, but I think that's the explanation. We have Keller, who is in it for profit, and our mad bomber . . . and the mad bomber is still at liberty.'

'Did you say the FBI and FAA investigation teams do not agree with you?'

'Yeah,' admitted Terrasino. 'I'm out on a limb on this one, Harry. It's just my suspicion. I can't substantiate anything yet.'

Harry Maclaren sighed.

'So what you are saying is that we haven't solved anything yet. That when the *Albatross* makes its first Transatlantic run tomorrow, we're going to be carrying some nutcase on board who is going to do his best to blow it sky high.'

'Can't you persuade Badrick to delay the flight?'

'No way,' replied Maclaren. 'He wasn't prepared to do so before we caught Keller and, sure as hell, he won't do so now everyone's running around saying that Keller is the bomber.'

'It would be easy to sit back and accept Keller is the man,' said Terrasino. 'But I can't say it, Harry. There's a pricking at the back of my skull which says Keller is telling the truth. It's going to be a hell of a thing to live with . . . the *Albatross* lifting off and knowing that someone on board is a lunatic who's going to try to blow the goddam thing up.'

PART THREE

Chapter One

John G. Badrick's Executive Sikorsky S-76 helicopter touched down at the project site at exactly 8.30 a.m. on Monday. Harry Maclaren stood leaning slightly forward into the wind created by the whirling rotor blades and watched impassively as Badrick climbed out, turned and helped his wife and then his secretary from the machine. Maclaren forced a wan smile to embrace them all as he held open the door of the limousine waiting to take them from the helicopter pad across the project site to the *Albatross*.

The high canvas windbreaks were still in position and only the giant silver tail of the mammoth aircraft could be seen.

'Your staterooms are all ready,' Maclaren said as the car neared the airship.

'Fine,' approved Badrick. 'No problems, eh?'

'We had to hustle some but—no problems.'

'Any word from London about a cargo for the return journey?'

By bringing the *Albatross*'s flying schedule forward four days, Badrick had been forced to sacrifice his first cargo. There was no way the manufacturers could guarantee supply or loading. According to Sir Ashley Ashton, Renard had been lucky and managed to organise a token cargo for the first flight of the *Charles de Gaulle*. Renault had declared its faith in the French project and provided him with $350,000 worth of agricultural machinery for mid-West suppliers.

'No,' replied Maclaren, 'we are still waiting to hear whether the English manufacturers can rearrange their supply times.'

Badrick nodded absently.

'I want a cargo waiting for the *Albatross* when we start the return flight from England. We've got to make this bird pay her way as soon as we can.'

The limousine drew to a halt before the main companionway.

As they climbed up, Badrick gazed up at the giant flying-ship. For the first time there was a slight look of awe on his face.

'History in the making, Harry. History in the making,' he whispered.

'Let's hope we don't regret it,' muttered Maclaren morosely.

Garry Carson climbed into his 1934 Cord and sat for a moment before switching on. He let his eyes glide over its sleek white lines before starting up and letting the machine purr out of his driveway, gathering speed along Edward Payson Park and into Ocean Avenue. It was a bright sunny morning and Carson felt strangely exhilarated. This was easily explained today, the day of the *Albatross* first major flight. Yet mingled with the exhilaration was relief. After the immediate anguish of the last few days, he realised that he was relieved that the situation with Helen had finally reached a state of catharsis; that she had, at last, decided to act.

He would have been a fool not to have admitted that his marriage had been intolerable during the last two years. There had been a total lack of communication between Helen and himself. What he had not been able to abide was the constant pretence that things were alright. At least Helen had made a decision to act. Now he could act in turn.

He was sure that Helen was mixed up with another man. Of course, he knew that she had moved in with the Terrasinos. Terry was a good friend of his. Perhaps when things were settled aboard the *Albatross*, he would have a word with the security chief. Maybe Helen had confided in Maria. He wondered briefly who the man was. For the moment, Carson had no intention of allowing Helen an easy divorce. He was too angry, his ego had been too hurt, to allow that.

Hell! He must try not to think about Helen during the next few days. His primary task was to nurse the *Albatross* over the Atlantic and back. The major problem, as he saw it, was Tom Saxon. He was beginning to regret his suggestion to Maclaren which had resulted in Saxon becoming the project's second test pilot. He didn't trust Saxon where booze was concerned. However, there was little that could be done until Saxon really blew his cover. Grounding a pilot without a hundred per cent watertight case was a dangerous business. That would bring down the Airline Pilots Association, Allied Pilots Association and all their cohorts. No one would like to take the responsibility, least of all Carson. Not until he had something definite. All the same, Art Stein would have made a more reliable number two pilot.

Carson swung his car over the New Fore River Bridge, drove along the Portland Airport perimeter fence and then turned off to the project site. The place was crowded with people, almost as many as had been there to witness the previous flights of the airship. They bunched along the wire perimeter fence of the project site and crowded around the main gate. The security guards, recognising Carson's Cord, waved back the crowd and motioned him through. The spectators didn't pay him a second glance. All eyes were on the visible parts of the grey monster, almost hidden behind the canvas windbreaks.

Terry Terrasino was feeling anxious as he threw some clothes into a suitcase and glanced at his wristwatch.

Maria Terrasino smiled at him from the doorway.

'Don't worry. There's plenty of time.'

It was not being late that was worrying the security chief; it was the idea that somewhere on board the *Albatross* was a maniac who was going to go for the 'grand slam' within the next two and a half days. Badrick was a *pazzo* to approve this flight. However, he could not tell Maria what was really on his mind. He turned and grinned.

'It's not the time I worry about, *cara* . . . it's you driving me to the project site.'

Maria reached down and threw a pillow at him.

'Chauvinist!' she smiled. 'Get a move on.'

She looked at her watch.

'Helen is supposed to come with us. We were going to watch the take-off together.'

'Where is she? I thought I heard her going out pretty early.'

Maria shrugged.

'Maybe she went to see Tom Saxon.'

Terrasino pulled a face.

'That *ubriacone*! I don't understand it. Garry is a good friend of mine, Maria. I hate to see his marriage break up because of a no-good *beone*!'

Maria bit her lip. Over the last two days she had regretted telling her husband the whole story. She was feeling guilty that she had not respected Helen's wish to keep Saxon out of the picture.

'Helen's marriage to Garry was over a long time ago, Helen says. It was not just because of Saxon.'

'Well, I wish it was someone else other than the Englishman,' replied Terrasino. 'He's going down the tubes fast and she'll go with him if she's not careful. How he hasn't been grounded, I'll never know. . . .'

There was a click at the front door and they heard Helen's voice cry: 'Hello!'

Maria frowned at Terrasino and then called: 'We're in here, Helen.'

Helen peered round the door. She looked tired and strained.

'I didn't hold you up or anything, did I?' she asked. 'I had to go for a walk this morning and nearly forgot the time.'

She didn't add that she had been wondering whether to go and see Tom Saxon but finally decided against it. It was up to Saxon to make the next move now.

'No,' smiled Terrasino. 'I'm only just ready. Shall we go?'

Tom Saxon was a little surprised when he reached the project site and found the besieging crowds. One would think that, having seen the airship take off on two previous flights, the experience would have paled. His cab nosed its way through to the main gates and the security guard, peering inside and recognising him, waved it through. Saxon directed the driver across to the main office complex, climbed out and paid the man. Dumping his bag on the tarmac he stood gazing up at the towering lines of the airship and slowly shook his head.

What a pantomime, he thought. For a moment he couldn't understand why he was bothered to be part of it. At one time—how long ago?—he had really liked flying, it had meant a great deal to him. Now he tried hard not to care, to be disinterested in the proceedings. Yet, deep within him, he felt the old excitement still. He was part of a momentous, historic flight. Damn! What was so good about that? He had other, more important things to think about. Helen immediately swam into his mind.

He had not expected that the old fires with Helen would be rekindled to the extent they had. He had not expected to realise that he still loved Helen or that she would be able to put the dim spectre of Jan to flight. He paused for a moment in surprise. Jan. Dammit! He had trouble even trying to conjure her face into vivid clarity. All he kept seeing was Helen. What was happening to him?

Part of him, the guilt-ridden part, wanted to hang on to the spectre of Jan, to the haunting memory, to wallow in the past and its consequences. Yet that part was beginning to fight a losing battle with reality, with life, with the here and now. With a sudden sigh of annoyance, he picked up his bag and turned into the administration building.

On board the *Albatross* John G. Badrick and his wife, with Badrick's secretary, Miss Shelley, and Harry Maclaren, were just finishing a working breakfast in the Badricks' stateroom.

Badrick glanced at his watch.

'Best get our helicopter over to the airport to meet the Washington flight, Harry. Our two VIPs will be arriving in fifteen minutes.'

Maclaren gave the order by the radio link. He had been surprised when Badrick had told him that the American Secretary for Air had agreed to change his entire working schedule and join the airship for its first Transatlantic flight; not only that, but he was bringing some senior British government official connected with transport, who had been visiting Washington for talks with the Air Secretary. Maclaren knew that Badrick was well connected, but it must have taken a lot of influence to get the government man to change his plans at the last minute.

As a matter of fact, Badrick knew the Air Secretary very well. Jimmy, as he called him, was a former USAF two-star general who had made it into the political arena. He was a blunt, ambitious Texan, with a first-class reputation as an administrator. Badrick had relied on his friendship to get the Secretary to cancel his appointments for the next three days and make the trip to England in the *Albatross*. It was certainly a good publicity angle to have such a highly-placed official on board. It had been thanks to Jimmy that the British official had been persuaded to come along.

'Any problems, Harry?' Badrick was demanding for the tenth time since he had come on board.

Maclaren shook his head.

'The crews are happy? No technical problems?'

'It's been a bit of a rush,' admitted Maclaren, 'but we're ready to go.'

'Great. We'll certainly teach that character Renard a lesson. Anglo-American isn't going to let itself be beaten at the last minute by a cheapskate outfit.'

'Renard is playing a dangerous game,' Maclaren agreed. 'Can he really make the flight? After all, he has made no proving flights and doesn't hold an airworthiness certificate.'

'The straight answer is—yes, he can, Harry. The French civil aviation authority are allowing him to use the Transatlantic crossing as a proving flight. Don't ask me how he wangled that. Our friend Renard has some very well-placed connections.'

'I just hope that his design team and flight crew are sure of their ship. I wouldn't like to send the *Albatross* across without the testing flights we've made.'

'Well, that's his problem, Harry.' Badrick lit up a cigar and smiled. 'We don't gamble at Anglo-American. We have a qualified crew working a ship that has all the certificates she needs. And we are going to be first across the Atlantic.'

His face a mask of annoyance, Oscar Van Kleef fought his way through the reporters who were now grouped around the administration building and sought sanctuary inside. Batteries of photographers and whirring television cameras seemed to be everywhere. The excitement was growing as thousands of people flocked out of the city to get vantage points around the project site to witness the historic flight of the *Albatross*.

Garry Carson was watching Van Kleef's perplexity as the designer came into the building.

'I guess you didn't think when you were scribbling down your ideas for the *Albatross* that it would create all this,' Carson grinned, waving his hand to embrace the crowds beyond the building.

The designer gave a sarcastic snort.

'People are morbid, Carson,' he said, before pushing his way to his office. 'Those crowds out there are not really here to witness an historic flight. They are simply here in the hope of seeing something go wrong; of seeing the *Albatross* crash or blow up!'

Carson frowned for a moment and then turned to make his way to the flight crew briefing room.

When Tom Saxon entered the room Danny Macmillan and Billy Heath were already there, going through the latest weather charts. They greeted Saxon with a lack of warmth, almost a curtness. Saxon knew they were aware of the rumours about his drinking and had not forgotten the mess-up he had made with the simulator flight. When he had first come to Anglo-American they had made friendly approaches, but Saxon liked to keep himself to himself. Eventually Macmillan and Heath had, in their turn, come to treat him with coldness. Well, the hell with them! thought Saxon. If they didn't like the way he was, didn't like the fact that he appreciated a drink now and then. . . . He suddenly realised that he was trying to justify himself to himself. He frowned and turned to inspect the mail slots. The company bulletins had to be read before the flight, following the standard procedure of any big airline company. Some bulletins contained information which had to be checked in the pilot's flight manuals.

There was a sudden burst of riotous noise as Art Stein and his crew came in. They exchanged ribald greetings with Macmillan and Billy Heath and then Art Stein came over and thumped Saxon on the arm.

'Lucky bastard!'

Saxon raised his eyebrows.

'You and Carson. You'll be lifting her off and bringing her down,' went on the younger captain.

Saxon understood. The *Albatross*'s two crews were divided into shifts. In ideal conditions the *Albatross* would have three full flight crews, but at the present time flying duties would alternate between Carson's crew and Stein's crew. Carson's crew with the most flying experience on the *Albatross* would take the first duty flight shift, lifting the airship from Portland and taking her along the coast towards the Cabot Strait and across Newfoundland. At the end of their shift, Art Stein's crew would take over. The shifts would alternate until they reached England and then Carson and his crew would bring the ship down to its pre-arranged landing at Cranfield Airport in Bedfordshire, just north of London.

'It's a routine job,' muttered Saxon, bending over his flight manual.

The corner of Art Stein's mouth drooped.

'Routine? Jesus!' he protested. 'Doesn't anything get you excited, Saxon?'

Carson came in and nodded approval as he saw that both flight deck crews were gathered.

'How's the weather, Garry?' asked Art Stein.

'Looks pretty fair,' answered Carson. 'I've just gathered the reports. There are some scattered disturbances in mid-Atlantic and right now there are storms over the British Isles and northern France, but these should clear by the time we reach those areas. There will be a few head winds over Greenland but we'll start making up time once we get past the Labrador Basin. There's a promise of a tail wind which should improve our flight performance. Our cruising height will be three thousand.'

An Air Traffic Control official came in with a clip-board.

'Here you are, captain,' the man smiled at Carson. 'The first official airship flight plan approved by ATC.'

Carson took the board and his pen raced over it, filling in the details which would be filed with ATC. Then, with a flourish he felt befitting the occasion, he signed it.

The ATC man grinned.

'And here's the confirmation of your airworthiness certificate, captain. You have been approved under the Federal Aviation Authority Regulations Part 91, General Operating and Flight Rules, and also Part 121. You're all clear now as regards the paperwork, captain. You can get aboard and start flying that baby.'

Chapter Two

There must have been fifty thousand people gathered around the fields of Agneaux on the outskirts of St. Lô to see the *Charles de Gaulle* take to the skies. They came mostly in cars and hired coaches, giving the local *gendarmerie* a headache, and the local farmers trouble. They came by train, flooding the local hotels, camping sites and caravan parks. There were batteries of television crews from all three French channels, vying with foreign television crews, as well as radio commentators and reporters from many countries. Renard looked down at them through the observation windows in the main lounge of the airship. He had spent the night aboard. Now he could afford to stand aloof from the unbearable tensions as the flight crew and ground crew made the final preparations for the take-off.

Carefully avoiding Villemur and his technicians, who were scurrying up and down making last-minute checks, Renard wandered into the Chief Purser's cabin to discuss the guest list. There were to be fifty passengers in addition to the flight crews and technical personnel. The most important man on board was a small, slightly-built man with greying hair. On him, with his distant, uncompromising manner, the future of Dirigeable-Commercial rested. He was Jean-Pierre Dubeaupuris of the Ministère des Transports department of civil aviation whose team of inspectors would certify the airworthiness of the *Charles de Gaulle*. There were important representatives of the press and officials from the ministries of commerce and defence, transportation unions and authorities and—Sir Ashley Ashton. The inclusion of Ashton on his list of guests had been a boost to Renard's vanity. It made him feel good to have a director of his closest rival firm on board to witness his triumph. He had already anticipated what he would say to Ashton as the *Charles de Gaulle* made its descent over New York.

The Chief Purser informed him that everyone was on board and checked into their cabins. Now the only thing that presented a problem was the weather.

Jacques Barjonet was already discussing that matter with François Chambrun, his navigator, when Renard pushed into the flight deck. Barjonet glanced up with a scowl. He was getting to dislike the way that Renard insisted on interfering in everything, especially in the running of the ship of which he knew nothing. Barjonet was sure that he was going to lose his temper before they reached New York.

'What's the weather going to be like, Barjonet?' demanded Renard, slipping into a seat and lighting a cigarette.

It was Chambrun who coughed and nodded towards the 'No Smoking' sign.

With a gesture of annoyance, Renard stubbed the cigarette out.

'The weather doesn't look bad,' replied the pilot evenly. 'There is a shallow depression off the north coast of Brittany but it's moving north-east and we should miss it. However, coming in from the Atlantic is another weather front which will probably bring a storm with it. We should meet it off the southern tip of Ireland. After that, the weather should improve.'

'What's the stormy area going to be like?'

It was Chambrun who answered.

'It could be rough. A trough of low pressure off southern Ireland will bring rain and winds up to thirty or forty miles an hour. Not an ideal picture. There will be lightning, clouds dropping to about a thousand feet and a visibility which will range from two to five miles. However, there should be no great velocity wind changes once we have weathered the storm front, and good conditions will prevail all the way to New York.'

'So there's nothing to worry about?'

Chambrun hesitated.

'I didn't say that, m'sieur. A maiden voyage, a storm . . . it is a foolish man who is never worried.'

Renard smiled and made a dismissive gesture.

'You can relax. Just navigate us across the Atlantic.'

Chambrun gave an uncomfortable glance at his captain and turned to roll up his weather charts.

'Are there any last-minute changes to our take-off time?' asked Renard.

Barjonet shook his head.

'No. But I would have liked to miss the start of the mistral winds. Is there any way we can resolve the problem of the airworthiness certificate? With the storm front approaching we should make an alternative course directly north across English airspace to Birmingham and then turn due west, running across Dublin to Galway and. . . .'

Renard was already shaking his head.

'No, we have to avoid foreign airspace until America . . . we have to chance the storm. Besides, your safer route will put an additional hour on our flying time, let alone the other problems. Remember that on this trip all time and fuel saved will be significant.'

Barjonet sighed. He had not really believed that Renard would take any notice.

'Alright, m'sieur,' he said. 'Under the present weather conditions, I will accept the situation. However, should the weather deteriorate then I will have to take action for the safety of the vessel.'

Renard gave Barjonet one of his disarming smiles.

'You are the captain. Yours is the last word for the safety of the ship.' He glanced at his watch. 'Well, I suppose we should be getting ready now.'

The interviewer on the television screen was enthusiastic as he poured forth a stream of praise for the *Charles de Gaulle,* its designers, builders and crew.

'And just before he went aboard for this historic maiden voyage,' the man was smiling like a conjuror about to produce a rabbit, 'I managed to get a brief word with Monsieur Charles Renard, the chief of Dirigeable-Commercial, the company which has produced this splendid monument to French genius and craftsmanship.'

Janine Renard, sprawling in front of the television, gave a short bark of laughter as the screen flickered and the face of her husband came into view trying to appear modest but succeeding only in looking more conceited than ever.

She poured herself a sherry.

'M'sieur Renard,' the interviewer was saying, 'for the past few months there has been a rivalry between your company and Anglo-American Airships. Even now we are told that their *Albatross* is preparing to take off in an obvious effort to race you across the Atlantic but from the other direction. How do you feel?'

'There is no question but the better designed and built ship will win that race.'

'You feel sure that the *Charles de Gaulle* can beat the American ship?'

'Of course. We did not ask for any childish race. We announced our intention of making the flight and Anglo-American's response was to announce their intention of racing us. Let them try!'

Renard smiled broadly into the camera.

'So a final comment, m'sieur . . . ?'

'I feel proud; proud of my team, my crew, and all those who have made this achievement possible. I feel proud to be French, for this is the achievement of French technology. France will be responsible for launching the first commercial airship transport in fifty years, and the first country to prove that it can be totally safe and a viable form of transport in the modern world.'

The smiling face of the interviewer filled the screen.

'That was Charles Renard speaking to me earlier before embarking on the *Charles de Gaulle* for this historic flight. And now. . . .'

Janine Renard flicked off the television with an angry gesture.

The airship's departure into the clouds was about to mark a turning-point in her life. She picked up her glass of sherry, went out onto the patio and stared up at the now cloudy early evening sky. She raised her glass in salute.

'Farewell, Charles. Farewell, you bastard!' She smiled sweetly, but her voice held a venom which belied the look on her face. 'May you fall overboard. I don't care. I won't be here when you come back. How's that going to look for your damned stupid image, eh?'

Tomorrow she would start packing. She would get Bernard to drive her down to her villa at Fréjus. After all, the Mercedes was Renard's and he could keep it. Jacques would join her there on his return. They would start a new life together. She smiled softly as she raised her glass once again towards the black threatening sky.

'*Au revoir*, Jacques, my love. Be careful!'

As if in distant answer came the faint rumble of thunder.

There was a discreet cough behind her.

It was Bernard.

'It's growing chilly, madame,' he said. 'You'd best come in.'

She smiled. As she returned to the living-room the man closed and bolted the windows.

'Was your dinner alright, madame?' he enquired politely, as he adjusted the curtains.

'Excellent, Bernard. You are lucky to have such a splendid cook as a wife.'

'I am lucky to have such a splendid wife to cook for me, madame,' Bernard replied with a ghost of a smile. He turned to leave, but Janine stayed him.

'I shall be using the Mercedes tomorrow, Bernard. I want you to drive me down to Fréjus and then you can bring the Mercedes back here.'

Bernard showed no surprise.

'Very good, madame. Will you be away for some time?'

Janine laughed, a deep throaty laugh.

'For a very long time, Bernard. For ever.'

There was comprehension in the man's compassionate eyes.

'Very well, madame,' he said imperturbably as he left the room, closing the door quietly behind him.

By seven o'clock, the scheduled time of take-off, it had grown dark and the field was lit with searchlights, bouncing their rays off the low-flying, scudding clouds. The gathering crowd waited in growing impatience, shivering with the cold wind and sudden patter of short showers. Then came the noise of the engines; one by one the great diesels were started, coughing and spluttering like ancient asthmatics, showing sparks before they began to run smoothly. Soon all the propellers on the great ship were turning and the hull seemed to shake with the engine vibration.

Barjonet sat in his command chair and let his eyes run over the array of dials and gauges which told him how the ship was reacting.

'Secondary checks okay, Hervé?' he asked Hervé Blanchard, his swarthy Corsican co-pilot.

'Everything is reading okay, captain,' replied Blanchard.

'Right. Let's take her up.'

Hervé flicked his radio switch.

'Georges Zero One,' he began, giving the *Charles de Gaulle*'s sign number. 'Georges Zero One to control. We are preparing to lift off. Release fore and aft moorings.'

The speaker crackled—they felt a slight shift in the displacement of the ship.

'Moorings released.'

Barjonet eased the boost on all engines, turning the vectoring propellers for vertical lift. There was a slight vibration.

'Release all mid-ship moorings,' cried Blanchard.

They could feel the ship move slightly and see the lights on the ground beginning to recede.

'Mid-ship gear released, Georges Zero One,' came the voice from the speaker. 'You are on your way. *Bonne chance. Bon voyage.*'

'*Merci, St. Lô. Merci,*' acknowledged Barjonet.

He watched the needle of the altimeter moving forward to five hundred feet before he decreased power in the vertical lift and swung the nose of the ship towards the north-west. He was just beginning the turn when, with an abruptness, the nose of the airship jerked downwards.

A warning light flashed on his control board.

'Drop two tons nose ballast!' he cried, reading the figures from the inboard computer. Blanchard stabbed at several switches.

Below, the watching crowds saw an enormous waterfall gush from the forward section of the ship, cascading to the ground and soaking many of them. The nose of the airship, lit by numerous searchlights, edged slowly upwards until the giant craft was on an even keel again. Then they heard the engines being gunned, and the ship began to rise slowly until its great black shape was lost in the darkness among the clouds; until, finally, all that could be seen of it were the red and green navigational lights, and here and there, the flicker of the lights from the airship's cabins.

Sitting on the floor of her apartment in the Rue Falguière, Tanya Le Solliec watched the departure of the airship on the television and let out a deep and troubled sigh. She was worried; oh, nothing that would make sense to a rational man like Charles Renard. It was a weird feeling of foreboding; a shiver of fear as she watched the great black bulk of the airship vanish into the clouds.

'. . . And so off it goes on its historic passage,' cried the voice of the reporter. 'And with it goes the pride of France.' The cameras panned across the crowds and caught the reporter struggling to face them, with the crowd behind him pushing good-naturedly that they might have their faces recorded on this epic occasion. 'This is Henri Tussard returning you to the studio in Paris.'

Tanya leant over and turned off the set.

She stood up and walked out on the tiny balcony which looked across to the Gare Maine-Montparnasse. A strong, cold, dry north-west wind was beginning to whisper and moan across the Parisian roof-tops. She shuddered in its icy breath and folded her arms tightly around her body, peering up at the sky. She could not dispel the feeling of gloom that settled over her.

'Charles,' she whispered softly into the sighing wind, 'Charles, *ma mie*, be careful!'

Chapter Three

The *Albatross* flight deck crew began their final checks twenty minutes later than scheduled. There had been some trouble with the forward mooring coupling which had to be checked out. It was nothing more serious than an oiling job. Now Carson was going through the final flight manifests while Saxon re-checked the fuelling systems for the last time. Macmillan was carrying out his own checks on his engineering control panels while Billy Heath was making last-minute adjustments to his radio equipment. Carson finally glanced at the chronometer in the panel in front of him.

'Okay; time for the final preflight check.'

He glanced at Saxon.

'You look a bit jaded, Tom,' he frowned.

Saxon bit his lip in annoyance.

'I'm okay,' he said shortly.

'Glad to hear it,' Carson lowered his voice. 'I don't want anything screwed up on this flight, Tom. If I catch a whiff of alcohol I'll have you replaced by Art Stein.'

Saxon controlled his anger.

'I'll do my job . . .' he began, and then stopped himself saying something that he'd regret.

Helen Carson sat with Maria Terrasino in the front of Maria's car, watching as the huge silver-grey airship rose into the sky. It was a spectacular sight, with the colossal construction nearly blackening out the blue of the heavens. Both women felt unease; both felt it for different reasons. Maria Terrasino was worried for her husband. Although he had not said much since Keller was arrested, Maria felt that he did not believe that Keller was the mad bomber; that he suspected that the psychotic saboteur was at large and possibly on board the airship. Helen's worry was, of course, Tom Saxon, mingled with anxiety about Garry. Her marriage had been a slow, rotting process but someone, somewhere, had written that friendship often ends in love but marriage in friendship never. She knew Garry could hold a grudge. She feared the consequences if he found out about her affairs with Saxon.

Maria, glancing at her sideways, tried to bring her mind away from her own problems.

'Are you making the right decision, Helen?' she asked.

Helen smiled without taking her eyes from the rising airship.

'About Garry and me? Or about Tom and me?'

'Terry doesn't think much of your Tom Saxon,' Maria said once again.

'I know.' Helen paused. 'Tom has to come to grips with his problem. I hope I'll be able to help him because . . . because I love him,' she added defensively.

'That means loving the bad as well as the good, Helen,' replied the Italian girl. 'Can you live with a drunk?'

Helen was a long time replying.

'I guess I'll have to,' she said finally, 'if there's no other option. But I hope there is another option.'

Maria Terrasino turned her gaze back to where the *Albatross* floated some five hundred feet in the sky.

'I hope it goes right for you, Helen . . . for both of us.'

The gigantic vessel moved ponderously eastward over the Fore River and, keeping mid-river, traced its path towards the sea, with downtown Portland to its port side and South Portland on its starboard. Carson gazed ahead to the Portland Bridge across which they would pass into the Portland Harbour complex. Below them the giant fingers of the wharf system, culminating in the Grand Trunk Docks, were already poking into the river. Soon they would be away from Portland and heading into Casco Bay. Carson now began to raise the ship to 1,500 feet, which was the regulation height for skirting the city limits. Down below, so he guessed, most of the city traffic would have come to a halt as the silver dart of the *Albatross* purred its way sedately through the sky. Most people would be pressing to the windows of their office blocks or crowding into the streets to see the now famous airship commence its historic flight.

For the next two and a half days a heavy responsibility would be Carson's. Although he would work the shifts normally with his crew he was still captain of the vessel on or off watch, like a captain of any ordinary seagoing ship. Should anything important occur while he was off watch, Art Stein would have to rouse him and summon him to the flight deck either to take command or approve of his command decisions. It was going to be a tough trip for Carson.

It had been a gentle, untraumatic take-off; few of the people on board had even noticed that the ship was airborne until it was officially announced by John G. Badrick in the main lounge to the gathering of pressmen, VIPs and other guests.

'Mr. Secretary,' Badrick had begun with his typical pomposity in public speaking, addressing himself to the Secretary for Air: 'Mr. Secretary, we have commenced an historic flight for the United States of America and the United Kingdom. The skill and enterprise of our two nations has resulted in the design and building of this great ship of the air—the *Albatross*. That which for years was just a dream is now fact; it is a reality!'

Terrasino glanced out of an observation port and saw the calm blue waters of Casco Bay below. Terrasino had decided that the bomber, equipped with the technical knowledge that 'Max Prüss' had displayed, would go for the vulnerable parts of the ship. Whoever the man was, he would surely strike soon. After his threats the bomber would not let the opportunity of this historic flight go by. Terrasino and his staff, Parish, Lindsay and Sands, had checked the likely places and, finally, he had reported to Harry Maclaren in the main lounge, where he sat listening half-heartedly to Badrick's speech-making. Badrick was already into histrionics.

'During the 1920s, ladies and gentlemen, a conference met to see if air transport systems could be evolved based on airships—in those days there was no possibility of such a system, especially a freight-carrying system, being based on aircraft. But as the 1930s advanced, the aeroplane and, more particularly, the flying boat began to provide a short-term satisfactory answer to freight transport requirements. After the Second World War, the aircraft, as a means of long-distance transport, came into its own. But today the aircraft is in trouble; costs are too high, there are problems about the supply of fuel and therefore new and more economic methods of transport have to be found. . . .'

The press listened in polite boredom, sipping their drinks. It was all in the handouts anyway. All they had to do was sit back, enjoy themselves and luxuriate in this new and unique form of air travel.

Maclaren shot an enquiring look at Terrasino; the security

chief shook his head and dropped into an empty chair beside him.

'You still don't believe that Keller is our man?' Maclaren smiled.

'Keller?' Terrasino grimaced. 'Keller is a stupid bastard; greedy, avaricious, the get-rich-quick type. I still believe we're looking for a psychopath, a real sick guy.'

Maclaren waved to one of the waiters and offered Terrasino a glass of champagne, which Badrick had ordered to be served to celebrate the take-off. Terrasino shook his head.

'It's going to be a pretty tense trip, Harry,' he said. 'I'm going to try to organise shifts between Parish, Lindsay, Sands and myself so that there will always be one of us on duty. Trouble is, this bird is so big it takes hours to get from one end to another.'

'I hope you're wrong, Terry,' Maclaren said.

'From where I stand now, Harry, so do I. We can always hope.'

Maclaren looked back to the chairman of Pan Continental.

'. . . since 1969 there has, in many quarters, been a growing pressure for the revival of the airship. Proposals and actual construction work have been going on in many different parts of the world, particularly in America, Britain and France. For the last four decades efforts to build commercial airships on a grand scale have ended in failure but only because of the complex interaction of politics and safety regulations. There have been technical weaknesses, admittedly. But given co-operation which was unknown in the 1930s, the differences could have been overcome. Today, technology has developed in many ways and there is now a much better understanding of the procedures necessary to operate in complete safety.'

Maclaren leaned towards Terrasino and smiled.

'Someone ought to tell Badrick to dry up. The Air Secretary looks about as bored as a eunuch in a harem.'

Badrick was apparently coming to a conclusion.

'The *Albatross*, my friends, is a creation of the new technology we possess. It has been designed by Doctor Oscar Van Kleef and is operated by a highly-trained crew. It is in every way a modern airship, in no way comparable with the old types. . . .'

Claire Ashton waited until the polite applause had died away and the Air Secretary and his British colleague had made congratulatory speeches. She could not say that she was enthralled at the prospect of being part of an historic trip; she was more excited about being with Danny Macmillan for the next few days. She smiled happily as she made her way along the lengthy promenades towards the cabin section. On the way she bumped into the elderly, grizzle-haired Chief Purser, Olsen.

'Hello, miss. How's the press party going?'

'Boring,' she grimaced. 'But it's over now.'

The Chief Purser grinned.

'Mr. Badrick's been making more speeches, has he?'

Claire nodded.

'Do you know what time the flight deck crew make their first change-over?' she asked.

Olsen peered at his watch.

'About another two hours, miss.'

Claire thanked him and went on to her cabin. Once inside she threw her clothes off and ran a shower. Thinking about Danny sent a tremendous thrill of desire through her which almost made her whimper. Perhaps it was a feeling mixed with the soft warm spray which caressed her body. She luxuriated with soap and water for a while then, stepping out, she spent ten minutes brushing her teeth before towelling herself. Then she began to unpack her bag and generally tidy the cabin.

Eventually there was a tap at her cabin door.

She opened it eagerly.

Danny Macmillan must have come straight from his duty period on the flight deck. He was tousle-haired and smiling.

'Hi. . . .' he began.

Claire hauled him into the cabin before he could get any further, flinging her arms about his neck, fastening her mouth to his, as the door swung shut behind them. She hung against his body, her mouth hungry against his. After a while she heaved a sigh.

'You do love me, don't you, Danny?'

Macmillan grinned broadly.

'I'm not exactly indifferent to you, Claire.'

She gave him a light punch on the shoulder and he pretended to grunt in protest.

'Tell me you love me,' she demanded.

Retrospectively, Macmillan was sure that the way he felt about Claire could be defined as 'love'. But 'love' was so difficult to define—was it affection, fondness, warmth, liking, attraction, closeness, intimacy, adoration, devotion, esteem? Claire, in her insecurity, was very fond of the word; she seemed to use it for any term of approbation and support. Macmillan gently patted her cheek.

'I like you, Claire, and that's more important.'

He felt her stiffen.

'You mean you don't . . .?'

'I mean that you can't demand love, Claire,' he interrupted her. 'Love is not a flip word. You can't switch it on every time you jump into bed with a person. You need time . . . time to let it grow, time to get to know each other. Loving is knowing someone, Claire. Knowing them really well. It is more important to like someone, really like someone, at this stage.'

She shook off his hand.

'You pig!' she hissed.

Macmillan gazed at her in astonishment. Her face was suddenly red and contorted with hysteria.

'Jesus, Claire! What's with you?' he demanded.

'You had me believe that you loved me!' she cried. 'Do you think you can use me like . . . like. . . .'

He gripped her firmly by the arms.

'You're being childish, Claire. If I said I loved you it wouldn't mean a goddam thing. I suppose all the guys who laid you said "I love you". What did they mean by it? We might have something going if only you give it time before making demands.'

She broke away from him and a hairbrush narrowly missed his cheek.

'Get out, you swine!'

Macmillan hesitated. Claire Ashton was more screwed-up than he had imagined.

'Alright, I'm going,' he said as a bottle of perfume slammed against the side of the cabin. 'But, Claire, you can't demand flip words and phrases to. . . .'

'Pig!'

The word screamed at him as a powder compact shattered against the door. Macmillan left.

As the door slammed, Claire's face seemed to dissolve and pucker. She started to give long gulping sobs and threw herself onto the bed, unconsciously drawing her body into the foetal position.

'Danny . . . Danny . . . daddy. . . .'

The words were mixed and oddly contorted amidst her sobs.

Charles Renard was in his stateroom going over some technical details with Jean-Pierre Dubeaupuris, the French government official, when Villemur burst in, red in the face and excited.

'So the *Albatross* did take off after all?' Renard mused, when the chief desigher had blurted out his news. So Keller had somehow screwed things up? One hundred thousand American dollars placed to his account in Geneva and the man had screwed things up. Hell! Well, Renard knew a few gentlemen of Corsican extraction who could be relied on to persuade Keller to return the money. Renard was not worried about that. He smiled thinly.

'Do you know their precise time of take-off, Villemur?' he asked.

'At one twenty-five eastern seaboard time,' replied the chief designer. 'That puts them exactly twenty-five minutes behind us.'

'Barjonet must try to gain on that twenty-five minutes.'

Dubeaupuris looked surprised.

'I did not think you were interested in racing the *Albatross*, m'sieur?' His voice was dry.

'Race?' Renard was suddenly expansive. He stood up, forcing the civil aviation official to stand with him, and guided him to his stateroom door. 'M'sieur Dubeaupuris, I did not invite a race. The Americans are pressing one on me. The honour of France is at stake if these Americans beat us. We must be the first to make that successful crossing.'

When Dubeaupuris had gone he spoke to Barjonet on the intercom and explained the situation.

'Well? Can we increase our speed?'

'It is possible,' returned the captain. 'But I would not attempt it. It is too early to take such liberties with this vessel, especially as we are approaching the storm front.'

'You are encountering running difficulties?' snapped Renard.

'No, but. . . .'

'Then there is no problem.' Renard's voice was harsh. 'We have Villemur and his team on board in case of problems. All you have to do is show us how fast this ship can travel.'

Chapter Four

The buzzing of the intercom caused Carson to jerk awake and grab for the instrument as a purely reflex action.

'Carson?'

It was the voice of the back-up crew captain, Art Stein.

'Yes, Art. What is it?'

'We seem to have a problem.' His voice was quiet. 'Can you get to the flight deck right away?'

Carson glanced at his wristwatch. It was five hours into his off-watch period. He was about to make a protest when he realised that Art Stein would not have called him had the problem not been a serious one. As captain of the *Albatross*, Carson had to be called to the flight deck for approval of any emergency decisions.

'I'll be right there,' he grunted.

It took him a few minutes to throw on his uniform and get to the flight deck.

Art Stein and his co-pilot were looking strained.

'What is it, Art?' asked Carson, leaning over his command seat and casting a quick look over the dials as if to pre-empt Stein's explanation.

'The buoyancy control systems seem to be causing a problem,' said the pilot. 'We're having trouble with the compensation for changes of flight pressure altitude and the temperature of the lifting gas.'

'What's our position?' Carson swung round to the red-haired navigator.

'We are still under Canadian Air Traffic Control from Gander. We're crossing the Labrador Basin, height three thousand, five hundred feet.' He leant forward and read off the longitudinal and latitudinal figures.

Carson acknowledged the information. They were too far

from land for any emergency landing. He motioned to Stein's co-pilot to leave his seat and slipped into his place. His eyes flickered to the appropriate dials and gauges and frowned.

'Have you been checking lift adjustment to compensate for fuel usage, Art?'

'Through the automatic feed,' replied the pilot.

Carson tapped the dials.

'Have you checked these figures—they don't seem to tally to me?'

Stein looked across and scribbled some figures on his knee pad and then made some rapid calculations.

'Sonofabitch!' swore Stein. 'It's one-five-two out of alignment.'

Carson grunted.

'We have a problem, Art. Sorry to do this to you, but I would like my own crew up here on the flight deck.'

'Alright, Garry. Can I sit in?'

'Yeah,' he turned to the navigator. 'Get Saxon, Macmillan and Heath up here fast. As soon as they are here, Art, your crew is relieved.'

'Fair enough. Do you want Van Kleef?'

Carson hesitated.

'Not for the moment. We'll try to sort out this foul-up ourselves.'

Within five minutes Carson's crew were at their places and Art Stein had removed himself to the spare crewman's chair, nicknamed the 'bucket seat', just behind the command chair. Carson led them through a quick check-list.

'So okay,' he said abruptly, 'we have a buoyancy control problem which seems to have affected the computer compensator controls.'

'That in itself is suspicious, Garry,' ventured Saxon. 'A control problem on the primary system can be bad luck; on both primary and secondary systems it can be a coincidence. On all five circuits . . . that's sabotage.'

There was a silence.

Carson glanced at him and grimaced.

'Okay, Tom. You and Art take over. I'm going to tell the big chiefs. We'll have to tackle the controls from the main gas-valve and control circuits.'

Badrick's face was white.

'Sabotage?' he sounded incredulous.

'It can't be mere coincidence.'

'Is it serious?' demanded Maclaren.

Oscar Van Kleef was doodling on a jotter as they sat round the table in Badrick's stateroom. The designer glanced up and bit his lip.

'It can be unless we fix it.'

'How bad?' demanded Badrick.

The door opened and Terrasino came in. His face was flushed.

'Is it true?' he asked Badrick. The Pan Continental chairman inclined his head.

'What's the situation?' Terrasino demanded.

Badrick turned to Van Kleef and raised an eyebrow in query.

'The longitudinal trim and control are essential to the stability of the ship, especially in turbulent air conditions. Basically, we have lost control of those areas and unless we can regain control, should we encounter storm conditions, this vessel will be thrown all over the sky. That's the problem in simple lay terms.'

Maclaren pursed his lips.

'How about the problem with the compensation for changes of flight pressure altitude and temperature of the lifting gases and the lift adjustment to compensate for fuel usage? From the figures Carson gives we are losing a lot of gas.'

Badrick and Terrasino looked bewildered.

Van Kleef tried to explain.

'What sustains the *Albatross*,' he began, 'is the amount of gas we have in our gas cells. You follow? Early rigid airships used somewhat uneconomic techniques when dealing with this problem. Normally the gas cells were initially under-flated by some five to ten per cent, so that as the airship climbed the gas expanded to just fill the cell volume at the operating pressure altitude. Both automatic and manual vent valves were used to ensure that the different pressures in the cells were effectively zero. The initial and any subsequent climbs were achieved by releasing water ballast which in some cases could be replenished in flight. During the cruising flight the not inconsiderable aerodynamic lift from the envelope and fins were used to maintain flight altitude in exactly the same way as an aeroplane. Descent for landing required venting of the lifting gas and fuel usage was usually counteracted in the same way. The loss of gas was expensive, not to mention the fact that with hydrogen it constituted a fire hazard which is unacceptable with today's technology.'

He paused, trying to make sure everyone was following him.

'The *Albatross* does away with the venting of expensive helium gas. As you know, we employ aerodynamic lift throughout its speed range by means of vectoring rotor systems. We use two other systems additionally. One is the incorporation of flexible ballonettes within the main gas cells which are filled with air. The pressure of these can be varied by the change in lifting gas volume, and this density adjusts the lift. That was a device commonly used on small non-rigid airships. Secondly, we also have a cryogenic technology which liquefies both helium or air on board, regassifying it as and when necessary to give precise control of buoyancy at all times.'

'Except,' broke in Carson, seeing the still puzzled expressions, 'the control systems to the gas cells have been fouled up.'

'Due to sabotage, you said?' pressed Terrasino.

Carson nodded.

'There can be no other explanation, Terry,' he said. 'All five computer systems are fouled up.'

Van Kleef was in agreement.

'We have five separate computer circuits for just this sort of unlikely emergency. If one of the circuits does not function, any one of the others can be used.'

Badrick passed his hand over a sweat-soaked brow.

'Can anything be done?'

Van Kleef smiled whimsically.

'That depends on exactly what is causing the malfunction. I suggest we go to Deck Level Ten to the main gas valve control circuits and see if we can trace the problem.'

As they trooped out Terrasino glanced at Maclaren almost in triumph.

'Sabotage, Harry! I told you that Keller wasn't our mad bomber, didn't I?'

'We are passing a mile south of the Scillies, captain,' François Chambrun broke in on Barjonet's troubled thoughts. 'The winds are pretty gusty now, velocity rate is over thirty-five miles an hour.'

Barjonet checked the readings. The vessel was beginning to pitch and roll slightly in spite of the stabilisers. The nose kept dipping unpredictably. Barjonet had already had to drop a further ton of water ballast from the bow tanks to keep the nose up. That, combined with the two tons he had dropped as they lifted off from St. Lô, left them with a small safety margin. They were still only at 2,500 feet, far lower than the ceiling of 4,000 feet which Barjonet wanted to make.

'How's the storm ahead, François?' he asked the navigator.

'We have a forecast of winds in excess of fifty miles an hour, cloudy and heavy rains with lightning, captain.'

'At least we won't be over land,' chimed in Hervé Blanchard, his co-pilot. 'That will eliminate the cross-currents and vertical draughts.'

'We will still be meeting winds of a velocity that this ship has not experienced before,' muttered Barjonet. 'Take over the con, Hervé. I'm going to have a word with Renard.'

Sir Ashley Ashton, sitting in a wicker chair in the spacious guest lounge of the *Charles de Gaulle*, sipping a whisky sour, noticed the rolling of the airship. He smiled across to Dubeaupuris.

'We must be heading into the storm,' he observed.

The grey-haired official put down his Campari. The drink splashed and tinkled with the ice as it stood on the table, and he frowned.

'The stabilisers should be correcting this,' he muttered.

Renard, who had been in the lounge chatting with reporters, paused by their table.

'Is everything alright, gentlemen?' he smiled. He was not too happy about the fact that Ashton and Dubeaupuris were apparently old friends and had spent most of the trip so far in each other's company. He wondered what they were saying about the *Charles de Gaulle*.

'She's pitching a bit, Renard,' remarked Ashton.

The Frenchman shrugged.

'Barjonet knows what he is doing. He'll probably take her above the storm soon. We have stabilisers, you know, which should reduce any discomfiture.'

Dubeaupuris raised an eyebrow but said nothing. Renard hesitated, then gave them an all-embracing smile and passed on. At the door of the lounge he met Barjonet. The pilot wore a worried expression.

'I'd like a word in private, Renard,' he said.

Renard glanced at him in annoyance.

'We're running into a storm. The ship is pitching. You should be on the flight deck.'

'If you have a moment . . . ?' pressed Barjonet.

Renard turned into the Chief Purser's cabin and motioned the startled man out. Barjonet came in and shut the door, taking off his peaked cap, placing it under his arm and standing at ease.

'Well, what's the problem?' Renard demanded.

'It is my recommendation that we should put back immediately.'

Renard stared at him in astonishment, his eyes widening.

'Why?'

'I do not feel that we have an adequate safety margin to continue our flight. Our gross lift was badly computed. At the moment we are flying too low and cannot increase our altitutde because of the early eviction of the ballast. I believe our load disposition is too great for a long, sustained flight. We will never be able to reach our correct cruising altitude and I have my fears as to whether we can outride the storm front.'

Renard looked at Barjonet long and thoughtfully. He reached for the intercom and switched to the ship's main communications room.

'This is Renard,' he said shortly. 'I'm in the Chief Purser's office. Ask Villemur and Le Braz to join me immediately.'

He turned back to Barjonet.

'I would like to see what our designers have to say.'

Barjonet made no reply.

'You realise the significance of this flight, Barjonet?' Renard asked impatiently. He hated being ignored. 'You know that the Anglo-American ship has taken off?'

'I am not interested in races when they conflict with the safety of my ship and its passengers.'

'Quite commendable, captain,' sneered Renard. He was about to say something else when Villemur came in, followed by Le Braz.

'Tell them what you suggest, Barjonet,' invited Renard.

Barjonet repeated why he felt the ship should turn back to St. Lô.

Renard waited until he had finished and then looked from Villemur to Le Braz.

'Well, gentlemen? Your reactions, please.'

Villemur looked uncomfortable but Le Braz plunged in immediately. He could see that Renard was not in favour of Barjonet's suggestion.

'Nonsense! There are certain minor problems which would naturally crop up on a proving flight. But there is absolutely no reason to abort the whole trip because one feels uneasy. The vectoring propeller system will surely take us above the storm.'

Barjonet shook his head emphatically.

'We can force up our altitude,' he agreed, 'but without the gas to sustain an even level flight path, we will sink down immediately to the present cruising altitude. Also, the engines are not performing well. I believe that the screws are too small and I am having fuel injector problems with number five engine. The bore capacity is not enough to raise the heavy load we have. It is entirely inadequate to the volume of the structure.'

Le Braz took Barjonet's comments as a personal attack on his technical capabilities.

'We can maintain a height of 2,500 feet and can ride out the storm at that height. That ceiling is all we need to complete a safe passage.'

Renard smiled slightly and swivelled to Villemur.

'Well, Villemur? You are the chief designer. You hold a casting vote.'

Villemur stood hesitantly. He had clashed with Renard in a confrontation once before and had been soundly beaten. Renard had his measure, knew his weaknesses. He glanced apologetically at Barjonet.

'I can sympathise with Captain Barjonet,' he mumbled. 'However, my colleague, Doctor Le Braz, is quite correct. If height is the only problem that we are not going to pass over any mountain ranges on this trip; therefore a safe height would certainly be 2,500 feet. We could even maintain a high safety altitude at 1,000 feet. Nowhere will our course take us over high terrain. The ship has the capacity of riding out the storm front and after that . . . well, it is clear weather to New York. The other problems are only minor irritants.'

Renard was smiling broadly.

'Well, Barjonet, you have heard the views of the designers. However, you are the captain. Your decision is the final one, after all.'

It was typical of Renard to throw the responsibility entirely onto his shoulders. If Barjonet made the decision to run for home and it was proved to be a wrong one then he would never get another job in aviation again. Renard would see to that, even if other employers were able to make allowances. France was littered with out-of-work aviation technicians with whom Renard had clashed and trapped into making wrong decisions. Renard, he knew, was ruthless. One had to be sure before going against him. Barjonet hunched his shoulders in defeat.

'I did say, in the first place, that I was merely making a

recommendation. I have placed you in possession of the facts as I see them. That is on record. I am prepared to go by the ruling of the designers. With your permission, I shall return to the flight deck.'

He replaced his cap, turned and left.

Kurt Nieman, the chief electrical engineer of the project, was standing before the master control panel on Deck Level Ten making notations on a clip-board. He turned in surprise as Van Kleef led Badrick, Maclean, Carson and Terrasino into the cabin.

'Doctor Van Kleef,' he said, 'I was just about to contact you. I think I have discovered a problem. . . .'

Carson grinned.

'You are too late, Nieman. We've already discovered it.'

The engineer pursed his lips and shrugged.

'You saw the readings on the flight deck control systems, I suppose?'

Van Kleef moved forward and started to examine the gauges.

Nieman handed him the clip-board. Van Kleef glanced at it and compared the figures with those Carson had handed him.

'What do you make of it, Kurt?'

'I believe we are losing gas at an intolerable rate,' replied the engineer. 'The gauge readings show an average loss of three per cent per gas cell. If we get below six per cent then we shall be in serious trouble.'

Van Kleef was already crouching beside a panel, unscrewing it with a small screwdriver. They watched him in silence as he adjusted several wires. He glanced up with a grin.

'Well, we can fix the loss of gas immediately. Some sonofabitch has re-wired these connections so that every time we compensate for flight altitude the gas valves jam wide open and we lose gas too fast.'

Terrasino peered forward at the mess of wiring in incomprehension.

'You can confirm it is definitely sabotage?'

'To re-wire like this you need to be an expert,' replied Van Kleef. 'Yeah, definitely sabotage.'

Nieman whistled softly.

'But I thought Keller. . . .'

'Keller was not our mad bomber,' said Terrasino decisively.

Nieman looked bewildered.

'You mean we have a saboteur on board?'

Van Kleef was hurriedly readjusting the wires and screwing the panel back into place.

'I'll have to check out the control circuits now.'

'And the buoyancy controls?' asked Carson.

'I'll get to them,' replied the designer, tightening the screws. 'I'll tell you one thing, Terrasino. The saboteur could only have re-wired after we took off or we would have discovered the fault immediately. This job could have been done only in the last three hours.'

Terrasino looked interested.

'What makes you say that?'

'Because of the gas loss,' grunted Van Kleef, as if stating the obvious.

'And you reckon he was an expert?' pressed Terrasino.

'He sure as hell wasn't a boy scout practising knots,' replied Van Kleef.

They watched him in silence as he unscrewed several other panels, checking the wiring behind them. It was on the fifth panel that he let out a long sigh.

'Here's the problem.'

They crowded round.

Nestling in the mess of wiring was a small, two-inch-square box. Some of the wires were connected to it.

'What in hell is that?' demanded Badrick.

Van Kleef was carefully removing it.

'That is a tiny transistor, battery-operated and transmitting just enough juice to throw out our control system by several micro-seconds—enough to screw up the whole goddam works.'

Terrasino stared at it curiously.

'I wish you hadn't disconnected it just yet, doctor,' he said slowly.

Van Kleef frowned.

'Why?'

'Because I could have had one of my men dust it for prints. As it stands now, it has your prints all over it.'

Van Kleef coloured and looked down in confusion.

'I guess I didn't think of that.'

'Never mind,' interrupted Badrick. 'The problem's been solved and, I presume, Colonel Carson now has full control of the *Albatross* again.'

'Yes, he does.'

'But we still have a problem,' said Terrasino. 'We have our saboteur on board who seems prepared to kill himself as well as us. Thank goodness that our psycho didn't go for the bomb option this time or we'd all be on a chartered flight to hell.'

'You'd better post one of your security men permanently on guard here,' suggested Badrick. 'This seems a vulnerable area if this madman should strike again.'

Nieman raised a worried face to Terrasino.

'Do you think that he will?'

Terrasino looked slowly around the anxious circle.

'This man is out to destroy the *Albatross* one way or another,' he said. 'He's not likely to give up yet.'

Danny Macmillan fell fully clothed and exhausted onto his bunk. The emergency flight deck shift had got everyone keyed up. He felt the tension in his body and tried a few isometric exercises to relax himself. Then he must have drifted off to sleep in his weariness. Abruptly he became aware of a persistent tapping on his cabin door. He stumbled from his bunk, half-expecting another emergency.

Claire Ashton stood outside. She looked a little strained and nervous.

'Danny,' she said hesitantly. 'Danny, may I come in for a moment?'

Macmillan silently held the door open for her. She entered the cabin and stood in the middle of the room in a nervous, undecided attitude.

'Danny, I want to apologise. I was stupid, immature . . . I behaved like a silly child.'

She looked lost, forlorn; exactly like a little girl.

Macmillan gently smiled and took her hands in his.

'Okay, Claire. It was as much my fault as yours. I like you a helluva a lot, but we mustn't rush things. We have to get to know each other better. Let's take it gently, eh?'

She forced a smile.

'Anything you say, Danny. Anything.'

'Right,' he kissed her forehead. 'That's better. Now I've got to get some shut-eye, Claire. I've nearly had a double shift and I'm exhausted.'

'Danny . . . can I remain with you for a while? I . . . I just don't want to be on my own.' She caught his glance. 'Nothing more . . . I promise.'

She was still a little girl, Macmillan thought, unable to deal with the process of growing up.

'Alright, but no funny business.'

They settled on the bunk together, fully clothed, and Claire curled herself against him, nestling into the crook of his shoulder, clinging tightly to him. Macmillan lay looking down at her. Poor kid; she must have had a hell of a relationship with her father because she was desperately trying to find a replacement. He hoped he could help her to grow up.

Chapter Five

Jacques Barjonet was very worried.

He should have forced Renard to put back to St. Lô hours ago. Now the fuel injector problem with number five engine was increasing and giving cause for concern. True that repairs could be effected in flight, but only when the storm had abated. Fouéré, the chief engineer, had already been up to the engine pod and found some of the aluminium pipes of the cooling system had cracked: they would have to be temporarily replaced with rubber hoses when the winds died down enough to allow the repair work to be carried out. At two thousand feet the *Charles de Gaulle* was beginning to encounter hurricane winds of over sixty-five miles an hour and the ship was not responding well to her stabiliser controls. Although she was putting up a sturdy resistance to the storm, the pitch and roll were becoming considerable.

François Chambrun suddenly swore aloud.

'We are just south of Carnsore Point, off the south coast of Ireland, captain,' he called.

That was fifty miles further north and nearly one hundred miles east of where they should have been. The head winds were tossing the airship all over the sky.

'Any possibility of getting round the storm, François?' asked Barjonet.

'No. Even fighting our way into it means that we will only edge our way along the Irish coast.'

Barjonet turned and asked Blanchard, the co-pilot, to take control of the flight deck. As he made to leave the cabin he met Renard.

'Ah, I wanted a word,' the head of Dirigeable-Commercial said, putting out a hand to steady himself as the great ship rolled in the wind.

'Yes?' demanded Barjonet unenthusiastically.

'The guests are trying to have their evening meal. Is there no way you can stabilise the ship, to steady it?'

Barjonet's face blanched. Up to this moment he had merely disliked Renard. Now he felt like punching him in the face.

'Well?' Renard was obviously waiting for a reply.

Barjonet pointed towards the observation ports.

'Outside you will see a storm. A bad storm. There is no way that this ship can be stabilised; unless, of course, you have some influence with the Almighty.'

Renard scowled.

'There is no need. . . .'

Barjonet did not let the man finish. He pushed by him.

'I am busy at the moment, Renard. I have a report that we are losing gas.'

'I'll come with you,' replied Renard, adding anxiously: 'Is there a problem?'

'I won't know until I have made an examination,' replied the pilot, as he entered the small service elevator from the control deck to the main gas cell service deck.

Baudouin, Le Braz's assistant and chief technician, met them with a worried face at the entrance to the cat-walk which ran between the giant gas cells. Their design was essentially the same as the old airships—loose balloon structures within the shell of the ship.

'How is it?' demanded Barjonet.

The technician gave an expressive lift of his shoulders.

'I don't like what I see, captain,' he replied.

He turned and led them stumbling along the cat-walk. The gas bags were surging from side to side in spite of the nylon mesh which was intended to secure each in its place. One of the bags was rubbing and chafing against the supports and radial struts. Two of Baudouin's men were trying to anchor the mesh to secure the bag more firmly. The rocking motion of the ship caused them to clutch every few seconds for support, making the work tedious and almost impossible.

'And that is not the worst of our worries, captain,' cried Baudouin, waving them forward.

They climbed up two more deck levels to the highest point of the ship where the main hydrogen bag stretched like a giant sleeping whale. Baudouin pointed. Barjonet's eyes narrowed as he saw a small rent of a few inches in length. He reached forward and felt the side of the bag. It was flabby, like a child's half-filled balloon.

'A lot of hydrogen must have escaped from that,' he yelled.

Up here the noise of the storm was so loud that they could hardly hear themselves shout.

Baudouin nodded violently and leant close to his ear.

'I only discovered it a few moments ago and have just ordered my men to patch it up but the hydrogen . . .' he gestured helplessly. 'Let's hope it has escaped into the night and not, well. . . .'

'Hydrogen gas rises,' pointed out Barjonet. 'It will have escaped through the vents.'

'The ship should never have been converted from helium. Hydrogen is much too tricky to use in jerry-rigged gas bags,' replied Baudouin, oblivious to Renard's white face.

'How much do you think we've lost?' demanded Barjonet.

'Thirteen per cent, roughly.'

'It's too much. We have to put back.'

Renard's mouth tightened.

'Are you telling me that we are in danger?'

Barjonet looked at him pityingly.

'I advised you to return to St. Lô before, Renard. Now I'm telling you.'

'Nonsense!' Renard was almost screaming to make himself heard. 'The company's whole future depends on our arriving in New York the day after tomorrow. I'm not jeopardising that. You are being over-cautious.'

Barjonet gritted his teeth.

'I am telling you that the safety factors on this aircraft are not adequate to ride out this storm, Renard. We have hydrogen aboard and escaping hydrogen at that. You care nothing about safety regulations—all you care about is being the first to cross the Atlantic.'

Renard was white in the face. His mouth was working, contorting.

'I am chairman of Dirigeable-Commercial, Barjonet! I'll have your resignation when we get back.'

'Delighted!' cried Barjonet, shoving him roughly aside and stalking off along the cat-walk to the gangway stairs.

Renard found himself trembling with rage: rage because some spark of humanity deep within him admitted that Barjonet was right. Even he could understand the danger of their position. He turned to see Baudouin and his men staring curiously at him.

'Well?' he screamed. 'Get on with your job!'

Blanchard greeted Barjonet morosely.

'The instruments are detecting large gas losses, captain,' he said, pointing to the gauges.

'I've already seen it,' returned Barjonet. 'We'll have to release a ton of water ballast to compensate.'

He began to compute the necessary changes.

'How's the weather?' he asked Chambrun.

The navigator did not look happy.

'Still running into one hell of a storm, captain. Rain's getting heavier and. . . .'

Just at that moment a streak of blind white lightning passed near, making them blink through the smoked perspex of the flight deck windows.

'That was close,' breathed Blanchard, adjusting the controls.

'Right, François, contact St. Lô and tell them we are putting back.'

The flight deck crew exchanged looks of relief as Barjonet made the order.

'Renard isn't going to like that, captain,' Blanchard said.

'He's already asked for and got my resignation,' replied Barjonet quietly.

'The bastard's mad,' said his co-pilot unemotionally.

'I know it, Hervé.'

Without warning the ship dived down two hundred feet by the altimeter. Blanchard swore and started fumbling for the lateral controls, forcing the nose slowly up.

'Dumping ballast!' cried Barjonet, stabbing at the switches. Over a ton of water and a ton of fuel oil cascaded down into the frothy seas below. The enormous hull jerked violently, but slowly the needle on the altimeter climbed upward. Barjonet looked around at his crew. They were shaken but seemed unhurt. He reached forward and snapped the intercom line to the Chief Purser.

'Give me a damage and injury report as soon as possible.'

'Yes captain.' The Chief Purser's voice was shaky.

Baudouin called in.

'I don't know what's holding this gas bag together, captain,' came the deep tones of the technician, 'so far as I see, there's nothing between us and the deep but a prayer . . . Any more tossing about and the rent will run the whole length of the bag.'

At that moment Renard burst angrily into the flight deck.

He was shaking like a leaf.

'What are you doing? Did you do that on purpose?'

Barjonet swore.

'Get that idiot off the deck,' he snapped at Chambrun. 'Then get on to St. Lô . . . no, get on to the nearest airport. . . .'

'You can't do that! I forbid it! You will not turn back!'

Renard took a step forward, clenching his fists.

Chambrun stood up and touched his arm.

'Now come on, m'sieur. We are in a little trouble up here and. . . .'

The intercom demanded Barjonet's attention. It was the Chief Purser.

'One passenger with a broken leg, captain. Three minor injuries. Two technicians also with minor injuries. Mostly people are a little shaken.'

'Alright. Can you send Monsieur Dubeaupuris to the flight deck?'

'Very well, captain.'

Barjonet turned back to Renard, who had tried to master self-control.

'Barjonet,' he said softly, 'I am the owner of this ship. I am relieving you of your command. You will hand over to Blanchard here.'

Barjonet smiled grimly.

'You cannot do that, Renard.'

Renard turned to Blanchard.

'Do as I say. You are appointed captain. Carry out my instructions.'

Blanchard shook his head.

'Sorry, m'sieur. SNLP regulations. . . .'

'We are turning back for St. Lô,' repeated Barjonet firmly.

'I warn you . . . you'll never work for another airline or aviation firm again. I will see to that, Barjonet. As soon as we get back, I'll see. . . .'

Barjonet interrupted him curtly.

'I shall call upon these gentlemen to witness that threat, Renard,' he said. 'Now will you leave this flight deck before I have you thrown off?'

Renard hesitated, his face working.

Dubeaupuris entered and looked around at the tableau.

'You wanted me, captain?' he asked.

'Yes, m'sieur. I am putting back to St. Lô with the utmost despatch.'

Dubeaupuris did not show any surprise.

'Very well, captain. You will, of course, let me have a written report as soon as possible?'

'Yes. I will enter specifics in my report but it has been my opinion for the last eight hours that this ship is not sufficiently airworthy to continue the projected flight.'

Dubeaupuris glanced at Renard.

'I concur with you, captain. I have done my own investigations and would say that your ballast and gases are in a dangerous state. I have also spoken to Doctor Villemur who is very unhappy with the current situation. I think, M'sieur Renard, we should have a talk about this matter.'

He turned and left.

Renard gave Barjonet a look of venomous hatred.

'You will pay, Barjonet!' he hissed, striding abruptly from the flight deck.

Barjonet was too busy with the controls to bother about him.

'We will make a half-circle to starboard, Hervé,' he said. 'Prepare to make the turn.'

'St. Lô have acknowledged our message, captain,' sang out Chambrun.

'Right. Plot us a course for St. Lô, then.'

The ship abruptly bucked and pitched dangerously. Chambrun was sent sprawling from his chair.

'What the hell?' cried Barjonet.

'Lightning!' cried Blanchard. 'We were struck by lightning, captain.'

Immediately the intercom buzzed.

It was Baudouin.

'Captain,' his voice sounded strange, 'we were struck on the starboard side, abaft Number Ten gas bag. A small fire has started . . . it looks pretty bad.'

'I'm coming up for an inspection,' replied Barjonet. 'Take control, Hervé, and tell Villemur and Le Braz to join me at . . . where is it?'

'Deck Level Six, observation post nine,' supplied Baudouin over the intercom.

Blanchard wrote down the co-ordinates.

A few moments later Barjonet met Villemur at the observation post. He had reached the spot first and was already getting the information from Baudouin. The chief designer looked anguishedly at Barjonet.

'I warned him. Renard. I warned him that this could happen.'

'What's happened?' demanded Barjonet, pausing as Le Braz came up.

'We were struck by lightning. The overload on the dispersal ducts was too much to contain the charge. The heat generated has caused structural failure on an area of about forty square feet of the ship's carbon-reinforced fibre shell. A fire has started.'

Barjonet glanced at Baudouin.

'Can we deal with it?'

'We are using both automatic and manual fire-fighting gear to contain it, captain, but it has taken a firm hold. Thank God that the lightning didn't strike twenty feet from the point it did . . . it would have struck right next to the main hydrogen bag. As it is, we'd better start containing the fire soon or else. . . .'

He made a popping sound with his lips.

'Do your damnedest, Baudouin,' said Barjonet and then turned back to Villemur. 'What did you mean, Villemur, when you said you warned Renard that this could happen?'

Villemur looked pointedly at Le Braz.

'Some weeks ago, when I joined Renard and was asked to go over his designs and point out possible faults, I told him that the hull of his ship, the skin, being made from carbon-reinforced plastic, would be heat-generating. In the event of a lightning strike in which the ducts did not spread the strike evenly over the ship's hull then structural damage could result. Le Braz disagreed with me. Renard told me to accept the design or leave the project.'

'Might have been better had you left,' muttered Barjonet, as he brushed the designer aside and climbed into the observation pod.

From this vantage point he could see the hull had been extensively damaged. The skin of the ship had been fractured and blackened over a large area, and great yellow and red tongued flames were licking backwards in the wind. The automatic jets of water from the fire-fighting controls were hissing over them but the flames were fierce and strong. They were dangerously near Number Six diesel engine. Barjonet crawled back into the ship and searched for the nearest intercom switch.

'Hervé,' he called, as soon as the co-pilot answered. 'Shut down Number Five engine and also Number Six engine. Dump all the oil and diesel fuel from Six immediately. There's a fire hazard.'

Blanchard acknowledged.

Baudouin reappeared. His face was already blackened by smoke.

'We are barely containing the fire, captain,' his voice was tight and rasping. 'I don't know how long it will be before . . . those damned flames are really feeding on the carbon.'

'Keep me informed on every development, Baudouin. I'm returning to the flight deck.'

Blanchard looked worried as Barjonet slumped into his command chair.

For a moment he did not say anything.

'How's the situation?' ventured Chambrun.

'Not good,' replied Barjonet. 'Can you raise the nearest airport? It will be Cork. Tell them who we are. Tell them we have an emergency and want permission to try to come down.'

Chambrun bent over his radio equipment.

'Cork are asking the exact nature of the emergency, captain,' said the navigator after a while.

'Patch me into them,' said Barjonet.

A few moments later he was speaking to the air controller at Cork International Airport and explaining the situation. There was only a few seconds' delay before the controller responded, issuing landing instructions.

Barjonet began to turn the wallowing airship slowly towards the Irish coast.

Chapter Six

It was a foul night with blustery winds sending huge sheets of rain sweeping across the rocky promontory of Mizen Head, which headland gave its name to the southernmost of the long south-western peninsulas of Ireland. It was a dark night; a rough night, with the winds whipping off the sea and causing the white foam-capped waves to roar and crash against the tall granite rocks. Below the squat headland the waves were rising to incredible heights and some of the lashing spray, mingled with rainwater, rose to flay the granite land. Every once in a while the heavens would suddenly rip open, showing blinding white sky, and the thunder would growl menacingly overhead.

Brian O'Mahoney put his head down into the teeth of the wild, wailing wind and tried to make his figure as small as possible. He cursed Davin, his son, for his carelessness. The boy, bringing the sheep in that evening, had left two ewes and a lamb unaccounted for. Now O'Mahoney had to go out in this sleety, leaden weather, and find them himself. He swung his flashlight forward as he climbed the steep path up Mizen Head, one of the three short spurs at the end of the long peninsula. He had farmed the area for twenty-five years. The O'Mahoneys had lived on the peninsula and farmed the land for longer than people could remember. O'Mahoney himself had often boasted that his ancestors had once owned the ancient castle which now lay in ruins on Three Castles Head, just to the north. He knew every foot, every chasm and hollow of the rocky promontory. And he knew more or less where his missing sheep would be, huddled in the rocks at the far end of the headland, sheltering against the storm. Nevertheless, he cursed Davin for his carelessness. Had it not been for his son he would have already been warm and dry, with a glass in his hand, holding forth at John-Joe Goleen's *ceile* over at Schule.

O'Mahoney gave an involuntary glance at the sky as lightning ripped across it. God, he thought, but the day was angry with itself now. It was a fearsome night and no mistake.

It was as he glanced up he saw it.

It was like a ball of fire hanging in the sky; just floating through the terrible storm. It seemed to be drifting towards the land from the black skies over the sea.

O'Mahoney halted and stared hard.

Was it an aeroplane? Sure, but it was going too slow, far too slow. Ach, but could it be one of those fiery chariots which the parish priest had been rumbling on about in his sermon only the other day?

'God between me and all evil!' he muttered reverently.

O'Mahoney turned and ran as fast as his clumsy rubber boots would allow him. He made it swiftly down to the old trackway where he had left his battered motor car and, without pausing, he scrambled in it and started up. The wheezing, rocking vehicle swayed down the track, along the rainswept vista of Barley Cove before joining the tarmac stretch of roadway which led into the village of Crookhaven. He sped dangerously along the single street of the village, it curved down to the quayside along which stood the few houses and bars which constituted the hamlet. Further along were the large sandy beaches and the holiday caravans which parked themselves on the dunes. But the tourist season had not yet begun and most of them were empty.

O'Mahoney's car screeched to a halt outside Kerrigan's Bar and he rushed inside.

'Is Christy Mike Tobin here?' he demanded.

There were half a dozen men in the bar who turned to look at the agitated farmer in surprise. Christy Mike Tobin, in the uniform of a policeman, turned and frowned.

'Where's the fire, O'Mahoney?' he smiled gravely.

'Sure, but never a truer word was said,' gasped O'Mahoney. ' 'Tis in the sky heading over Mizen Head. I never saw the like.'

A couple of the men laughed coarsely.

'Now then, now then, O'Mahoney,' growled Christy Mike. 'Do you not know that you must have more respect for a member of the *Garda Siochana*?'

'Aye, that's why I've come to you. 'Tis a job for the po'lis.'

The burly policeman stood up and looked at the farmer suspiciously.

'What are you talking about?' he asked, authority in his voice.

Excitedly, O'Mahoney explained what he had seen.

'Take me to where you saw this fire, O'Mahoney,' said Christy Mike, buttoning his jacket. 'And heaven help you if you are pulling my leg.'

'I swear I am not.'

A couple of men followed the policeman and farmer outside. Even from the village they could now see the fireball in the sky.

'Begod!' wailed a man. 'What is it?'

'An aircraft,' hazarded one man.

'No; 'tis flying too slow. Why . . . Holy Mother!' Christy Mike suddenly shouted. 'It's the airship . . . it's on fire. It must be that French airship that was flying to America . . . the one we saw on the television. Kerrigan, will you get on the phone to Cork airport and tell them what we see?'

'It's coming down, Christy Mike!' cried O'Mahoney. 'I tell you, it's coming down on the hills.'

A woman who had joined the group started wailing.

'Ah, heaven help the poor souls! Heaven help them!'

The policeman dived across the road to a phone box and frantically started to dial his headquarters.

O'Mahoney, one hand over his eyes to keep off the blustering rain, peered into the sky.

'It's going to come down. If it keeps like that it'll come down in Clonagam's meadows. The poor wretches will be needing help.'

Christy Mike Tobin was running back from the telephone box.

'Take us up there, O'Mahoney,' he cried, flinging himself into O'Mahoney's car. 'Help's on its way but I don't give much hope for those poor souls if they are blown into the rocks.'

O'Mahoney and a couple of men jumped into the car and the farmer gunned the engine, roaring out of the village and up the road towards the hills. Overhead the great black shape, like a giant cigar, grew bigger and bigger. Along one side flames were licking, lighting up the ship in a strange eerie glow.

'We'd best not get under her,' muttered Christy Mike Tobin, 'just in case she comes down suddenly.'

'Well, I can't leave the roadway, can I?' shouted the aggrieved O'Mahoney.

Christy Mike Tobin gazed up at the black shape above him in awe.

In the spacious main lounge of the *Charles de Gaulle* Sir Ashley Ashton clung tightly to the bar and forced a smile at the white-faced barman.

'I think a double scotch is in order,' he forced himself to say evenly.

The barman looked at him blankly.

'If we are going to crash,' persisted Sir Ashley, 'then it does seem a pity to waste all that liquor.'

The barman pursed his lips and, with an effort, pushed the bottle of whisky across the bar.

'Drink all you want, m'sieur,' he said. The tone of his voice betrayed what he thought about eccentric Englishmen. 'I'm going to my emergency station.'

Ashton picked up the bottle and moved through the panic-stricken people who were even now deserting the lounge, struggling and shouting, demanding to know what was happening. Along the observation ports on one side of the lounge they could see hungry flames lapping along the side of the ship. The vessel still bucked and pitched alarmingly and Ashton had a hard job to make it to the seat where Dubeaupuris was hunched, white-faced but forcing himself to remain calm.

Dubeaupuris looked up.

'Aren't you going to go to the emergency stations, Sir Ashley?' he asked.

Ashton smiled tightly and shook his head.

'No point,' he replied. 'If the captain can't get this thing down, you know as well as I do that there is no safe place on board.'

Dubeaupuris made a gesture of resignation and pushed an empty glass towards Ashton.

'I agree. So, in that case, I will indulge. . . .'

Barjonet was peering through the windscreen of the flight deck into the darkness of the Irish night. His face was pale, his lips merely a thin line.

'We are coming down, captain,' cried Blanchard.

'Stand by to blow the gas valves as soon as you can,' Barjonet answered grimly. 'Try and release as much hydrogen as possible before we make contact. François,' he turned to the navigator, 'contact Cork, say we can't make the airport and are coming down on a rocky promontory. . . .'

'It's Mizen Head, captain,' shouted the navigator. 'It's not suitable ground for. . . .'

'Damn it! Any ground is suitable at this moment,' snapped Barjonet.

He glanced at his co-pilot.

'Close down all portside engines . . . vectoring thrust on the main starboard engines.'

Blanchard nodded.

The airship began to sink rapidly towards the black gloomy headland.

'Too fast! Too fast!' yelled Barjonet. 'Throttle back!'

The ship was going into a long dive. The pilots threw themselves at the controls. The ship began to pitch dangerously.

'Christ!' cried Chambrun. 'We're going into the side of a mountain!'

Barjonet breathed a prayer as he felt the craft struggling with the storm.

'Dump all ballast, all fuel oils and release the gas valves!' he shouted.

Blanchard reached towards the switches.

The ship suddenly tossed and bucked and began to swing tail-on to the mountainside. Barjonet could actually feel the tailplanes scraping across the rocks. Then his heart caught —there came an ominous crack, the crack of a fractured girder or strut. His world exploded into a searing white flame.

Sitting unsteadily with his drink, Sir Ashley Ashton was aware of a blast of hot air; hot air, like a whirlwind, gusted through the lounge and everything about him began to burn wildly. He felt a crash and was thrown from his seat. Dazed for a moment, he clambered unsteadily to his feet and peered about in the bright inferno that had once been the ship's main recreational centre. A short time ago it had been crowded with passengers, chatting, drinking and laughing. He looked round for Dubeaupuris. The Frenchman was struggling to his feet, his jacket on fire.

Ashton looked round, spied a soda syphon on the bar, grabbed it and squirted it over the burning garment. Then, as it was extinguished, Ashton tore a curtain, ripping it in two, and squirted the rest of the syphon over it.

'Hold that across your face,' he cried above the crackle and roar of the fire, which mingled with the screams of twisting girders. 'It'll protect you.'

He gazed round, wondering what to do next, trying to cover his own face and mouth from the terrible heat—looking for some avenue of escape. Somewhere in the back of his mind a small voice was saying quite clearly: 'This is it, Ashley. Too bad, eh?'

Abruptly, a weighty cascade of water came roaring down into the lounge from the burning hull above. Even as it swamped through the great cabin, Ashton realised that it must be part of the water ballast. It splashed and hissed its way through the lounge, sweeping them off their feet. Such was the speed of the water that it crashed against the hull, tearing it apart, and Ashton found himself smashing through the crumpled structure. Then he was lying face downward in the cold rainswept heather, smelling the tangy odour of peat.

He stood up gingerly. Nothing appeared to be broken. He peered round. Flames and black shadows were everywhere, like a scene from Dante's *Inferno*.

'Dubeaupuris!' he cried.

There was no answer.

O'Mahoney shoved his foot down on the accelerator as the car climbed the twisting roadway up the mountainside. Then, turning a corner, above the noise of the engine they heard a rumbling, crashing sound that terrified them. O'Mahoney braked the car so hard that it nearly swivelled within its own length. There came a tremendous explosion. Flames shot up all over the place, flames that were orange and blue. The entire hillside had suddenly become a roaring furnace. Wreckage lay strewn and blazing everywhere.

Christy Mike Tobin, O'Mahoney and the others climbed slowly out of the vehicle and gazed about them in horror. Slowly, one after the other, they crossed themselves.

'God have mercy on them,' whispered O'Mahoney.

'Christ have mercy on them,' answered Christy Mike Tobin with equal reverence.

They turned, aware of screaming in the distance. The air was unbearably hot. Everywhere they looked they could see fires big and small, the smaller ones hissing in the sleeting rain. On the hillside they could see part of the main structure was silhouetted by flames. The intensity of the fire held them back.

Then, to their horror, someone came staggering out of the inferno towards them—a blazing torch.

Christy Mike Tobin ripped off his jacket and rolled the man on the ground.

Already in the distance, along the coast road, they could hear the screaming wail of an ambulance and a police siren.

The man on the ground had mercifully sunk into unconsciousness.

O'Mahoney saw another figure moving down the hill, staggering, falling and picking itself up again.

He called out but the figure ignored him. O'Mahoney turned and picked his way down the hill at a rapid pace.

Turning his flashlight on the man, O'Mahoney saw that his jacket was badly burnt and his face was scorched and dirty. His eyes were wide and staring.

'Are you alright, mister?' O'Mahoney demanded, suddenly realising it was a ridiculous question to ask in the circumstances.

The man gazed at him and began to laugh hysterically.

'Whist now, enough of that,' chided O'Mahoney helplessly. 'Come away up to the roadway. There's an ambulance nearly here.'

The man continued to laugh uncontrollably.

'Savvy? Ambulance. Hospital.' O'Mahoney raised his voice, remembering that Christy Mike had said the airship was French. Perhaps the man did not understand him.

The man suddenly was serious.

'I am Renard,' he said slowly in accented English. 'Charles Renard.'

O'Mahoney patted his shoulder.

'Well, you are safe, Mr. Renard. You are safe now.'

Renard's face suddenly dissolved and he started to sob and wail like a baby.

O'Mahoney had heard that shock did strange things to people and so he gently led the man back to the roadway where the ambulance had pulled up. He handed him over to a young official.

The man kept mumbling in French as they ushered him into the back of the ambulance. As they made him lie down on a stretcher he turned and looked at them with bright pleading eyes. Then, in halting English, he said:

'I am Charles Renard. It is my fault. My fault.'

Ashton heard a roar and was knocked sideways as a pocket of hydrogen ignited nearby. He picked himself up again from the heather and peered into the ghastly scene. The heat was excruciating. He heard a voice crying from somewhere behind the flames. It was calling on God for help. It sounded like Dubeaupuris. Ashton was sure it was his voice. He turned towards the flaming walls of the wrecked airship.

Miraculously, out of the blazing mass, stumbled a figure —clothes alight. It staggered towards him, screaming. Ashton seized it and threw it to the ground, rolling it over and over in the damp heather until the flames were extinguished. He looked down. The flickering light of the flames lit up the face. Ashton retched immediately. There was no recognising the scorched features.

His head jerked as there came another scream nearby. He turned towards the inferno again.

A hand fell on his shoulder.

'Are you alright, sir?' A dark shape, a man in uniform, appeared.

'Who are you?'

'I'm a policeman, sir,' replied the figure. 'Would you come down to the ambulance, sir?'

Ashton shook off the man's restraining hand.

'There are others—trapped. I've got to help.'

'You've done enough, sir,' pacified the policeman. 'Come away now, sir. You can't reach the rest of them.'

Ashton turned back to the flaming tomb.

'No. I must help. Dubeaupuris!'

Christy Mike Tobin made a grab at him but Ashton had run forward.

'Come back, sir. Sir! Watch out!'

Ashton heard the creaking noise, a descending, rushing sound like that of an express train.

He glanced upwards and started to scream.

Several tons of blazing girders and carbon plastic thundered down.

Christy Mike Tobin blinked and felt sick.

O'Mahoney came up and looked at the mess. The fires were dying down a little except around the main structure, high up in the hull.

'Grief,' he said, 'is there anything more to be done here?'

The policeman shook his head slowly.

'The army is on the way, Christy Mike,' O'Mahoney said, 'and the fire engines and ambulance men from Bantry and Cork City itself.'

Christy Mike Tobin stood staring at the flames roaring round the wreckage.

'They'll not find much of the bodies left either,' he said, as if musing aloud. 'There are a few scattered about—haven't I counted twelve already?'

O'Mahoney nodded slowly.

'God be merciful to them,' he muttered.

Chapter Seven

It was Billy Heath who received the news first. Garry Carson and his crew had just started their second scheduled watch on the flight deck when the news came through. Billy Heath asked for the message to be repeated in a tone which caused the rest of the crew to look round with surprise.

'It's . . . it's the *Charles de Gaulle*,' he told them. 'She crashed somewhere in the south-west of Ireland. There are only twelve survivors.'

There was an absolute silence on the flight deck. Then Carson asked:

'How many was she carrying?'

'Her manifest listed seventy-five.'

This time the silence was more prolonged as each wrestled with their thoughts.

'Jesus!' Danny Macmillan said at last, 'the press are going to crucify us. We have been assuring them about the safety of airships and then this happens. No one will take any notice of us now.'

'What about the sixty-three poor sods who have just got themselves killed?' snapped Saxon.

Macmillan looked contrite.

'I didn't mean . . .' he began.

Carson silenced him.

'Billy, can you get a casualty list? And is there any information about the cause of the crash?'

Saxon gave him a puzzled glance.

'Why the casualty list?'

'Because I understood that Sir Ashley Ashton was flying on the *Charles de Gaulle*.'

Saxon had forgotten that Claire Ashton was aboard.

It was a short time later that Billy Heath passed Carson a clip-board. The name of Ashton was at the top.

'Those are the confirmed dead so far, skipper,' said the navigator.

Carson bit his lip.

'Poor bitch,' he said compassionately.

'Claire's old man?' asked Macmillan.

'Yeah,' nodded Carson, levering himself from the command chair. 'The con is all yours, Tom. Billy, ask Badrick, Maclaren and Van Kleef to join me in my cabin in ten minutes and tell them it's urgent. And let me know if any more details come in.'

Billy Heath nodded.

'They say the media are already screaming about another R101 but the only thing known so far is that the French went down in a storm . . . burst into flames and practically incinerated themselves.'

Carson did not reply as he left the flight deck.

There was a brooding silence among the passengers of the *Albatross*. The news of the *Charles de Gaulle* had been broadcast on the ship's internal communications system and any updated bulletins that came into the ship were immediately rebroadcast. The passengers sat about the lounges in glum morbidity. Maclaren had insisted that the canned music should continue to be piped through the ship and an atmosphere of false gaiety prevailed, which was given lie to by the long faces of those who sat about in small groups, talking in whispers. Even the press corps seemed unusually silent.

Badrick had not stirred from his cabin after the first news bulletin. A number of cablegrams of sympathy in his name had been despatched; prominently among them was one to Lady Ashton. But Badrick had not been able to face Claire Ashton. In the end his wife, Alice, had gone to break the news. Claire had stood quietly, solemn-eyed, showing neither surprise, horror or regret. She had simply said, in a small voice: 'Thank you'. Then she had turned into her cabin and closed the door. Mrs. Badrick wondered whether it was just shock and if she ought to contact the Chief Purser.

In a corner of the main lounge of the *Albatross*, the Secretary for Air sat gazing thoughtfully at a tumbler of rye which he had been nursing for the last half-hour without touching. His British colleague leant forward in his seat, looking uncomfortable and nervous, sipping a gin and tonic. He kept fingering his moustache in an irritating fashion. Maclaren and Van Kleef sat with them but no one spoke. Occasionally the canned music would stop and the latest news broadcast concerning the crash would be read. There were few facts to go on. The storm. The fire. The crash. Not much else. They sat as if they were at their own wake; like worshippers in a church during a particularly boring sermon. Finally, after one newscast describing the fire, Maclaren cleared his throat.

'It's obvious from the description that Renard must have filled his tanks with hydrogen instead of helium.'

The Air Secretary glanced up in surprise.

'Would that be allowed?' he asked incredulously.

'It's only public opinion which doesn't allow it,' Maclaren replied. 'The memories of the past dictate the use of an inert gas for the operation. We have often stated that it is not inconceivable to design a safe ship employing an inflammable gas like hydrogen. But so far as our project was concerned the only acceptable gas was helium which uniquely combines low density with non-inflammability.'

Van Kleef looked up from his brooding.

'The trouble is the cost and relative scarcity factor. A ready access to the gas is essential. I understand Renard was having trouble getting his shipment of helium. Perhaps he decided to go for an easy option and fill his gas cells with hydrogen.'

The British government official coughed nervously.

'Wouldn't that, er, be dangerous?'

'It depends on the conversion of the gas cells. Maybe Renard did a hurried job.'

'So faced with the prospect of not getting helium,' the Air Secretary recapped ponderously, 'helium being inert but expensive and rare, he opted for hydrogen, which is inflammable but relatively cheap and easy to come by?'

'That's about the size of it, Mr. Secretary,' agreed Maclaren.

'But surely if Renard did not have access to helium,' said the Britisher, 'there are other gases he could have used?'

Van Kleef grimaced.

'Let's face it, hydrogen has the best lifting capacity when all's said and done. Helium comes second. Other gases like neon, ammonia, which is very dangerous, coal gas, natural gas, and methane are simply not on. Neon is the only inert gas out of the whole bunch, while coal gas, natural gas and methane, although cheap, are highly inflammable and the ratio of their density to lift makes them impracticable.'

Both government men looked bemused.

'So what is your theory about the *Charles de Gaulle*'s crash, doctor?' demanded the Air Secretary.

Van Kleef reflected.

'I don't like giving judgments without facts but, on the facts we know from the newscasts, I would say that Renard opted for hydrogen; that his safety levels in converting his gas cells to the new gas were insufficient. That there was probably some fire or explosion on board, or maybe even a lightning strike, and. . . .'

He gave a gesture of finality.

'A lightning strike?' The British official sounded dubious.

'Certainly. An airship can be expected to receive a significantly higher number of lightning strikes than an aircraft, due to the much greater surface area. Our experiments have estimated a strike rate of once every six hundred hours in ordinary travelling conditions.'

The American politician pulled a face.

'Say, that ain't much.'

'One strike, just one, not adequately spread is enough, Mr. Secretary,' replied Van Kleef. 'And if you have leaking hydrogen, well. . . .'

The British official looked very pale.

'What would happen if the lightning struck the *Albatross*?' he asked nervously.

It was Maclaren, smiling, who replied.

'Don't worry. We have spent a good deal of time on that subject. You are perfectly safe. Before Doctor Van Kleef chose the final material for the structure we conducted several experiments. For example, early on we found that a lightning strike could actually blow a six-inch diameter hole clean through a sheet of high-tensile stainless steel. We had been thinking of making our outer skin with 0.060-inch-thick stainless steel. So we had to change our minds.'

Van Kleef leant forward nodding.

'With our special honeycomb structure, with the disposition of the core depth, skin material and preparation and earthing arrangement, a direct strike only penetrated the honeycomb to a third the depth of the panel. So we proved that the design was safe from the viewpoint of a lightning strike. A direct strike would just allow the outer skin to burn feebly for a time. We experimented with outer skin strikes to the density of 550 coulombs, considerably in excess of existing CAA requirements . . . and these left our inner skin completely unmarked.'

The Air Secretary was bewildered.

'Come again?' he queried. 'Coo-what?'

Maclaren explained.

'Coulombs, Mr. Secretary. It's the unity of quantity in measuring current electricity—the quantity furnished by a current of one ampere in one second.'

The politician sighed.

'I guess I'll leave the technical side to you boys. But what you are saying is, as I understand it, that Renard set off with a dangerous ship.'

Maclaren glanced at Van Kleef.

'Is that what you're saying, Oscar?'

'I suppose it is,' replied the chief designer, smiling thinly. 'Sorry if I disguised it with too much technical data.'

The Air Secretary sniffed.

'Well, so long as you boys know the cause. Trouble is, the crash is going to set airship aviation behind again, unless you can prove the reasons behind the crash and make the public understand them. The public are already scared stiff of airships. This French crash will really turn the screws.'

Maclaren sighed.

'We have to convince the public that airships can be safe and economical and that modern technology has reached the point where airships can be safely and successfully constructed. We must show that we can overcome the difficulties of lighter than air flight because airships can economically fulfil a necessary role in the future.'

The Air Secretary smiled whimsically.

'You wouldn't like a job writing my speeches, mister?' he said, then as he saw Maclaren's offended expression, he reached forward and laid a hand on his arm. 'Don't get me wrong. I'm with you all the way. Trouble is, when Joe Public is yelling his head off—scared to death—how do you turn round and tell him that he has no need to worry? In a democracy you have to move along at the rate of common prejudice and not informed opinion. If such things were left to you and I . . .' he sighed deeply. 'But, hell, Joe Public out there, he's a pretty dumb animal and he has to be pandered to, especially around election time.'

Terrasino was lying on his bunk, hands behind his head, gazing up at the bulkheads in his cabin. His mind was not on the shocking news of the *Charles de Gaulle* but on a more immediate problem.

The bomber was going to strike soon and Terrasino was trying to figure out what his likely target would be. It was quite obvious that he was a skilled technician and that he was highly placed in the project. Terrasino must know him well, or thought he knew him well. But who was it? Van Kleef? He certainly looked guilty when Terrasino rebuked him for destroying the fingerprints on the transistor scrambling device. Damn it, though. It could be anyone; any one of the flight deck crew, any one of the back-up engineers aboard, any one of them could be capable of screwing up the control circuits. Shit! If this were some cheap dime novel, he would now have a brilliant flash of intuition and be able to name the culprit. But this was real life, and in real-life detective work nothing came easy. It depended on checking and re-checking the facts.

His mind kept going back to the letters which the bomber had written. They must surely present a clue. He suddenly swung his legs over the side of the bunk and reached towards his attaché case. He had brought photostats of the notes with him. For the hundredth time he scanned each page, trying to seek a fresh clue. There was nothing. Yet those letters must provide a key to the personality of the man.

Terrasino tried to visualise what the bomber could be like. The late famous German psychiatrist, Ernest Kretschmer, had made a study of ten thousand patients in mental hospitals and noted that roughly eighty-five per cent of paranoiacs had an athletic body type. Alright, so fifteen per cent had other body types but the law of averages would be in favour. Seventeen to twenty, Terrasino reckoned, that the bomber was symmetrically built, well-developed with only few, if any, physical oddities. Terrasino wished he had a copy of Kretschmer's *Physique and Character* with him. He couldn't remember much about the actual correlation between physique and psychosis apart from some generalisations, and they were not really a help. A hell of a lot of people on board the *Albatross* were not only athletic types but also had the right technical qualifications to be the bomber.

He turned back to the letters and the signature 'Max Prüss'. Why Max Prüss? Prüss had been captain of the ill-fated *Hindenburg*. But what was the connection between Max Prüss and the bomber? The FBI had already run a check for any connection between Prüss and the personnel working on the project. Nothing. A big fat zero. Terrasino suddenly started. A computer would only come up with an answer on the basis of the information fed to it. Hayes had said that. What if they weren't asking it the right question? What was the connection between the *Hindenburg* and the bomber? Perhaps the bomber was taking the name of the old airship captain as a symbol. Why Prüss? Why not the captain of American airships like the *Shenandoah*, the *Akron* and *Macon*. . . . Why use the name of the skipper of a German airship? Terrasino had thought the connection must have been between the bomber and Prüss, but what if the bomber was merely connected with the airship itself? That was it!

He grabbed the inter-stateroom telephone and called Billy Heath.

'This is Terrasino, Billy. I want you to patch me through to the following Portland number. . . .'

He reeled off Hayes' number and added: 'This is a number one security priority.'

It took some time before a sleepy voice answered.

'Hayes? This is Terrasino.'

'Yeah?' answered the FBI agent. Then, as if suddenly coming awake: 'Jesus! It's three o'clock in the morning. Aren't you supposed to be in mid-Atlantic?'

'I am,' answered Terrasino. 'Now listen. You recall we checked the entire personnel for a connection with Max Prüss?'

'Is that what you've hauled me out of bed for?'

Terrasino ignored the protest.

'I know the time,' he grunted. 'But you might like to know the saboteur has struck again and that knocks your theory about Keller on the head. The screwball is on board and we have to find him.'

Hayes started to talk but Terrasino shut him up.

'I want you to run a list of Anglo-American personnel currently on board the *Albatross* against a list of all the passengers and crew who were on board the *Hindenburg* when it crashed. I want the data cross-checked against the names of survivors, their descendants and especially where a name change occurred. I want marriages, adoptions, anything. Got it?'

'It's going to be a long job.'

'We don't have much time. You federal guys have access to some pretty good hardware in computers. There has to be a link between our bomber and the *Hindenburg*.'

'It's still going to take some time,' sighed Hayes. Then: 'We'll get cracking on it.'

'It's a long shot,' admitted the security chief, 'but we've got to get the bastard before he initiates a repeat performance of the *Hindenburg* disaster.'

Danny Macmillan paused outside the cabin occupied by Claire Ashton and knocked gently. There was no reply. He called urgently through the door.

'It's me, Claire. I've just got half an hour. It's me—Danny.'

There was still no answer. He tried the handle and, to his surprise, found that it turned and the door was open. The cabin was in darkness. He closed the door behind him and peered round, letting his eyes adjust to the dimness. Claire was lying face down on her bunk.

'Claire?'

He walked across and sat uncomfortably on the edge of the bunk, letting his hand lie gently on her shoulder. Her shoulders were heaving; deep, rasping sobs shook her whole body. He had a momentary feeling of helplessness.

'I'm sorry, Claire. I wanted to be the one to tell you but I was on duty. I've only a few minutes before I have to go back.'

She did not speak. They remained in a silent tableau for a while. Only the sound of the deep, racking sobs broke the stillness.

'Let me get you a drink,' Macmillan said after a while.

'No, no . . .' she turned hurriedly on her back and held out a hand to him. 'Don't go, Danny. Please!'

He could not see her face in the gloom. It was a mass of shadows. He reached forward and gently traced her cheekbone. He could feel the salty wetness on her cheeks.

'I'm here, Claire,' he said. 'Don't worry.'

She reached up a hand to grasp his, gripping it so tightly that Macmillan nearly winced.

'He never thought I loved him, Danny,' she said, after a long silence. 'I never acted as though I did.'

Macmillan did not reply. He could not intrude himself into this world of hers—not yet. His role was merely to support and help her.

'All my life I wanted his love,' she went on. 'He was too remote, too austere. He wasn't a man who displayed his emotions. I suppose that's why I always tried to draw attention to myself, so that he would notice me, love me. I wanted him to love me more than anything.'

Macmillan patted her hand.

'We all have to grow up eventually, Claire.'

'But he's dead now. He never knew. . . .'

She stopped and gulped, flinging herself into Macmillan's arms and moaning softly. Macmillan sat there, arms around her shaking body, making soft comforting noises in his throat and feeling totally inadequate.

Chapter Eight

Billy Heath, working over his navigational charts, checking figures, glanced up.

'We need a five-degree starboard course change, skipper.'

Carson acknowledged and looked across at Saxon.

'Disengage automatic pilot, Tom.'

Saxon reached forward, flicking switches in the required pattern.

'Disengaged,' he grunted when the green light came on.

'Starboard five, commencing the turn now,' Carson began and then frowned. 'Is the auto-pilot fully disengaged?'

Saxon checked.

'I'm getting no response on rudder and elevator controls.'

Behind them, Macmillan and Billy Heath exchanged anxious glances.

Carson fiddled with the controls.

'Still no response,' he muttered. 'Switching to the secondary circuit.'

There was a silence.

'No response.'

Saxon began to go through the checks and then examined the secondary circuit responses. The computer controls showed that the elevator and rudder controls on the tail section were perfectly aligned and should be responding normally but were not; the course correction data which Carson was now feeding into the circuit was simply being ignored.

'Danny,' called Carson, 'check out the systems on your monitor.'

Macmillan started to go over the procedural checks. The elevator and rudder controls of the vessel were the main steerage systems. The controls worked through five computer circuits, as most of the important control systems did. All computer circuits had to be running in synchronisation or a warning light would start blinking in the flight deck control panel. However, even with four of the synchronised circuits knocked out, the *Albatross* could still be flown on the fifth. But it was to be a rule of airship flight that all five systems had to be working in synchronisation before take-off.

Macmillan was looking worried.

'According to the check-out, everything should be working fine,' he reported. 'Trouble is, there's just no reaction from the tail section.'

'Jesus!' breathed Billy Heath, 'does that mean we're stuck at this course and altitude forever?'

Carson grinned.

'We can make course changes by shutting down our engines and using them to turn. It's a cumbersome technique but efficient. Also, we can change our altitude with gas and ballast. However, our primary control systems should make those old-fashioned methods obsolete. The worry is—what is wrong with the systems?'

Saxon gazed at him anxiously.

'The mad bomber again? Sabotage?'

'Could be,' replied Carson as he sat puzzling over the controls. 'Switch back to auto-pilot, Tom. Billy, keep an eye on our course and make sure you know by how much we are deviating from our flight plan. Before I start any cumbersome method of course changing I want to check out the tail section controls.'

Saxon went through the procedure to bring the auto-pilot into action again and then, with an acknowledgment that it was done, he turned to Carson.

'You reckon you know where the problem lies, Garry?'

'The only place I can think of is the tail maintenance section terminal, that's where the computer feeds into an induction control which then gives information to the tail section. I think I'd better go down there for a look.'

'If it's our saboteur you better not go alone,' advised Saxon.

Carson half-nodded.

'Billy, patch me through to Van Kleef.'

A moment later he was explaining the problem to the chief designer of the *Albatross*.

'I am going to the tail maintenance section terminal now.'

'Okay, Garry,' acknowledged Van Kleef. 'I'll join you there.'

Carson was just about to stand up when the ship lurched. He was pushed back into his chair.

'What the. . . .'

The gigantic vessel was trembling slightly and peering across the control board to the altimeter, Carson saw its needle swinging downwards. Saxon was staring at the controls, his hands still resting on his knees.

A red warning light and bell came on simultaneously. Saxon automatically reached across to silence the bell, leaving the red light winking like a baleful eye.

'The auto-pilot has just taken us down five hundred feet,' he whispered in disbelief.

Carson stabbed at several buttons.

'The auto-pilot override warning has come on,' sang out Saxon.

Carson was checking the systems again.

'Indicator says that the auto-pilot is being overridden manually,' he gasped.

'Skipper!' It was Maxmillan. 'Rudder control is in operation now.'

'We've just made a ten-degree port course change!' cried Billy Heath from his navigation console.

Carson swore softly.

'Disengage auto-pilot, Tom.'

Saxon had broke out into a sweat.

'Auto-pilot off but . . . damn it! . . . we're climbing. The damn controls are operating themselves!'

'Get me Van Kleef again, Billy,' snapped Carson. There was a moment's pause.

'Oscar . . . the control systems on rudder and elevators are being controlled manually. We can't control the ship!'

There was a long pause before Van Kleef replied.

'Alright, something is interfering with the signals. Something is giving spurious signals on all five computer control systems . . . hell, even if those controls are fourteen microseconds out they could destroy the *Albatross*.'

'I'm on my way to the tail section now!' said Carson. He began to climb out of his seat. 'Tom, you have the con. Put her back on auto-pilot but there's not much we can do until we get the control systems back.'

Saxon looked up with a pinched expression.

'Let's hope the auto-pilot doesn't decide to take the *Albatross* down any further, otherwise we'll be the first airship to go through undersea trials.'

No one laughed.

In the lounge, the Secretary for Air shifted his weight in his armchair and tried to mop up the remains of his drink.

'That was some air pocket we must have hit,' he grinned ruefully to Maclaren.

Maclaren nodded absently and glanced across to where Oscar Van Kleef was taking a phone call at the bar.

The British government official followed his eyes and smiled.

'Doctor Van Kleef is rather a strange man, isn't he?'

Maclaren swung his gaze back to the man.

'Oscar? I suppose all inventors are a bit goofy. Oscar is quite a genius. After all, we have the proof of his genius about us.'

He gestured round the luxurious lounge of the airship.

'Strikes me that you were all a little goofy,' said the Air Secretary. 'Attempting to make airships viable again when you have to fight against history.'

Maclaren sighed. The Air Secretary's favourite theme was airship disasters, especially since the news of the *Charles de Gaulle*.

'Remember the American Navy R38?'

'That was 1921, Mr. Secretary, and this is slightly larger and designed with a higher degree of technology.'

'Yes, but the point is that during its trial flight it broke in two and killed thirty-two of its crew of thirty-seven. Then the USS *Shenandoah*, our own one hundred per cent American-built airship, broke in two. . . .'

'After flying more than nine thousand miles in complete safety,' Maclaren pointed out. 'And even when it did break, its forward section managed to land in safety and twenty-nine out of its forty-three crew members were saved.'

The Air Secretary smiled.

'Okay, so you've done your homework on the history of these things. The point is, with all the disasters, how are you going to convince Joe Public that airships are safe?'

'Example, I suppose,' replied Maclaren. 'But it sounds as if you've changed your mind about airship safety since you spoke at the press conference when we took off at Portland.'

'Me? Don't get me wrong. It's Joe Public out there. What is he going to say after the disaster of the *Charles de Gaulle*, eh? I would be putting my political career on the line if I stood up and started telling him how safe airship travel was in the face of that disaster.'

'Why not tell your Joe Public the truth?'

The Air Secretary looked surprised.

'The truth is a heady wine, Maclaren.'

Maclaren was distracted by Van Kleef leaving the lounge in a hurry. There was a look on his face which the project manager did not like. He stood up and excused himself. Outside the lounge was the Chief Purser's office. He went in and called the flight deck.

Saxon explained the position.

'We just had another altimeter drop,' he said. 'We are now down to one thousand feet above sea level. Another couple of drops like that. . . .'

He didn't finish.

'You say Carson and Van Kleef are headed towards the tail unit?'

'Yes.'

'So am I,' snapped Maclaren.

Carson groped his way along the darkened catwalk towards the tail section of the *Albatross*. Away from the insulated and protected areas of the main part of the vessel, he could hear the whistling of the wind over the skin of the airship. He shivered slightly, more in reaction to the noise than to the drop in temperature.

It was dark in this part of the ship, apart from the occasional inspection light. There was no need for anyone to enter the area except the technicians who made regular inspections when the ship was at her moorings. The entire working of the elevators and rudder section on the tail was governed by computer control and, usually, it was unnecessary for anyone to go near the manual override section.

Carson paused to light his flashlamp and peer round in the darkness.

The induction control was on the third level and he climbed one-handed up the metal service ladders. The control was housed in a black metal casing, its cover held in place by half a dozen butterfly nuts. It was the work of a few moments for Carson to undo them and shine his torch among the wiring circuits that led from the main computer controls to the actual mechanism of the tail section.

He whistled softly.

Someone had obviously re-wired the circuits and there, nestling among them, was a small black transistor pack, identical to that which Van Kleef had removed from the gas valve controls. The saboteur had re-wired so that the auto-pilot would appear to be working normally, yet the transistor could give its own orders. That required a lot of electrical and technical knowledge.

Carson swung his torch round, looking for the intercom.

He pressed the button code for the bridge.

'Tom? I've found the fault. Someone had re-wired the induction synchronisations into a transistor sender and that's the device which is creating the spurious signals.'

'Repairable?' Saxon sounded casual.

'I think so. Van Kleef hasn't got here yet. Maybe you'd better send Macmillan along.'

'Alright, skipper.'

Carson turned back to the transistor and tried to see how it was wired up. He shivered slightly in the colder temperature.

A scraping sound on the ladder caused him to glance up.

'Oscar? Is that you?'

A figure emerged into the semi-gloom. Carson recognised the figure and turned away.

'Have you been sent to help me sort out this mess?' he asked.

He suddenly felt a sharp pain just below his ribs. He stared down in astonishment at the dark object which protruded from his body. He opened his mouth to protest but his world seemed to turn black and he sank slowly to the floor.

The figure bent over him and, with a quick jerk, withdrew the sharp chisel from Carson's inert body. The figure paused and then began to climb upwards to the higher levels.

Chapter Nine

Harry Maclaren swung swiftly along the catwalk into the dark tail section of the airship, scrambling up the service ladders into the induction control area. As he climbed into the section, he abruptly halted in the gloom. A figure was bending over something which lay slumped on the deck. The figure started and turned. It was Oscar Van Kleef.

'Who's that?' he demanded, his voice high-pitched with tension.

'Maclaren,' answered the project manager. 'What in hell's going on?'

Van Kleef's face was drawn and white.

'It's Carson . . . he's dead.'

'Dead?'

Maclaren's voice cracked with disbelief. He moved forward. The pilot lay crumpled on the deck. Maclaren bent forward and felt for a pulse on the man's neck, just behind the ear. Van Kleef was right. Garry Carson lay lifeless.

'What happened, Oscar?' Maclaren asked, staring at the chief designer curiously.

'There was a problem with the tail unit control. Carson asked me to meet him here. When I arrived he was just lying there.'

He moved his hand into the light of Maclaren's flashlight.

It was covered in a red sticky substance.

'He's been wounded in the chest.'

Maclaren swung his torch back to the body.

'Looks like a knife wound.'

He gave a swift inspection of the compartment and then unhooked the intercom.

'Terrasino? Yeah, Maclaren. Come to the tail section maintenance area. We have a problem. Yeah. Carson—someone has killed him.'

There was a movement on the ladder below. Both men tensed as a shape came up the ladder into the section.

'Macmillan!'

Danny Macmillan stared up, his flashlight swinging towards Maclaren.

'Oh, it's you. Where's Garry?'

Maclaren stood aside and pointed.

'Someone's killed him, Danny. Our mad bomber most likely. We're waiting for Terrasino.'

Macmillan looked as if someone had punched him in the jaw. He shook his head like a prizefighter recovering from a blow.

Before he had time to say anything the intercom buzzed. Maclaren answered. It was Tom Saxon.

'Hello, Maclaren. I didn't realise you were down there. How are Carson and Macmillan doing with the control override? We've just taken another five-degree starboard course change and are decreasing our height slowly.'

'One moment, Saxon,' replied the project manager. 'We'll get back to you.'

He looked at Macmillan.

'Did Carson ask you to come here and help out?'

The flight engineer nodded.

'Garry had found a transistor overriding the elevator and rudder controls.'

Maclaren shone his torch to the induction control unit. It was still open where Carson had been inspecting. It did not take long to locate the small black transistor.

'Can you re-wire?' demanded Maclaren.

Macmillan examined the box.

'Yeah; easy.'

'Let me help,' muttered the chief designer and found a special emergency light switch which bathed the induction control box in a white glow.

'Sabotage?' asked Maclaren, as he watched the two men bending over it.

Van Kleef nodded.

'But why did the saboteur kill Carson?' he demanded.

Terrasino burst into the compartment. One of his men, Parish, was hard on his heels. The security chief went straight to the pilot's body and examined it carefully without touching it.

'Stabbed with something, eh, Harry? I guess it went through the upper stomach and under the rib-cage into the heart.'

The security chief gazed up.

'Our mad bomber?'

'We have a sabotage problem here,' affirmed Maclaren.

'Okay,' said Macmillan, standing up. He handed Terrasino the small transistor. 'It's fixed now but mad or not, that was a neat bit of wiring that he did.'

Terrasino took the transistor. It was no use talking about prints. He glanced at it as he thrust it in his pocket.

'Same as before?' he asked Van Kleef.

The chief designer nodded.

'So what have we got?' mused Terrasino. 'Carson came here to investigate?'

'Yeah,' affirmed Macmillan. He explained briefly the control problem. 'Our tail section was all fouled up. He found the trouble and then asked me to come down to help him clear it.'

'I was already on my way but by the time I got here. . . .' Van Kleef shrugged.

'The screwball must have surprised him or he surprised the screwball,' said Terrasino. He frowned, gazing around, and then exhaled deeply.

'Okay, Danny. You'd better get back to the flight deck.'

Macmillan gave a brief nod.

'I'll tell Saxon he has control,' he said. He reached for the intercom.

'Tell Art Stein to take the co-pilot's seat for the rest of this watch; we'll have to work out something permanent later,' Maclaren told him.

'Do I take it that Tom Saxon is now skipper?' asked Macmillan.

Maclaren hesitated.

'Yeah; tell him to meet me in Mr. Badrick's cabin as soon as he can.'

Tom Saxon felt a numbness.

'Garry Carson is dead, you say?'

'Yes,' replied Danny Macmillan. 'This makes you skipper from here on.'

Saxon was gazing blankly at the controls in front of him. His mind was a whirlpool of conflicting emotions. God! What would Helen feel? For the first time in a couple of years he felt suddenly cold and completely sober. He felt as if an ice-cold bucket of water had been poured over him, as if someone had slapped him across the face and altered his perspective of life.

'Did Terrasino get whoever did it?' he asked at length.

'Terrasino is investigating,' replied Macmillan. 'They are taking Garry's body to the sickbay.'

Saxon forced himself to think about the ship.

'The tail section is now fully functional?' He tried to put a crispness in his voice.

'Yeah; should be.'

'Right, I want some course changes to ensure full functionability.'

Macmillan and Billy Heath exchanged a surprised glance at his tone. They watched as Saxon slipped out of the co-pilot's seat into the command chair.

'Don't you want to wait for Art Stein?'

'We can make the course changes ourselves.'

Macmillan sighed and moved to the co-pilot's seat.

'I'm releasing the auto-pilot . . . now!' snapped Saxon. There was no appreciable difference in the feel of the controls. He flicked the switches and turned on the computer link for the tailplane elevators.

'Climbing,' he murmured, as he drew back on the short stick which gave instructions to the computer control. The needle on the altimeter began to rise slowly. After a short while, Saxon returned the control to normal setting.

'Levelling off. Climb satisfactory.'

He glanced over his shoulder.

'What's our new position?'

Billy Heath hesitated.

'Navigator! Christ, man, I want information now! What is our new height and position?'

Danny Macmillan shot a look of dislike towards Saxon. Why should he start bullying Billy Heath at a time like this? There was no need. . . . Even as the thought crossed his mind, Macmillan suddenly realised there was a need. Saxon could not let his crew fall apart with shock at the death of Garry Carson. There was a screwball on board whose intention it was to destroy them all. The crew had to be in top form. They could not be allowed to give way to their emotions until the *Albatross* was safely on the ground. Macmillan studied Saxon out of the corner of his eye with a new respect.

Billy Heath was stammering out the new height and position.

'Right,' acknowledged Saxon. 'I am going to make a half-turn to port now.'

The great ship reacted almost immediately. Saxon made a

further turn, bringing the vessel back to its original true course. Then he locked on the auto-pilot again.

'The tail section is working fine,' he said, with false satisfaction.

Art Stein came on to the flight deck. He looked grim.

'I've just heard,' he said.

No one spoke for a moment and then Saxon motioned Art to take over from Macmillan in the co-pilot's seat.

'I've engaged auto-pilot, Art,' Saxon said. 'Keep an eye on the shop. I have to talk with Maclaren and Badrick. Just let her run on auto but if there are any problems buzz me immediately.'

Maclaren and Badrick were arguing animatedly when Saxon knocked on Badrick's stateroom door. He entered on Badrick's invitation.

'Hi, Saxon. Take a seat. Drink?'

The rotund face of the chairman of Pan Continental was anxious.

Saxon declined the drink and saw Maclaren stare hard at him.

'Danny Macmillan has filled you in about Carson?' asked Badrick.

'Yes,' said Saxon, dropping into the chair which Badrick indicated. 'Has the murderer been caught?'

Before Badrick could reply there was a knock on the door and Terrasino came in, grey-faced. No one spoke while he seized a glass and poured himself a shot of whisky.

'No sign of the bastard or the murder weapon,' he muttered. 'He's probably dumped it overboard. Parish and Sands are searching the ship and Lindsay is on stand-by in case he has another try at the tail section.'

Saxon frowned.

'Just who are your men looking for, Terrasino?'

Terrasino shot him a look of annoyance.

'Anything unusual, that's all.'

Saxon nodded.

'It's a bit of a waste of time. All they will find is the people they expect to find because this mad bomber is one of us. Isn't that right?'

'A search might turn up the murder weapon. . . .'

'But you say it has probably been thrown overboard.'

'Jesus, Saxon!' snapped the security chief, 'just what do you suggest I do?'

Badrick held up his hands, trying to adopt a reassuring posture.

‘I am sure Terrasino is doing everything he can.’

‘There is not much we can do in the circumstances,’ admitted the security man. ‘Just be prepared for anything.’

‘We have to make an important decision,’ Badrick’s voice was heavy. ‘In case you haven’t realised it we have come to the point of no return . . . the halfway mark between our take-off and our set-down point. In view of what has happened we have to make a decision—do we go on or do we turn back?’

Maclaren spoke for the first time.

‘I have suggested we go back. The odds are too heavily stacked against us. Now that Carson is dead we haven’t the expertise to. . . .’ His voice trailed off as he met Saxon’s gaze.

Saxon’s face was impassive. He knew what Maclaren wanted to say.

Badrick waited for Maclaren to finish and when he did not he asked:

‘Is that all, Harry?’

Maclaren shrugged.

Badrick turned to Saxon.

‘How is the ship handling now? Have you any problems on the flight deck that I should know of?’

‘None. The ship flies beautifully. It’s everything Van Kleef said it would be. So far as I am concerned you have the same problems going back as going forward—so why not go forward?’

Terrasino nodded.

‘I have to admit that I’m in agreement with Saxon there. It’s six to one and half a dozen of the other, isn’t it? Anyway, why isn’t Van Kleef here to make the decision? It’s his ship.’

Badrick coughed.

‘Harry Maclaren and I decided that the decision should be confined to us four. At least we can be sure that none of us is the saboteur.’

Terrasino gestured in agreement.

‘I guess you’re right.’

Badrick was tugging at his lower lip.

‘Saxon is right,’ he said at last, ‘going forward or backward we will have the same problems. At this stage I’m for going forward, too. Sorry, Harry,’ he turned to Maclaren, ‘I’m being commercial about this but, dammit, it’s the only way to handle it. Whichever way we go we are over twenty-four hours from landing.’

Saxon stood up.

'Right. I take it that I am now in command of the *Albatross*?'

Badrick lit a cigar thoughtfully, glancing briefly at Maclaren.

'That's right. You're the captain.'

Saxon smiled shortly.

'So long as Terrasino can keep this psycho off our backs, I'll drop you nice and safe in the grounds of Buckingham Palace.'

'Cranfield Airport will do just fine, Saxon,' interrupted Maclaren, dryly.

Saxon turned and left Badrick's stateroom.

Maclaren caught up with him further down the corridor and halted him.

'I'm not a fool, Saxon,' he said shortly.

Saxon returned his gaze evenly.

'I never thought you were, Maclaren,' he replied.

'Alright. So let's level. I know you've been having a problem. I know Garry Carson covered for you and I know you fouled up a simulator run. I know the cause. Booze. Do you deny it?'

Saxon smiled thinly.

'Booze is the symptom, not the cause. Anyway, in essence you are right.'

Maclaren's eyes widened a little. He had expected Saxon to deny it. Drunks always denied they were drunks.

'Unfortunately I don't have proof enough to get you grounded, Saxon, nor to get Art Stein made captain. So let me tell you this . . . if I smell alcohol during the next twenty-four hours, I'll personally haul you off that flight deck.'

Saxon's eyes were smouldering.

'It's a deal, Maclaren. Give me the next twenty-four hours and I'll show you that your fears are groundless.'

Maclaren stared hard at the English pilot. Somehow, in spite of the haggard features of the man, the blood-tinged eyes and his unkempt appearance, which a few moments ago Maclaren had put down as a sign of his alcoholic condition, Maclaren saw something else. There was a ghost of a man there . . . the ghost of a man who had once been one of the Royal Air Force's top test pilots and holder of the Air Force Cross.

'I'll stay off your back for the next twenty-four hours, Saxon,' he said. 'But that's on condition you don't give me cause. If you give me a tinge of suspicion that you are knocking back the booze then I'll hit so fast it will make a cyclone seem like a summer's breeze.'

He turned and walked rapidly away.

Chapter Ten

Flames. Wreckage. Searing, unbearable heat. Tom Saxon groaned in his sleep and threshed in his bunk, waving his arms in a futile effort to keep the images away. They came—sharply clear, relentlessly. Faces drifting before him, swimming in and out of focus. The compassionate face of the policeman; the implacable face of the young terrorist; the accusing stare of Jan; the bewildered gaze of Tom Junior; the tender expression of Helen and the suspicious glance of Garry Carson. The faces twisted and turned in voiceless recrimination. And eventually the circle of faces dissolved into blazing wreckage. The mangled remains of the helicopter with its gruesome cadavers. Before it was in focus the image was replaced by the debris of Jan's car with its terrifying contents, the indictment of his wife's staring dead eyes. Then this, too, dissolved into the shattered twisted girders of the airship—the *Charles de Gaulle*, no, the *Albatross*—they seemed to merge into one awesome spectre. And then the faces came back again, swirling before him in soundless denunciation.

Sweating, Tom Saxon awoke and stared fearfully round his darkened cabin. He was suddenly very frightened. He lay, heart beating wildly, panic-stricken. He sat up abruptly, having reached a decision.

His thought processes of recent weeks had suddenly crystallised. He came to the realisation that he was still the lord of his fate and had not entirely resigned the job to alcohol. He was in control of his own thoughts. He was not a slave; he had not resigned his role just yet. He could still make valid judgments.

It felt as if he were coming into the sunlight out of a long, dark tunnel. He began to recognise that he had been having an affair—an affair with the enemy of life, the slayer, the pedlar of murky dreams, the king of lies whose tricks and deceits introduced maggots into the apple of truth. He had spent two years of unknowing apprenticeship to Lord Drunk, an apprenticeship of trying to accustom his system to the poison he was injecting into it. The apprenticeship had failed. He sat up and smiled and thanked the fates for that failure.

He was lucky. He was alive. Others had died. Jan, Tom Junior, Garry Carson . . . they all wanted to live, wanted to enjoy life's experiences whether they were sad or happy. Those sixty-three people on the *Charles de Gaulle*, hadn't they wanted to live? A few days ago he wouldn't have given a damn had he been on the French airship. Now he suddenly realised that he did care. He wanted to remain alive. He had a duty to the dead to remain alive and enjoy life. He wanted—more than anything—to go back to Portland to see Helen.

He swung out of bed and breathed in the stale tobacco and alcohol fumes which permeated the atmosphere. With an abrupt anger he swept the half-empty bottle of Old Grand-dad and the dirty glass off the side table and dropped them into the waste-basket. He drew fresh underwear and socks out of the closet drawer and a clean uniform from the cupboard. Then he stripped off and stepped into the shower cubicle, letting the warm water run over his aching body. He reached into a side cupboard and took out a fresh carton of *Lait de Chèvre* soap, tearing off the wrappings and letting the sweet-smelling lather foam over his chest. He smiled as he remembered that Helen had always teased him about his habit of using expensive perfumed soaps to wash with. It made him feel good. Other men liked deodorants, toilet waters, after-shaves . . . he preferred soaps.

He started thinking about Garry Carson and wondered whether he had ever known about Helen and himself. Then he found himself wondering how Helen was going to react when she heard the news about Garry. What would. . . .

It was like a breath of hot air passing close to his chest.

He saw the hole appear chest-high in the wall of the cubicle. For several moments he stared at it in incomprehension. Then he dropped as flat as the tiny cubicle would allow him to, knocking the shower switch off with his arm as he did so. There were two more dull thuds and two more holes appeared, coupled with the whine of bullets.

Someone had fired three shots through the cubicle wall; fired three shots at him! By a fluke the first shot had missed, though it was fired at chest height. Had he not dropped to the floor the second and third shots would surely have hit him.

His old reflexes woke after many dormant months.

He flicked open the catch of the shower cubicle and did a near-perfect parachute roll out of it onto the floor of his cabin and then leapt to his feet. There was no one in his cabin. Without pausing he jerked open the passageway door and peered outside. The corridor was deserted. Disregarding his nakedness he went cautiously into the corridor and moved along it, peering at the wall. At a spot obviously level with the shower cubicle there were three neat holes in the wall surrounded by powder marks. Whoever had shot at him had stood here, in the corridor, and fired deliberately through the wall.

A frown creased his forehead.

Whoever had done so must have had a thorough knowledge of the design of the ship to be able to fire exactly through the soft fibreglass walls into the shower. He shivered and looked carefully around. Then, aware of his undressed condition, he returned to his cabin, grabbed a towel and folded it around his waist before raising Terrasino on the intercom.

By the time the security chief arrived, Saxon had dried and dressed himself.

Terrasino examined the bullet holes with a fixed expression on his face. He examined them from the corridor and then from the inside of the shower.

'It's a damned lucky thing you dropped after the first shot, Saxon,' he said.

'Damned lucky!' echoed Saxon.

'Do you realise that whoever fired those shots had a pretty good knowledge of how far a .38 slug can penetrate through this material?' He tapped gently on the side of the cubicle.

'It did cross my mind, Terrasino,' agreed Saxon. 'But how do you know what calibre slugs they were?'

Terrasino smiled.

'By the size of the holes and allowing for the slug to fan out a fraction. Anything smaller would have drilled a neater hole and anything larger would have widened it out all over the place.'

'Pretty smart detective work,' admitted Saxon.

'There is one thing I can't figure,' went on Terrasino. 'How come whoever fired the shots knew you were taking a shower?'

Saxon shrugged.

'I suppose the person opened the door to my cabin and saw I was in the shower. My door wasn't locked.'

'Yes . . . but then why didn't they shoot you through the

shower door instead of going out into the corridor and firing through the wall?'

Saxon was startled.

'That didn't occur to me.'

Terrasino pursed his lips. He went back to the shower cubicle and peered at the bullet holes.

'It looks like the bullets have passed right through the skin of the *Albatross*. There's no chance of making any ballistic tests.'

The cabin telephone buzzed.

'Skipper,' it was Danny Macmillan. 'You're on watch, I'm afraid.'

Saxon grunted.

'I'll be on the flight deck immediately, Danny.'

Terrasino closed the shower cubicle door.

'I'll walk along to the flight deck with you, Saxon.'

'You think I need looking after?' grinned Saxon as they left the cabin.

'There's someone aboard who killed Garry Carson and has made a damned good attempt to kill you,' Terrasino replied evenly. 'Whoever it is knows this ship intimately. Whoever it is also happens to be one of us.'

'He might even be you,' joked Saxon but Terrasino's face was serious.

'That's right, Saxon. It might be me. But it's not. And I know damn well it isn't you because you didn't join until well after this madman started his act. So stay alert and stay alive, okay?'

They halted before the flight deck door. Terrasino smiled crookedly and walked on. For a moment Saxon stood looking thoughtfully after him before moving to join his crew.

For the first time in his life John G. Badrick felt nervous. He went into his private stateroom and made for the drinks cabinet. His wife, Alice, looked up in surprise. She glanced at the travelling clock on the table.

'It's unlike you to drink at this time, John,' she said quietly.

Alice Badrick was a gentle person, long resigned to her role as a business widow. She preferred to lead her own life, pursue her own interests and enjoy her husband's company when he could spare the time. She made no demands on him and accepted the long separations as a matter of course.

Badrick shrugged and poured himself a shot of malt whisky.

'I think we'll go on vacation after we get to London, Alice,' he said suddenly.

She stared in astonishment.

'Vacation? But you've been saying it was out of the question this year—what with the merger of Brasil Airfreight with Pan Continental and the *Albatross* project. . . .'

Badrick tossed back his whisky.

'I reckon it's about time I decided to take a vacation, don't you? Here am I, fat and sixty and with one coronary down. Hell, I've made a pile, Alice. It's time I started slowing down.'

Alice Badrick smiled a little. She knew her husband well. It was his way of saying that he was damned scared. She was not a stupid woman. She had heard the scuttlebutt; she knew all about the mad bomber and the threat to the *Albatross*. She shivered slightly. Still, if John wanted to play it this way. She smiled evenly.

'Where do you suggest, dear?'

Badrick frowned, his mind obviously elsewhere.

'What's that?'

'Where do you suggest we go for a vacation?'

'Oh . . . maybe a cruise in the Med. Maybe a Greek island or something.'

Alice Badrick nodded calmly.

'Yes, we could book from London and go straight on.'

Badrick smiled but it was clear her words had not registered.

'I'll just go and have a word with Harry Maclaren, dear,' he said, setting down his empty glass.

She watched him leave the cabin with a worried sigh.

Danny Macmillan had seized the opportunity to go to Claire Ashton's cabin before he went on watch.

The girl was half-lying, half-sitting on her bunk, red-eyed and ugly. On a side table stood the food which had been brought to her some hours before lay untouched. Macmillan sat down and kissed the girl gently on the forehead.

'Come on, Claire,' he admonished her lightly. 'You must eat.'

She gazed at him through bloodshot eyes.

'I feel awful, Danny,' she muttered.

'That's natural,' he replied. 'But you'll feel even worse if you don't get some food down you. I'll ask the purser to bring you something light and hot.'

Without waiting to hear her protests, he telephoned Olsen and ordered a hot snack.

'Have you spoken with your mother?' he asked her.

She nodded.

'Things are pretty incoherent,' she said. 'The reporters said that my father survived the crash but insisted on going back into the blazing wreckage to look for survivors. A policeman identified him.'

Macmillan pressed her hand gently.

'Your father sounds quite a guy.'

He felt her stiffen.

'He was . . . a pig!'

His eyes widened at the vehemence in her voice.

'He never loved me, never displayed any affection towards me. He always wanted a boy—he tried to make me into a boy when I was little and hated it because I was a girl. Him with his silly discipline. I . . . I wanted to be close to him. I wanted to love him. He rejected me. He was a pig!'

She started sobbing again.

'I wanted to love him, Danny. I wanted to love him!'

There was a gentle tap at the door. It was Olsen with a tray. Macmillan took it and placed it by her bed, then persuaded her to eat the food. She did so reluctantly, mouthful by mouthful, forcing each piece down. When she had finished, Macmillan glanced at his watch.

'I've got to go, Claire. I'm on watch.'

The girl nodded morosely.

'Thanks for coming by, Danny. I don't know what I'd have done without your support.'

She lay back, pale, withdrawn and distant. He wished he could touch her, really touch her, mentally. Communicate. He sighed and smiled softly.

'I'll be back to see you soon.'

Macmillan bent and kissed her lightly on the forehead but she made no response.

Chapter Eleven

Art Stein glanced at his watch. He had half an hour to go before the start of his next flight deck duty and he had a sharp, needling pain in his lower jaw. He realised that he should have had the filling seen to before leaving Portland. He had just never found the time. Now he was having to live with a god-awful toothache. He swung himself from his bunk, showered, dressed and went in search of the Chief Purser, Olsen. The man was apologetic.

'We've only a few aspirin in the emergency kit, Captain Stein,' he said.

'That isn't going to do me any good,' groaned Stein. 'Surely you have something stronger on board?'

Olsen thought for a moment and then broke into a smile.

'Yes; there's some pain-killers in the medical store-room on level seven, abaft the food storage rooms. But I won't be able to get them at the moment. Mr. Badrick has just called for me.'

'Never mind,' said Stein, 'I'll get them.'

Olsen reached into a cupboard.

'Well, here's the key . . . . the container number is marked on the label.'

Art Stein grimaced with gratitude and made his way to Deck Level Seven. He had no trouble in finding the store-room nor locating the container. He took out a strip of pain-killers, relocked the container and store-room and made his way to the nearby washroom. He threw back a couple of pills with the aid of the drinking fountain.

As he was coming out he heard a muffled clatter and peered cautiously along the corridor. This area of Deck Level Seven was basically a stores area, containing store-rooms for the ship's in-flight maintenance, food, ancillary items and other supplies. Theoretically, the Chief Purser was in charge of this deck area and no one other than the purser and his staff had business there.

His inquisitive instincts aroused, Art Stein walked down the corridor and found a store-room door half-open. He reached out a hand and pushed it slightly. It swung inward.

Stein was in no way prepared for what happened next.

As he made to grasp the door handle, the door flew wide open and, with an inarticulate cry, a figure leapt upon him, punching and kicking him. In the initial momentum, Art Stein was carried backwards and only by colliding against the far wall of the corridor did he manage to remain upright. Stein was fairly athletic and once he had recovered from his surprise, which was the main cause of his being bowled backwards, he was able to push the attacker away. As he did so he gaped with astonishment.

'Nieman!'

The project's chief electrical engineer was beetroot-red in the face. It was contorted with a fury such as Stein had never seen before. In the man's right hand he grasped something which glittered. It was a knife.

'Swine! Swine! Swine!' screamed Nieman. 'Spy! You saw me! You saw me!'

He swung the knife up but Art Stein rocked away and, almost in the same movement, kicked out at Nieman. His shoe caught the engineer's thigh. The man screamed in agony. The knife went clattering across the corridor.

'I'll get you! I'll get you all!'

Before Stein could do anything, Nieman had turned and fled up a service ladder.

Art Stein stood for a moment to catch his breath, puzzled and a little shocked. What in hell had come over Nieman? Was he crazy or something? The polite little engineer had never displayed temperament before. He had always been quiet, courteous and respectful. What in blazes had caused him to launch an unprovoked attack? Frowning, Stein moved to the door of the store-room. It was full of electrical equipment. He gazed about as if seeking an answer to Nieman's incredible behaviour.

There was a work-bench in the corner with a lamp hanging over it. Kurt Nieman had obviously been working at something when Art Stein had disturbed him. Curiously, the pilot walked forward and peered down at the collection of odds and ends on the bench. A box, a battery, a clock and wiring and . . . God! Art Stein had never seen sticks of dynamite before, but he had seen enough bad 'B' movies to know what they looked like. Slowly, he backed out of the store-room and peered around. His foot caught something. It was Nieman's knife. He gazed down at it. No, it wasn't exactly a knife. It was a chisel, a long, sharp chisel, equally as wicked and deadly as a knife. It was then the realisation hit him.

He turned to the nearest intercom and demanded Terrasino.

'This is Stein,' he said quietly, giving his location. 'I've found your mad bomber . . . yeah, that's what I said. Get up here immediately.'

In a few moments Terrasino was staring at Art Stein in amazement.

'Nieman?' he asked slowly.

Stein was leaning back against the store-room wall.

'I feel lousy,' he said. 'You haven't got a drink on you by any chance?'

Terrasino shook his head.

'Are you sure it was Nieman?'

'Sure, I'm sure,' replied the pilot indignantly. 'The guy's cuckoo, out of his skull.'

'Where is he now?'

'He went up the service ladder to Deck Eight.'

'Damn it, we've got to find him,' muttered Terrasino.

The intercom buzzed.

'Terrasino,' snapped the security chief, grabbing the receiver.

It was Billy Heath.

'I've a priority one signal from the FBI in Portland. I'm patching it through.'

Hayes's voice came on the line.

'We've been re-running the checks on the *Hindenburg* and *Albatross* personnel,' he said.

'And?' prompted Terrasino as Hayes paused.

'We've come up with something interesting. There was a rigger named Schmidt on the *Hindenburg*. Just before the last voyage of the airship in '37 this guy Schmidt moved his wife and kid to the States. His kid was about eight years old. Schmidt didn't like the way things were shaping up in Germany. He was a member of the Socialist Workers' Party which had been proscribed in 1933. Schmidt had seen its leaders and many of his fellow members being taken off to concentration camps in the mid-thirties. He apparently felt his time was going to come. So he made plans to emigrate with his family. However, having smuggled his wife and kid out, Schmidt decided that the *Hindenburg* trip of '37 was to be his last on the airship. He was right, but not in the way he planned. His wife and kid were waiting at Lakehurst when the *Hindenburg* began to land . . . and burst into flames.'

Terrasino interrupted impatiently.

'What has this to do with Anglo-American personnel?'

'Hold your horses, son,' went on Hayes imperturbably. 'Frau Schmidt remarried during the war years. Like most of the German nationals, she and her son were interned from 1941-45. In the camp she met a man and married and her son was legally adopted, changing his name from Schmidt to. . . .'

'Kurt Nieman,' interposed Terrasino.

There was a long pause at the other end of the wire.

'How did you know?' gasped Hayes.

'Because Nieman has just crawled out of the woodwork. We are searching for him now.'

'It seems you were right about Keller,' said Hayes. 'Keller was just playing with industrial sabotage. But Nieman . . . Nieman has lost his marbles. Seeing his father burnt to death when the *Hindenburg* went up must have affected the boy, and that is why he signs his notes with the name of the *Hindenburg*'s captain. The trouble is, after the war, something else happened to the kid. He became attached to his mother, of course. But he had a good relationship with his step-father who, by coincidence, was also an aeronautical engineer. Nieman Senior became involved in the experiments being conducted by the U.S. Navy Department into non-rigid airships. There was an accident. He was killed when the ship he was working on burnt up in 1949. The mother was unable to cope and committed suicide. Although we can't be sure, reports say that she did so in front of the boy; flung herself off Brooklyn Bridge just like a bad movie story.'

'Which places Nieman around the age of twenty at that time?' mused Terrasino.

'A very immature twenty with a strong attachment to his mother. He was broken up and had to spend a year in a sanatorium. That's where we managed to track down the early records.'

'So I was right? Nieman is a paranoiac and now he is a very dangerous one.'

'Can you handle it?'

Terrasino grinned wryly.

'Ain't no one else up here to do it. I'll be in touch.'

He put down the receiver and took his Walther PPK out of its holster, checked a cartridge clip and thrust it back.

Stein watched him with a frown.

'Art,' said Terrasino, 'you better go and tell Saxon what's happening. Tell him that I'm trying to find Nieman.'

Stein nodded.

'He's crazy—watch out.'

'Yeah,' replied Terrasino shortly as he turned to call his security team.

When Stein reported to Saxon on the flight deck, he was met with incredulous stares from Danny Macmillan and Billy Heath. Saxon's face was imperturbable.

'You're joking? Kurt Nieman?' Macmillan was saying.

'Terrasino has gone after him. He told me to tell you, skipper,' replied Stein.

Saxon nodded.

'Are you fit enough to stand watch?' he asked Stein.

'If you can give me five minutes to wash up, I'll be okay.'

Danny Macmillan smiled cynically as Stein left.

'Looks like flight deck crews need extra insurance on this trip, skipper.'

Saxon didn't reply but re-checked the auto-pilot setting before relaxing. He glanced at Macmillan.

'Did you know Nieman well, Danny?' he asked.

'No, not really,' replied the flight engineer. 'He always kept himself to himself. We only spoke to exchange technical data. Even so . . . he seemed such an ineffectual person; wouldn't say boo to a goose.'

'Guess someone said that about Mr. Hitler once,' observed Billy Heath.

The intercom buzzed and Saxon reached forward.

'What?' His tone caused Macmillan and Billy Heath to glance up. 'Right. I'll be with you in a moment.'

Art Stein came on to the flight deck as Saxon was putting down the intercom.

'The con is all yours, Art,' said Saxon, easing himself from the command chair. 'Terrasino and his men have cornered Nieman up on Deck Level Fifteen by the gas compartments. Nieman has a gun and has already wounded one of Terrasino's men. I'm going up there.'

Billy Heath held up a hand, thumb upwards, while Macmillan muttered a soft 'Good luck, skipper.'

Chapter Twelve

Terrasino came crouching low along the corridor and halted beside the prone figure of one of his guards. It was Parish.

'He's up at the end,' whispered Parish, 'just behind Number Seven Tank.'

Terrasino squinted along the corridor.

In the darkness there came a blinding flash, the report of an automatic and a bullet whined dangerously close to his head. Beside him Parish grimaced.

'Careful. He knows how to shoot. Lindsay took a slug in the arm and he's in sickbay.'

'Bad?' asked Terrasino.

'Naw. A flesh wound.'

Terrasino glanced around.

'I want this section completely sealed off. Go tell Maclaren to keep everyone away from here.'

Parish nodded and began to slide backwards along the corridor. Another shot pinged into the fabric near his body.

Terrasino brushed his hair back from his forehead and squinted again into the darkness.

'Kurt!' he called softly. Then, more loudly. 'Kurt! It's me Terry Terrasino. Can you hear me?'

There was a silence before Nieman's voice echoed hollowly along the corridor.

'I hear you perfectly, Terrasino,' came his precise voice.

'Can we talk?'

'Well?'

Terrasino sighed, trying to remember all the text-book advice he had learnt about dealing with psychopaths.

'Come on, Kurt. This is no way to behave. People are going to get hurt.'

He knew it sounded ridiculous. After all, Nieman had already killed Alec and Jane Westbrook and Garry Carson and Jack Lane. What did he care if people were going to get hurt?

'They brought it upon themselves. I am sorry that people have to be hurt but there is no other way.'

Terrasino tried to adopt a sorrowful father attitude.

'But what do you hope to achieve by this, Kurt?'

'My wishes were made plain all along, Terrasino. By ignoring them you have brought death upon yourselves. It is nothing to do with me.'

Kurt Nieman's voice was even, conversational. Terrasino shuddered slightly.

'You said you want us to destroy the *Albatross*. . . .'

'Work on these terrible engines of destruction must cease.' For the first time Nieman's voice rose in anger. 'It is God's will! His hand was raised against these airships from the beginning. Man ignores God at his own peril.'

'If you want to destroy the *Albatross* why do you kill people —why the Westbrooks, why Jack Lane, why Garry Carson? Surely God does not approve of destroying people?'

'It is sad that people must die but God understands. When there is a greater good to be achieved, people do not matter. Didn't God destroy the people of Sodom and Gomorrah for the greater good? Fire must root out evil. Those who refuse to obey the commands of God must perish.'

Terrasino bit his lip.

'Okay, Kurt. But how do you know that God commands man not to work on airships?'

Nieman's voice rose a fraction, almost pityingly, like a teacher trying to explain a simple problem to a particularly dumb pupil.

'God speaks to me, Terrasino. He tells me. Did he not send all the great airships of the past crashing to a fiery doom as a sign of his displeasure? Was he not ignored? And the French ship, yesterday? Is that not his sign? Yet man does not heed him. My own father, my step-father . . . they did not heed the signs. Innocent people suffered. No more shall the innocent suffer. No more. . . .'

For the first time there was a catch in Nieman's voice.

Terrasino realised that it was hopeless trying to reason with the man. He tried to force his voice to stay calm and friendly.

'So what do you want us to do, Kurt? Just tell us what you want?'

There was a bark of laughter from Nieman.

'Don't think that I will fall for any tricks,' he called. 'It is too late. The *Albatross* is doomed. It, too, will end its life amid the fires of hell like all the rest!'

He punctuated his statement with another shot.

A figure abruptly threw itself down beside Terrasino. It was Tom Saxon. The security chief glanced hopelessly at him.

'This creep is really out of his skull, Saxon,' he whispered. 'I've tried talking with him but it's useless.'

Saxon peered along the corridor.

'We've cordoned off this section so far as we are able, using members of the project's technical crew. There are men on the level below and in the parallel corridors.'

'Then it's probably a question of just waiting,' said Terrasino. 'He's got an automatic with him and I don't know how much ammunition.'

'You can't fool me,' suddenly came Nieman's voice. 'I know you are plotting to capture me, whispering about me.'

'We're just trying to talk with you, Nieman,' called Saxon. 'We're just trying to find out what you want of us?'

Nieman's laughter was much higher-pitched now.

'I want nothing more—it is too late, too late for all of you. I have placed my incendiary device. Soon the *Albatross* will be destroyed and God's will be done.'

Saxon felt himself go cold and beside him Terrasino exhaled slowly.

'So the bastard has planted a bomb,' Terrasino said.

'We've got to get that maniac and find it,' hissed Saxon.

'Damned right?' the security chief snapped back, easing from his holster his Walther PPK automatic. 'Are you sure that this section is blocked off?'

'Yes.'

'Okay. We only have one chance. I'm going to rush him while you try to distract him by talking.'

Saxon grabbed Terrasino's arm.

'That's bloody ridiculous! He'll gun you down before you're halfway along the corridor.'

'All I need is one clear shot at the bastard,' returned Terrasino. 'There's a recess five yards up. If I can get there, I stand a chance.'

Saxon was dubious.

'Christ, man!' swore Terrasino. 'It's the only chance we've got. We can play it cool and hang around until his bomb goes off or we can make a fighting chance of it.'

Saxon shrugged. He supposed Terrasino was right. They had to do something to try to avert a catastrophe.

He leant forward.

'Nieman,' he called. 'This is Tom Saxon. Look, why don't we—you and I—meet in the corridor and talk about this?'

'What for?' sneered Nieman's voice.

'Well, we can talk this thing through. You don't really want to kill yourself, do you? And that's what will happen if we sit around waiting for the bomb to go off.'

'I am prepared. I have made my peace with my maker. It is God's will.'

'Now, surely you've mistaken what it is God really wants you to. . . .'

Terrasino touched his arm lightly, sprang to his feet and sent two shots blazing down the corridor, at the same time making a crouching sprint towards the recess.

There came a snarl of rage, almost a scream, and three shots blazed back.

Terrasino gave a cry and collapsed before he had gone two yards.

Saxon grabbed him by the leg and hauled him back to cover.

There was blood all over Terrasino's right thigh, staining his pants. His face was white, teeth gritted against the pain. He still held his automatic in his hand.

'I told you, I warned you not to try anything!' came Nieman's cry of rage.

Saxon ignored him and hauled off his neck-tie, twisting a make-shift tourniquet around Terrasino's leg.

'Flesh wound, I think,' he muttered, trying to sound encouraging.

There was a scrabbling noise at Nieman's end of the corridor.

Saxon frowned as he glanced along towards the sound.

'I think he's going up the service ladder,' he muttered.

'We've got to get him, to find that bomb,' groaned Terrasino.

Saxon glanced over his shoulder, then back into the blackness. He stood up carefully, still slightly crouching, and began to haul Terrasino back towards the section doorway. No more shots rang out as they reached it and Parish bent forward to help drag the security chief through.

Badrick was there, looking white-faced, along with Maclaren and the other security man, Sands.

'Get Terrasino to sickbay,' snapped Saxon to Parish.

'No way!' snarled Terrasino. 'It's my job to nail that bastard.'

'Get to sickbay,' returned Saxon. 'I'm responsible for the safety of this ship. Get going,' he added to Parish.

Terrasino tried to haul himself up but his shoulders slumped. He had fainted. His automatic fell from his grasp. Saxon bent and picked it up. It was many years since he had handled a gun. It seemed unfamiliar. He checked the mechanism to refresh his memory and pocketed the weapon.

'I'm going after Nieman,' he said as Parish, using a fireman's lift, carried the security chief away.

Maclaren and Badrick said nothing as Saxon turned and began to walk slowly along the corridor. There were no shots from the darkness. Nieman had moved upwards, towards the central inspection ladder which led out onto the ship's skin. Halfway along the corridor, Saxon turned and beckoned to Sands, the other security guard, to move forward as a back-up. Then he moved on to the small section which led to the stairwell. The door was marked 'maintenance crew only'. It was swinging open. Saxon thrust his hand into his pocket and drew out the automatic. In the semi-gloom he again checked the safety catch and then, flattening himself against the wall, he edged to the open door. He could hear nothing except a strange sighing, whistling noise. A cold draught of air was coming from somewhere. Swiftly, he jerked his head into the stairwell section. It was empty.

Where was Nieman?

There was only one way he could have gone—upwards; up the ladder to the maintenance inspection gallery which ran along the 'spine' of the airship's upper surface from nose to tail. It was a small flat walkway, three feet wide, which, when the ship was grounded, engineers could walk along while checking the surfaces for skin damage.

Nieman must be crazy. They were flying at five thousand feet. Saxon suddenly realised the irony of his thought. Nieman *was* crazy.

Badrick and Maclaren had joined Sands behind him.

Saxon looked at them and shrugged.

'The crazy bastard has gone topsides,' he announced.

Badrick looked relieved.

'Well, at least he's taken his damned bomb out of the ship. If it explodes out there, damage will be negligible.'

'We don't know that, Mr. Badrick,' replied Saxon. 'We don't know if he was carrying the bomb or not. While Nieman is insane, he is certainly no fool. He may have already planted his bomb somewhere in the ship. I'll have to follow him out there and make sure.'

Maclaren shook his head.

'Not in these weather conditions, Saxon. It's too dangerous.'

'No more dangerous than sitting on a time-bomb,' replied Saxon.

He turned and began to climb up the ladder. Maclaren laid a hand on his arm. Saxon gave him a questioning glance.

'Saxon . . . Tom . . . I'm sorry about what I said earlier. About you being a lush.'

Saxon grinned.

'Forget it. It was true anyway.'

He resumed his climb upwards and found that the hatch leading out onto the giant vessel's upper surface was open. Saxon raised his eyes cautiously over the hatchway rim. It was just twilight outside and he could make out the figure of Nieman about ten yards away, one hand only gripping the safety lines which stretched along the walkway. The wind was blustering and strong. In his other hand Nieman still held his revolver. Saxon found his mind detached enough to recognise the type of gun Nieman was carrying. It was a .38. A Smith and Wesson Centennial Airweight. Nieman was leaning into the air flow, almost holding himself upright in the slip-stream. Gently, slowly, Saxon began to climb outside.

The movement must have been caught in the corner of Nieman's eye because the man turned and sent a bullet crashing in his direction.

'Keep back! Keep back, blast you!' came his snarl of rage.

Saxon ducked back below the hatch rim.

'It's alright, Nieman,' he called. 'No one wants to hurt you.'

Privately he thought: if I get my hands on you I'll personally throw you overboard!

'Hurt me?' Nieman gave a hysterical laugh. 'Nothing can hurt me now. I have accomplished my holy task.'

'How about your bomb, Kurt? It'll just blow you to pieces and not even touch the ship. So why stay out there freezing?'

The answer was a coarse laugh.

Saxon ventured his head up again, ducking as the black muzzle of the .38 swung in his direction. Even as he dodged below the hatch rim he heard the hammer fall on an empty chamber; heard Nieman, with a curse, depress the trigger twice more and then fling the useless weapon towards the hatch.

Saxon raised himself up, grasping one of the safety lines, and pressed himself forward in the sudden cold rush of air that thrust at his body.

Nieman was backing along the catwalk, crouching low in the slip-stream.

Behind him, Maclaren yelled for him to come back but Saxon ignored him. His mind was alert and determined. He had to get to Nieman and make sure whether the man carried his bomb. If he had already planted it. . . .

'It's all over, Nieman,' he cried as loudly as he could into the wind.

He came within a few yards of the man and then, without warning, Nieman lashed out at him with his foot. Saxon swayed backwards, the wind pushing him hard so that he swung out of reach of Nieman's boot with little effort. Nieman slipped forward and nearly lost hold of the safety line.

'It's over, Nieman,' cried Saxon again.

'No!' The word was just a scream.

Nieman tried to kick out at Saxon again; again Saxon dodged and reached out a hand towards the man. Nieman darted backwards; as he did so, he stumbled, tried to regain his balance and fell, his hands clutching in the air, letting go of the safety line. To Saxon's horror, the man began to slide across the surface of the gigantic hull, his hands feebly scrabbling for a hold against the smooth fibreglass skin. His figure gathered momentum and then . . . then it had stopped and lay spread-eagled about ten yards away from Saxon. Saxon could see his white face staring upwards, the eyes large and piercing.

'Hang on, Nieman!' he cried, turning to look for a rope or safety line to throw down to the engineer.

Sands was peering out of the hatch behind him. Saxon edged backwards.

'I need a rope, a safety line. . . .'

Sands ducked below the hatch rim and swiftly reappeared with a bundle of thick yellow nylon climbing rope, which was hooked with safety clips. Grabbing it, Saxon made his way back to the point above Nieman and hooked the rope onto the safety lines, testing it cautiously with his weight. Then he let the rope slip down gently towards Nieman's spread-eagled figure.

'Grab the rope!'

The man didn't seem to hear. He made no move.

Biting his lips, Saxon twisted the rope over his shoulder and began to edge across the curving surface of the hull. He had a bad moment when his shoes slipped against the smooth fibreglass and he nearly fell but, using rock-climbing techniques, he leant backwards, edging down the outer surface of the ship, trying not to look into the vista of the foaming ocean five thousand feet below in the grey twilight.

He was a yard away from Nieman.

He turned and reached out a hand.

'Come on, Nieman,' he cried.

A crazed face peered back with a maniacal gleam.

'You are all doomed! I have already planted my bomb . . . inside the ship . . . doomed!'

Saxon saw the smile of exultation on the man's face.

'Grab the rope, Nieman!' he called.

'No! I go to my rest now . . . to my God! His will be done!'

Without warning, Nieman suddenly released his hold on the skin surface and seemed to push himself backwards into space. His body bounced and tumbled down the hull until it was lost to Saxon's vision. He could imagine it as a black speck falling thousands of feet into the ocean below.

For a while he hung at the end of the rope drained of energy, sick with strain.

Slowly he began to haul himself back towards the catwalk. Sands and Maclaren were there to help him up and through the hatch. When he had climbed back down into the maintenance section stairwell he turned towards their white anxious faces —Badrick, Maclaren and the security man. He stood for a while trying to regain his breath, then he forced himself to speak.

'He didn't have the bomb with him. He's already planted it somewhere on the ship. We don't even know when it's due to go up!'

Chapter Thirteen

They gathered in John G. Badrick's stateroom; Maclaren, Oscar Van Kleef, Saxon and Terrasino. Terrasino was white-faced and limping but the flesh wound was not serious, just painful, and he had insisted on attending. Strain and tension told on every face as the chairman of Pan Continental offered drinks.

'So we have a bomb on board,' Badrick said heavily. 'We don't know where it is or when it is timed to go off. And we are ten hours out from the Irish coast.'

Terrasino spoke first.

'Nieman was mad but clever. There was a certain logic in his madness.'

'Logic?' grunted Maclaren cynically.

'Let's work on the thesis that Nieman was paranoid. It seems to have held up so far. The paranoiac is, as I have said before, the world's champion grudge holder. He is subject to unalterable, systematised and logically constructed delusions. Nothing you can say will cause him to change his mind, and he defends his arguments with a degree of logic once his central premise is accepted.'

'So where does that get us?' demanded Badrick.

'What I am saying,' continued Terrasino, 'is that once you accept the central premise of the man's paranoia then everything follows a logical pattern. He often has a superior intellect and sharp perceptions, so we are not dealing with anyone who is haphazard in his thinking. The only difference lies in our interpretation of what is reality.'

'How does this help us find where Nieman planted his bomb?' asked Saxon.

Terrasino wiped the beads of sweat from his forehead. His leg was painful and sore and he kept feeling sick.

'Nieman was convinced he had been ordered by God to

destroy this airship, right? Nieman said it was God's will that the *Albatross* go up in flames. He alluded to Sodom and Gomorrah. I reckon he wants a public demonstration of his faith.'

'A public demonstration?' frowned Van Kleef. 'What do you mean by that?'

'The *Albatross* must not only go up in flames but must be seen to go up in flames. I believe that his bomb will be timed to go off when we are somewhere over England, so that people can witness what Nieman would call "the hand of God" at work.'

Badrick glanced at his watch.

'In other words, we have about fourteen hours to find and defuse the bomb.'

Terrasino shrugged.

'I'm not saying that is the word of the law, but I am saying it is a probability rather than a possibility.'

'Alright,' agreed Saxon. 'So we have fourteen hours . . . perhaps. But where do we start looking? This vessel is as big as a small town.'

Terrasino looked at Van Kleef.

'That is a question which you are best able to answer, Oscar.'

The chief designer frowned.

'What do you mean?'

'Get back to Nieman's logic. He knew this ship as well as anyone. He was the chief electrical engineer on the project. If he wanted to incinerate the ship in a great, spectacular fire, how would he accomplish it?'

'With difficulty, seeing that this is a helium-filled ship and inert gas is not going to make a spectacular fire,' interposed Maclaren.

'Are you sure that your deductions are right—that Nieman wants to create a holocaust fire?' asked Badrick.

'We are not sure of anything,' replied Terrasino. 'We can only work on probabilities.'

He turned back to Oscar Van Kleef who was stroking his forehead with a puzzled expression.

'Well?' prompted the security chief. 'How would Nieman go about it?'

'The only area where you would get a sustained fire on this ship is where the power and fuel storage is, on the lower levels, abaft the centre. A bomb elsewhere would do considerable damage, even cause the ship to break up in the right circumstances, but an incendiary device placed in the fuel storage area would create a fire sufficient to cause the type of holocaust which Terrasino is contemplating.'

Terrasino sat back with a sigh.

'Then that is the place I think we should concentrate on,' he said. 'Get everyone away from the area as far as possible and let us start a search. On no account is anyone to touch the device when it is found. It may be boobytrapped—in fact, that's very likely, knowing Nieman.'

It was Maclaren who started to issue the instructions. But Badrick was frowning.

'Just a minute. If, as you say, Nieman's idea is to ignite the bomb over England and the logical place is in the fuel storage, surely the fuel tanks would be empty at that time.'

Terrasino found himself nodding. It was a point he hadn't thought of.

Van Kleef looked rather annoyed.

'Mr. Badrick,' he said dryly, 'I thought you knew the design of the ship thoroughly. The tanks of the *Albatross* carry sufficient fuel for the return trip. We contain enough fuel to make a very thorough blaze.'

Saxon rose to his feet.

'What shall I do?' he demanded.

Terrasino grinned.

'Reckon you've done enough, Saxon. Just fly this bloody contraption and let me handle things from now on.'

Saxon caught sight of Van Kleef's pained expression and gave an answering grin.

'Right. And if you can't deal with the bloody bomb, just tell me when to jump.'

As Saxon entered the flight deck Art Stein glanced up.

'How's things, skipper?'

Saxon looked round at the anxious expressions of the flight deck crew.

'Terrasino has things in hand,' he replied shortly as he slipped into the command chair. 'At the moment we have a bomb on board but we think we know where it is.'

Danny Macmillan exchanged an anxious look with Billy Heath.

'Terrasino only *thinks* he knows where it is?' asked Heath.

'That's right. It was Nieman's farewell gift to us. But as we can't do anything about it, let's fly this airship. Give me our position, Billy.'

Billy Heath seemed to have a little difficulty in articulating. Finally, he stammered out their position.

'Good,' answered Saxon. 'That makes just nine hours and thirty minutes from the Irish coast. How's the wind velocity, Art?'

Art Stein checked some figures.

'We are picking up a ten-mile-an-hour tail wind, skipper, so we're coasting along at the moment.'

'What's the weather like ahead?'

'Pretty fair,' replied Billy Heath, checking his charts. 'There's a low pressure over Ireland and we might run into some localised rain but it's more or less okay.'

'How about the engine systems and controls, Danny?'

The flight engineer grinned.

'No problems. She's running like a dream.'

Saxon sat back satisfied. It was like old times. The accents were different but the *espirit de corps* was the same. The old days. He felt like a man emerging from some dark nightmare. The old days. . . .

It was Parish who actually found the device.

'It's housed in a black rectangular box, chief,' his voice crackled over the intercom in Terrasino's ear.

'Where is it placed?'

'It's wired up to the computer control system next to Fuel Storage Tank Seven.'

Van Kleef, standing next to Terrasino, banged his fist into the middle of his hand in agitation.

'Okay, Parish,' replied Terrasino. 'Stand by. I'll be down.'

He turned to look quizzically at the chief designer.

'It's next to the middle storage tank,' explained Van Kleef. 'If that goes up then everything goes up.'

Badrick moved forward angrily.

'How are we going to handle it?'

'I'll see if I can deal with it.'

Maclaren pursed his lips and shook his head.

'Dammit, man! You're running round with a gunshot wound.'

'Have you anyone else in mind for the job of defusing it?'

Badrick started and frowned.

'Defusing?'

'You don't reckon that now we've found it, we are just going to sit round staring at it until it goes off?' Terrasino demanded sarcastically. 'Someone has got to disconnect it from the computer section and drop it overboard.'

'Are you up to it? Can you do it?' Badrick stared at him, with worried expression growing more acute.

'Terrasino has had bomb-disposal experience in Air Force security,' pointed out Maclaren.

Terrasino was grinning at Badrick.

'With the sort of stakes that we are playing for, Mr. Badrick, I can make myself up to it.'

The explosive device was perched high on a small ledge near the control gauge panel which showed the fuel pressures from the main storage tanks to the power units. As Parish had stated, it was a small black rectangular box; a tin box. It reminded Terrasino of a small cash box. Even from his position six feet beneath the ledge Terrasino could see some coloured electrical wires snaking out of the tin and disappearing into the fuel-vent control panel which he knew was activated by computer controls from the main flight deck.

A movable maintenance ladder stood nearby.

'Put that in place for me,' he asked Parish.

The security guard did so and then looked dubiously at his chief.

'You can't go up there with that leg,' he said.

Terrasino raised a shoulder and let it fall.

'I'll have a damn good try because it's the only ball game in town.'

He began to climb up. It hurt. It hurt like hell but he forced himself to climb slowly. He could feel the blood oozing from his wound, seeping through the bandages. It seemed an age before his eyes drew level with the small box. He found himself drenched in sweat.

'Throw me up a towel,' he called.

Parish frowned but put his head into the corridor and repeated the request. A few moments later he thrust a small towel up to Terrasino who, holding on with one hand, wiped his face and then his hands, changing hands to hang on to the bars of the steel ladder.

'Okay, Parish, I'm going to start now,' he said evenly. 'It's no good telling you to get the hell out . . . if this baby goes up then we all go up with her.'

He peered closely at the box. It looked so innocuous, apart from the coloured wires at the back. Why connect the box to the computer terminals? Terrasino frowned a little as he studied the connections. It seemed odd, terribly odd. A thought struck him which he immediately dismissed as nonsensical; the box was in a clear vantage point, could so easily be seen and discovered. He moved his hand to test whether the lid of the box was secured or open. It moved a fraction. He let his hand fall away and turned to Parish waiting below.

'Can you find me an engineering plan of what's behind that control panel? I want to see where those wires are likely to terminate.'

Parish nodded, turned and left.

Terrasino looked once more at the coloured wires. If the wires, as seemed likely, were fixed to an electrical charge, then they would have to be cut simultaneously. But to do that he would have to have both hands free and synchronised. Not easy; even if he didn't have this ferocious stabbing pain in his leg it would not be easy.

'Here you are, chief,' came Parish's voice from below.

With an effort, Terrasino bent down and took the small clip-board from the security guard. Stuck on it was a plan of the control board system. Hell! He was right. The two wires were obviously fixed into an electronic power circuit. Well, there was only one thing to do.

'I want two pairs of very sharp pliers and a strong leather belt.'

Parish looked amazed.

'A leather belt, chief?'

'Yeah.'

Terrasino winced in pain and forced himself to turn back to the plan. He examined it, trying to figure out how the charge would be ignited.

'Hey,' he called, 'is Van Kleef out there?'

The chief designer looked into the cabin section. He was pale and nervous.

Terrasino, groaning inwardly, climbed down the ladder and thrust the plan at him.

'Oscar, what would cause a charge of electricity to pass along these terminals?'

He pointed. The designer looked at the diagram and frowned.

'The only time those wires become live is when the fuel tanks are changed. The pilot or co-pilot or engineer would switch over the fuel supply tanks and the vents are operated by a charge of electricity.'

'So until the fuel tanks are changed there is no power on the line at all? You're sure?'

Van Kleef smiled thinly.

'I designed the system. There's no power until the switches are pulled.'

Parish returned with the pliers and the belt.

Terrasino shoved both pairs of pliers in his pockets, draped the belt around his neck and began to climb slowly up the ladder again. Once on a level with the box he halted and then, still holding on with one hand, managed to wrap the belt around his waist and over the rungs of the ladder. Leaning backwards a little, he was able to use both hands to tighten the belt so that he could perch securely against the ladder, leaving both hands free to work. Next, he took out both pairs of pliers and gently laid them by the box.

'Towel,' he snapped and Parish threw it up again.

Once more Terrasino wiped the sweat from his face and hands and threw the towel down to Parish.

'Okay, the moment of truth, fellers,' he breathed.

Taking a pair of pliers in each hand, he manoeuvred them into position over the two wires at the back of the box. Then, gritting his teeth, he snapped them shut. The wires cut cleanly in two simultaneously.

Nothing happened.

Terrasino breathed a long shuddering inhalation.

Slowly he replaced the pliers on the ledge beside the box and turned to scrutinise it again.

Using one hand only, he eased up the lid a fraction, cautiously peering for any tell-tale signs which would indicate the box was boobytrapped. He could see nothing and raised the lid carefully. Inside, taped together, were three sticks of dynamite, each one eight inches long and about an inch and a quarter in diameter. He had seen the type before. They were Du Pont Red Cross Extra, very powerful charges containing forty per cent nitroglycerine. The wires were effectively attached. Any charge passing from the terminals in the control board would have set off the explosive.

Savagely, Terrasino tore the wires from the control board and handed the entire contraption down to Parish. The security man took it gingerly.

Terrasino untied his belt and climbed painfully down.

Van Kleef had been joined by Badrick and Maclaren. All three clapped him on the back and voiced their congratulations.

'Put that over the side, Parish,' Terrasino advised him as he tried to shrug off their words of praise.

'Brilliantly done, Terrasino,' said Badrick.

'Yeah,' grunted Van Kleef. 'I wouldn't like to go through that experience again.'

Terrasino smiled wryly.

'Let's hope we don't have to.'

Saxon smiled broadly at the news over the intercom.

'Damn good show!' he said, and turning towards the others added: 'Terrasino has defused the bomb.'

There was a chorus of congratulatory shouts on the flight deck which Saxon tried to still.

'Now we can relax,' breathed Billy Heath.

'We've still got to fly this thing,' admonished Saxon.

'Okay, skipper,' smiled Macmillan, 'just point the way.'

Saxon glanced at the ship's chronometer.

'The way for this crew is our respective bunks for the next six hours. The relief crew should be here in a moment. And I want you all spruced up when we land in dear old Blighty.'

Macmillan gazed at him in incomprehension.

'Land *where?*'

'Ignorant man,' smiled Saxon, raising his voice to a theatrical pitch. 'I mean that royal throne of kings, this sceptred isle, this earth of majesty, this seat of Mars . . . this precious stone, set in the silver sea. . . .'

Billy Heath grinned.

'He means England.'

Macmillan sighed.

'I always knew Limeys were crazy.'

Terrasino lay back on his bunk and tried to ignore the throbbing of his painful leg.

He was not relaxed. He was worried. He could not fully understand why. He had defused the bomb. It was a fairly simple device compared with the others he had handled in the Air Force. The only thing that had made it complicated had been the bullet wound in his leg. Apart from that the bomb had been a fairly crude affair, as if put together hastily. A crude affair! That's what did not fit in with Nieman's character. He remembered seeing the hoax bombs which Nieman had set before.

There was nothing crude about them. This device was not in keeping with Nieman's precise and careful workmanship.

Terrasino suddenly sat bolt upright on his bunk.

'Oh, sweet Jesus!' he muttered.

Chapter Fourteen

Terrasino paused outside his cabin door and groaned as the pain in his leg hit him. He looked up and down the corridor. There was no point in arousing Badrick, Maclaren or Van Kleef. If his surmise was wrong then he would look a damn fool. He turned and began to limp towards the centre of the ship.

'Terrasino!'

Tom Saxon came round the corner from the flight deck elevator.

'Oughtn't you to be in sickbay?'

'I ought to be in a nursery school,' growled Terrasino sarcastically. 'I reckon Nieman is laughing at us from hell.'

Saxon gazed at Terrasino in puzzlement.

The security chief decided to confide in the Englishman.

'The bomb I defused . . . I reckon it was a phoney.'

'What do you mean?'

'I reckon that Nieman planted a decoy. All the while I was defusing the bomb I felt something was wrong. I've seen his work before—he doesn't go in for crudely constructed devices and this one was crude. Then it was wired to an electrical circuit which would never have been used on this flight. I thought that Nieman might have tampered with the circuits but he hadn't. No, the sonofabitch put a dummy device where we'd find it and easily defuse it, then—thinking how clever we were—we'd go away and forget all about it until the real device went off.'

Saxon's mouth gaped.

'Do you know where the real device is?'

'I've an idea,' said the security chief. 'Come with me.'

He led Saxon down to the lower levels of the ship, to the cabin where he had defused the dummy bomb. The maintenance ladder was still in place. Terrasino glanced round and found a tool-kit locker. He bent, swearing in pain as he did so, and extracted a screwdriver before he began to haul himself up towards the control gauge panel.

Saxon tried to stop him.

'Tell me what you want doing and I'll do it.'

Terrasino was about to ignore him when the pain in his leg caused him to slip from the ladder, groaning.

Saxon reached out and took the screwdriver.

'I reckon I'll pass out anyway if I have to spend any more time scrambling up and down that goddam ladder,' admitted Terrasino, gritting his teeth.

'What am I to do?' demanded Saxon as he clambered up towards the panelling.

'Straight ahead of you, on that ledge, is where we found the tin box with Nieman's crude device. The fake bomb. Right? He had wired it into an electrical circuit in the panel straight ahead of you.'

'Yes. Now what?'

'My guess is that Nieman's convoluted mind told him that we would spot his bomb, defuse it and, breathing thanks, would not look any further. I reckon that Nieman placed his real bomb behind the control panel immediately to the right of his fake bomb.'

'Why not immediately behind the fake?' demanded Saxon.

'Because the wires lead into the panel. If we had decided to defuse the fake bomb by unscrewing that panel we would have found the other bomb.'

'Well, we'll soon see,' muttered Saxon. One hand grasping the ladder, he began to loosen the dozen screws which kept the panel frontage in place. It took him some time, for many of the screws were machine-tightened. Finally, the panel—a section of thin metal about two feet square—came away.

'Go easy,' Terrasino called up anxiously. 'It might be boobytrapped.'

Saxon broke into a sweat and nervously craned his head to peer behind the panel.

'The panel covering is free but . . . by God!' He was suddenly quiet.

'What is it?' demanded Terrasino anxiously.

'You were right. There is something behind it . . . here, I'm passing the panel covering down.'

Terrasino caught it and placed it on the deck.

'What do you see?' he called up.

'It's a device, right enough. God help me, I can't make head nor tail of it.'

'Okay, Saxon. Come on down. I'll take over.'

Saxon slipped down the ladder.

'You sure you can make it?' he asked.

Terrasino, his pale face pinched with pain, nodded.

'Quit worrying about me,' he grunted. 'That's a live bomb up there.'

Gritting his teeth once more, Terrasino hauled himself up the ladder. It was lucky that he had left the leather belt on the ladder after he had used it earlier. It took him a while to fix it around his waist so that he could have both hands free. Then he leant forward to peer into the panelling.

There were four main components to the device. There were four dynamite cartridges, again the Du Pont Red Cross Extra, taped together with insulating tape, wired up to a blasting cap, a twin cell transistor radio battery and a small travelling clock. Terrasino grinned savagely. This was fairly simple but still sophisticated. It was certainly more like Nieman's usual devices. The minute hand had been removed from the clock and close to the figure of 10 was a small metal plate which had been screwed down. When the hour hand came up to it, it would form a circuit and the dynamite would blow. Small, simple and deadly. He looked curiously at the clock face. Four hours to go.

'Hey Saxon,' he called down. 'Where will we be in four hours?'

Saxon stared up, puzzled.

'Give or take a few minutes, I'd say we'd be over Dublin. Why?'

'Dublin, eh?' Terrasino sighed. 'Guess I was wrong again. Nieman didn't set the bomb to go off while we were over England but over Dublin.'

'Dublin? Well, it's a European capital,' replied Saxon. 'That would be good enough to demonstrate Nieman's idea of God's will.'

Terrasino turned to the device.

It was, as he had seen, a fairly simple device with no secondary circuits, boobytraps nor back-up systems. He reached forward and gave the connecting wire a sharp tug. It came away with ease. Then Terrasino disconnected the battery and blasting cap. He turned and dropped the components one by one to Saxon who caught them and stared at them.

'Could these few odds and ends have really sent the *Albatross* to kingdom come?'

Terrasino nodded wearily.

'That dynamite plus the fuel tanks would have created quite a blaze,' he said.

'What are we going to tell Badrick?'

Terrasino shook his head and climbed down the ladder.

'If it's all the same with you, Saxon, I think we'll just drop this over the side and forget all about it.'

Saxon smiled.

'What's the matter? Can't you stand being a hero twice in one day?'

Terrasino groaned and stumbled.

'Me? I can't even stand, period. Let me get back to my cabin and get some shut-eye.'

'Alright, Terrasino. I'll go up to the observation deck and drop the explosives over the side. Can you make it back to your cabin on your own?'

'Yeah—that I can do, I think.'

Terrasino squeezed the Englishman's arm in gratitude.

'I was wrong about you, Saxon. You're an okay guy.'

He turned and limped away. Saxon watched him go before turning to the service elevator up to the observation deck. It was a vented section where the bolder passengers could actually step outside the airship onto a short promenade deck which, although it was three-quarters enclosed, had one side open to the elements, with a low barrier and transparent netting to prevent any accidents.

It was deserted as Saxon stepped out and walked across to the rail. The promenade deck, or observation deck as it was generally called, was a strip eight feet wide and some fifty feet in length. The netting was big enough for Saxon to squeeze through the components of Nieman's bomb.

He turned sharply at the sound of a cough.

Macmillan emerged from the shadows.

'Hi, skipper. I thought you were getting some shut-eye.'

Saxon shook his head.

'My brain is still at full revs, Danny. I thought a walk would do me good.'

Macmillan nodded and lowered himself into one of the fixed promenade deck chairs.

'Guess we gave you a pretty rough ride, skipper, until . . . well, you know.'

Saxon inclined his head.

'I deserved what I got, Danny.'

'Well, I wanted to say that I'm sorry. You've been a damned good skipper in a tough spot.'

Saxon smiled.

'It was about time I got my act together, chum. Come on, I'll treat you to a drink . . . I gather Olsen can rustle up a pretty good brew of tea.'

Macmillan grinned.

'I'll take a rain check on that. I must go and see how Claire's making out.'

'Has the news of her father's death upset her very much?' Saxon looked sympathetic. He knew Macmillan and Claire had something going for them.

'Yeah. She's in a sort of state of shock.'

'Sorry. It was a bad business—the French crash.'

'Pretty bad,' agreed Macmillan. 'I gather that Renard survived the crash but the news is that he's had to go into a sanatorium. A total breakdown. The Irish government have ordered an enquiry into the cause of the crash.'

'Of course,' Saxon said, 'it would be their jurisdiction.'

Macmillan climbed to his feet.

'See you on the next shift, skipper.'

'Well,' said Saxon, looking at the darkened sky, 'at least we'll be landing in time for a good English breakfast.'

Macmillan nodded and ambled away.

Saxon turned back to the rail, gazing into the dark coldness of the night. Well, whatever the future now held, he felt he could face it, could face it without the synthetic courage of the bottle. What was it that André Gide had said: 'Drunkenness is never anything but a substitute for happiness. It amounts to buying the dream of a thing when you haven't money enough to buy the dreamed-of thing materially.' Funny how those lines sprang so easily to his mind. Sad that it took Garry Carson's death to shock him into complete sobriety. But he couldn't feel guilty about him. In fact, he felt merely gratitude to Carson, for out of the tragedy of his death he—Saxon—had been given a chance for rebirth. He wondered whether Helen would see it that way. He hoped she would.

He started suddenly.

Far across the blackness of the sea, silver-speckled with

moonlight, there was a sudden flash of white in the velvet night sky. A shooting star. What did that portend? Didn't you have to make a wish? He closed his eyes briefly. He wished for strength to build his life anew.

Chapter Fifteen

The *Albatross* was down to one thousand feet as she swung over the M1 motorway which snaked northward from London. The journey across Ireland, Cardigan Bay and Wales and into the English Midlands had been almost an anticlimax to the journey. The ship had run without the slightest hitch, the auto-pilot computers measuring and adjusting trim and elevation with ease. As they crossed into the county of Bedfordshire, Saxon found himself tired but less tense than at any time during the last two days. He glanced across to Danny Macmillan, seated before the engineering control console.

'How are we doing, Danny?' he asked.

'Everything is fine, skipper,' replied Macmillan. 'This bird is coasting like a dream.'

Saxon gazed for a moment at the cloudy blue canopy of sky before them and the green and brown mottled fields of the English countryside below.

'Was it worth the lives?' he mused aloud.

Art Stein, sitting in the co-pilot's seat for the landing, frowned at him.

'Nieman was a madman. There wasn't much we could do about it.'

'I don't mean that,' replied Saxon. 'I mean generally . . . the lives of the people on the *Charles de Gaulle* as well as our own personnel.'

No one replied.

'We need a ten-degree course change, skipper,' ventured Billy Heath, glancing up from his instruments. 'Then we should be able to get a visual fix on Cranfield.'

'Alright,' acknowledged Saxon, shaking himself and turning towards his instruments to make the necessary adjustments.

Peering through the forward observation windows he could see the level green swathe stretching far ahead—the slow, flat countryside of Bedfordshire. There it was. He caught the tell-tale signs of an aerodrome. Anglo-American had chosen Cranfield as a terminal site because it was near the motorway, connecting London and other major British cities, where freight could be offloaded onto motor transport for despatch across the country. It was also away from major air traffic routes, which fact kept the British Civil Aviation Authority happy—so far the British were keeping a low profile until Anglo-American could prove the safety of their giant airship. However, Cranfield was not too far from Luton airport for any airship passenger who wished to make regular airline connections, or wished to transport goods from the airship terminal to a regular freight airline.

The *Albatross* began to move steadily towards the landing site. Saxon could see, as he brought the airship down to six hundred feet, large crowds gathered on the outskirts of the airfield. There were the landing beacons and mooring poles. Saxon buzzed the Chief Purser, Olsen, on the intercom.

'Warn the passengers that we are about to dock,' he ordered.

'Very well, captain.'

Art Stein began his checks.

'All systems functioning, skipper.'

'I'm bringing the vectoring propellers into play within thirty seconds. How are the cross winds?'

'Minimal, skipper,' sang out Billy Heath, checking the readings. 'No swing at all.'

He paused, then punched a series of buttons.

'You are patched into Cranfield ground control, skipper.'

A harsh voice crackled in Saxon's ears.

'Starboard half a point, captain.'

'Roger,' acknowledged Saxon.

'*Albatross*,' came the voice, 'you are looking beautiful from down here. Coming in nice and level.'

'We are at five hundred feet, Cranfield . . . what's our position to the docking bay?'

'Dead above, captain,' came the voice. 'Start coming down.'

'Roger . . . coming down.'

Saxon increased the thrust of the vectoring propellers, so that the great airship began to descend straight and true like a helicopter. It was the work of fifteen minutes or so to bring it down to its dock and secure the gangways, switching off all the engines. The first Transatlantic crossing by an airship in nearly fifty years had been completed in safety. Saxon heaved a long drawn-out sigh.

Art Stein looked across and grinned.

'Made it, skipper. Safe and sound.'

'Yes,' muttered Saxon. 'Safe and sound.'

He avoided the welcoming party, the British government ministers, the aviation authority officials and civil dignatories and other guests; he avoided the media and camera crews and the RAF band who played them a rousing welcome. He slipped away past the eager police and customs officials who were now questioning the security officials of Anglo-American, and entered the Anglo-American terminal building. The aircrew debriefing room was easy to find. It was empty. He found a telephone and put through a call to Portland.

Maria Terrasino answered.

'Terry?'

'No, sorry, Maria. This is Tom Saxon. Can I speak with Helen?'

'Oh,' the voice was disappointed. 'Sure. Is Terry alright, Signor Saxon?'

'Yes,' Saxon decided Terrasino could tell her the full story when he rang her. 'Yes, he's okay.'

'Tom?'

Helen's voice was breathless as if she had run to the telephone.

'Hello, Helen.'

'Tom. Are you alright?'

'Yes. We've landed in England safely. Have you . . . ?'

He felt awkward; not knowing how to tell her.

There was an uncomfortable pause.

'They told me about Garry, Tom.'

'I'm sorry, Helen.'

'I can't pretend that I don't feel anything about him,' Helen went on. 'But I can't pretend that it alters anything, anything about me, about you . . . anything. . . .'

There was a silence.

'When will you be back, Tom?'

Saxon shrugged, realising that the gesture was futile.

'We are going to lie over in England for a week for tests and refitting. Also, we'll wait until another pilot can be flown out to complete the crew. We'll probably be back about the middle of next week.'

'I'll look forward to that, Tom. Take care now.'

'I love you, Helen.'

Saxon stood listening to the buzzing static in the receiver for several minutes before he hung up.

The black Daimler cruised down the motorway towards London. John G. Badrick sat back with a contented smile on his face. He turned to Harry Maclaren who was sitting on the other side of his wife in the back of the car.

'Well, Harry . . . we've done it.'

Maclaren looked morose.

'Yes; I suppose so.'

Badrick looked surprised.

'You don't seem happy.'

'I can't help thinking about the cost—Jack Lane, the Westbrooks, Garry Carson. And the people on the *Charles de Gaulle*.'

Badrick waved a hand in dismissal.

'Unfortunate, yes. But we are in no way responsible. How can we be responsible for the actions of a lunatic? How can we be responsible for what happened on Renard's project?'

Badrick was oblivious to Maclaren's look.

'Anyway, now we've proven the capabilities of the *Albatross* there will be a lot of work to do,' went on the chairman of Pan Continental. 'I shall have to fly back to New York first thing tomorrow to organise. . . .'

Alice Badrick bit her lip.

'But John . . . what about the vacation?'

Badrick frowned.

'Vacation? Vacation? Good God, Alice, I haven't time . . . not now. There is far too much work to do. Maybe we can grab a week or so later on.'

Alice Badrick sighed with resignation.

Maclaren stared out across the white ribbon of motorway to the green vista beyond. He felt no elation, no triumph—just tired, emotionally exhausted. He would have given anything to avoid the celebration party at the Dorchester that evening. In spite of what Badrick had said he realised that he did feel responsible—if he was not responsible, who was?

Oscar Van Kleef was sitting in the command chair on the deserted flight deck of the *Albatross*. A terrible sad feeling of anticlimax overwhelmed him. Years of work, of struggle, of arguing had finally given birth to the airship. It was a success. Yet now, what else was there left to do? He gazed about him in dismay. He realised that he was alone. He had dedicated himself to the *Albatross* with such a singleness of mind and now there was nothing left for him to worry about. Lesley had gone; the kids had gone. Friendless and solitary, he felt an almost overpowering isolation.

The buzzing intercom startled him.

It was a member of the ground staff.

'Your car is here to take you to London, Doctor Van Kleef.'

Van Kleef acknowledged the information, sighed deeply and, with a final glance, rose and left.

Terrasino had finally managed to escape from the company officials, the American Embassy and the British police. For two hours they had questioned him and taken statements. Now all the red tape was over. In spite of the expert dressing by a hastily summoned doctor, his wound was throbbing with an excruciating pain. At least it would heal, and that was reassuring. However, all he wanted to do right now was crawl away to a telephone and then a bed. He managed to slip across to the Anglo-American building. Parish was already there and guided him to a telephone in an empty office.

Terrasino sprawled in a chair and picked up the receiver. It was a few minutes before he heard her voice.

'*Pronto* . . . er, hello?'

He smiled.

'Hello, *cara mia*.'

'Terry!' Maria Terrasino's voice was apprehensive. 'I hear on the news that terrible things happen. Are you alright?'

Terrasino glanced down at his throbbing leg.

'Fine,' he smiled. 'Just fine. I might be needed here for a day or two but I shall try to get the next available flight home. I'll telephone you tomorrow and let you know when. How are you?'

'I'm better now.'

'I love you, *cara*.'

'I love you too,' cried Maria, laughing with relief.

Danny Macmillan walked slowly with Claire Ashton to the hire car. Her eyes, he noticed, were still red and her lips tight, forming a thin line. The car delivery man thrust a board and a pen at her. Automatically, she signed but Macmillan reached forward and took the car keys.

'I think that I'd better drive you down to Kent, Claire,' he said.

For a moment he did not think she had heard him, then she nodded.

'I'd . . . I'd like that, Danny.'

Macmillan gave her a comforting smile and put her bag into the boot of the car, opened the door to allow her to slide into the passenger seat. Then he climbed in behind the wheel and started the engine.

'Danny,' she turned, a hand on his arm. 'Danny, I need you very badly now.'

'Your mother will need you very badly, Claire.'

She bent her head.

'I know,' she said contritely. 'I don't think I shall be able to cope alone.'

'Don't worry,' Macmillan said, suddenly feeling an overwhelming compassion for her waif-like look. 'I'll be around as long as you need me.'

He put the car into gear and sent it off down the road towards the motorway.

Behind them rose the great sleek silver-grey body of the *Albatross*, towering like some gigantic floating whale in the sky; a strange phantom in the semi-gloom of the cloudy English day, coming alive in bursts of shining silver as the rays of the weak sun broke through the low cloud cover. It rose like a giant silver sausage. The people stared upwards with mouths agape. They had come by motor car, omnibus, train, coach and bicycle to see the first huge airship fly across the country in fifty years. They had come in hundreds and in thousands, swarming into the sleepy Bedfordshire countryside, filling the hotels, the bed and breakfast cottages and the local pubs which offered rooms. They carried picnic packs and thermos flasks, exuding an air of festivity as they packed the fields and lined the perimeter fences which bordered the Cranfield aerodrome. They crowded round, only held back by barriers and efficient security guards; they crowded round to gaze in wonder and awe at the sleek shape of the *Albatross*, to gaze in reverence at this great ghost from the past and shadow of the future. They stood in respect before the man-made construction, almost in veneration as if it was some god, some vehicle from another world.

THE END